LIFE

on

MARS

LIFE on MARS

TALES FROM THE NEW FRONTIER

AN ORIGINAL SCIENCE FICTION ANTHOLOGY

EDITED BY

JONATHAN STRAHAN

VIKING

AN IMPRINT OF PENGUIN GROUP (USA) INC.

VIKING

Published by Penguin Group

Penguin Group (USA) Inc., 345 Hudson Street, New York, New York 10014, U.S.A.

Penguin Group (Canada), 90 Eglinton Avenue East, Suite 700, Toronto, Ontario, Canada M4P 2Y3
(a division of Pearson Penguin Canada Inc.)

Penguin Books Ltd, 80 Strand, London WC2R 0RL, England

Penguin Ireland, 25 St Stephen's Green, Dublin 2, Ireland (a division of Penguin Books Ltd)

Penguin Group (Australia), 250 Camberwell Road, Camberwell, Victoria 3124, Australia
(a division of Pearson Australia Group Pty Ltd)

Penguin Books India Pvt Ltd, 11 Community Centre, Panchsheel Park, New Delhi – 110 017, India

Penguin Group (NZ), 67 Apollo Drive, Rosedale, North Shore 0632, New Zealand
(a division of Pearson New Zealand Ltd.)

Penguin Books (South Africa) (Pty) Ltd, 24 Sturdee Avenue, Rosebank, Johannesburg 2196, South Africa

Penguin Books Ltd, Registered Offices: 80 Strand, London WC2R 0RL, England

First published in 2011 by Viking, a member of Penguin Group (USA) Inc.

1 3 5 7 9 10 8 6 4 2

Introduction, story notes, and arrangement copyright © Jonathan Strahan, 2011

"Attlee and the Long Walk" copyright © Kage Baker, 2011
"Martian Heart" copyright © John Barnes, 2011
"On Chryse Plain" copyright © Stephen Baxter, 2011
"Martian Chronicles" copyright © Cory Doctorow, 2011
"Goodnight Moons" copyright © Ellen Klages, 2011
"First Principle" copyright © Nancy Kress, 2011
"Digging" copyright © Ian McDonald, 2011
"LARP on Mars" copyright © Monkeybrain, Inc., 2011
"Wahala" copyright © Nnedi Okorafor, 2011
"The Old Man and the Martian Sea" copyright © Alastair Reynolds, 2011
"Discovering Life" copyright © Kim Stanley Robinson, 2000
"The Taste of Promises" copyright © Rachel Swirsky, 2011

LIBRARY OF CONGRESS CATALOGING-IN-PUBLICATION DATA IS AVAILABLE
ISBN 978-0-670-01216-9

Printed in the U.S.A.   •   Set in Granjon   •   Book design by Sam Kim

For my brother Stephen, again, with gratitude
for his endless willingness to share his frontiers with me.

LIFE
on
MARS

CONTENTS

INTRODUCTION: LIFE ON MARS

❀

Jonathan Strahan

Mars has traditionally been the setting for grand tales of romance and adventure: stories of powerful gods of war, beautiful maidens, and mysterious aliens. Tellingly, those tales have grown and changed with each passing year as what we know about the red planet has increased.

Our nearest planetary neighbor has had many names: the ancient Romans called it Mars, but it was known as Nergal by the Babylonians, Ares by the ancient Greeks, Mangala by the ancient Hindus, Ma'adim in Hebrew, Bahram by the ancient Persians, and Sakit by ancient Turks, while the Chinese, Japanese, Korean, and Vietnamese cultures referred to the planet as the fire star, a name based on the ancient Chinese mythological cycle.

Although Mars was known to many of Earth's ancient cultures, it is only in the past few centuries—since telescopes improved to the point where we could begin to make out its image clearly—that we have begun to learn much about it. The astronomers Giovanni Schiaparelli and Percival Lowell named Martian seas and continents in the late nineteenth century, creating a world that fired the imagination of H. G. Wells, who in *The War of the Worlds* described an ancient race casting envious eyes across the gulfs of space at our young and vibrant blue world. In *A Princess of Mars,* Edgar Rice Burroughs told of the swashbuckling adventures of a Virginian soldier on the sweeping plains of Barsoom, a savage frontier world filled with honor, noble sacrifice, and constant struggle, where martial prowess is paramount, and where strange Martian races fight over dwindling resources. Mars often appeared in early twentieth-century science fiction stories, providing either a threatening nemesis or an exotic locale for many, many classic tales.

Then, in 1964, the United States launched the space probe Mariner 4, followed by Mariner 9 in 1971, as well as Soviet probes Mars 2 and Mars 3, and then most significantly Viking 1 and Viking 2 in 1976. They sent back images that swept away any grand visions of a romantic world filled with ancient civilizations, replacing them with photographs of what may be the largest mountain in our solar system—so tall it reaches through the atmosphere into space itself!—the longest, deepest valleys, and many other awe-inspiring sights.

Wonder after wonder . . . but no sign of life.

Our knowledge of the planet changed permanently, and this changed the kind of stories we told. Instead of stirring adventures with four-armed green giants fighting shoulder to shoulder with heroes on dead seabeds, we were treated to tales of shattered, isolated expeditions traversing cold, distant deserts, or epic visions of vast engineering projects to make Mars more Earthlike, with Mars turning first blue as its oceans filled and then green as its forests grew. But, alas, all of those tales were merely dreams.

Or were they?

In early 2004 the president of the United States, George W. Bush, announced that they would send astronauts to the moon by 2020, establish a permanent base on the surface of the moon—and then turn its attention to Mars, with a goal of putting people on the planet. NASA now estimates it can send a manned mission to Mars by 2037. It was a grand vision, and one that looks like it could come true, if not quite as we might have anticipated. In 2001 the Mars Odyssey orbiter was launched, and remains in orbit as I write. It was followed by further probes—the European Space Agency's Mars Express Orbiter, the Spirit and Opportunity probes and then the Mars Reconnaissance Orbiter—all of which added more and more to our knowledge of the planet. The European Space Agency announced that it too intended to put humans on Mars, sometime between 2030 and 2035. There's even a Google Mars.

And yet nothing's assured. Political plans change. There's no way of knowing exactly when, or if, humans will land on Mars.

Whatever human exploration of Mars turns out to be like, though, we can be sure it won't be easy or safe. Half the size of Earth, Mars has almost no atmosphere, and what little it has is constantly being stripped away by the solar wind. Relentlessly bombarded by radiation, its gravity is about a third of Earth's, and it receives only half the amount of light we're used to, and . . .

. . . and yet it's Mars! Another world! Modern dreams of Mars are dreams of a cold, hostile place initially made bearable and then possibly made wonderful. In response to former President Bush's bold and optimistic presidential decree, I challenged some of science fiction's finest writers to imagine stories set in a world where the mission was a success, and humanity gained a permanent foothold on a new world. Some set their tales on the journey, some soon after colonization, and others in a far, far distant future. The tales that follow are very different from the kind of stories that were being written about Mars one hundred years ago, but they are still filled with stirring adventure and grand romance. I hope you enjoy them as much as I have.

Jonathan Strahan
Perth, Australia

ATTLEE AND THE LONG WALK

❖

Kage Baker

I t was close and foul in the shed as the kids packed in, giggling.
Attlee wrinkled her nose. Some of the stink came from the sacks
of chemical fertilizer being used as seats, and some of it was
the goaty sweat of children, but most of it was the ever-present
methane fug of the Long Acres.

"Ayck-oh!" said Stot Richards, ducking inside and pulling the
door to. "All clear, Supreme Council." The Supreme Council of the
Martian Shadowcats was presently only Hobby Augustus and Jennifer Langshank, since Eddie Penton had started working grown-up
hours and attending Collective meetings. Jennifer would probably
follow soon, since she had begun to grow interested in boys and was
getting a little impatient with the rules and regs of the Shadowcats.
Attlee figured that Hobby would stay until she dropped, though,
because Hobby loved being in charge.

You could see it in the way she held up her hands now for
silence, like she was an Ephesian Mother from the mission up the

hill, and in the way she pursed her lips in disapproval when Dinky Purett farted and everyone around him started laughing.

"This is not a laughing matter," said Hobby. "This is a deadly serious matter! So you just listen up, brother and sister Shadowcats. Because you won't be laughing when it's *your* turn, I can tell you."

The snickering died down. Hobby leaned forward and lowered her voice dramatically.

"This is the story as we heard it from Blackie Atkins, who heard it from Sharn Penny, who heard it from Pollitt Gardiner, who heard it from Bill Haversham who is dead and gone and killed in the Strawberry cyclone. They *say*. But some people say that the Old Roach got him, just for knowing that he was there and letting on. So you think about that as you listen. The Old Roach might be listening too.

"It was long years ago, when our mums and dads and our granddads and grandmams first formed the Collective and came up here to Mars. And there was a lazy sod came along among them and he was a Backslider. And in his crate of personal stuff some cockroaches stowed away, and the frozen cold of space didn't get them, and they didn't starve neither on the trip. And when the Backslider opened his crate, the cockroaches all ran out and ran away down the Tubes. And everybody thought they'd die, on account of they were Earth bugs.

"But no!

"The black night frozenness didn't kill them: they changed their blood so they were full of antifreeze. The Ultraviolet didn't kill them: their scritchy armor got hard and thick and kept it out. The Outside didn't kill them, either: they learned how to breathe without any air out there. And where they'd been little chippy things on Earth, up here they grew big and strong; big as your hand, big as dinner plates. And they laid their eggs everywhere and ate the insulation off wires and started fires.

"So it was War. And the brave heroes of the Collective gave every kid a hammer, and said, 'It's your duty to hunt and kill these enemies of the people, and that ought to be enough for you, but if you're really good at it you'll earn threepence for each one you kill.' So that was when the Bug Hunting started. The kids killed hundreds and thousands of cockroaches, and the smashed corpses was ground up into fertilizer, in aid of making the new perfect world. And so it goes on to this very day.

"But!

"There was one cockroach we didn't get. One cockroach that was bigger and faster and smarter and meaner than the rest. And he kept growing! Rays from space made him extra big. He got smart enough to pick up commcodes on his long, long antennas, so he listened like a spy to everything the Collective done, and waved his whippy antennas in the air and picked up signals from the shuttles coming in, and from the capitalists up on the mountain, and he learned human ways. There's even talk he learned to steal clothes, disguise himself as a man, and sneak up the Tubes at night to gamble and drink on Mons Olympus. But that's just talk.

"Because everybody knows that what he done was, he hid himself far out, way out, at the farthest, farthest ends of the Long Acres. Four times four kilometers and then some. Way out there where there's nothing but algae bubbling in the canals. That's where the Old Roach hides, and he only comes creeping back at night when we're all asleep in our beds. He knows how to steal from the fields. When you go out in the morning to feed your rabbits, and the screen's torn and maybe a rabbit or two is gone—well, it was the Old Roach done it."

There was dead silence in the shed as the younger kids listened open-mouthed. Leo Grindell looked as though he was about to cry. Hobby surveyed them triumphantly. She leaned forward and continued:

"And, ever since there's been Shadowcats, we Shadowcats have had one test, and only one test, for admission to the Supreme Council. And what it is is, any kid that comes of age has to go out to the very end of the Long Acres, all by themselves. All the way. They have to brave the Old Roach. Then they have to come back alive. Not everybody comes back alive. When my cousin Shree was on the Supreme Council, there was one kid who went out and didn't come home again. And when the mums and dads went looking for him, *all they found was his bones.*"

That did it for Leo Grindell, who started to bawl. He was only two (in Collective years; the people who lived up on Mons Olympus still measured time in Earth years and would have said he was four), so nobody laughed at him, but some of the older kids looked good and scared. Hobby turned slowly, pointing with her finger, and Attlee braced herself.

"And now it's *your* time, Attlee Bonser!"

"I 'n't scared," said Attlee defiantly, standing up. She had turned six a month ago and been expecting this. She folded her arms and stared Hobby in the eye.

"Well, you will be," said Hobby. "Being a smarty-pants won't help you when you have to go all alone into the farthest, farthest fields. When you're huddling all by yourself in the dark and cold, waiting to hear the Old Roach coming along down the canalside— *skitter skitter skitter!* What'll you do then?"

"Expect I'll do as well as you did," Attlee retorted. She hated it when people made fun of her for being smart.

"Yeah, well. We'll see." Hobby stood up and folded her arms too. She wasn't quite as tall as Attlee, in that crowd of stringbean youth, so neither Attlee nor anybody else there was as impressed as they might have been. "Tonight after Lights Out. At Besant Fields. Be there."

Attlee trudged home to the allotment shelter where she had lived with her mum since her dad had been killed. It was smaller than the place they'd lived in before, of course; as the Council had said, there was no reason to waste a good shelter on just two people when a family could make better use of it. Attlee's mum had sighed and nodded in agreement, too weary with grief to argue about it. Later— in private, to Attlee, on the understanding that Attlee would never ever tell anyone—she had laughed sadly and remarked that neither the old place nor the new would have done for a garden shed back on Earth anyway. Attlee had just shrugged. She'd never seen Earth.

Now, she stepped in through the lock and unmasked. Before sitting down with her lesson plan, Attlee knelt in the kitchen space and rummaged through the locker where they'd stashed her dad's things. His psuit was in there; so was the billy-can he'd used to take out with him to the fields. The heating element was broken in the billy, and the psuit had some damaged sensors so it didn't work very well (otherwise both would have gone back into the Collective's store of goods), but Attlee was good at fixing things.

It took only a little tinkering to fix the billy, swapping out the element from an old hand-warmer. The psuit took a bit more work. In addition to repairing what she could of its broken connections, Attlee had to mend the couple of long gashes where her dad's mates had tried to cut him out of the psuit when they still thought they could save his life. But what was duct tape for? She'd finished the job and stowed both the psuit and the billy together with some ration packets and a canteen in her pack, and got dinner on besides, by the time her mum came home from work.

They ate dinner in near silence, seated side-by-side on the fold-down, taking turns dipping into the casserole with their spoons. Nobody wasted resources on individual plates in the Collective.

"Done your lessons?" said Attlee's mum at last.

Attlee nodded. "I finished extraordinarily fast."

Attlee's mum winced at the big word. "Don't brag, girl."

"Sorry." Attlee looked sidelong at her mum. "Hobby and Jennifer asked me to a sleepover tonight. Ayck-oh if I go?"

"Thought you didn't like them," said her mum in surprise, turning to stare at Attlee.

"We made up," said Attlee.

"That's nice," said Attlee's mum.

"Might sleep over two days."

"Having a party, are they?"

"Working on lesson plan project."

"Oh. Well, that's nice too."

They scraped up the corner crust with their spoons, savoring it. "How's Uncle Dave?" Attlee inquired.

"Busy," her mum replied.

Busy went without saying in the Collective, but in this case it meant that Attlee's mum wasn't likely to be seeing Uncle Dave for walks along the Tube anytime soon. Uncle Dave wasn't an uncle really; he had just been friends with Attlee's mum before she'd married Attlee's dad. Uncle Dave was kind and besides was a boffin in a white coat, doing science stuff. Boffins earned perks within the Collective because they worked with their brains. Uncle Dave had told Attlee that she had a good mind too. Attlee thought that if her mum married Uncle Dave, life would get a lot nicer for all three of them. Attlee had loved her dad, but he was gone. Attlee was a realist.

Attlee put the dish and the two spoons in the sink and carefully measured water to soak them, while her mum stretched out on the bed and opened a buke. She was absorbed in watching her holos by the time Attlee shouldered her pack, masked up, and crept out.

The little bluish sun had set and the temperature was dropping fast out in the black night out there beyond the vizio roof. Shivering, Attlee found a storage shed and ducked into it long enough to strip down to her thermals and pull on the psuit. It was too big, of course, but a few loops of duct tape (no Martian ever went anywhere without a roll of duct tape) around the wrists and ankles snugged it close. If it bulked awkwardly under her outer clothes, Attlee didn't care. Even with half its sensors broken, it still kept her deliciously warm.

The wind had picked up Outside and was howling, hissing sand against the vizio by the time Attlee got to the lock by Besant Fields. Hobby and Jennifer were huddled together in the red light of the warning lamp. As Attlee drew near, Jennifer reached up and turned her speaker on.

"You took your time," she complained.

"I'm here, 'n't I?"

"All arranged with your mum?" demanded Hobby. Attlee nodded. "All right, then. You go in there and you go *all the way to the end*. You may not even get there before morning. *If* you get to the end you need to look for a rock that's got SHADOWCATS scratched on it. You need to take it and put this in its place." Hobby drew a big flattish chip of stone from her pocket and thrust it at Attlee. Attlee took it and glanced at it briefly. It was marked s-c.

"Then, *if* you make it back you have to bring it straight to the secret shed," Hobby said.

"You lot waiting here for me?" Attlee shoved the stone into her pocket.

"As if!" cried Jennifer. "We done our test, thank you very much. I'm not standing out here freezing all night."

"So you both went all the way out there and had it out with the Old Roach, huh?" Attlee looked hard at Hobby.

"Of course we did!"

"How big is he?"

"I couldn't see him very well," said Jennifer, after a moment's hesitation.

"Big as a tractor," said Hobby. "But I can't say anything else. That would be telling."

"Right," said Attlee, putting as much scorn as she knew how into her voice. "Ayck-oh. Step aside, then."

They moved and Attlee palmed the lockpad and stepped through as it irised aside. Then it had shut behind her and she was alone in the dark, staring down the long passage into Besant Fields.

The canal ran down the passage's center, from the place just in front of her where the pipes fed it, to the far vanishing point in the darkness. The moisture in the air was rich, heavy, like perfume. Attlee lifted her mask cautiously, then slid it off her face. She gulped in a breath. She could taste the oxygen, the water droplets. It was just the sort of lush pleasure the kids of the Collective were taught to distrust. *That's sensual, that is. Bad for you.* As if to underscore the admonition, something flickered with movement far ahead.

Nothing really there, Attlee told herself. *Nothing to be scared of anyway. Except Mars. And Mars is enough.*

Every Martian kid knew that there had once been a time when ancient Mars had been like ancient Earth, a little blue planet with water and an atmosphere, but something had smashed Mars into— what had the book said?—into its own Permian Extinction that never ended. Only algae had survived, down in the frozen water. But just as Earth had healed itself of its Permian catastrophe, Mars might be healed too, and that was why everybody had to work self- lessly at the Great Work of giving him back an atmosphere and freeing his water to fill his vanished seas. . . .

Attlee stepped forward, clenching her fists on the straps of her pack. Nothing jumped out at her, and so she took another step, and another, and after that she just put her head down and kept walking.

At Besant Fields the domed area widened out, with rows of beets on one side of the canal and rows of cabbage on the other. Attlee paused here and looked around suspiciously. Though the wind howled outside beyond the vizio transparence, though it moaned and spattered the walls with blown sand, no breath of air moved in here. The beets and cabbage were as immobile as though they were painted on the rows. Only the water moved, flowing down the canal, throwing little glints of green around the walls where a safety light reflected off its surface. Had that been what she'd seen?

Of course it had been. Must have been. Attlee marched on along the service path next to the canal, resolutely ignoring all the sneaking memories that came creeping to mind now. Hadn't it been Besant Fields that had been hit by the first-ever Strawberry the Collective had faced, a long time ago when they were newly arrived on the planet? The cyclone of pink sand and red boulders roaring up out of the west was very rare here on the Tharsis Bulge, but came paying a special visit to the Collective to test its resolve. It had destroyed the temple the Ephesians had built, it had picked up another building and whirled it like a hat until it landed on a ledge far up Mons Olympus, and it had ripped through Besant Fields.

Don't think about that. Useless memories make you weak.

But it was hard not to remember the whispers passed among the adults when they thought children were asleep: *It tore away the vizio like it was cobwebs. The cabbages froze and dried in an instant, they looked like green glass and shattered to bits if you kicked them. The boulders came smashing down and bashed the canals so the water froze and blew away as frost; you can still see the places where the concrete was replaced. And we hadn't learned yet to wear psuits, see? There was only one man, Alf Higgins, who had traded for one. And he was wearing it, and he was one of the five who was in Besant Fields when it happened.*

He saw it all and lived to tell it. Saw the others, heroes of the Collective all, picked up and whirled away like straws. They all hung on to the vizio frames but one by one their hands froze and they lost hold, all except Alf. The gloves of his psuit kept his hands from freezing. But whether they were scoured to death or froze or were smashed by rocks going 'round and 'round, all of them died, see? Except Alf. Which is why we always wear psuits in the fields now.

And we went out weeping and found the heroes' bodies, one by one, with their clothes shredded away and the black blood frozen in their mouths, and those four red polished stones mark where we buried them, and those are the graves of the heroes of Mars. They're shrines, that's what they are, to the first who gave their lives in the great work of making this planet the perfect world.

Attlee hated that story. It was a lot of talk to give you the shivers, the same way Hobby was always talking to impress the kids. Making up things. The Strawberry had been real enough, that was even in their history lesson plans and you could still see the foundations where the Ephesian Temple had stood. The other bits, though . . . people becoming heroes with shrines just because they were in an accident and got killed . . . that was stupid.

It wasn't like they had wanted to die. It wasn't like their deaths had done any good. Attlee's dad hadn't wanted to die either, when the tractor fell down the dune and onto him, but there had been the same kind of talk at his funeral. Fat lot of good a fancy tombstone did anybody.

Attlee shrugged and quickened her pace now, reaching the lock into Besant Annex. It was loud here, where the canal dove into pipes that took it underground and up again into the Annex. She palmed the lockpad and went through hastily.

Besant Annex ran on for kilometers and kilometers, striking north. Someday, when the Collective had terraformed the whole planet, it would be only one of thousands of vizioed canals crossing the face of Mars, carrying water everywhere. For now it was the most that had been managed, a long, long tube of air over cultivated soil, with the canal running down its center like an artery. If the Collective had a good year there might be enough money to drill more wells, extend the annex. *Someday it'll be too long for the Shadowcats to send kids walkabout like this. Wonder what we'll do then?*

Attlee walked for hours, going through lock after lock. To her left, beyond the vizio, Mons Olympus blotted out the stars. Before her, rows of cabbage gave way at last to potatoes, and then gradually to barley. The smell of the air changed too; just as wet, but not so heavy with fertilizer. Attlee didn't know what sort of smell it was. She was wondering about it, half in a dream as she paced along, when the cockroach darted out at her.

It had scuttled up her leg and was making straight for her face before she coordinated herself enough to beat it off, smacking it away into the vizio wall in a frenzy of disgust. Acting on a lifetime of habit, Attlee had her mask down and had pulled a hammer from her belt in one smooth motion. She watched the roach, which lay immobile where it had fallen. It was a big one, maybe the size of a rabbit. A faint hiss and a warning pulse on the safety light told Attlee there was a puncture in the vizio, probably from one of the roach's spurred legs. She took her eyes off the roach for a split second, just long enough to glance at the light. When she glanced back the roach had flipped itself over and was coming at her again.

Attlee leaped into the air and stamped on it, but the roach whistled in fury and pushed back under her boot, refusing to be crushed. It took several blows with her hammer before she was sure she'd killed it. The spiked legs kept flailing, slowly now. Attlee turned, gasping for breath, looking to see if any others were lurking about. Seeing none—and Attlee knew how to spot the curve of a shiny carapace, the involuntary twitch of an antenna—she put away her hammer and dug out her roll of duct tape. The vizio puncture was easy to find by the needle-jet of burning cold it was admitting. Attlee patched it and stepped back into the comparative warmth of the potato field.

She eyed the dead roach distrustfully. *You're not so big,* she thought. *Are you the Old Roach? No wonder the likes of Hobby and Jennifer saw you and lived to tell the tale.*

Looking ahead, though, Attlee saw that Besant Annex stretched on a long way yet, curving slightly as it veered northwest, its vizio panels glittering faintly in the starlight. Closer to she saw that some of the potato plants were dying, pulled up, their roots all gnawed through and tubers dug out of the sand. Had one roach done all that?

Wary, hammer in hand, Attlee searched along the rows for any other insects, but nothing attacked her. It wasn't until she got to the end of that section of the canal that she saw the black hole in the ground, right by the conduit pipes. After a long staring moment of incomprehension, she realized what it must be. Snarling in disgust, Attlee scuffed sand into it to close it, stamped hard to collapse it. *Bloody roaches!*

She jumped through the lock into the next length of the annex, holding her hammer high. Nothing but the peaceful trickle of water along the canal, seeping under its layer of algae, and the boom and sigh of the wind Outside. Silvering barley stood tall and motionless along both lengths of the fields. Anything might be hiding back in there. Anything might come rushing out at knee level.

So that's it, thought Attlee. *It 'n't one big old roach, it's a bunch of regular ones, only biggish, and they've learned to dig the ground. And they hide in the day, when the grown-ups come out here, so that's why only Shadowcats ever see them, here at night.*

And that would be why those stories might be true, about some kid that went missing and all they found was his gnawed bones out here. Some kid who maybe pushed his mask up, same as Attlee had, so he could smell all the sweet wet air, but he maybe hadn't had the sense to pull it back into place. And maybe he'd got tired and lay down for a sleep. With his face and hands uncovered, and no psuit like Attlee had, and then the roaches came.

Attlee shuddered. Something bright yellow was flashing in her field of vision; one of the working sensors in her psuit was telling her that her heart was beating fast. She clenched her fists.

"Listen! You don't understand me, because you're stupid roaches. But any of you takes me on, I'll kill you, see?"

Nothing answered her. Blown sand gusted against the vizio. She raised her hammer in the darkness, gripping it tight. "Shadowcats rule OK!" she cried, and immediately felt silly. Oddly, it diminished her fear.

She began to run along the canal footpath, jogging steadily, counting her strides as she went. Each stride was a meter; five hundred meters brought her to another lock; five hundred more took her down the next bit of canal and all the way to the next lock.

All this, she thought, *just so I can join the Supreme Council.* Had she ever actually wanted to join the Supreme Council? What was so great about sitting in on private meetings with Hobby and Jennifer? It was the first time Attlee had ever thought about it objectively. Then again, thinking objectively wasn't really encouraged, was it?

You got born and your parents dropped you off at the Collective's baby-minders, so they could work while you got fed your pabulum. As soon as you were old enough you got put to work doing baby stuff for the Collective, feeding rabbits and chickens or cutting air filters out of paper—anything a little kid could do—so you'd learn to be a good worker. As you got stronger you were given your roach hammer and set to harder jobs, learning to repair tractors or pick cotton. Until you were fifteen Earth years old, though, the work day ended at two in the afternoon.

It was supposed to give kids a chance to play, before settling down with their lesson plans; a chance to have some "unstructured time" so they could just be kids. The only problem was, most kids in the Collective didn't know what to make of unstructured time. They wandered listlessly in the Tubes, uneasy without someone shoving chores at them. And so the Shadowcats had been founded.

Bill Haversham had started them. He had been born on old Earth and he had said a cat was a kind of animal you didn't eat, but people had used to keep them because they hunted rats, which were like roaches only not bugs. So the Shadowcats were the great roach hunters, the kids who were best with their hammers, fast and brave and smart.

That had been the idea, at least. Shadowcats were supposed to band together and have exciting adventures stalking and killing roaches. Sometimes that happened, it was true, but mostly they held meetings that were just like little Collective meetings, where everyone sat around and listened to Council members talk on and on. But at least it was something to do, until you turned eight—sixteen in Earth years—and went to work full-time.

Attlee had begun to suspect that she'd be bored by the Shadowcats long before she came of age. She wasn't sure they didn't bore her now, actually.

But what'll I do with the next two years if I drop out of the Shadowcats?

She thought about it as she pounded grimly along. She liked books. Attlee was good at her lesson plans. Everyone said she was smart, though they usually said it with a slight sneer, as though cleverness was something to be ashamed of. Uncle Dave didn't, though. What if she had the brains to be a boffin? Wear a white coat like Uncle Dave, get a nicer place to live, work with clean hands in the Collective's laboratory instead of grubbing in the fields like her dad and mum? You weren't supposed to be ashamed of grubwork, because it was honest labor and a noble sacrifice that would transform the planet. Attlee wasn't ashamed of it, but she didn't fancy being crushed to death in a stupid accident because Earth tractors didn't work well in Martian gravity, or for some other fool reason.

Wrong to think that way. That's practically criminal. Selfish. You don't get to have a future; the future belongs to everybody. Somebody has to work in the fields. Your mum and dad did. Think you're too good for that? Pride'll be your downfall.

But some kids were smart enough to become interns, and learn to work alongside the boffins. If she spent more time on her lesson plans, took some extra courses instead of hanging out with the Shadowcats, would Attlee qualify to become an intern?

Is that why you want Mum to marry Uncle Dave? So you can get a soft job?

No! Attlee wanted her mum to marry so she'd be alive again, instead of the dead-eyed low-priority field mule she'd been since Attlee's dad had died. Rise up in the dark and spend your days cutting irrigation trenches in the clay with a shovel, and come home worn out and only too glad to do nothing but watch old holos until you fell asleep, every night for the rest of your life until you died, when you got called a hero. Her mum had used to laugh sometimes. Now she never even smiled.

And it was obvious that Uncle Dave cared about Attlee's mum, the way he looked at her, the way he'd asked her out to walk in the Tubes, the way he'd invited them over to his shelter and cooked them dinner. Boffins got allotted a lot of good food. But Attlee's mum seemed content to disappear inside a cocoon of apathy and exhaustion, as though her life was already over and there was no point hoping for anything new.

Still, if Attlee worked with Uncle Dave, that would make reasons for Attlee's mum seeing him more often, wouldn't it? And then she'd have to come back to life. She could be proud of Attlee being smart, instead of apologetic. She'd have a reason for taking an interest in things.

Attlee Bonser, Backslider.

She wasn't a Backslider! Wanting a better life wasn't the same as if she planned on ditching the Collective, the way some traitors had done, and going to live up on Mons Olympus with the rich people or, worse, going back to Earth. Attlee would stay on Mars and use her brains to make the terraforming go faster. She'd be a hero too. Just not a dead one.

But the jeering voice in her mind wouldn't shut up, and finally she stopped arguing with it as she loped along through the darkness. She was a long way out now, and though Mons Olympus still obscured stars to the west, different stars whirled and burned to the east; the others had long since sunk behind the jagged ridges of Ceraunius.

When she felt her strength flagging, Attlee stopped and pulled off her pack. She set up the billy-can, filled it with water, and dumped in a packet of dehydrated broth and noodles before activating the heating element. The pounding of her heart took a while to slow down, as did her gasping breath, but they did, and so it was fairly quiet when she heard the scuttling run of another roach.

Attlee looked up in time to see it streaking straight for the billy, a big bold roach. Rising from her crouch, she grabbed the billy and set it high on the edge of the canal. The roach halted for a second. She was pulling out her hammer when it darted right up the side of the canal. Outraged, Attlee kicked at it to knock it off, but it dropped before she connected and her boot hit the canal wall with a painful thud. She chased it down the canal path, slamming at it repeatedly with her hammer, until she killed it at last. Limping, she turned and went back. She drank the broth and ate the noodles standing, dipping them out with two fingers as she glared around, daring anything else to surprise her.

Nothing more did. As she packed up the billy, Attlee spotted another couple of holes in the ground at the far edge of the field. The beets all around looked chewed and plundered. Muttering to herself, she stamped in the holes and continued her journey.

During her rest, the cold had begun to sink in a little, even through her psuit. Attlee could see the frost patterns on the vizio now, and here and there as she jogged along, the vibration of her passage knocked little flakes of ice from the ceiling or walls.

Got to be somewhere close now. Nobody's ever frozen to death going to see the Old Roach, at least. Attlee halted in her tracks as she heard a low gurgling roar in the darkness, echoing along the canal. She fumbled for her hammer and gripped it, half-crouched as she waited.

The roar grew louder, but as it did Attlee realized that it was coming from the fields behind her, rather than ahead. *He's back of me! How? How'm I getting past him to get home again?*

Attlee trembled as she waited, swinging her hammer to brace her nerves. *Big as a tractor, Hobby said. Can't be true. Just big. Jump high, hit hard. Don't let him knock you down—*

She saw the wave of steam racing along the pipe before she understood what it was. When she realized that the roar was coming with the steam, Attlee almost dropped her hammer, she was so relieved. She laughed out loud as the noise and the heat caught up with her and passed her, racing mindlessly on down the canal.

"Big as a tractor!" she cried. "You liar, Hobby!"

As clouds of warmth rose from the heating pipe, the ice on the vizio melted and began to fall in little drops, plinking into the canal and spattering on the path. The crops in this particular bit of the annex—oats, still green—seemed to wake up, seemed to crane eagerly toward the falling water. *They must be remembering rain,* thought Attlee in wonder. She slid her mask up and turned her face toward the ceiling. A big drop hit her cheek. *Is this what it feels like?*

She'd never seen rain. Rain was the blessing of old Earth, it fell from the sky everywhere down there. On Attlee's planet, water had to be melted and pumped from below, every drop, or brought in by Haulers from the poles. Mars had no blessings; every good thing here had to be earned. *But someday it* will *rain.*

Feeling light-headed from the moist warmth, Attlee trudged on. More often, now, she saw the black mouths of dug burrows, always in fields that looked neglected and chewed. The crops out at this distance were all stuff that didn't need to be tended much, oats and barley and sugar beets, and the burrows looked fresh. Attlee supposed they had all been dug since the last time the planting crews had been out here. Dutifully she stamped in each one, as a Shadow-cat ought to do, but there were more and more of them now.

What if the Old Roach laid eggs and they hatched, and these are his kids? He's a she then. Attlee thought briefly of an Old Roach dressing itself up like one of the posh ladies on holos, disguising itself with makeup, drawing red lips around its mouthparts and simpering. Somehow that made it scarier. And what if thousands of giant roaches were down this end of the fields, now, with Attlee was out here all alone?

She began to run again, not too fast, determined to keep control.

I'll do it. I'll fetch back their stupid rock, just to show I wasn't scared, and then I'll ditch the Shadowcats. I don't need the likes of Hobby and Jennifer always telling me what to do. Jennifer's going to leave soon anyway and that'll just make Hobby bossier. I'll go to Uncle Dave and tell him I want to be an intern and ask him what classes I have to take.

The sneering voice in her head called her a coward, called her lazy, told her she wasn't worthy to clean the canal-mud off the boots of the noble field workers, and asked moreover what would happen to the Great Work if everyone tried to get themselves soft jobs?

Attlee came to the next lock, smacked it, and jumped through. There, far off but clearly visible, was the far wall with no lock, the end of the annex. And that was dawn light filtering in, over a wretched ragged field of sugar beets so chewed up the field looked already harvested.

If the Old Roach is anywhere, Attlee thought, *it's here.*

She was suddenly acutely aware of how tired she was, and what a long way she had to go to get home. She thought of Hobby's scary stories, all the kids nodding solemnly and believing every word. You were *supposed* to believe, weren't you? Believe and shut up and do what everybody else did. Not question the ones like Hobby, who liked to boss everyone around. Not *know* things by finding them out for yourself.

But it's good to know things.

Attlee took the stone from her pocket with one hand as she walked forward and swung her hammer in the other. All around her, black things were springing out of the ruined field and streaking for . . . streaking for the biggest den Attlee had seen yet, a mass of holes and thrown-off dirt.

There's dozens of them. Not one big one, but lots. One slip and they'd be on you in a second, biting and hooking you with their spikes. So this was it, this was the real danger you had to face. This was the truth behind the stories.

Attlee walked straight and steady, keeping to the canal path. She got all the way to the end and looked out at the vizio wall. The sun must be coming up, far away on the other side of the eastern hills. She could just glimpse frost glittering on the Ceraunius tops, though stars were still visible. Lowering her gaze, she saw the rock marked SHADOWCATS lying in front of her boots.

Attlee bent, dropped the rock she was carrying, and scooped up the one she had come so far to find. As she was putting it in her pocket, she saw something beginning to emerge from one of the holes.

Shuddering, she ran and stamped at it with her boot, as hard as she could. The soil gave way under her and she fell.

Attlee didn't fall far. But it was pitch-black where she landed, somewhere warm and stinking of . . . what was that smell? Her arm was buried but she thrashed free, smacked on her mask's light, and swung her hammer.

It didn't connect with anything. Attlee looked around wildly, expecting her light to flash across clicking mandibles, waving antennae. She saw none. There was only a glimpse of a pair of legs vanishing into a wall of holes . . . black-furred legs . . . and the wall was obscured by branching spindly stuff, whitish-yellowish. . . .

Attlee followed the branches with her spotlight, down to the floor where they sprouted from a dense carpet of pellety things, black and squashy.

She remembered being little and working at the baby-minders', working with the animals the Collective farmed because kids were supposed to like animals, only she never had liked cleaning out the pens full of . . . rabbit poo.

Rabbits vanished, and everyone assumed something was taking them. But hadn't they lived in the ground, back on Earth? They dug under fences and ate carrots. Attlee remembered an illustration in a lesson plan that showed rabbits doing just that.

And here on Mars they had gotten away and dug down into the Martian soil, where the cold and the ultraviolet couldn't hurt them. Some would burrow out into Outside and they'd die, of course, but some would learn to burrow only under the domed fields where there was air, and they'd survive to have babies. Lots of babies, because rabbits did that too, they bred fast. It was why the Collective raised them for meat.

Old Roach is rabbits! Attlee struggled to her feet, laughing, but with her mouth closed because of the smell. Were Hobby and Jennifer in on the joke? Or had they never dared to step off the canal path? Hadn't the grown-ups noticed? Or didn't they pay attention, sending the harvester machines in?

She was about to scramble out of the pit when her attention was caught again by the spindly branches. What were they? Was it some kind of mushroom? . . .

Wondering, she put out her hand and swept a bunch toward her. Not mushrooms at all. Thin scaly stems, no leaves, unlike any plant that grew on Mars where there were no weeds ever, nothing that the Collective hadn't planted. Attlee had seen a picture of something a little like this, something primitive that once grew on Earth. What had its name been? *Cooksonia*. But it was extinct. And this was different, and alive.

It was something that had lived underground away from the

UV glare, casting out spores, and had finally perished as the planet got colder and dryer. Except for its spores, which lay dormant. Who knew how long?

Until something dug down where they were and gave them warmth and damp and fertilizer.

Well, so what? It's not something you can eat, is it?

"It's a Discovery," said Attlee out loud. She put away her hammer and pulled out her fieldman, unfolding the sharpest blade. She cut a bunch of the branches free. It was awkward climbing from the pit holding them before her, but she managed.

It was a miracle. Something *Martian* finally growing again on Mars, instead of cabbages and beets. Something that would make Attlee's mum proud. Something to show Uncle Dave and maybe get Attlee an internship in the laboratory.

Attlee emerged by the canal path just as the first sunlight was spreading out over the high valley, and the frost on the mountains blazed like bright windows. She slid her mask up and ran for home, holding her future in front of her like a bouquet.

KAGE BAKER grew up in the Hollywood Hills amid glamorous houses, ruins, and the ruins of glamorous houses. Her aunt and uncle, Anne Jeffreys and Robert Sterling, played the cosmopolitan ghosts on television's *Topper*, endowing the young Kage with a permanent and uniquely flexible view of time, reality, and immortality. This resulted in the concept of Dr. Zeus, Inc.—an all-powerful cabal responsible for a secret history of the human race—the source of her acclaimed Company series (*In the Garden of Iden*, *Sky Coyote*, et al). She won the Theodore Sturgeon Memorial Award in 2004 for "The Empress of Mars," and was nominated several times for both Hugos and Nebulas. The novel length version of this story is a nominee for the 2010 Locus Awards, and has just won the *Romantic Times* SF Novel of the Year Award. Her novella *The Women of Nell Gwynne* is a nominee for both the 2010 Nebula and Hugo. Her fantasies include the novels *The Anvil of the World* and *The House of the Stag* (a 2009 World Fantasy Award finalist and winner of the 2009 *Romantic Times* Best Fantasy Novel of the Year Award). She contributed stories to numerous anthologies, including tribute collections for Robert Silverberg and Jack Vance, and published extensively in the developing steampunk genre. She also wrote a children's book, *The Hotel Under the Sand*, in the classical traditions of E. Nesbit, Edward Eager, and Kenneth Grahame.

Her upcoming novels are *Not Less Than Gods*, a Company/steampunk novel, and *The Bird of the River*, set in the universe of *The Anvil of the World*. They will be published posthumously.

Kage Baker lived her entire life in the numerous environments of California. She died in Pismo Beach, her home for the last fifteen years, in January 2010 after a brief and heroic battle with cancer, whence she departed for the Uttermost West. She is assumed to be sailing over the horizon now, dining at the Captain's table, drinking the kinds of cocktails that feature rum and fruit spears, and slow dancing on the aft deck with God.

Visit her Web site at www.kagebaker.com.

AUTHOR'S NOTE

"The biggest inspiration for this story was the fact that new lands are settled by courageous idealists and sturdy pioneers—but their kids have to live with that decision, willy nilly. Most kids do rebel in some way against their parents, but they still end up living essentially the same lives Mom and Dad did. The kids of Mars 1 are like that too: and if you aren't by nature a heroine of the Revolution, you're pretty much out of luck unless you can invent your own way. Attlee is one of those people who has to navigate life on their own. Her parents are among the dedicated socialists who have emigrated to Mars to make a new and perfect world; and while Attlee loves her parents and her home, she doesn't much like her society.

"Attlee is named for Clement Attlee, Labour Prime Minister of the UK from 1945 to 1951. Her parents name her Attlee because he's a heroic Labour politician; I called her that because Clement was a rather cool guy, actually. He helped develop the National Health Program, and was instrumental in India, Burma, Pakistan, Sri Lanka, and Jordan all winning their independence from Britain. He was independent, smart, and resourceful, and I've tried to give Attlee some of those characteristics. The big difference, though, is that she finds her parents' socialist paradise stagnant and boring, and she wants to strike out on her own."

✳ ✳ ✳

"Attlee and the Long Walk" was conceived of and written during Kage Baker's last few months, when she was undergoing therapy for the cancer that finally took her life. She was hopeful and stubborn and sure she would win, and that attitude is reflected in self-sufficient, determined Attlee. It's also largely the way Kage lived. She made her own worlds and quietly insisted on living there, and so succeeded in accomplishing things that elude most people. She's off on her own Long Walk now, and Old Roach had better watch his ass.

—Kathleen Bartholomew

(Kage Baker's sister)

THE OLD MAN AND THE MARTIAN SEA

Alastair Reynolds

In the belly of the airship, alone except for freight pods and dirt-smeared machines, Yukimi dug into her satchel and pulled out her companion. She had been given it on her thirteenth birthday, by her older sister. It had been just before Shirin left Mars, so the companion had been a farewell present as well as a birthday gift.

It wasn't the smartest companion in the world. It had all the usual recording functions, and enough wit to arrange and categorize Yukimi's entries, but when it spoke back to her she never had the impression that there was a living mind trapped inside the floral-patterned—and now slightly dog-eared—hardback covers. And when it tried to engage her in conversation, when it tried to act like a friend or even a sister, it wasn't clever enough to come out with the sort of thing a real person would have said. But Yukimi didn't mind, really. It had still been a gift from Shirin, and if she stopped the companion talking back to her—which she mostly did, unless there was something she absolutely had to know—then it was still a place to record her thoughts and observations, and a useful window into the aug. When she was seventeen she would be legally entitled to receive the implants that gave her direct access to that shifting, teeming sea of universal knowledge. For now, all she had was the glowing portal of the companion.

"I've done it now," she told it. "After all those times where we used to dare each other to sneak aboard, I've actually stayed behind until after the doors are closed. And now we're in the air." She paused, tiptoeing to peer through a grubby, dust-scoured window as her home fell slowly away. "I can see Shalbatana now, Shirin—it looks much smaller from up here. I can see Sagan Park and the causeway and the school. I can't believe that was our whole world, everything we knew. Not that that's any surprise to you, I suppose."

It wasn't Shirin she was talking to, of course. It was just the companion. But early on she had fallen into the habit of making the entries as if she was telling them to her sister, and she had never broken it.

"I couldn't have done it if we hadn't played those games," Yukimi went on. "It was pretty hard, even then. Easy enough to sneak onto the docks—not much has changed since you left—but much harder to get aboard the airship. I waited until there was a lot going on, with everyone running around trying to get it loaded on time. Then I just made a run for it, dodging between robots and dock workers. I kept thinking: what's the worse that can happen? They'll find me and take me home. But I won't be in any more trouble than if I do manage to sneak aboard. I know they'll find me sooner or later anyway. I bet you're shaking your head now, wondering what the point of all this is. But it's easy for you, Shirin. You're on another planet, with your job, so you don't have to deal with any of this. I'm stuck back here and I can't even escape into the aug. So I'm doing something stupid and childish: I'm running away. It's your fault for showing me how easy it would be to get aboard one of the airships. You'd better be ready to take some of the blame."

It was too much effort to keep on tiptoe so she lowered down. "I know it won't make any difference: I'm not a baby. But they keep telling me I'll be fine and I know I won't be, and everything they say is exactly what I don't want to hear. *It's not you, it's us. We still love you, darling daughter. We've just grown apart.* As if any of that makes it all right. God, I hate being me."

She felt a lurch then, as if the airship had punched its way through the pressure bubble that surrounded the whole of Shalbatana City and its suburbs. A ghost of resistance, and then they were through. Behind, the bubble would reseal instantly so that not even a whisper of breathable air was able to leak out into the thin atmosphere beyond.

"I'm through now," she said, going back on tiptoe. "On the other side. I guess this is the farthest from home I've ever been." The sun was catching the bubble's edge, picking it out in a bow of pale pink. Her home, everything she really knew, was inside that pocket of air, and now it looked like a cheap plastic snow globe, like the one her aunt had sent back from Paris with the Eiffel Tower.

It hit her then. Not the dizzy sense of adventure she had been expecting, but an awful, knife-twisting sense of wrongness. As if, only now that the airship was outside the bubble, was she grasping the mistake she had made.

But it was much too late to do anything about it now.

"I'm doing the right thing, Shirin. Please tell me I'm doing the right thing."

She slumped down with her back against the sloping wall of

the cargo hold. She felt sorry for herself, but she was too drained to cry. She knew it would be a good idea to eat, but she had no appetite for the apple she had brought with her in the satchel. She closed the covers on the companion and let it slip to the hard metal deck, gaining another dent or dog-ear in the process. Sensing her mood, the cartoon characters on the side of the satchel started singing and dancing, trying in their idiotic way to perk her up.

Yukimi scrunched the satchel until they shut up.

She listened to the drone of the airship's engines. It was a different sound now that the air outside was so much colder and thinner than inside Shalbatana City's dome. She knew from school that the air had once been even thinner, before the changes began. But it was still not enough to keep anyone alive for very long.

There was enough air inside the cargo hold to last for the journey, though.

At least that was what Shirin had always said, and Shirin had never lied about anything. Had she?

"I think something's happening," Yukimi told the companion. "We're changing course."

They had been flying high and steady for eight hours, Mars unrolling below in all its savage dreariness, all its endless rust-red monotony. Adults were always going on about how there were already too many people on the planet, but as far as Yukimi could tell there was still a lot of empty space between the warm, wet bubbles of the settlements. Aside from the pale, arrow-straight scratch of the occasional road or pipeline, there had been precious little evidence of civilization since their departure. Unless one counted the lakes, which were made by rain, and rain was made by people—

but lakes weren't civilization, as far as Yukimi was concerned. How anyone could think this world was crowded, or even beginning to be crowded, was beyond her.

Yukimi closed the book and strained to look through the window again. It was hard to tell, but the ground looked nearer than it had been all afternoon. They didn't seem to be anywhere near a dome. That made sense, because in the time she had been in the air, there was no way that the airship could have made it to Vikingville, let alone anywhere farther away than that.

"It's a good sign," she went on. "It has to be. Someone must have figured out what I did, and now they've recalled the airship. Maybe they even got in touch with you, Shirin. You'd have told them about our game, how easy it would be for me to escape. I'm going to be in a lot of trouble now, but I always knew that was coming sooner or later. At least I'll have made my point."

That was going to cost someone a lot of money, Yukimi thought. She could see her father now, shaking his head at the shame she had brought on him with her antics. Making him look bad in front of his rich friends like Uncle Otto. Well, if that was what it took to get through to her parents, so be it.

But as the airship lowered, so her certainty evaporated. It didn't seem to be turning around, or be in any kind of a hurry to continue its journey. The engine note had changed to a dawdling throb, just enough to hold station against the wind.

What was going on?

She looked through the window again, straining hard to look down, and, yes, there was something under them. It wasn't a bubble like the one around Shalbatana, though, or even one of those settlements that was built straight onto the ground with no protection from the atmosphere. It was a machine, a huge, metallic-green, beetle-shaped juggernaut inching slowly along the surface. It was bigger than the airship, bigger than any moving thing she had ever seen with her own eyes. The machine was as long as a city district, as wide as Sagan Park. It had eight solid wheels, each of which was large enough to roll over not just her home but the entire apartment complex. And although it seemed to be crawling, that was only an illusion caused by its size. It was probably moving faster than she could run.

"I can see a Scaper," she told the book. "That's what I think it is, anyway. One of those old terraforming mechs." She held the companion open and aimed down through the window, so that it could capture the view of the enormous machine, with chimneys sprouting in double rows along its back, angled slightly rearward like the smokestacks on an ocean liner. "I didn't think there were many of them left now. I don't think they actually do anything anymore; it's just too much bother to shut them down."

But for the life of her she could not imagine why the airship was now descending to rendezvous with a Scaper. How exactly was that going to get her home any quicker?

"I'm not sure about this," she told the companion and then closed it quietly.

Through the window, she could see the airship lowering itself between the twin rows of atmosphere stacks. They were soot black and sheer, as tall as the highest buildings in Shalbatana City. The airship stopped with a jerk, the freight pods creaking in their harnesses, and then a series of bangs and thuds sounded in rapid succession, as if restraining devices were locking into place. The engine note faded away, leaving only a distant throb, one that came up from the floor. It was the sound of the Scaper, transmitted to the cargo hold.

For long minutes, nothing happened.

Yukimi was by now quite uneasy, not at all sure that this rendezvous had anything to do with her being rescued. Halting on the back of a Scaper—kilometers from anywhere—had not figured in her plans. She had always assumed that the airships went from A to B as quickly as possible. No one had ever mentioned anything about them indulging in this kind of detour.

None of this would be happening anywhere else in the solar system, she told herself. Mars was the only place where a girl could run away from home and not be found. Everywhere else, the aug was so thick, so all-pervasive, it was impossible to do anything illegal without someone knowing more or less instantly. You couldn't hide away inside things. You couldn't get lost.

Mars was different, as everyone liked to say. Mars was a Descrutinized Zone. The aug was purposefully thin, and that meant people had to take responsibility for their own actions. You could get into trouble on Mars. Easily.

Yukimi was pacing around, wondering what to do—with all sorts of impractical ideas flashing through her head—when the cargo doors began to open. She took in a deep breath, as if that was going to help her. But apart from a slight breeze there wasn't any loss of pressure. As hard blue light pushed through the widening gaps where the doors were rising open, she slunk back into the shadows, hiding between two freight pods. She had put the companion back into her satchel, and she hoped neither of them would make a sound. She very much wanted to be discovered, but she also very much wanted not to be.

For a long time nothing at all happened. All she heard was faint mechanical sounds in the distance, and the continuing throb of the Scaper. She was aware now of a very slight undulation to their motion, as the colossal machine followed the terrain under its wheels.

Then she heard something approaching. The noise was patient, rhythmic, wheezing, and it was accompanied by a labored shuffling. Yukimi tensed and pushed herself even farther back, but not quite so far that she couldn't see the cargo doors. With an agonizing slowness, something horrible came up the ramp.

It was a monster.

Silhouetted, huge and bulbous against the blue light beyond, came something like a man, but swollen out of all proportion, with the head no more than a bulge between wide, ogrelike shoulders. Yukimi's fear sharpened into a very precise kind of terror.

She had never seen anything like this before.

The figure stepped into the bay, and at last she saw it properly. It was wearing armor, but the armor was scratched and scabbed and rusty, and bits of it didn't fit correctly. There were pipes and cables all over the misshapen form, with wisps of steam coming out of its joints. Green fluid dribbled out one of the knees. The bulge where its head should have been was a low bronze dome, caked in grease and dirt, with nothing at all that could pass for a face. It didn't even have eyes. It just had cylinders sticking out of it at various angles, glassy with lenses, and some filth-smeared grills in the side of the dome. She couldn't tell if it was a robot or some ancient, grotesquely cumbersome space suit. All she knew was that she was very, very frightened by it, and she didn't want to know who—or what—was inside.

The figure clanked and wheezed as it moved through the cargo bay. It paused by one of the cargo pods, not far from where she was hiding. She hardly dared move in case it saw or heard her.

The figure raised one of its huge arms and scraped dirt off a shipping label. Its armored hand was big enough to crush a chair. One of the lenses sticking out of its head swiveled into place, telescoping out to peer at the label. Yukimi felt herself caught between possibilities. She wanted to be found now, no doubt about it. But she did not want to be found by this *thing*, whatever it was.

No one had ever told her there were monsters like this on Mars, not even Shirin, when she had been trying to scare her little sister. And Shirin had never missed a trick in that regard.

The figure moved sideways, to the next pod. It peered at the next label. If it kept that up, there was no way it was going to fail to notice Yukimi. Yet in that moment she saw her chance. There was an open-topped cargo pallet behind the two pods she was hiding between—it was only partly filled with plastic sacks of some agricultural or biomedical product. She could conceal herself in that easily—if only she could get into it without being noticed.

She listened to the figure's wheezing. It was regular enough that she had a chance to move during the exhalation phase, when the figure was making enough noise to cover her movements. There was not going to be time to agonize about it, though. It was already moving to the next pod, and the one after that would bring it right next to her.

She moved, timing things expertly. Shirin would have been proud. She was into the open-topped pallet before the wheeze ended, and nothing in the ensuing moments suggested that she had been discovered. The figure made a sound as of another label being scuffed clean. Yukimi crouched low, cushioned on the bed of plastic sacks. They squeaked a little under her, but if she stayed still there was no sound.

She had done the right thing, she told herself. Better to take her chances on the airship than to put herself at the mercy of the creature, whatever it was. The airship would be on its way again soon. They didn't just go missing between cities.

Did they?

The figure left. She heard it clanking and wheezing out of the bay, down the ramp, back into the Scaper. But she dared not move just yet. Perhaps it had sensed her somewhere in the bay and was just waiting for her to leave her hiding place.

Shortly afterward, something else came. It wasn't the shuffling, wheezing figure this time. It was something big and mechanical, something that whined and whirred and made pneumatic hissing sounds. Quite suddenly, one of the freight pods was moving. Yukimi snuggled down deeper. The machine went away and then came back. She caught a glimpse of it this time as it locked onto the next pod and hauled it out of the cargo bay. It was a handler robot, similar to the ones she had seen fussing around at the docks, except maybe a bit older and less cared for. It was a big stupid lunk of a robot: yellow and greasy and easily powerful enough to crush a little girl without even realizing what it had done.

Then it came back. Yukimi felt a jolt as the robot coupled onto the open-topped pallet. Then the ceiling started moving, and she realized that she was being unloaded. For a moment she was paralyzed with fear, but even when the moment passed she didn't know what to do. She dared move enough to look over the edge of the pallet. The floor was moving past very quickly, racing by faster than she could run. Even if she risked climbing out and managed not to break anything or knock herself out as she hit the deck, there was still a danger that the robot would run over her with one of its wheels.

No, that wasn't a plan. It hadn't been a good idea to hide inside the pallet, but then again it hadn't been a good idea to sneak aboard the airship in the first place. It had been a day of bad ideas, and she wasn't going to make things worse now.

But what could be worse than being taken into the same place as the wheezing, goggle-eyed thing?

The robot took her out of the bay, down a ramp, into some kind of enclosed storage room inside the Scaper. There were lights in the ceilings and the suspended rails of an overhead crane. Even lying down in the pallet, she could see other freight pods stacked around. With a jolt the robot lowered the open-topped pallet and disengaged. It whirred away. Yukimi lay still, wondering what to do next. It seemed likely that the airship had stopped off to make a delivery to the Scaper. If that was the case it would be on its way quite soon, and she would much rather be on it than stay behind here, inside the Scaper, with the thing. But to get back aboard now she would have to make sure the thing didn't see her, and lying down in the pallet she had no idea if the thing was waiting nearby.

She heard a noise that sounded awfully like the cargo doors closing again.

It was now or never. She scrambled out of the pallet, catching her trousers on the sharp lip, ripping them at the knee, but not caring. She got her feet onto the floor, dragged her satchel with her, oriented herself—she could see the loading ramp, and the doors above it lowering shut—and started running. Really running now, not the pretend running she had done all her life until this moment. She had to get inside the airship again, before the doors shut. She had to get away from the Scaper.

The thing stepped in front of the ramp, blocking her escape. With dreadful slowness it raised one of its hands. Yukimi skidded to a halt, heart racing in her chest, panic overwhelming her.

The thing raised its other hand. They came together where its neck should have been, under the shallow dome that passed for its head. The huge fingers worked two rust-colored toggles and then moved up slightly to grasp the dome by the grills on either side of it. Yukimi was now more terrified than she had ever thought possible. She did not even think of running in the other direction. The thing was slow, but this was its lair and she knew that she could never escape it for good. Plodding and wheezing and slow as it might be, it would always find her.

It took off the helmet, lifting it up above its shoulders.

There was a tiny head inside the armor. She could only see the top of it, from the eyes up. It had lots of age spots and blemishes and a few sparse tufts of very white hair. The rest of it was hidden by the armor.

An unseen mouth said, "Hello."

Yukimi couldn't answer. She was just standing there trembling. The thing looked at her for several seconds, the eyes blinking as if it, too, was not quite sure what to make of this meeting. "It is, at least in polite circles, customary to reciprocate a greeting," the thing—the old man inside the armor—said. "Which is to say, you might consider giving me a 'hello' in return. I'm not going to hurt you."

Yukimi moved her mouth and forced herself to say, "Hello."

"Hello back." The man turned slightly, his armor huffing and puffing. "I don't want to seem discourteous—we haven't even introduced ourselves—but that airship's on a tight schedule and it'll be lifting off very shortly. Do you want to get back aboard it? I won't stop you if you do, but it'd be remiss of me not to make sure you're absolutely certain of it. It's continuing on to Milankovic, and that's a long way from here—at least two days' travel. Have you come from Shalbatana?"

Yukimi nodded.

"I can feed you and get you back there a sight quicker than you'll reach Milankovic. Of course you'll have to trust me when I tell you that, but—well—we all have to trust someone sooner or later, don't we?"

"Who are you?" Yukimi asked.

"They call me Corax," the old man said. "I work out here, doing odd jobs. I'm sorry if the armor scared you, but there wasn't time for me to get out of it when I learned that the airship was coming in. I'd just come back from the lake, you see. I'd been scouting around, checking out the old place one last time before the waters rise . . ." He paused. "I'm wittering. I do that sometimes—it comes of spending a lot of time on my own. What's your name?"

"Yukimi."

"Well, Yukimi—which is a very nice name, by the way—it's your call. Back on the airship and take your chances until you reach Milankovic—miserable arse-end of nowhere that it is. You'll need warm clothing and enough food and water to get you through two days, and maybe some supplementary oxygen in case cabin pressure drops. You've got all that, haven't you? Silly question, really. A clever looking girl like you wouldn't have stowed away on a cargo airship without the necessary provisions."

Yukimi held up her satchel. "I've just got this."

"Ah. And in that would be—what, exactly?"

"An apple. And a companion." She observed the faint flicker of incomprehension on the old man's forehead. "My diary," she added. "From my sister, Shirin. She's a terraforming engineer on Venus. She's working with the change-clouds, to make the atmosphere breathable. . . ."

"Now which of us is doing the wittering?" Corax shook the visible part of his head. "No, there's nothing for it, I'm afraid. I can't let you go now. You'll have to stay here and wait for the flier. I'm afraid you're going to be in rather a lot of hot water."

"I know," Yukimi said resignedly.

"You don't seem to care very much. Is everything all right? I suppose it can't be, or you wouldn't have stowed away on an airship."

"Can you get me home?"

"Undoubtedly. And in the meantime I can certainly see that you're taken care of. There's a catch, of course: you'll have to put up with my inane ramblings until then. Do you think you can manage that? I can be something of a bore, when the mood takes me. It comes with age."

Behind Corax, the cargo doors were closed. The loading ramps had retracted and now even larger doors—belonging to the Scaper— were sealing off Yukimi's view of the airship.

"I suppose it's too late now anyway," Yukimi said.

She followed Corax's stomping, wheezing suit down into the deeper levels of the Scaper. By the time they got anywhere near a window the airship was a distant, dwindling dot, turned the color of brass by the setting sun. Yukimi considered herself lucky now not to be stuck on it all the way to Milankovic. She was sure she could do without food and water for two days (not that it would be fun, even with the apple for rations) but it had never occurred to her that it might get seriously cold. But then, given that the airships had not been built for the convenience of stowaways, it was hardly surprising.

Yukimi was glad when Corax got out of the armor. At the back of her mind had been the worry that he was something other than fully human—she had, after all, only been able to see the top of his head—but apart from being scrawnier and older than almost anyone she could ever remember meeting, he was normal enough. Small by Martian standards—they were about the same height, and Yukimi hadn't stopped growing. The only person that small Yukimi had ever met had been her aunt, the one who sent the snow globe, and she had been born on Earth, under the iron press of too much gravity.

Under the armor Corax had been wearing several layers of padded clothing, with many belts and clips, from which dangled an assortment of rattling, chinking tools.

"Why do you live out here?" she asked, as Corax prepared her some tea down in the Scaper's galley.

"Someone has to. When big stuff like this goes wrong, who do you think fixes it? I'm the one who's drawn the short straw." He turned around, conveying two steaming mugs of tea. "Actually it's really not that bad. I'm not one for the hustle and bustle of modern Martian civilization, so the cities don't suit me. There are a lot like us, leftovers from the old days, when the place was emptier. We keep to the margins, try not to get in anyone's way. Bit like this Scaper, really. As long as we don't interfere, they let us be."

"You live in the Scaper?"

"Most of the time." He sat down opposite Yukimi, tapping a knuckle against the metal tabletop. "These things were made two hundred years ago, during the first flush of terraforming."

"The table?"

"The Scaper. Built to last, and to self-repair. They were supposed to keep processing the atmosphere, sucking in soil and air, for as long as it took. A thousand years, maybe more. They were designed so that they'd keep functioning—keep looking after themselves, locked on the same program—even if the rest of human civilization crashed back to Earth. Their makers were thinking long-term, making plans for things they had no real expectation of ever living to see. A bit like cathedral builders, diligently laying down stones even though the cathedral might take lifetimes to finish." He paused and smiled, years falling from his face, albeit only for an instant. "I don't suppose you've ever seen a cathedral, have you, Yukimi?"

"Have you?"

"Once or twice."

"The Scapers were a bad idea," Yukimi said. "That's what my sister told me. A relic from history. The wrong way to do things."

"Easy to say that now." He drew a finger around the rim of his tea mug. "But it was a grand plan at the time. The grandest. At its peak, there were thousands of machines like this, crisscrossing Mars from pole to pole. It was a marvelous sight. Herds of iron buffalo. Engines of creation, forging a new world."

"You saw them?"

He seemed to catch himself before answering. "No; I'd have to be quite impossibly old for that to be the case. But the reports were glorious. Your sister's quite right. It was the wrong approach. But it was the only way we—they—could see at the time. So we mustn't mock them for their mistakes. In two hundred years, someone will be just as quick to mock us for ours, if we're not careful."

"I still don't see why you have to live out here."

"I keep this Scaper from falling apart," Corax explained. "Once upon a time the self-repair systems were adequate, but eventually even they stopped working properly. Now the Scaper has to be nursed, treated with kindness. She's an old machine and she needs help to keep going."

"Why?"

"There are people who care about such things. They live on Mars, but also elsewhere in the system. Rich sponsors, for the most part. With enough money that they can afford to sprinkle a little of it on vanity projects, like keeping this machine operational. Partly out of a sense of historical indebtedness, partly out of a cautionary attitude that we ought not to throw away something that worked, albeit imperfectly, and partly for the sheer pointless hell of it. It pleases them to keep this Scaper running, and the others still trundling around. It's Martian history. We shouldn't let it slip through our fingers."

Yukimi had no idea who these people were, but even among her father's friends there were individuals with—in her opinion—rather more money than sense. Like Uncle Otto with his expensive private sunjammer that he liked to take guests in for spins around Earth and the inner worlds. So she could believe it, at least provisionally.

"For them," Corax went on, "it's a form of art as much as anything else. And the cost really isn't that much compared to some of the things they're involved in. As for me—I'm just the man they hire to do the dirty work. They don't even care who I am, as long as I get the stuff done. They arrange for the airships to drop off supplies and parts, as well as provisions for me. It's been a pretty good life, actually. I get to see a lot of Mars and I don't have to spend every waking hour keeping the Scaper running. The rest, it's my own time to do as I please."

Looking around the dingy confines of the galley, Yukimi couldn't think of a worse place to spend a week, let alone a lifetime.

"So what do you do?" she asked politely. "When you're not working?"

"A little industrial archaeology of my own, actually." Corax put down his tea cup. "I need to make some calls, so people know where you are. They're sending out a flier tomorrow anyway, so we should be able to get you back home before too long. Hopefully it won't arrive until the afternoon. If there's time, I'd like to show you something beforehand."

"What?"

"Something no one else will ever see again," Corax said. "At least, not for a little while."

He made the calls and assured Yukimi that all would be well tomorrow. "I didn't speak to your parents, but I understand they'll be informed that you're safe and sound. We can try and put you through later, if you'd like to talk?"

"No thanks," Yukimi said. "Not now."

"That doesn't sound like someone in any great hurry to be reunited. Was everything all right at home?"

"No," Yukimi said.

"And is it something you'd like to talk about?"

"Not really." She would, actually. But not to Corax; not to this scraggy old man with tufts of white hair who lived alone in a giant, obsolete terraforming machine. He might not be an ogre, but he couldn't possibly grasp what she was going through.

"So tell me about your sister, the one on Venus. You said she was involved in the terraforming program. Is she much older than you?"

"Six years," Yukimi said. She meant Earth years, of course. A year on Mars was twice as long, but everyone still used Earth years when they were talking about how old they were. It got messy otherwise. "She left Mars when she was nineteen. I was thirteen." She reached into her satchel and pulled out the companion. "This is the thing I was talking about, the diary. It was a present from Shirin."

He moved to open the book. "Might I?"

"Go ahead."

He touched the covers with his old man's fingers, which were bony and yellow nailed and sprouted white hairs in odd places. The companion came alive under his touch, blocks of text and illustration appearing on the revealed pages. The text was in an approximation of Yukimi's handwriting, tinted a dark mauve, the pictures rendered in the form of woodcuts and stenciled drawings, and the entries were organized by date and theme, with punctilious cross-referencing.

Corax picked at the edge of the book with his fingernail. "I can't turn to the next page."

"That's not how you do it. Haven't you ever read a book before?"

He gave her a tolerant smile. "Not like this."

Yukimi showed him the way. She touched her finger to the bottom right corner and dragged it sideways, so that the book revealed the next pair of pages. "That's how you turn to the next page. If you want to turn ten pages, you use two fingers. Hundred pages, three fingers. And the same to go backward."

"It seems very complicated."

"It's just like a diary. I tell it what I've been doing, or let it record things for me. Then it sorts it all out and makes me fill in the gaps."

"Sounds horrendous," Corax said, pulling a face as if he had just bitten into a lemon. "I was never very good at diary keeping."

"It's meant to be more than just a diary, though. Shirin had one as well—she bought it at the same time. She was leaving, so we wouldn't be able to talk normally anymore because of the lag. I was sad because she'd always been my best friend, even though she was older than me. She said our companions would help us bridge the distance."

"I'm not sure I understand."

"We were both supposed to use our companions all the time. Make entries whenever we could. I would talk to my companion as if Shirin was there, and Shirin would talk to hers as if I was there. Then, every now and again, the companions would—I can't remember the word." Yukimi frowned. "Connect up. Exchange entries. So that my companion got better at copying Shirin and hers got better at copying me. And then if we kept on doing that, eventually it would be like having Shirin with me all the time, so that I could talk to her whenever I wanted. Even if Venus was on the other side of the sun. It wouldn't be the same as Shirin—it wasn't meant to replace her—but just make it so that we didn't always feel apart."

"It seems like a good idea," Corax said.

"It wasn't. We promised we'd keep talking to our companions, but Shirin didn't. For a while, yes. But once she'd been away from Mars for a few months she stopped doing it. Every now and again, yes—but you could tell only because she was feeling bad about not doing it before."

"I suppose she was busy."

"We promised each other. I kept up my side of the promise. I still talk to Shirin. I still tell her everything. But because she doesn't talk to me enough, my companion can't pretend to be her." Yukimi felt a wave of sadness slide over her. "I could have really used her lately."

"It doesn't mean she doesn't love you. It just means she's an adult with a lot of people making demands on her. Terraforming's very important work. It requires great responsibility."

"That's what my parents keep saying."

"It's the truth. It always has been. The people who made the Scapers understood that, even if they didn't get the technology quite right. It's the same with—what they call them? Those things in the air, swirling around?"

"Change-clouds," Yukimi said.

He nodded. "I see them sometimes at dusk. Just another machine, really. In a thousand years, there won't seem much difference between them and this. But they make me feel very old. Even your book makes me feel like an old relic from prehistory." He stood up, his knees creaking with the effort. "Speaking of recording devices, let me show you something." He moved to one of the shelves and pushed aside some junk to expose an old-looking space helmet. He brought it back to the table, blowing the dust off it in the progress, coughing as he breathed some of it in, and set the helmet down before Yukimi.

"It looks ancient," she said, trying hard not to show too much disappointment. It was scratched and dented and the white paint was coming off in places. There had once been colorful markings around the visor and crest, but they were mostly faded or rubbed away now. She could just make out the ghostly impressions where they had been.

"It is. Unquestionably. Older even than this Scaper. I know because I found it and . . . well." He stroked the helmet lovingly, leaving dust tracks where his fingers had been. "There's serious provenance here. It used to belong to someone very famous, before he went missing."

"Who?"

"We'll come to that tomorrow. In the meantime I thought it might be of interest. The helmet's still in good nick—built to last. I had to swap out the power cells, but other than that I've done nothing to it. Do you want to try it on?"

She didn't, really, but it seemed rude to say so. She gave an encouraging nod. Corax picked up the helmet again and shuffled around the table until he was behind her. He lowered it down gently, until the cushioned rim was resting on her shoulders. She could still breathe perfectly normally because the helmet was open at the bottom. "It smells moldy," she said.

"Like its owner. But watch this. I'm going to activate the head-up display playback, using the external controls." He pressed some studs on the outside of the helmet and Yukimi heard soft clicks and beeps inside.

Then everything changed.

She was still looking at Corax, still inside the galley. But overlaid on that was a transparent view of something else entirely. It was a landscape, a Martian landscape, moving slowly, rocking side to side as if someone was walking. They were coming to the edge of something, a sharp drop in the terrain. The pace slowed as the edge came nearer, and then the point of view dipped, so that Yukimi was looking down, down at her chest-pack, which looked ridiculously old and clunky, down at her heavy, dust-stained boots, down at the Martian soil, and the point where—just beyond her toes—it fell savagely away.

"The edge of Valles Marineris," Corax told her. "The deepest canyon on Mars. It's a long way down, isn't it?"

Yukimi agreed. Even though she was sitting down, she still felt a twinge of vertigo.

"You can still go there, but it's not the same," Corax went on. "Mostly filled with water now—and it'll only get deeper as the sea levels keep rising. Where I'm standing—where you're standing—is now a chain of domed resort hotels. They'll tear down the domes when the atmosphere gets thick enough to breathe, but they won't tear down the hotels." He paused. "Not that I'm complaining, or arguing against the terraforming program. It'll be marvelous to see boats sailing across Martian seas, under Martian skies. To see people walking around under that sky without needing suits or domes to keep them alive. To see Earth in the morning light. We'll have gained something incredible. But we'll have lost something as well. I just think we should be careful not to lose sight of that."

"We could always go back," Yukimi said. "If we didn't like the new Mars."

"No," Corax said. "That we wouldn't be able to do. Not even if we wanted it more than anything in the world. Because once we've touched a world, it stays touched." He reached over and turned off the head-up display. "Now. Shall we think about eating?"

In the morning they left the Scaper, traveling out in a small, four-wheeled buggy that came down from a ramp in the great machine's belly. "Just a little sightseeing trip," Corax said, evidently detecting Yukimi's anxiety about not being back when the flier—scheduled for the afternoon—came to collect her. They were snug and warm in the buggy's pressurized cabin, Yukimi wearing the same clothes as the day before, Corax in the same outfit he had been wearing under the armor, which—for reasons not yet clear to Yukimi—he had stowed in the buggy's rear storage compartment.

"Will the Scaper be all right without you aboard?" Yukimi asked, as they powered out of its shadow, bouncing over small rocks and ridges.

"She'll take care of herself for a few hours, don't you worry."

An awkward question pushed itself to the front of Yukimi's mind. "Will you always be the one in charge of it?"

Corax steered the buggy around a crater before answering. "Until the people who pay for my upkeep decide otherwise." He glanced sideways, a cockeyed grin on his face. "Why? You think old Corax's getting too old for the job?"

"I don't know," she answered truthfully. "How old are you, exactly?"

"How old do you reckon?"

"Older than my aunt, and I'm not sure how old she is. She's from Earth as well."

"Did I say I was from Earth?"

"You mentioned cathedrals," Yukimi said.

"I could have been there as a tourist."

"But you weren't."

"No," he said eventually. "I wasn't. Here I'm the tourist."

They drove on, crossing kilometers of Martian terrain. Most of the time Corax didn't have his hands on the controls, the buggy navigating by itself. Yukimi saw tire tracks in the soil and guessed that Corax had come this way before, maybe within the last few days. As the route wound its way around obstacles, the Scaper became little more than a dark, chimney-backed hump on the horizon, seemingly fixed in place. And then even the dark hump was gone.

The ground began to dip down. Ahead, reflecting back the sun like a sheet of polished metal, was what appeared to be a large lake or even a small sea. It had a complicated, meandering shoreline. Yukimi could not see the far side, even with the buggy raised high above sea level. She did her best to memorize the shape of the lake, the way it would look from above, so that she could find it on a map. That was hard, though, so she took out the companion and opened the covers so that it recorded the view through the buggy's forward window.

"You want to know where we are?" Corax asked.

Yukimi nodded.

"Approaching Crowe's Landing. You ever hear of it?"

"I don't think so."

"Doesn't surprise me. It's been a ghost town for decades; I'd be surprised if it's on any of the recent maps. It certainly won't be on them for much longer."

"Why not?"

"Because it'll soon be under water."

Corax took control of the buggy again as it completed its descent to the edge of the lake, following a zigzagging path down the sloping terrain. As they neared the water, Yukimi made out a series of sketchy shapes floating just beneath the surface: pale rectangles and circles, some of them deeper than others, and reaching a considerable distance from the shore. They looked like the shapes on some weird game board. They were, she realized, the roofs and walls of submerged buildings.

"This was a town?"

Corax nodded. "Way back when. Mars is on its second wave of history now—maybe even its third. I remember when Shalbatana was nothing, just a weather station that wasn't even manned half the time. Crowe's Landing was a major settlement. Not the main one, but one of the four or five largest colonies on the surface. Yes, we called them colonies back then. It was a different time. A different age." Slowly, he guided the buggy into the waters, picking his way down what must have been a thoroughfare between two rows of buildings. With some apprehension, Yukimi watched the water lap over the tops of the wheels, and then against the side of the cabin. "It's all right," Corax said. "She's fully submersible. I've taken her a full kilometer out, but we're not going anywhere so far today."

They were driving along a hard surface, so even though the buggy's wheels were underwater, they didn't stir up much material. The water was clear enough that Yukimi could see for tens of meters in all directions. As the road sloped down, the sea gradually closed over the cockpit bubble and it was almost possible to believe that they were just driving through a normal, albeit strangely unpopulated, district of Shalbatana City. The buildings were rectangles, cylinders, and domes, all with small black windows and circular, airlock style doors set out from the main structure in rounded porches. There must never have been a bubble around Crowe's Landing, so the buildings would have been the inhabitants' only protection from the atmosphere. Yukimi guessed that there were tunnels linking them together, sunk under the road level. Even the newer communities like Shalbatana—and it was strange now to think of her hometown as "new"—had underground tunnels, maintained to provide emergency shelter and communication should something untoward happen to the bubble. Yukimi had been down into them during school field trips.

She wasn't alone—she was in the cabin with Corax—but there was still something spooky about driving slowly through this deserted colony. She wished Corax hadn't called it a ghost town, and while she understood that he hadn't meant that the place was literally haunted, she couldn't turn her imagination off. As the light wavered down from the overlying sea, she kept seeing faces appear in the windows, brief and spectral like paper cutouts held there for a moment. Once they turned a corner and passed another kind of buggy, left parked there as if its owners had only just abandoned it. But it was a very old-fashioned looking buggy, and the symbols painted on its side reminded her of the faded markings on the old space helmet.

Eventually Corax brought the buggy to a halt.

"We're here," he said grandly. "The objective. You see that building to our right, the one shaped like an old-fashioned hat box?"

"Yes," Yukimi said dubiously.

"It's still airtight, unlike most of the others. Because of that, it's watertight as well. And the air lock's still functioning—there's just enough power in the mechanism for another cycle. Do you see where I'm headed?"

"Not really."

"Crowe's Landing is almost gone now, and in a hundred years it'll be completely forgotten. The seas will rise, Mars will be greened. A whole new civilization will bloom and prosper. You'll be part of that, Yukimi—when you're older. You'll see wonderful things and live to tell your grandchildren of the way it used to be, before the change-clouds finished their work." He smiled. "I envy you. I've lived a very long time—the drugs weren't always the best, but at least I had a ready supply—but my time's coming to an end now and you'll outlive me by centuries, if luck's on your side."

Yukimi thought of all the things in her life that were not the way she wanted. "I don't think it is."

"I'm not sure. That airship could have carried on to Milankovic, and then where would you be?"

"Hm," she said, remaining to be convinced.

"I had an idea," Corax said. "Not long after I found this place and this building. Mars is changing now and the seas will rise. But they won't stay that way forever. One day—a thousand or ten thousand years from now, maybe more—the seas will shrink again. People will have other worlds to green by then, and maybe they'll let Mars return to its primal state. Whatever happens, Crowe's Landing will eventually come out of the waters. And that building will still be there. Still airtight."

"You can't be sure."

"It's a fair bet. Stronger odds of surviving than anything left on the surface, with everything that's to come. Soon there'll be woods and forests out there, and where there aren't woods and forests there'll be cities and people. There'll be weather and storms and history. But none of that will reach down here. This building's as close to a time capsule as we're going to find. Which is why we've come." He tapped a few commands into the buggy's console and stood up creakily. "That helmet I found? It used to belong to Crowe, one of the very first explorers."

"Can you be sure?"

"Reasonably. As I said, it's got provenance." He paused. "I'm going to put the helmet in there. It's a piece of the past, a memento of the way Mars used to be. Not just a chunk of metal and plastic but a historical document, a living record. I only played back a tiny part of what's stored in that helmet. That old fool captured thousands of hours, and that's not including all the log entries he made, all the thoughts he put down for posterity. An old man's ramblings . . . but maybe it'll be of interest to someone. And it'll all still be inside that helmet when they find it again."

Yukimi had trouble thinking much further in the future than her seventeenth birthday, when she would receive the golden gateway into the aug. Everything was a blank after that. Centuries, thousands of years—what difference did it make?

"Will anyone understand it?"

"They may have to work at it," Corax allowed. "But that's what historians and archaeologists do. And I was thinking: while we're at it, why don't we give them something else to puzzle over, in addition to the helmet?"

Yukimi thought for a moment. "You mean my companion?"

"Your thoughts and observations aren't any less valid than Corax's. You'll miss your diary, of course, and maybe you'll have some explaining to do to your sister when she finds out what happened to it—assuming you tell her, of course. But in the meantime, think what you'll have done. You'll have sent a message to the future. A gift from the past to a Martian civilization that doesn't even exist yet. No matter what happens, you'll have made your mark."

"No one's interested in what I have to say," Yukimi said.

"Don't put yourself down. Look, there's still time to make another entry. Tell them how you got here. Tell them how you feel today, tell them what made you run away from home yesterday. Be angry. Be sad. Get it out of your system."

"I've got to go back to it later."

"Believe me, this will help. When everything seems like it couldn't get any worse, you'll always be able to tell yourself: I did this one brilliant thing, this one brilliant thing that no one else has ever or will ever do. And that makes me special."

She thought about the companion. It had been a gift from Shirin and—for all that it was dog-eared, and not the smartest in the world—she had treated it with fondness. It reminded her of her older sister. It reminded her of the good times they had spent together, before Shirin bored of childhood games and started looking to the skies, dreaming of worlds to make anew.

But had Shirin really cared? It had been easy for her to promise to keep her side of the bargain, before she said good-bye. Yukimi sometimes wondered if her sister had given her more than a moment's thought except for the times when her conscience prickled her into sending a message.

"I cared," Yukimi said to herself. "Even if you didn't."

She still had the companion in her hands from when she had shown it the lake.

"You want a moment to yourself?" Corax asked.

Yukimi nodded.

She stayed in the submerged buggy while he took the helmet and the companion into the airtight building. He went out in the under-water armor, a monster born anew. But when he had taken a few paces away from the buggy and turned back to wave, Yukimi waved back. She couldn't see his face, but she knew it was Corax inside now, and while the armor was still monstrous, it was no longer frightening. Corax had been kind to her, and on some level he had seemed to understand what she was going through.

She watched him enter the building via the porch air lock. Some bubbles erupted out of the dark mouth of the door, and then there was nothing. She didn't think it would take him long to place the helmet and the companion, especially if he already knew his way around the building.

The buggy started moving.

It was sudden, purposeful activity, not the result of the brakes being loose or some underwater current stirring it into motion. It began to turn, steering back the way they had come. This wasn't right. Yukimi looked despairingly at the console, with its many controls. She didn't know which one to hit. There was a red panel, lit up as if it was some kind of emergency stop. She whacked it with her palm and then when there was no response she whacked it again and again. She grabbed hold of the steering joystick Corax had been using and tried yanking it left and right. But nothing she did had any effect on the buggy's progress. It was already climbing out of the lake, the water beginning to drain off the top of the canopy as it pushed into air. "Stop!" she shouted. "Corax isn't back yet!"

But either the buggy was too stupid to realize what was happening or Corax had programmed it to ignore her.

Soon it was out of the lake. Once the ripples had settled, Yukimi could see the outline of Crowe's Landing exactly as it had been before. Nothing had changed. Except now Corax was down there, inside the armor, inside the watertight building.

She remembered him punching commands into the buggy before he had stood up. Had he been telling it to return to the Scaper after a set interval with Yukimi was still aboard?

Numb, but knowing there was nothing she could do, she sat in silence for the rest of the journey.

✳ ✳ ✳

The flier came not long after the buggy climbed back into the Scaper's belly. She was sitting alone in the galley, barely able to speak, when she heard footsteps echoing down the long metal corridors from the landing bay. Eventually two adults came into the galley. One was a young-looking man carrying a heavy bag. The other was her father, looking worried and gray. She braced herself for a stinging reproof, but instead her father rushed to Yukimi and hugged her. "I'm sorry," he said. "We didn't realize."

When she could find the words she asked, "Am I in trouble?"

"No," her father said soothingly. "I am. But you're not. Not now. Not ever." He hugged her again, as if he couldn't quite believe he had her in his arms, that it wasn't a dream.

"Where's the old guy?" asked the other man.

"I presume you mean Corax?" Yukimi asked.

"Yeah, Corax." The young-looking man set his bag down on the table and began unloading it. "I'm his replacement. That's why the flier was scheduled, so I could take over from him. The sponsors were worried he was getting a little too old for this kind of thing."

"Corax isn't coming back," Yukimi said.

The man looked impatient with her, as if she wasn't showing sufficient deference. "What do you mean, not coming back? What happened to him? Where is he?"

She looked him straight in the face, daring him to dismiss what she was about to say. "That's between me and Corax."

"Are you all right, Yukimi?" her father asked gently.

"I'm fine," she said. Which, for the moment at least, was the truth. She was sad for Corax, sad that she wouldn't see him again. But whatever he had done, he must have planned on doing it long before she took her airship ride. That he had shared it with her, that he had allowed her to place the companion in the time capsule, and to record her thoughts before doing so—her angry, bitter, wounded thoughts—was a privilege and a secret she would always carry with her. And whatever happened next, however hard it got with her family, she would have the knowledge that she had participated in something wonderful and unique, something no one else would know about until the seas retreated, on some impossibly distant day in the future of Mars, her Mars.

The flier took off, leaving the other man alone on the Scaper. Her father let Yukimi sit by the window as the flier accelerated back toward Shalbatana City. Nose pressed to glass, she studied the wheeling, rushing landscape for the lake where Crowe's Landing used to be. She saw a few patches of water, some vehicle tracks, and some of them looked vaguely familiar. But from up above, with an entirely different perspective, she couldn't be certain.

"Shirin's coming back from Venus," her father said, breaking the long silence.

"Oh," Yukimi answered.

"She says she's sorry she hasn't been in touch as often as she'd have liked."

"I'm sorry as well."

"She means it, Yukimi. I saw how upset she was."

Yukimi didn't answer immediately. She watched the ground hurtle by, thinking of Corax in his armor, the old man and the Martian sea. Then she reached out and took her father's hand in hers. "It'll be good to see Shirin," she said.

ALASTAIR REYNOLDS was born in Barry, South Wales, in 1966. He has lived in Cornwall, Scotland, and—since 1991—the Netherlands, where he spent twelve years working as a scientist for the European Space Agency. He became a full-time writer in 2004 and recently married his longtime partner, Josette. Reynolds has been publishing short fiction since his first sale to *Interzone* in 1990. Since 2000 he has published eight novels: the Inhibitor trilogy, British Science Fiction Association Award–winner *Chasm City, Century Rain, Pushing Ice,* and *The Prefect*. His most recent novel is *Terminal World*. His short fiction has been collected in *Zima Blue and Other Stories* and *Galactic North*. In his spare time he rides horses.

His Web site is www.alastairreynolds.com.

AUTHOR'S NOTE

I looked forward to the challenge of writing my *Life on Mars* story. Given the freedom offered by the submission guidelines, I opted to tell a story about a Mars that's already been colonized for several centuries, and a girl growing up who has never known anything *other* than Mars and, to tell the truth, is a bit jaded by it all. Wanting a reason for her to run away from home—so that she could get on the airship, have an adventure, and learn something about her world—I remembered how I'd felt at sixteen, when my parents split up and it felt like my universe had been chiseled in two. I never ran away but I certainly fantasized about being able to climb into a spaceship and leave it all behind. Instead, I climbed into the mental escape pod of writing.

Above all else what I wanted to convey in this story is the notion of change sweeping away the past, and how that's not always going to be good for everyone.

WAHALA

✦

Nnedi Okorafor

I wasn't lost. I *wanted* to cross "The Frying Pan of the World, Where Hell Meets Earth." I was fighting my way through this part of the Sahara on purpose. I needed to prove to my parents that I could do it. That I, their sixteen-year-old abomination of a daughter, could survive in a place where many people died. My parents believed I was meant to die easily because I shouldn't have been born in the first place. If I survived, it would prove to them wrong.

The sun was going down and the "frying pan" was thankfully cooling. Plantain, my camel, was walking at her usual steady pace. We'd left Jos three days ago and we were still days from our destination, Agadez. I'd traveled the desert many times . . . well, with my parents, though, and not here. I was okay, for now.

I was staring at the small screen of my e-legba, trying to forget the fact that I might have made a terrible mistake in running away and coming out here. It was picking up the only netcast available in the region, *Naija News*.

"Breaking News! *Breaking News, o!*" a sweating newscaster said in English. He stared into the camera with bulging eyes. He was wearing an ill-fitting Western-style suit. It was obviously the reason for his profuse sweating.

I chuckled. *Everything* on *Naija News* was "breaking news." Drama was the bread and butter of Nigerians. Even our news was suspenseful and theatrical. It was why our movies were the best and our government was the worst. I laughed. I missed home.

"Make sure you listen to what I am about to say, *o!* Then turn to those beside you and tell them! Tell *every*body," the man stressed. Spit flew from his mouth, hitting the camera lens as he spoke. He wiped his brow with a white handkerchief. I could see individual beads of sweat forming on his forehead. "This is no laughing matter, o!"

"Let me guess," I muttered. "Another *farmer!* has lost his flock of goats in a spontaneous forest. Someone's *house!* is infested with a sparkling lizard. Another *boy!* turned into a giant yam." I smiled, ignoring my chapped lips. This kind of "breaking news" happened all the time.

"It's heading this way *right now!*" the anchorman said. He clumsily held the microphone and wiped his brow again. He switched to Igbo. "This is utterly unbelievable!"

I laughed loudly. So unprofessional! How many of his viewers would understand that?

He coughed, smiled sheepishly, and switched back to English. "A *space shuttle* carrying people from the *Mars Colony* is going to land in the *Sahara*, o! These people had been on a spacecraft for months! Cooped up like chicken! It landed on the moon. From there they got on to the space shuttle to return to Earth. Communication with the shuttle has been spotty but we know where it will land." He moved closer to the camera, turned his head to the side, and opened his eyes wider. "If you encounter it, do *not* approach. *Biko nu,* stay away! Help will arrive. Officials will be there in two or three days! Don't—"

The picture distorted and the sound cut off. From far off came a deep *boom!* I felt the vibration in my chest, like a huge talking drum. Plantain growled. "Shh." I patted her hump. "Relax."

She stopped and I jumped off, looking to the south. I saw nothing but sky and sand for miles. A startled desert fox family was running across the sand about two miles away. I looked into the sky with my sharp eyes. There. About fifteen miles away.

"Oh," I whispered.

Within seconds, it zoomed overhead like a giant white eagle. Plantain groaned loudly as she dropped to the sand. I knelt beside her, craning my head and shielding my eyes from the dust it whipped up. It was flying so low that I could have hit it with a stone. This was the first flying aircraft I'd ever seen. I watched it land a few miles away, sliding to a stop in the sand.

It was a snap judgment, though it came from deep within me. "Let's go see!" I said to my camel, climbing on. "Before all the ambulances, government officials, technicians, and journalists show up!" I was in the middle of nowhere. It really would be days before anyone got here. I couldn't believe my luck. People from Mars!

As we headed there, I felt a pinch of embarrassment. I wondered if those onboard knew what we had done to ourselves here on Earth while they were away. People had been living on Mars for decades *before* the Great Change. We should have been super advanced like the people in those old science fiction books, jumping from planet to planet, that sort of thing. Instead we had destroyed the Earth because of stupid politics and misunderstandings.

I wanted to go inside the shuttle and breathe its trapped air. After so many years, that air wouldn't be Earth air. I am a shadow speaker. My large catlike eyes, my "reading" abilities, they're extraordinary, but they are all *because* of the Great Change, aka stupid human error. I'm as tainted by nuclear and peace bombs as one can get. I was born this way. But those on that ship hadn't *been* here when it happened. They were untouched. I wanted to see and touch them. And I wanted to *read* them.

Some of them were probably born on Mars. What had it been, over forty years since anyone last heard from the colonies?

"Faster, Plantain!" I shouted, laughing.

"I don't believe this," I muttered, my heart sinking.

Already, a small spontaneous forest had sprung up around the shuttle, enshrouding it with palm trees, bushes, and a small pond to its left. Vines had even begun to creep up the sides of the shuttle. I guess this was the Earth's way of welcoming it home. The sun was now completely down and there were several sunflowers opening up near the bottom of the ship.

Plantain slowed her stride when we reached the trees. An owl hooted and crickets and katydids sang. An instant oasis in the middle of the Sahara. Yet another result of human idiocy. I'd known spontaneous forests all my life, but their spontaneity and inappropriateness always bothered me. It wasn't hard to imagine a time when this was *not* normal.

I looked around cautiously, ready for anything. I couldn't tell if this was the type of forest that was full of stuff like stinging insects and rotten fruit or stuff like succulent strange vegetables and color-ful butterflies. We passed a tree heavy with rather normal looking green mangos. That was a good sign.

The shuttle was about the size of an American football field. It took us a while to amble all the way around it. Not one opening. It was night, but I could see perfectly in the dark, another shadow speaker privilege. I knocked on the ship's white metal skin. No response. Minutes passed. Nothing happened.

I was exhausted. We'd been traveling for hours before seeing the ship. I'd been so excited that I hadn't eaten or been hydrating myself properly. Stupid. Suddenly, all at once, my neglect disarmed me. I fell to my knees, weak. Plantain trotted to the small pond and started drinking. Eventually, Plantain returned to me, gently clasped the collar of my dress with her teeth, dragged me to the water, and dumped me in the shallow part.

I laughed weakly. The water was cold. "Okay, okay," I said, pushing myself up. Cupping some of the water in my hands, I looked closely at it, searching for bacteria or strange microorganisms that might make me sick. The water was wonderfully fresh and clean, so much better than the water my capture station pulled from the clouds. I drank like crazy.

After having my fill, I laid my mat under a tree, sat down, and ate some bread and dried goat meat as I gazed at the ship. *Don't they want to come out?* I wondered. They had to have been on that shuttle for weeks. I brushed my teeth and lay down. As I drifted off to sleep, I thought, *Tomorrow.*

I woke an hour later to Plantain's soft warning grunt. I opened my eyed to a star-filled sky. Something was humming and splashing in the pond. I listened harder. It sounded like a person. *Finally.*

Someone's come out, I thought, sitting up. But the shuttle looked as it had an hour ago, no openings anywhere. *Maybe the door's on the other side?* I crept to the pond for a better look.

He was standing thigh deep in the water wearing only his blue pants. As he waded deeper in, he hissed with pain. The way he moved, with his hands out, it didn't seem like he could see in the dark at all. I stood up for a better look. His things were on the ground, closer to me than him. A ripped satchel, a tattered blue shirt, and a silver, very sharp looking dagger.

Quietly, I snuck to his things. I was about to reach for his dagger when he suddenly stopped. He was up to his belly; his back to me. He whirled around and before I realized what was happening, he *flew* at me. Fast like a hawk! I leapt to the side, grabbing his satchel. Items fell from its large opening.

He landed and snatched another small dagger from his wet pocket. Then he eyed me with such rage and disgust that I stumbled back. He addressed me in Arabic, his dagger pointed at me. "Filthy *abid* bitch," he spat. "I'll slice your belly open just for *touching* my things." His wet face was scratched up, and one of his eyes was nearly swollen shut. There were more fresh scratches and bruises on his arms and his chest.

I blinked, understanding several things at once. First, he'd been recently beaten. Second, he was a windseeker, one born with the ability to fly, a product of the Great Change, tainted like me. Third, this meant he could not have been from the ship.

I was so appalled by his mauled condition and his words that I just stood there. He took this as further evidence that I couldn't possibly understand him.

"Allah protect me," he said, lowering his dagger. "Can this night get any worse?" He looked my age, had skin the color of milky tea and a hint of a beard capping his chin. And he had the usual wind-seeker features: somewhat large wild eyes and long onyx black hair braided into seven very thick braids with copper bands on the ends.

"What is wrong with you?" I asked in Arabic, regaining my composure. He looked obviously shocked that I could speak his oh-so-sacred language. Most black Africans in Niger spoke Hausa or Fulanese. I deliberately looked him up and down and slowly enunciating my words said, "There are no *slaves* in these lands." *Abid* meant slave in Arabic.

"Hand me my things," he demanded. "*Now.*"

Instead, I read him. I was close enough to him. The first thing was the scent of turmeric. I tasted something spicy, garlicky . . . *a dish called* muhammara. *Ahmed, that is his name. He's from . . . Saudi Arabia.*

He flew this far? I wondered as I swam within his past, seeing, hearing, tasting, touching, smelling. I was me but I was him. Duality. My heart was slamming in my chest as it always did when I read people.

As fast as I could, I soaked information from him like a sponge. . . . *From a lavish home. The seventh of five sons and four daughters. All normal. Except him.* Ahmed's father loomed large to me. Larger than Ahmed. *Father did not smoke or drink. Father prayed five times a day. Father hated spontaneous forests and the fact that the way to the nearby village was not always the same whenever he walked there. Father owned three black African slaves and he often cursed their black skin and burned hair.*

Father hated how the quality of the air was different. And he constantly dreamed of Mars. The new world, a fresh world, the place of his birth. He was an important man in the crumbling local government. Too important to have a windseeker son, one of those strange troublesome polluted children. Ahmed understood that Father thought him ruined.

As I looked into Ahmed, I heard him step toward me. When in a reading state, I'm basically helpless. I can't pull out of it quickly. One day, I will learn to not be so vulnerable.

Looking into Ahmed, I was surprised to find poetry and gentleness, too. *Ahmed loved salty olives. Short, curvy women. The beaded necklaces around the necks of black-skinned women he'd see working at the market. The open sky. Music moved him. His quiet mother, whose hands were always writing adventure stories in the notebook she hid from Father* . . .

It came as it always did. In disorganized fragments, details, like a sentient puzzle more concerned with the shape of its pieces than putting itself together.

The day Father drove him away was the day news came about his grandfather on the shuttle returning to Earth. The first since the Great Change. Ahmed had assumed he'd never see Grandfather. During the celebration of the news, Father had turned to Ahmed. Had sneered at Ahmed. Father was ashamed of the bizarre son he'd have to present to his father whom he hadn't seen since he was four years old. Ahmed ran away that night. A windseeker must fly . . . *not even Father's heavy hand and words could change that.*

"You *abeed* are the lowliest of all Mankind," Ahmed was telling me. "A polluted *abid* . . . you are an aberration of the devil." These wicked words against the compelling melancholy of his past made my head ache. I fought to pull myself from him. A last fragment came to me, just before he shoved me to the ground . . . *As Ahmed flew from the only home he'd ever known, he received a message on his e-legba. From Grandma. The attachment she'd sent took up half the space on his hard drive. Coordinates, linked tracking applications, schedules . . . for Grandfather's space shuttle arrival. "Meet him," Grandma's message said. "He will love you."*

"Stop it!" he shouted, shoving me so hard that my breath was struck from my chest. I fell to the sand.

"Your father drove you away," I said, quickly getting up. I backed away from him and dusted the sand from my long dress. My heart was still pounding as I fought for breath. "Yet . . . you speak to me . . . with the same words that you fled."

"You're Nigerian," he growled, looking a little crazed. "I can hear it in your accent! You all are nothing but *thieves!*" He pointed to his pummeled face. "Who do you think did this to me? They didn't just take my money, they tried to put a virus on my e-legba to empty my bank account! Double thievery!"

His motions, again, were so quick. Before I realized it, he'd grabbed a flashlight from the ground and flashed in my face.

"Ah!" I exclaimed, shielding my sensitive eyes, temporarily blinded. He clicked it off. "What are you doing here?" He began using his feet to gather to himself the other items that had fallen from his satchel.

For a few seconds, all I could see was red, figuratively and literally.

"Give me my bag," he snapped, when I didn't respond to his stupid question. I threw it at him, more things falling out of it. He glared at me and I glared back.

My mother grew up in northern Nigeria and had traveled with her parents all over the Middle East before the Great Change. She'd told me about how black Africans were often treated in these places, but I'd never encountered it with the Arabs I met in Nigeria. My mother said it was an old, old, old problem, stemming from the trans-Saharan slave trade and before that. I only half-believed it was real. But I knew the words *abeed* and *abid,* the Arabic singular and plural forms for *black* or *slave*. Ugly, cruel words.

"What is it you're doing here?" he suddenly asked again, once he had all his things in his satchel. "How did you know to be here?"

"I didn't," I snapped.

"Then get out of here," he said. "Didn't you hear it on the news? You people never know what's best for you!"

"You know what? I'm here to see what's in that ship, so stay out of my way!" I said. He stepped forward. I stood my ground. He glanced over my shoulder at the ship.

"We'll see," he said. He flew up into the air and eventually descended behind some trees.

"Don't mind him," I muttered to Plantain, who was yards away, preoccupied with a patch of fennel she'd found near a tree. "I'm not going anywhere." I returned to my spot on my mat and sat staring at the ship, listening. Waiting.

Seven hours later, I woke to Ahmed crouching over me, a rock in his raised hand. Every part of my body flexed. I stayed still.

He had the wild look of someone about to do something terrible in the name of those who raised him. I stared at him, willing him with all my might to look into my eyes. *Look,* I demanded with my mind. It was my only chance. If he didn't, he'd kill me, I knew . . . and it was not going to be a painless, quick death. I strained for his eyes. *Look, now! PLEASE!*

He looked into my eyes.

He looked for a long long time.

His face went from intense to slack to horribly troubled. He dropped the stone beside my head. He whimpered. Tears welled in his eyes. I smirked. Good. To look into the eyes of a shadow speaker is to court madness. Or so the rumor went. All I knew was that people who looked right into my eyes for more than a second were never the same afterward.

He sat before me, his hands not over his eyes but over his ears, terror on his face. I began to feel a little ill. Not guilty. No. I hadn't done anything. I was actually awash in rage. He'd been ready to cave my head in and now while he grieved over whatever he was grieving, I wanted to kick his teeth in. He wasn't paying attention to me. He was just sitting there holding his head. I could do it. But to do such a thing was not in me; it was evil. Unlike him, I *couldn't* murder. But he'd almost brutally killed me. My conflicted feelings made my stomach lurch.

Naked faced, he started weeping. His eyebrows crinkled in, his mouth turned downward, and his eyes narrowed as he wept softly.

"Look at me! I deserved to be robbed and beaten by your people!" he sobbed. "They should. . . ."

I didn't know what to say, so I didn't say anything.

"Fisayo," he whispered. It was odd to hear him speak my name. The sun was just coming up. "I . . ."

There was a loud hissing sound and we both looked toward the ship. A door had appeared on its side. The shuttle was finally opening.

Wiping his face with the heel of his hand, Ahmed got up. I scowled at him as I got up, too, wishing he'd stop his sniveling.

"Get it together," I snapped. "Goodness." He nodded, sobbed loudly, but then quieted a bit.

He was still weeping as we approached the shuttle. The sunlight was quickly bathing the desert. In the Sahara, the sun rises fast and steady. Even in a spontaneous forest. As we walked, I noticed many of the trees and bushes in the forest had disappeared or were withering, and the pond had gone foul and brackish.

"Will you *stop* it?" I whispered. I didn't know why I was whispering but it seemed right. "Tell me what we should expect. Do you have information about how many are on board?"

He brought out his e-legba, clicked it on, and read for a moment. He took a deep breath. "Your eyes are evil," he whined.

I scoffed. "It's not my eyes, Ahmed. It was you."

He sniffed loudly. "It says here that there are . . ." His voice cracked. He sniffled again. "There are supposed to be thirty-one people onboard."

As the sunlight and the heat increased, the vines on the shuttle quickly dried and began falling off, leaving the shuttle exposed. The door that had opened gave way to darkness inside. I could see only the wall, as the passageway went directly to the right.

"Why isn't anyone coming out?" I asked.

As we moved closer, Ahmed pulled himself together . . . at least he stopped weeping. "So really," he asked. "Why are you here?"

I hesitated. Then I shrugged. "I just happened to be a few miles away when I heard about it on my e-legba."

He wiped at his eyes again. "You're not here to steal from them?"

"No! Of course not!" I was getting more nervous the closer we got; it was good to talk about something else. "You were going to *kill* me."

"I was." He paused. He frowned as more tears began to dribble from his eyes. "I . . . I'm sorry." He rubbed his temples. "I don't think you're human."

"I don't think *you* are either."

We were standing at the door. Inside the shuttle, the walls were plush red and busy with buttons, small blank screens, and other things. To the right, the corridor went well into the ship. Ahmed sobbed loudly. He turned to the side, pressed a finger to his left nostril, and blew out a large amount of snot. "I'm sorry," he said, looking distraught again, his voice strained as he tried to hold back more sobs.

"Ugh," I said, turning to the side. I couldn't look at him anymore. "Look . . . I'm going in, are . . ."

Ahmed had stopped weeping entirely. I frowned, turning back to him. He looked as if he was seeing a ghost. He grabbed my hand. I turned to the door just as something large and red slammed me to the ground. *Hot glass! Hot glass!* I frantically thought. Ahmed hadn't released my hand and was thus yanked back as I fell. I could hear Ahmed yelling but all I saw was a layer of red and all I felt were pain and heat. It was as if the world was submerged under soft ripples of red tinted waters. I could see a wavy red sun, the ship, and Ahmed kicking and kicking at whatever was on top of me.

I heard it hissing in my ear. A creature with a heavy solid body like glass. Dry, hot, and buzzing. No, not buzzing. Vibrating. I could feel it, down deep inside me. I struggled to understand. But it was pressing on my throat. A part of me could only think one thing: *Look into my eyes! Please look into my eyes!* If it was a thing, a creature maybe . . .

I was looking through . . . its head. Oblong but empty. Then I was falling. Shaking. Vibrating. Falling. Into. Red. *The CoLoRs it knew and loved. The CoLoRs of HoME. Where everything was all kinds of RED. Until it was fOuNd. For VIbRAtINg too much with CuriosItY.* I fell deeper. Beyond myself. I have no words to describe it. But it was alive. Not in the same way that I knew life, but it was alive.

As its weight lifted off me, my entire body flared with pain. Nevertheless, I lived. And I knew why. I knew what the creature was. I knew many things about it now. I tried to laugh. Instead I coughed hard and everything around me throbbed red.

It stood before me. Too heavy now and sinking into the sand. It looked like a crude glass bipedal grasshopper. It was impervious to Ahmed's attacks. Kicking it was like kicking transparent stone.

"From Mars," I breathed as I got to my feet. My neck ached painfully and I had to bend forward. "It's a . . ."

It suddenly turned to Ahmed and sent out so much vibration that I could feel it in my chest. I coughed, pressing my hands to my chest. Then it leapt at him.

"No!" I croaked. "Stop, wait!'

But Ahmed was ready. He jumped back and shot into the sky. The creature fell forward and started sinking fast into the sand. I shielded my eyes, searching for Ahmed. The creature had sunk halfway into the sand before Ahmed returned. "What is it?" he asked, hovering several feet above my head.

I laughed, rubbing my neck. I was beginning to feel a little better. "It's an alien." Then I sat down hard on the sand.

In a matter of minutes, I'd gone from fighting off a racist wind-seeker armed with a rock to fighting off a Martian alien. As I sat there contemplating this, I stared at the door.

"You know why it didn't kill me?" I asked, rubbing my temples and shutting my eyes. Ahmed sat beside me, anxiously looking at where the alien had sunk.

"Why?" he muttered. He hacked loudly and spit to the side. He was done crying.

"Because I'm Nigerian," I said.

"What?" Ahmed said, frowning at me. "How would it know that? Why would it *care*?"

"It was held captive, and the only person to treat it with any respect before it managed to escape was a man named Arinze Tunde, a Nigerian."

"How do you . . ." His eyes widened. "You read an alien?"

"It read me more," I said.

"That cursed thing could read genetics or something?"

"Guess so," I said. "That's what the vibrating was. You felt it, right?"

"Yeah, like being touched by sound."

I got up and waited a moment to make sure I was steady. Ahmed got up, too. For a moment, I felt dizzy, then everything stabilized. As I dusted off my dress, I said, "And you know why it wanted to kill you?"

Ahmed shrugged.

"Your grandpa was the one who captured it."

He stared at me blankly as I quickly walked to the ship. I turned to him. "Come on!" I said. "The passengers are locked in some room. We need to get everyone off *right now*. The alien is going to make the shuttle take off again."

"My grandfather?" Ahmed said as I ran inside. "Alien? Didn't it just sink into the sand? There's another one??"

The soft humming was continuous and the lights flickered as we walked down the narrow corridor single file. The padded walls added to the narrowness. Everything was spotless, no dust or dirt in any corners. And everything smelled like face powder.

"I don't like this," Ahmed said, moving faster. "Not at all."

I smiled. Windseekers hate tight places. "Inhale, exhale," I said. "We'll find the passengers and then get out. Relax."

As he loudly inhaled and exhaled as he walked, I took a moment to look behind us. So far we'd moved in a straight line and I could still see the sun shining in from the open door. I felt a little better. If it was a trap, the door probably would have shut. Eventually, the corridor did break off in three different directions. We took the one in the middle and came to a large metal door with a sign on it that said CONFERENCE ROOM B. Ahmed was about to touch the blue button beside the door. I grabbed his hand.

"What?" he said, accidently looking into my eyes. He quickly looked away, squeezing his face as if I'd stuck a pin in his arm.

"Don't start that again," I snapped.

"It's your damn eyes!"

I rolled my eyes. "Let's knock first."

"Fine," he said, gritting his teeth. He knocked three times. The sound was absorbed by the hallway's padding. We stood there, listening hard.

I sighed, "Maybe, we could . . ."

"Arinze?" a woman called from behind the door.

Ahmed grabbed my arm, and I stepped closer to him.

"Please!" a man shouted in English, banging on the door. I couldn't place his accent. "Open up. Just . . ."

"Is that English? What are they saying?" Ahmed asked me in Arabic. "I can't understand."

"They want us to open the door," I said. I stepped up to the door. "We're . . . we're not him!" I responded in English. I turned to Ahmed and switched back to Arabic. "I told them we're not Arinze."

"Let's open it," he said.

"Okay."

He was about to and then stopped. He turned to me, looking guilty. "You should step back."

I understood. My eyes. Who knew what they'd think? And I didn't want anyone looking into them.

"Okay," I said, stepping behind him. "Makes sense."

He touched the blue button and there we were facing about thirty sweaty dirty people all crammed at the door. Hot air wafted out. It reeked of sweat, urine, feces, and rotten fruit. Ahmed and I coughed.

Ahmed stood up straight. "We're here to—"

"Take her down!" a man shouted in English. There was a mad rush as they all tried to lunge for me through the narrow corridor. I stumbled back as Ahmed jumped in front of me, using his body to block the way. Five men tried to shove him aside but he somehow managed to remain lodged.

"Stop it!" he shouted in Arabic.

"We can handle her!" someone said in Igbo. "Just get out of the way!"

"We're getting off this damn shuttle!" another said in English.

"Stop!" Ahmed screamed in Arabic, pushing them back with all his might. "She's not—she's human!"

No one listened or maybe they didn't understand. Everyone started shouting at the same time. Sweat gleamed on Ahmed's face as he fought to keep himself in the passageway. I ran back several feet but I wasn't about to leave Ahmed.

Suddenly, out of nowhere, a blast of wind flew through the passageway. It knocked me off my feet and I slid several feet back. Then everything went silent. I slowly sat up. Everyone in the passageway had been blown back into the conference room. They murmured as they sat up, rubbing their heads, arms, confused.

Only Ahmed remained, hovering, his seven long thick braids undulating as the windseeker breeze circulated his body. The passengers stared at him. I smiled broadly, though once again, I was shaking all over.

"She, *we* are not . . ." Ahmed switched to French as he landed on his feet. "We are not whatever you've been dealing with! Does anyone understand me? We're here to get you out!"

"How do we know that?" some woman asked in French from behind everyone. *Good*, I thought. Someone understood.

"Speak in French," I said. "I can speak that, too."

Ahmed looked at me. I winked. I can speak six languages, Arabic, Hausa, French, Igbo, Yoruba, and English. My father liked to call me the daughter of Legba—the Yoruba deity of language, communication, and the crossroads—because I picked up languages so easily.

"Why else would we *unlock* the door?" Ahmed snapped. The woman translated for those who couldn't understand.

Silence.

"Stupid," I muttered, stepping closer to Ahmed.

"This is Fisayo and I'm Ahmed," he said. "We're . . . Do you know what's happened on Earth since you left?"

More confused murmuring. The general consensus was that they knew something bad had happened but they weren't sure what.

"She and I have been . . . affected. We're not aliens. One of you is my . . . my grandfather. Zaid Fakhr Mohammed Uday al-Rammah." Before the woman could translate for the others, Ahmed repeated himself in Arabic, listing his name, his grandmother's name, and his village. There was a soft gasp from near the back and the crowd slowly parted, allowing a tall wizened man to come forth. He was about eighty and wore blue garments whose armpits were dirty with sweat, and a deep blue turban.

There was a long pause as the two stared at each other.

"Why do you look like a punching bag?" Ahmed's grandfather asked in Arabic. He motioned to me. "Is this girl your wife? Have you two been quarreling?" A few people chuckled.

"Uh . . ." Ahmed said. "We're . . ."

"Come here," his grandfather said.

Ahmed slowly stepped up to him and the old man looked him up and down. "You don't look like my son."

Ahmed scoffed. "The last time you saw him he was about four years old."

I held my breath. Then I let it out with relief as the old man smiled and laughed softly. "You are really my grandson?"

Ahmed brought a picture from his pocket. "This is you, Grandma, and my father just before they left for Earth."

His grandfather stared at it for a very long time.

"That . . . monster will let us out now?" someone impatiently asked behind them.

Ahmed's grandfather was crying. "I haven't seen this photo in . . . such a long time. It's why I came back."

"There's one more of us," an African woman said in Igbo, pushing to the front. She wore jeans and a dirty purple sweater. Ahmed looked back at me and I stepped forward. The woman hesitated, glancing at and looking away from my eyes and said, "He's being held captive in the cockpit, I think." She pointed behind her. "It's through the conference room."

"Arinze," I said.

She nodded.

"Troublesome sellout," Ahmed's grandpa mumbled. "Nigerians." He spoke the name of my people like he was spitting dirt from
his mouth. I frowned.

The women who'd spoken Igbo sucked her teeth loudly and
deliberately. "Keep talking and see *wahala*, old man."

Even when they lived and were born on Mars, people were still
people.

Ahmed's and my eyes met for a half second. Then he looked
away. "I'll go," I said.

"I'll go with you," the Igbo woman said.

"It's okay," I told her. "I know what's going on. Just . . . wait for
him outside." This time, I was the one who didn't want to meet her
eyes. I switched to English. She spoke Igbo with an English accent,
so I suspected she'd understand, as would more of the others. "You
all need to get off. There isn't time. This shuttle is going to take off
soon."

"What!" a man said. "Impossible! There can't be any fuel
left. . . ."

People started translating for each other, and there were more
exclamations of surprise.

"Who cares," a woman said. "Show us out of here! I can't stand
being on a shuttle any longer!"

Everyone began pushing forward again. As they crammed
past me, I told Ahmed, "Go with them. They need someone who
knows . . . Earth."

"Okay. But hurry out," he said, taking and squeezing my hand.
His other was holding the hand of his grandfather.

"I'll be all right."

I watched them all file down the corridor. Then I walked into the conference room to attend the strangest meeting of my life.

The conference room was spacious with a high ceiling and windows the size of the walls (which were currently covered with the ship's protective white metal exterior). Near the back were shelves of books and three exercise bicycles. This large room was probably normally beautiful. But at the moment it was filthy and stinky. There were plastic tubs brimming with urine and feces and sacks of garbage. Had they been allowed to leave the room for anything? How long had they been trapped in there? I hurried to the door on the other side.

It easily opened and led into another passageway that was even narrower than the other one. It went on and on. I passed sealed doorways on my left and right. I frowned, realizing something. Maybe the creature was allowing the doors to open. Maybe it had opened the door to the outside so that Ahmed and I could come in and rescue the people. I had so many answers, yet I had even more questions.

Finally, I reached a small round door. It felt like metal but it looked like wood. Nervous, I took a deep breath, tugging at one of my long braids. Suddenly the door slid open and I was standing before a tall very dark-skinned Nigerian man. Behind him was a round sunshine-filled room. The cockpit window must have been recently opened, for I hadn't seen this on the outside. Every inch of wall was packed with virtual sensors, small and large screens, and soft buttons.

In the middle of it all, manipulating the ship's virtual controls, was the . . . thing. It looked like something out of the deep ocean. Wet, red, bloblike, formless. I imagined that it would have fit perfectly into the glasslike thing that had attacked Ahmed and me outside.

It smoothly pulled its many filamentlike appendages in, rose up, and molded itself into an exact replica of my face, shifting and changing colors to even imitate my dark skin tone. I gasped, clapping my hands over my mouth. It smiled at me.

Terrified, I looked up at Arinze, who was still standing there. "I—"

His face curled, and he grabbed me. He pushed me back and slammed me against the wall. For the third time in the last hour all the air left my chest. I grabbed at his hands and dug my nails into them. His grip loosened and I seized the opportunity to slide away.

My eyes located a wrench. I grabbed it and raised it toward one of the screens. Arinze froze and the creature melted from my shape back into a blob.

"I swear I'll . . . I'll smash this!" I screamed, utterly hysterical by this point. "May the fleas of a thousand camels nest in your hair!" I was hurting all over, shaking, full of too much adrenaline and there was a red alien in the middle of the room with appendages snaking out in multiple directions like some sort of giant amoeba! I strained to keep the tears from dribbling for my eyes. The last thing I needed was for my vision to blur. I focused on the alien, sharpening to a molecular level. . . . I immediately pulled back, further shaken. I hadn't seen cells; I saw something more like metal balls.

"Please don't break that," Arinze said in Igbo. His accent was vaguely Nigerian, Yoruba. But not quite. How long had he been on Mars? He had to have been born there. He looked about thirty. Yet he had three short vertical tribal makings on each cheek. So they were still practicing that tradition even on Mars?

"We need that to navigate properly," he said.

"You just nearly *killed* me!"

"I'm sorry," he said. "I was . . . I thought you were going to hurt it. It's . . . it's like a snail without a shell until it makes a new living shell."

I didn't lower my wrench.

"That's . . . that's why it attacked you," he said. "Then we realized a lot of things." He paused. "What are you?"

"I'm human. A shadow speaker." I shook my head. "It's a long story."

He stared at me. I knew he was making up his mind. I'd made mine up. If he tried anything, I'd smash the screen and then smash his head. "Arinze," I said quickly. "I know who you are. I know you have befriended this creature. You understand each other."

"How do you know?" he snapped. "What can you know?"

The creature stretched a narrow filament and touched Arinze's forehead. Affectionately. Arinze seemed to relax.

I felt a pinch of envy. I was constantly getting attacked because of what I looked like. This creature had no shape and could look like anything it wanted. And then it could create an exo-skin that it could wear or send to do what it asked . . . at least until it sunk into the sand on a planet with stronger gravity than it was used to. I wondered why it had chosen to make its exo-skin look like a giant bipedal grasshopper.

"It 'reads' things through vibration," I said. "I am similar. I read things by closeness and focusing. I read it as it read me. You know I'm right. It has told you. Trust it."

"Put the wrench down," he said. "I'm not going to hurt you."

"How do I know?"

He sighed and sat on a stool, now rubbing his own temples. "You know. You both know."

I didn't put it down. "Please," I said. "I'm tired of fighting." I leaned against the controls, feeling very, very tired. "What is it about me that everyone wants to attack? I just came here to *greet* you people. To see." I sighed, tears finally falling from my eyes. Why did everyone think I was evil? One of the last things my mother had said to me before I ran away was that I was *wahala*, trouble.

He frowned. "Did I hurt you?"

I waved a hand at him. It was too much to explain.

"I'm sorry," he said again.

"So am I," I said, sitting on the floor.

There was a clicking sound as the alien's appendage screwed something in beneath the front window controls. There was a soft whirring. The creature's body twisted up and leaned toward Arinze.

"I'm not held captive here," he said. "They all think I am but I'm not."

"I know."

"It's been ugly on this shuttle," he said. "We had to lock them up. Were they all okay?"

I nodded.

"Good. I'm . . . I'm going to go back with it. It's not the only one that's been discovered by the Mars government and there were some government officials on this shuttle who will alert those here on Earth. If I don't go with this one, to help it speak to its people, there will be a war. It tells me so. Like here. It was war, right?"

"Yes. Nuclear and something else."

He nodded. "I have to go back."

"You've never been outdoors, have you?"

"No. But . . ." he said. He looked at the creature, a sadness passing over his face. The creature was focused on getting home. "What's happened to Earth?"

"It's a long story."

He chuckled. "Have you heard news of Nigeria? My grandparents are from there."

I smiled, "Nigeria is still Nigeria."

"One day . . ." He took my hands. "You'd better get off the ship."

The creature moved a filament across the green virtual grid above it and the shuttle shook hard enough to make me stumble.

"Go!" Arinze said. "Hurry!"

I made for the door and then turned back. I ran to Arinze and shook his hand. "I hope you come back," I said.

Before I ran off, quickly like a striking snake, the creature reached out and touched my forehead with a moist appendage. It was neither warm nor cold, hard nor soft, absolutely foreign. Only one image came to me from its touch: an empire of red dust in a place that looked like the Sahara desert. Here strange things grew and withered spontaneously. As they did now on Earth. The communities of these creatures were more like the Earth of now, especially in the Sahara. I breathed a sigh of surprise. Then I could feel it more than I heard it. A vibration that tickled my ears. *My people do not understand Mars Earthlings, but they will understand when I tell about you, Fisayo. You are not* wahala. *You are the information I needed.*

Arinze was pushing me. "Go!" he shouted.

I went.

✳ ✳ ✳

I barely made it off the shuttle before it started rumbling. Plantain was there, waiting. I jumped on her and she took off. We joined the others two miles from the shuttle as it launched into the sky with impossible power and speed. I'd seen what the alien did to the shuttle when I read it, but I didn't have the capacity to understand its science. The Igbo woman who'd wanted to come to the cockpit with me cried and cried when she didn't see Arinze with me. Ahmed stood close to his grandfather. His grandfather had his arm over his shoulder.

Ahmed and I did not say good-bye. As they were all deciding if they should wait for officials to arrive or try to make it to the next town, Plantain and I left. There was too much to say and no space to say it. Plantain and I headed south, back home, to Jos. Crossing the Sahara to Agadez was a silly idea. I needed to have long talk with my parents.

There was other life on Mars. Even after all that had happened here on Earth, I had to work to wrap my mind around that. *Allah protect Arinze and the one he's befriended; provide them with success. There's been more than enough* wahala.

NNEDI OKORAFOR was born in Cincinnati, Ohio. She earned a BA in rhetoric from the University of Illinois, Champaign-Urbana and an MA in journalism from Michigan State University. She attended the University of Illinois in Chicago, getting her MA in English in 2002 and completing her PhD in 2007.

She is the author of the acclaimed science fantasy novels *Zahrah the Windseeker* and *The Shadow Speaker*. *Zahrah the Windseeker* was the winner of the Wole Soyinka Prize for Literature in Africa, was shortlisted for the Carl Brandon Parallax and Kindred awards, and was a Golden Duck Award finalist. *The Shadow Speaker*, winner of the Carl Brandon Society Parallax Award, was a Book Sense Selection, a James Tiptree Jr. Honor Book, and a finalist for the *Essence* Magazine Literary Award, the Andre Norton Award, the Golden Duck Award, and the NAACP Image Award. Her children's book, *Long Juju Man*, won the Macmillan Writer's Prize for Africa.

Her most recent work is the adult magical realist novel *Who Fears Death*, and forthcoming is her young adult novel *Akata Witch*. She is a professor of creative writing at Chicago State University and lives with her family in Illinois.

Visit her Web site at www.nnedi.com.

AUTHOR'S NOTE

"Wahala" deals with a lot of heavy issues, including racism, discrimination, cultural conflict, rebellion, yearning, embracing one's self, and. . . the apocalypse. Even when I'm writing science fiction, I like to keep the "camera" really close to my characters. In this way, I maintain realism within all the bizarreness that springs from my imagination. Nevertheless, what is most memorable for me with this story is the fact that it is my first alien story. I smile because my alien is partial to Nigerians; Fisayo's Nigerian-ness is the reason it does not kill her. This is me paying angry homage to the 2009 film *District 9*, a unique, innovative alien flick that portrayed Nigerians terribly. In *District 9*, it was only "the Nigerians" (this is how they were dismissively referred to) who could relate enough to the aliens to closely interact with them. In the film, this made Nigerians an ugly, corrupt people; in my story, it saves Fisayo's life. I have a habit of turning lemons into lemonade. (Oh, and in case you were wondering, *wahala* means *trouble* in Nigerian pidgin English. It's a word I am quite familiar with and defiantly relate to.)

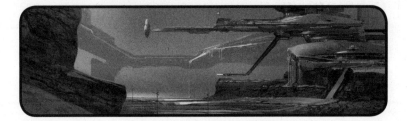

ON CHRYSE PLAIN

Stephen Baxter

"You haven't even seen a picture of her," Jonno said, panting as he pedaled.

"She's called Hiroe," Vikram said.

"Your bride-to-be in Hellas Basin!"

"Shut up."

Jonno laughed, wheezing.

The flycycle dipped, and Vikram had to push harder to bring them back up to their proper altitude. It was always like this with Jonno. At fifteen he was the same age as Vikram, but a few centimeters shorter and a good few kilos heavier, enough to unbalance the cycle. He didn't have enough breath to talk and cycle. But he talked anyhow.

Vikram didn't mind taking the strain for his friend. He liked the feel of his legs pumping at the pedals, his breath deepening, the skinsuit snug around him, the slow unwinding of the crumpled landscape under them, the way the translucent wings above the cycle frame caught the buttery light of the Martian afternoon. He liked the idea that it was his muscles and his muscles alone propelling them across the sky.

Jonno kept on about Hiroe. "You worry too much. Just because you haven't seen a picture doesn't *necessarily* mean she looks like she was hatched by a rock bug."

"Shut up! Where are we anyhow?"

Jonno glanced down and tapped his wristmate. "That's Chryse Plain, I think. We just crossed the highland boundary. Wow, look at those outflow channels." Where, billions of years ago, vast rivers had briefly flowed from Mars's southern highlands into the basin of the northern sea, cutting deep valleys and spilling megatons of rocks over the plains. "What a sight it must have been, once."

"Yeah."

"You don't care, do you?"

Vikram shrugged, pedaling. "It's all about the journey, for me. Getting the job done."

"Checking out those weather stations at Acidalia. Getting together the credits for another A grade. You've got no imagination, man."

Something distracted Vikram. Odd lights in the sky. He squinted and tapped his faceplate to reduce the tint.

"Or," Jonno said, "you've got the wrong kind of imagination. Such as about Hiroe. You could always wear a disguise in the wedding photos—"

Vikram pointed. "What's that?"

The sky was full of glowing trails.

When the plasma glow cleared from around her clamshell, and the gnarly landscape of Mars was revealed beneath her, Natalie whooped. She couldn't help it. She'd made it. She'd dived down from orbit, lying flat on the broad disk of the clamshell, and had got through the heat of atmospheric entry, and now she was skimming through the air of another world. The air of Mars is thinner than Earth, but it is taller, and she was high, so high the world was curved beneath her. The shrunken sun, off to her left, was low and cast long shadows over the channeled plains.

And all around her she saw the contrails scratched across the sky by the rest of her school group, dozens of them on their shells.

Benedicte's voice crackled in her ears. "You stayed on your shell this time, Nat?"

"Yes, Benedicte, I stayed on."

"Well, we're over the Chryse Plain, as advertised. Betcha I get the first sighting of the Viking lander."

"Not a chance!" And Natalie lunged forward, shifting her weight, so her clamshell cut into the thickening air.

But she wasn't used to the Martian air. She didn't get the angle quite right. She could feel it immediately.

"Natalie, you're too steep. Pull out. . . . I lost you. Natalie. Natalie! Oh, I think I see you. . . ."

But whatever Benedicte saw it wasn't Natalie, who continued to fall, far beneath the rest of the group. The clamshell dug deeper into the air and started to shudder.

This wasn't good.

"Clamshell trails," Jonno said. He leaned sideways so he could see the sky, around the edge of the wing. "Earthworm tourists."

They hit a pocket of turbulence and the flycycle bucked and shuddered, the rigging creaking. Vikram said, "Hey, get back in, man. I'm having trouble keeping us on line."

"Look at those babies," Jonno said wistfully, still leaning out. "You know, someday, if I can afford it—"

It came out of the sky, almost vertically, a bright green disk with somebody clinging to its back. Vikram actually saw a head turned toward him, a shocked face behind a visor, a mouth opened in an O. He hauled at the joystick. The flycycle's big fragile rudder turned, creaking. It wasn't enough. It was never going to be enough.

The clamshell cut through the flycycle like a blade through paper. The cycle folded up, crumpling, and started to fall, spiraling down toward the plain of Chryse.

Jonno groaned. Vikram saw the instrument console had jammed into his chest. Vikram couldn't even reach him.

He tried the controls. Nothing responded, and the machine was bent out of shape anyhow. They were going down. Their best hope was that the cycle's fragile structure would slow down their fall enough for them to walk away from the crash. But as they descended the spinning increased, and the structure creaked and snapped.

The clamshell was in trouble too. Vikram glimpsed it tumbling down out of the air.

And the rock-strewn ground of Chryse loomed beneath them, the detail exploding. Vikram braced.

Natalie took a step forward, then another. Red dust scattered at her feet.

She was walking on Mars, for the first time in her life. In the low Martian gravity, she felt like she was floating. She was on a plain of dusty sand strewn with rocks. The sun was small and low in a deep red sky, and there were long, sharp shadows cast by rocks that looked as if they hadn't been disturbed for a billion years. She saw nothing, nobody, no vehicles or buildings. She was alone.

She wasn't supposed to be here.

She didn't remember climbing out of the clamshell. Just the looming ground, her fight to bring up the rim of the shell, the punch in the gut as the shell's underside hit the ground and began to scrape through the dust. . . .

She turned around. There was the clamshell, cracked and crumpled. And a gully, hundreds of meters long, cut through the dust where she had crashed and skidded. The clamshell had a small liquid-rocket pack that should have kicked her back to orbit when she was done skimming in the air. But the small, spherical fuel tanks were broken open. It couldn't have got her to orbit anyhow, not from here.

Her suit was comfortable, warm. She could hear the whir of the fans in her backpack. She tested her legs and arms, her fingers. Nothing broken, and her suit was working, keeping her alive. It was a miracle she'd walked away from the crash, but she had. Now she just needed to get off this rock.

"Benedicte," she called. "Doctor Poulson? I'm down. Somewhere on Chryse Plain, I guess. . . ."

Nothing. No reply. Her suit comms were very short range. The structure of the clamshell contained amplifier boosters and an antenna . . . but the clamshell was wrecked.

She was out of touch. She couldn't talk to anybody.

The shock hit her like a punch, worse even than the crash. It must have been the first time in her life she had been cut out of the nets that spanned Earth and moon and beyond. It was an eerie feeling, as if she didn't exist.

But they would be looking for her. Benedicte had seen her duck down, hunting the Viking. And from orbit they ought to see the clamshell, and the trench she'd cut when she crashed. . . . But she remembered Benedicte's last words to her. *Oh, I think I see you.* Benedicte thought she had pulled out of the dive. And Natalie had a habit of shutting up when she was intent on some quest, like finding the Viking.

Even Benedicte didn't know she was missing. It might be a long time before anybody noticed she wasn't around.

The clamshell flight wasn't supposed to last long. She had no food, no water save in the sachet in her suit, a few mouthfuls. No shelter, save maybe her emergency pressure bag. The power in her suit wouldn't last more than a few hours.

It seemed to be getting darker. How long was a Martian day? How cold did it get on Mars at night? She felt a touch of panic, a black shadow crossing her mind.

She turned and walked away from the shell, distracting herself.

"Well, Benedicte," she said, "if you can't hear me now you can listen to me later, if I'm picked up. *When* I'm picked up. So here I am, walking on Mars. Who'd have thought it? So what can I see? Well, the surface is very fine, powdery." She kicked at the soil, leaving furrows. "It's easy for me to dig little trenches with my toe. The surface crunches when I walk. The dust is clinging in fine layers to the sole and sides of my boots. . . ." She wished she could take her shoes off, press her bare toes into the sand of this Martian beach, feel it for herself.

She took a few more steps. She bounced across the surface. Moving on Mars was dreamlike, somewhere between walking and floating. "I have no difficulty in moving around, Benedicte. It's easier than walking on the moon, actually; you don't bounce so high. But my backpack is making me feel top-heavy, as if I might fall backward on every step. . . ."

She stopped, panting. Sunlight shone into her face, casting reflections from the surface of her faceplate. "Sunset on Mars. The sky here is different from on Earth. Oh, I should take some pictures." She tapped a control on the side of her faceplate. The sun was surrounded by an elliptical patch of yellow light, suspended in a brown sky. It looked unreal. The sun was small, feeble, only two-thirds of its size as seen from Earth. She shivered, although her suit temperature couldn't have varied. The shrunken sun made Mars seem a cold, remote place.

She walked farther away from the shell, letting her view pan across the landscape. "I'm walking on sand littered with rocks. There are small bubbles in the surface of the rocks. The rocks are pitted and fluted, I would guess by wind erosion. I can see smaller formations that look like pebbles. Actually this stuff is not like sand. It's dust, very fine grained. Dust everywhere. Nothing gets rid of dust on Mars. Didn't Doctor Poulson tell us that? There's nothing to turn dust and sand back into rock, like on Earth. It just washes around the planet forever."

On impulse, she bent down and picked up a pebble. She lifted it up to her face to get a closer look. The pebble was very light, so light she couldn't even feel its weight, and she couldn't feel its texture because of the thickness of her gloves. It was oddly frustrating. She closed her fingers. The pebble burst and shattered. She dropped the dust from her hand. It wasn't even a real pebble, just dust stuck together somehow.

She looked back at the crumpled clamshell. A single set of footsteps, crisp in the dust, led to where she stood. They looked like the first steps on a beach after the tide went out. She felt as if the long, thin line attaching her to home was fraying, leaving her stranded on this high, cool plain.

Nobody knew she was here. She was walking around, breathing, talking. But was she already effectively dead?

Keep walking, Natalie. Walk, don't think.

The land wasn't completely flat, she saw now. She made out low sand dunes. And away to the west, toward the sun, she saw a line, a soft shadow in the sand. It looked like a shallow ridge.

She walked forward, toward the ridge. It was somewhere else to go.

When she climbed the ridge she found she was looking down across a shallow valley scoured out of the landscape. There was a crater in the valley floor, maybe thirty meters across. And from up here she could see something off to the north, on the horizon. Like a pile of rocks. A cairn, maybe? Something made by humans. It didn't excite her too much. A pile of rocks wouldn't keep her alive. But maybe she should walk over. There could be a beacon.

She was curious about the crater, though. She'd seen craters before, on the moon, but not on Mars. She scraped her way down the valley side, kicking up a flurry of dust that sparkled yellow in the pale daylight.

The crater was a shallow, regular bowl, its rim sharp and fragile. Her faceplate was misted up, her breath rapid. She leaned forward. In the lee of the crater rim, something sparkled.

It was frost. Frost in a crater. "Well, you don't see *that* on the moon, Benedicte—"

"Who are you talking to?"

✳ ✳ ✳

The girl in the valley whirled around, kicking up dust.

"So did she hear us this time?" Jonno was leaning on Vikram. They were limping forward, toward the girl and the wreck of her clamshell, step-by-step through the clinging dust.

"I think so," Vikram said. "Her comms setup must be really short range. We were practically on top of her before she heard us."

The girl replied, "My main comms system is in the clamshell. And that's smashed up."

"Funny kind of accent," Vikram said.

"That's Earth girls for you." Jonno tried to lift his head. "I can't see her too well."

"She's wearing a kind of skinsuit," Vikram said scornfully. "Bright green stripes. Looks like it's painted on. Typical Earthworm."

They were only meters apart now. The girl put her hands on her hips and glared at them. "Martians, are you?"

"What do you think?" Vikram set Jonno down in the soft dirt and glanced around theatrically. "So who's Benedicte? Your imaginary friend?"

"I'm recording my observations," she said defensively. "My name is Natalie Rivers."

"I'm Jonno. This is Vikram," Jonno gasped, massaging his chest through his suit.

Vikram could make out her face through a dusty, scarred visor. High cheekbones, picked out by the low sun. She was frowning, uncertain.

"Are you from Kahra?"

Kahra is the capital of Mars. Jonno laughed, but it hurt him and he groaned. "Why do Earthworms think every Martian is from Kahra? No. We're from Argyre. South of here."

"One of those domed towns."

"Yes, one of those domed towns."

"So what do you want? Have you come to rescue me?"

Vikram snorted. "Do we look like it? I'll tell you who we are. We're the two guys you nearly killed with your dumb clamshell."

Her mouth opened in an O, and Vikram clearly remembered the face he had glimpsed at the moment of collision. "There was something in the way as I came down."

"That," Jonno said, "was our flycycle. Now it's smashed to pieces."

Vikram snapped, "You Earthworms should keep out of our airspace."

"And you should have got out of the way," she shot back. "There was a whole swarm of us. Why didn't you just—"

"Why didn't *you*—"

"Not helping," Jonno wheezed. "It's not helping, to argue about blame. Let's work out whose fault it is after we're all safe. Agreed?"

Natalie stayed silent, and Vikram nodded curtly.

"So," she said. "What's the plan?"

Vikram laughed. "Plan? What plan?"

"*You* must have comms. Do your people know where you are?"

Vikram hesitated.

"Tell her the truth," Jonno said.

"No," Vikram admitted. "Our primary comms system was built into the flycycle."

She nodded. "As mine was built into the clamshell. So where's your backup?"

Vikram took a breath. "In my room, back in Argyre."

Natalie stared. "Why, of all the stupid—"

"Save it," Vikram said, chagrined. "I've been getting that from Jonno since the crash."

"We all make mistakes," Jonno said. "What's important is what we do now."

Natalie said, "Maybe there's some kind of beacon at that cairn."

Vikram frowned. "What cairn?"

"I saw it before." She climbed the bank and pointed. "Over there. Come on." She strode away without hesitation, although Vikram was spitefully glad to see she stumbled a couple of times in the apparently unfamiliar gravity.

With no better idea, Vikram helped Jonno to his feet and trudged after her.

"I never heard of a cairn," Jonno wheezed. "Or a beacon."

"No."

"Confident, isn't she?"

"Yes. But she'll be wrong about the cairn. It'll just be a pile of rocks."

As it turned out, it was more than a pile of rocks.

Natalie stood there, looking at the "cairn." Vikram helped Jonno sit down in a bank of soft dust.

The cairn was a machine—a big one, topped off by a dust-filled dish antenna about two meters off the ground, above their heads. Its body was a six-sided box that stood on four legs. On the box's upper surface was a forest of gadgets, and an arm thrust out the side, with a trenching tool on the end stuck in the dirt. Dust had drifted up against the machine, and its surfaces were yellowed and cracked from long exposure to the sunlight. It had evidently been here a long time.

A blue plaque stood on a post, a marker left by the planetary preservation authorities. Vikram didn't bother to read it. It didn't matter what it said.

"Here's your cairn," he said to Natalie. "Here's your beacon. A stupid old space probe."

"Not just any probe." Vikram saw she was taking images with her visor. "This is Viking One. The first successful lander."

A thin wind kicked up dust that sifted against the silent carcass. "Been here centuries.

"Well—about a hundred and fifty years. It's what I was looking for when I dipped down in the clamshell."

"Looks like you found it," Vikram said. "Congratulations. Some kind of robot, is it? So it's got no water tank or first aid kit. This is going to save us?"

"Oh, shut up, dust-digger," she said, her cultivated voice full of withering contempt. "At least I tried. What have you done but moan and bitch?"

Vikram would have replied, but Jonno cut him off. "She's got a point. It will be night soon."

Natalie frowned. "We'll be found before dark. Surely."

"Maybe. Maybe not," Jonno said. "Does anybody know you're down here? No? Nobody's going to miss us either, not for a couple of days until our next check-in time."

"You only have to check in every couple of days?"

Vikram shrugged. "We 'dust-diggers' are self-reliant."

"You don't look very self-reliant to me. They'll see us." She glanced up. "Surely you have surveillance satellites."

"Few and far between," Jonno said. "This isn't Earth. This is Mars. The frontier."

"But this stupid little rock of a planet—it's so small! How can you possibly get lost?"

"It's a rock with about as much land area as Earth," Vikram

said. "Most of it unexplored. There are only a few thousand of us, you know. Martians. Plenty of room to get lost in. And besides, just how visible do you think we are from space?"

She laughed. "Look at the color of my suit!" But when she looked down she saw that the bright green and blue design was already obscured by rust-colored dust. She brushed at it with her gloved hands, but it stuck.

Vikram smiled. "Clingy stuff, isn't it? Natural camouflage."

Jonno said, "Look, surely we'll be missed in a day, two days, by your people or ours, and they will come looking for us. But we're going to have to get through at least one night. Mars gets cold quickly. We're already down to minus twenty-five. It's liable to fall to minus ninety before dawn—"

"I get the picture," Natalie said. Vikram grudgingly admired the way she was staying calm. "So what do we do?"

Vikram said, "We've got a little food and water in our packs. Some basic first aid stuff. But we've no shelter. We should have reached our camp before nightfall."

"I've got a pressurization bag," Natalie said. "But I've got nothing else, no food."

"So we share," Jonno said, and he grimly tried to get to his feet. "Because if we don't share, we've all had it. Maybe we can use the Viking to rig up some kind of tent. . . ."

Natalie got her pressurization bag out of her backpack. It was a sack of silvered material that folded down to a mass smaller than her fist, but when she shook it out it opened up into a spherical bag about two meters across.

Jonno suggested they set it up on the Viking platform. When

Natalie asked why, Vikram said, "So we don't get chewed by the rock bugs. They come up at night, you know."

Natalie glanced down. Everybody knew there was life deep in the rocks of Mars, native life, microbes with some kind of relationship to Earth life. But she'd never heard of it rising up in the dark.

Jonno took pity on her. "He's teasing you. It's just to keep us off the cold ground, that's all."

Vikram laughed, and Natalie turned away, fuming.

They used a bit of cable that the boys had scavenged from their wrecked flycycle to attach the sack to the Viking's antenna pole. Then, clumsy in their suits, they all clambered onto the platform and inside the bag, and Natalie fumbled to zip it up. There was a hiss of air, and the bag inflated to a sphere, slightly distorted where it was pushed up against the old probe's instruments. There was a faint glow from light filaments embedded in the bag walls, and the air rapidly got warmer.

Cautiously Natalie lifted her faceplate. The air was cold, and had a tang of industrial chemicals, and it was thin, so thin her lungs seemed to drag at it. But it was breathable. She pushed back her hood and unzipped the neck of her suit. She caught Vikram staring at the stubbly pink hair that coated one half of her scalp, the latest London fashion.

She and the boys were sitting cross-legged. There was so little room they were pushed up against each other, and every move brought them into contact. As Vikram opened his own suit, and helped Jonno with his, he kept brushing against Natalie, which they both put up with in stiff silence.

Jonno let Vikram remove his faceplate, but he kept his suit closed up, and he clutched his chest, breathing raggedly. It was obvious he'd been hurt in the crash, but he wouldn't let Vikram see the wound. Vikram was patient with his friend, calm, reassuring, even gentle. When he behaved that way, Natalie thought reluctantly, unlike when he was snapping at her, Vikram didn't seem so bad. Almost decent-looking, if he'd had a wash, and a sensible haircut with a shade of some modern color like silver or electric blue, instead of that drab natural brown.

Vikram dug food bars out of his pack and passed them around. Natalie bit into her bar. It was tough, stringy stuff, faintly like meat, but she was pretty sure there were no cows or sheep on Mars. It had probably come out of a tank of seaweed. She preferred not to ask. There wasn't much to the food, but it was filling.

At least the lack of a bathroom wasn't a problem. All their suits had facilities for processing waste. But when Vikram offered her water she learned it was the product of his suit's recycling system—it was, in fact, Vikram's pee. She politely declined.

Vikram touched the wall of the bag. "Nice piece of kit," he said grudgingly.

"Thanks."

"How does it store its air, in that little packet you opened it out of? And the energy for the heat and light."

Natalie shrugged. "I have no idea."

"Some kind of chemical reactions," Jonno said. "Probably." He winced with every word.

Natalie said, "It's an emergency pressurization bag. Meant for space, really. You suffer a blowout, you zip yourself in and wait for rescue. Meant for one person, which is why it's a bit snug. It should last twelve hours."

Jonno grunted. "Then it's no use for more than one night."

Vikram studied her. "So you're a space traveler, are you?"

"I'm here on a school trip," Natalie said, refusing to be riled again. "But I've been to the moon and on a Venus flyby cruise, and I'm here, of course. I suppose *you've* traveled all over."

Jonno laughed, though it clearly hurt him. "Earthworms always think Martians spend their time whizzing through space. We've got too much to do down here."

"I've been to Phobos," Vikram said defensively. "One of Mars's moons."

"When you were two years old!" Jonno said.

Vikram, embarrassed, turned on Natalie. "And you never set foot down here before today, did you? I could tell by the way you were stumbling around in the gravity."

She shrugged. "Landing wasn't in our itinerary at all for this trip. Mars is so pricey. Even the wilderness areas, now that the whole place is a planetary park."

"What about the cities?"

"The dome towns? I know people who've been there. Expensive again. And, you know, small." Stuck in this bag for the night with these two boys, she didn't want to give any more offense. "Look, you have to see it from my point of view. I grew up in London! You don't want to come all the way to Mars and stay in some poky little village in a bubble."

"No," Jonno said. "So you don't spend your euros in our shops and inns, you just muck about in the upper atmosphere and then you go home again. No wonder you're so popular."

"Well, it's not my fault," she said, feeling defensive. "Look, my family has connections to Mars. My grandfather was a trader here for a while. He's the reason I'm called Natalie. I was named after the heroine of some old book that was published a hundred years before I was born. The first human on Mars, in the book . . . Anyway, where were you going, cycling across Mars?"

Vikram began to say something about community duties, doing maintenance on weather stations around the north pole water-ice cap.

But Jonno cut in, "I'll tell you where Vikram was going. Anywhere but Hellas."

"Jonno—"

Natalie asked quickly. "What's in Hellas?"

Jonno said, "The question is *who* is in Hellas. And the answer is, a lovely lady called Hiroe."

Natalie felt her face redden, and she was glad the lighting was dim. "Your girlfriend."

"No!" Vikram said. "*Not* my girlfriend. I never even met her—"

"His fiancée," Jonno said slyly. "His wife-to-be."

"Shut up."

Natalie was discovering she knew even less about these Martians than she had imagined. "You're engaged? How old are you?"

"Fifteen," Vikram said. "How old are you?"

"Not much younger."

"It's an arranged marriage," Jonno said. "Their fathers are business partners. They sorted out the arrangement, and had it cleared with the genetic health people. All Vikram's got to do is marry her. Oh, and produce lots of healthy little dust-diggers."

Vikram didn't look happy about this deal at all.

"And he never even met her? *Eeeww.* That's so weird. We don't have arranged marriages on Earth. Well, *we* don't, in Britain. Maybe they still do in some cultures. Why do it on Mars? It seems— old-fashioned."

"There aren't enough of us," Vikram said. "Simple as that. Only a few thousand on the whole planet. We have to avoid inbreeding. So we have systems to ensure that doesn't happen."

"Inbreeding? *Eeeww!* And you'll go through with this?"

Jonno answered for Vikram. "Unless he finds a better option before his sixteenth birthday, yes. And a better option means somebody else he likes more, but who has at least the same degree of genetic difference from him as the lovely Hiroe."

"It's the law," Vikram said miserably. "It's my responsibility—everybody's responsibility to the future. Oh, shut up, Jonno. Let's get some sleep. Because unless we have a good day tomorrow, it's not going to make any difference anyhow, is it?"

"That's the first intelligent thing you've said all day," Jonno said. "Good night."

So they scrunched around in the bag, the three of them curled up like fetuses, head to toe, and tried to sleep. Knobbly bits of the old Viking stuck into Natalie's sides. Even in the low gravity it was uncomfortable. She thought she could hear Jonno sobbing softly, under his breath—sobbing at the pain of the injury he wouldn't let the others see. But she was aware of Vikram's presence, strong and warm and calm.

And she heard the thin wind of Mars, just millimeters away from her head, a thin hiss as sand sifted against the bag's fabric. She wondered if that was normal. She kept thinking about Vikram's Martian rock bugs, a whole world of bacterial communities kilometers deep beneath her.

Under all this was the fear, the fundamental gnawing fear that she'd tried to distract herself from since the moment the clamshell went down. The fear that she wasn't going to live through this, that this desolate Martian plain was where she would die.

She'd never been so alone in her life. She wished she could talk to Benedicte or her parents. She wished she could hold somebody's hand. Even Vikram's.

She didn't sleep well.

And when they woke, things looked even worse.

It started with Jonno. He still wouldn't let Vikram look at his injury. He had weakened, his face pale from a loss of blood.

At least Natalie continued to look calm and composed, under that silly pink hairstyle. Vikram supposed all this was even stranger, more scary, for her than it was for the two of them.

They sealed up their pressure suits and zipped open Natalie's bag. The dimming lights of the bag's power supply were over-whelmed by the thin Martian dawn, and a sifting of crimson dust caught the light.

They pushed out of the collapsing bag and found that every-thing, the bag, the old Viking, was covered with a fine layer of dust, blown by the wind.

"They can't see us under this," Natalie said, fretfully shaking the dust off her bag.

"Could have been worse," Jonno wheezed. He was sitting on a corner of the Viking. "Mars has dust storms all the time. We could have been hidden altogether, under a storm kilometers high."

"She's right, though," Vikram said. "Even if they're looking, they won't have seen us. The bag isn't going to get us through another night, is it?" And then there was the food. They had half a ration bar left each. He was already hungry. "We can't just stand here waiting to be rescued. We're going to have to do something."

Jonno snorted, despairing. "Like what?"

Natalie said, "What about the Viking?"

Vikram stood back and looked at the yellowed old craft. "It's just a relic."

"But it's also a big heavy chunk of engineering. There must be something we can do with it. The trouble is, I don't know how it works, what all these bits on top of it do." She looked up at the empty sky. "If only I could get online and do some searching!"

Jonno tapped at his wrist. "No need. Give me a minute."

She frowned. "What's that?"

"Wristmate," Vikram said. "Multiple functions—including a wide database. He can look up the Viking in there."

She stared. "You carry a database around *on your wrist*?"

"When Mars is as crowded as Earth and there's a wireless node under every rock," Vikram said acidly, "maybe we won't need to."

Jonno pointed at the equipment on the Viking's upper surface. "This canister here is a mass spectrometer. This is a seismometer. These pillarlike things are cameras. Stereoscopic."

To Vikram, everything looked big and clumsy and clunky. "I never saw cameras like that."

"Maybe there's something we can use. . . ." Jonno started to tap at his wristmate, muttering.

Natalie walked around the lander. "I suppose some of it is obvious. This arm, for instance, must be for taking samples from the soil. Maybe there's some kind of lab inside."

Vikram bent down to see. "Look, you can see the trench it dug."

"After all these years?"

He shrugged. "The dust blows about, but Mars doesn't change much. Look at this." He found a faded painted flag, and the words

UNITED STATES. "What's this, the company that built it?"

"No. The nation that sent it. This is its flag."

"I never heard of it."

"America. You've heard of America. Of course America doesn't exist anymore, not since the oil wars and the partition. . . . But here's its flag, sitting on Mars. My grandfather said the Americans landed this thing to celebrate a hundred years of independence. Or maybe it was two hundred."

Vikram laughed. "How can any part of Earth be independent of anywhere else? And anyhow, independence from what?"

She shrugged. "Canada, I think."

Jonno coughed and staggered. He had to hang onto the Viking to avoid falling.

Vikram ran to him and helped him settled down in the dust. "What's wrong, buddy?"

"It's not working."

"What isn't?"

"Look, the lander's got a comms system. Obviously. The big dish antenna is for speaking directly to Earth, and the little spoke thing over there is an ultra-high-frequency antenna for talking to an orbiter. I tried to interface my suit's systems to the lander's. But the electronics is shot to pieces by a hundred and fifty years of Martian winters. And, look at this—" He showed Vikram an image on his wristmate. "Transistors! They used transistors! They may as well have sent up a blanket and sent smoke signals with that robot arm."

Natalie said, "So we can't use its comms system to send a signal."

"Not without a museum full of old electronic parts, no. . . . *Oww*." He slumped over, clutching his chest.

Vikram lay Jonno down in the dust, by one of the Viking's foot-pads. "It's all right."

Natalie hurried over with her decompression bag. "Here. I'll blow this up a little way. We can use it as a sleeping bag, a pillow."

"I'm not going to make it," Jonno whispered.

"Just save your strength," Vikram said.

"What for? I let you down, man. If I could have figured out some way of using the Viking to get us out of here—"

"I might still work something out."

"You?" Jonno laughed, and something gurgled in his throat.

They pulled the bag around Jonno's body. Wordless, Natalie pointed at Jonno's neck, the inner seal of his suit. There was a line of red there. Blood. His suit was filling up with blood.

Natalie said, "I'll go and take a look at the Viking. Can I use your watch? I mean your—"

"Wristmate?" Vikram said. "Sure."

"Give her mine," Jonno whispered. "No use to me now."

"Don't talk like that."

Natalie took Jonno's wristmate and backed away, poking at its screen to access its functions.

Jonno's voice was a rasp now. "I'm just sorry I won't meet the lovely Hiroe in person."

"Shut up."

"But let me tell you something. . . . Listen. . . ."

Natalie saw Vikram bending over his friend, listening to some snippet of private conversation. He had to touch faceplates to hear.

Natalie didn't want to know what they were saying. And besides, it made no difference. Unless they figured out a way out of here, she and Vikram were likely to follow Jonno into some shallow Martian grave, taking any secrets with them.

But she wasn't prepared to accept that. Not yet. Not with this Viking, sitting here on Chryse Plain like a gift from the gods. There had to be some way of using it to get out of here.

She suspected the Martian boys didn't think the right way about the probe. Vikram lived on an inhabited Mars, a human Mars. But there had been nobody on Mars when the Viking arrived here. Nobody had brought the probe here in a truck and set it up. It was a robot that had sailed, unmanned, across the solar system and landed here by itself.

How had it landed? She checked the wristmate again. She learned that the Viking had come down from orbit using a combination of heat shield, parachute—and landing rockets. Rockets!

She got down on her hands and knees so she could see underneath the main body. She found rocket nozzles—a whole bunch of them, eighteen.

What if she started the rocket system up again?

She sat back on her heels and tried to think. She knew very little about liquid rockets, but she knew you needed a propellant, a fuel, something like liquid hydrogen, and an oxidizer, a chemical containing oxygen to make the fuel burn. And if there was fuel, there must be fuel tanks. She got to her feet and searched.

She quickly found one big spherical tank on one side of the lander. She rapped it and thought it felt like it still contained some liquid. But there had to be a second tank. . . .

She spent long minutes hunting for the other tank, feeling increasingly stupid. Then she looked up Viking on Jonno's wristmate again. And she discovered that the rockets had been powered by a "monopropellant" called hydrazine. A bit more searching told her how that had worked.

It was a system you'd use if you needed extremely reliable engines, for instance on a robot spacecraft a hundred million kilometers away from the nearest engineer. Hydrazine was like fuel and propellant all in one chemical. It didn't even need an ignition system, a spark. You just squirted it over a catalyst, a special kind of metal. That made the hydrazine break down into other chemicals, ammonia, nitrogen, and hydrogen. And it released a huge amount of heat too. Suddenly you had a bunch of hot, expanding gases—and if you fired the gases out of your nozzles, you had your rocket.

Her heart beat faster. There was some hydrazine left in the tank. All she had to do was figure out how the hydrazine got to its catalyst and to the nozzles.

She got down in the Martian dust and crawled under the lander, tracing pipes and valves.

"We need to move him away from the lander."

Vikram, cradling Jonno, had forgotten Natalie was even here. "Huh? Why? We don't know what this injury is. It's probably best not to move him."

"Trust me. Look, we'll keep him wrapped in the bag. You take his legs and I'll take his shoulders. We'll be gentle." She moved to Jonno's head and got her hands under his shoulders.

Vikram didn't see any option but to go along with it. "He's kind of heavy."

"I've got Earth muscles. On Mars, I'm superstrong."

He snorted. "After months in microgravity? I don't think so."

But she was strong enough to lift Jonno. "Okay. We'll take him behind that ridge, so he's sheltered from the lander."

Bemused, Vikram followed her instructions.

They soon got Jonno settled again. He didn't regain consciousness. Then Vikram copied Natalie when she got down in the red dirt, sheltering behind the ridge, facing the lander. "I suppose this has all got some point."

"Oh, yes." She held up Jonno's wristmate. "I hope I got this right. I found a valve under the lander, leading from the fuel tank. I fixed it up to a switch from a spare pump from my backpack. When I touch the wristmate, that switch should open the valve."

"And then what?"

"You'll see. Do you space boys still have countdowns?"

"What's a countdown?"

"Three, two, one." She touched the wristmate.

Dust gushed out from under the lander, billowing clouds that raced away, falling back in the thin air. And then the lander lifted off, wobbling, shaking away a hundred and fifty years of accumulated Martian dirt.

Vikram was astonished. He yelled, "Wow!" He grabbed Natalie's shoulders. "What a stunt!"

"Thanks." Natalie waited patiently until, embarrassed, he let her go.

The Viking was still rising, wobbling and spinning under the unequal thrust from dust-clogged nozzles.

Natalie said, "I'm hoping that a rocket launch will attract a bit of attention, even on a low-tech planet like this one. I was worried that the whole thing would just blow up, which was why I thought we should get some cover. But even that would have made a splash."

"You're a genius." He watched the Viking. "It's still rising. But I think the fuel has run out already. When it comes down it's going to be wrecked."

"Oops. I hope the park authorities will forgive me. And the ghosts of the engineers who built the thing." Suddenly she sounded doubtful. "You think this will work, then."

"I think you've saved my life. I hope they come in time for Jonno too." He said awkwardly, "Thank you. Look, we got off on the wrong foot."

"Well, you did crash into me."

"You crashed into *us*—never mind. When this is all over, why don't you stay on Mars a bit? I, I mean we, could show you the sights. Hellas, the poles, the Mariner valley. Even some of the domed towns aren't bad. You could bring Benedicte."

"And I could meet Hiroe."

He felt his cheeks burn. "I'm trying to be nice here."

"I'll stay on one condition."

"What?"

"Tell me what Jonno whispered before he lost consciousness."

"That was private. They could be his last words."

"Spill it, dust-digger."

"He said if I didn't want Hiroe, I could always marry a girl from outside the Martian gene pool altogether. That would be legal."

"Such as?"

"A girl from Earth."

"Shut up."

"You asked."

"Shut up!"

"With pleasure."

In silence, they lay in the dirt and watched as the Viking reached the top of its trajectory, and, almost gracefully, fell back through the light of the Martian morning, heading for its second, and final, landing on Mars.

And, minutes later, a contrail arced across the sky, banking as the rescuers searched Chryse Plain.

STEPHEN BAXTER is the author of more than forty books and over one hundred short stories. His most recent books are the near-future disaster duology *Flood* and *Ark*. Upcoming is a new novel, *Stone Spring*, first of a new alternate prehistory saga, and a major omnibus of his acclaimed Xeelee novels.

His Web site is www.stephen-baxter.com.

AUTHOR'S NOTE

I liked the idea that Mars is already a human world. The robot spacecraft we sent are sitting up there; there are already trackmarks and scoop scars. When humans get there, these will play a role as the first human monuments—and maybe more.

FIRST PRINCIPLE

Nancy Kress

He was even bigger than I expected. All three of them were. Barb and I watched on the link screen as they waited for the transport bay to pressurize, as they climbed out of the rover. Dr. Langley, in his rotation as council leader, made a welcome speech. The parents managed exhausted smiles, but the boy scowled.

"He's so *ugly*," Barb said. "And look at him—he hates us already."

"He's scared," I said. "Wouldn't you be, if you got taken away to Earth?"

Barb made a vomiting sound and folded her small arms across her chest. "Don't be so good all the time, Gina. It's wearying."

I didn't answer her. I'm not "good," just reasonable. If Mom had ever dragged me to Earth from Mars, I'd be just as scared as this boy looked. Not that anyone would be so insane as to leave Mars for Earth.

Barb said, "They should stay where they belong. Hell, Gina, that reco we saw just last night!"

"We don't know that this kid watches that sort of reco."

"We don't know that he doesn't."

Now Dr. Langley and the "immigrants"—such a strange word, we haven't had immigration to Mars in decades and never to Mangala—walked through the rover bay and into Level 1. More people to greet them, more speeches. I tugged on Barb's hand, and we moved to the boy to do our part. *"It would be nice if someone his own age were there to greet David Hansen,"* my mother had said, in the tone that meant *You're elected.* I'd made Barb go with me. Now that didn't seem like such a good idea. She radiated contempt.

Maybe David Hansen felt it. Or maybe he was just stupid. This was our world; he was the outsider, and he didn't even try to fake good manners. After the adult introductions, while the officials chatted warily, stumbling over each other's strange accents, David and Barb and I stared at each other, silent. But the message in his eyes was clear. *You're ugly, you're deformed, you're monsters, you're not even human.* Last night's reco lay on my mind.

Does he have any idea how he looks to *us?*

"Hello," I said finally. "I'm Gina Mellit and this is Barb Fu. I understand you play chess."

He wasn't stupid. He had manners when he chose to use them, although even then a sneer underlay the polite phrases. He was a better chess player than I am, and I'd been Valles Marineris junior champion. He hated Mars, and I hated him.

But not at first. "He's scared," I said to Barb and Hai-Yan and Andre and Ezra until I was tired of saying it and they were tired of hearing it. David wasn't scared, he was a sick, supercilious son-of-a-bitch. But at first he was just plain sick. They took his family down to Level 2 and gave them a room on the terrace—which Mom and

I wouldn't get until our rotation came up next year—and specially designated a bot to take care of him while his parents, who weren't sick, went to work in the labs. And then they urged me to play chess with him.

"Why can't he play against the computer?" I said.

"He can," Mom said. "He does. But I'm sure he needs human company, Gina. Wouldn't you, in his place?"

I didn't say, *I'm not in his place*. I didn't say, *I wouldn't ever be in his place*. I didn't say, *His place made those recos about us*. All those things were true, but you didn't say them to Mom, who was a Spiritual Guide when she wasn't a geneticist. The First Principle was even stronger in our family than in my friends', especially since my father was killed a year ago in an accident on the surface. So I didn't say any of it. I went to play chess with David Hansen.

The bot let me in. I nodded to it and said, "Gina Mellit to visit David Hansen. Chessboard, please."

From his bed David said, "Why are so polite to it? It's just a machine."

"Why not be polite?" I said.

He did something with his tongue that I knew from the recos meant extreme contempt. And because that kind of reco was the only Earth feed where I'd ever seen that tongue thing, I knew then that he watched them.

The bot handed me an old-fashioned chess set, carved of some heavy Terran wood. I put it on the table beside David's bed, he sat up shakily, and I held out my closed fists. "Right one," he said. It held the white pawn. He opened with the Sicilian, I responded, and we played in a thick, ugly silence. He was a romantic player, making bold attacks and sacrifices, and I should have been able to counter that style of play. But somehow the advantage eluded me. Two pawns down, I lifted my eyes from the board to rest them on Mars.

The terrace rooms on Level 2 have a wonderful view. Mangala, a fairly new settlement although I've lived in it my whole life, is built against a south-facing cliff. The cliff face is terraced in four levels, each set back from the one below, with steps on the outside that mean you don't have to wait for the elevators if you don't want to. Pots on the terraces hold genemod flowers designed by my mother, and at the bottom is the park, full of the genemod plants and trees that the wizards are always improving. The clear plastic of the shield slants down from the top of the cliff, Level 1, to the ground, and then beyond that is the shallow dome of the farm. From David's bed he could see the green of the park and the farm, and beyond them the red landscape and glorious pink sky.

David followed my gaze. "It's so ugly."

"*Ugly?*" My and Mom's current quarters were in the worst part of our rotation, at the back of Level 4 where the sound of the excavation bots droned, night and day, even through the stone.

"You don't even know how ugly it is, do you? You've never seen the ocean, or a beach, or mist at morning. . . ." He stopped, bent over the board, and coughed. My anger morphed into pity. Despite being so big—he must top 170 centimeters!— he looked frail. I was never sick.

I said, "Did you live near an ocean? With mists at morning? I've seen recos."

"You've seen nothing. A reco can't capture it."

"Maybe not. But I know that—"

"You know nothing."

I stood up. "Finish the game by yourself."

"Leaving because you're losing?" he taunted.

I glared at him. But I sat down again.

The First Principle governs Mars. It's a spiritual principle, not a legal one, and absolutely necessary for survival in any closed environment with limited resources: *Put yourself in the other person's place.* David was sick, uprooted, longing for the pestilence that was Earth, despite how hard that was for me to imagine. I advanced my bishop.

We finished the game in silence. He won. I left without looking at him. But as the bot let me out, I heard him breathe behind me, so soft that maybe he didn't mean for me to hear. But I think he did mean it.

"Bug."

I didn't turn around. *Neanderthal*, I wanted to say, but didn't. *Don't be so good all the time, Gina. It's wearying.*

We don't look like bugs. He does look like a Neanderthal. Too big, too hairy, too few arms.

My great-great-great-grandfather was on the initial genemod team. I'm proud of that, and why wouldn't I be? On Mars there is no room for waste or excess or stupid ostentation. Form follows function. The beauty which that creates is so much better than any Earth beauty; it's filled with unity and grace. We have softer colors—through a telescope Earth always looks to me too gaudy, all that bright blue and white. On Mars variations are fashioned with subtlety and for the beauty of perfect fit with the environment. My genes are exactly what they need to be for this gravity, this level of radiation, this type of light. And I am a pretty girl. I see it in the eyes of my friends, my mother, other people. The thick, short bones of my legs don't lose calcium and strength in this gravity, as David

Hansen's will. My big arms, engineered for strength, could break his too-long neck. The flexible tentacles of my small arms can manipulate objects that his clumsy fingers would crush. The light green of my epidermal photosynthetic cells uses the weak Martian sunlight to augment the energy from my food intake. I can see farther than David Hansen, hear better, use fuel more efficiently. Who the hell is he to presume to condescend?

"I'm not going to play any more chess with David," I said to my mother. We were on our way to the women's baths, walking along a corridor deep inside the Level 3 rock. I had my coming-of-age ceremony several weeks ago, and most of my friends have already moved into their adult quarters, but I'm in no hurry. I like my mother. It's pleasant to have someone to come home to, and there's no one yet that I'd like to set up a partnership with.

"I wish you would continue the chess, Gina."

"No. He's awful."

"He's dying."

I stopped cold. She said it quietly, factually, the way she recites genetic data. I blurted, "Why would anybody bring a dying man all the way to Mars? Especially one who doesn't even want to be here?"

"David isn't yet a man."

"He's the same age I am!"

"But it's different there, you know that. David can't make any decisions on his own and his parents wanted to be here. Earth is dying. You know that, too."

Of course I knew that. We all knew that. It was the reason immigration had resumed at all. Three generations of arrivals at Mars, five generations when Earth was in too much crisis to fund expeditions and we were left to become ourselves in peace. And now another desperate influx by people frantic to get away while they still could. A phrase from literature came to mind: *rats leaving a sinking ship*. But I had never seen a rat nor a water ship, and Earth literature mostly bored me.

I said, "Mom—"

"Put yourself in David's place, Gina."

David's place was watching bug recos. Vile, stomach-turning things. And the computer games were worse. Win points by pulling tentacles off the "bugs." Crush them under big robotic feet. Hit them with "pesticides" that make that tough green skin blister and molt. Tie the girl bugs down and rape them. Pack them naked into a "bug jar" and see how many you can fit. But Mom didn't know my friends and I had seen bug recos and bug games, and I couldn't tell her. We had them off an illegal feed that Ezra, who was some sort of electronic genius, had cobbled together during a mapping expo in a surface rover and then narrow-beamed to his receiver.

In my opinion, Earth *should* die.

"I think," Mom said carefully, "that maybe there's a little xeno-phobia going both ways here. Will you promise me to think about that, Gina?"

"All right," I said, without enthusiasm. "I'll think about it. What's David Hansen dying of?"

"Brain blight."

She had me, and she knew it. We'd all learned about brain blight. Earthers caught it from one of the microbes that had been engineered in the Second Bio Wars; it created neurotoxins that ate away at the cerebral areas that controlled basic bodily functions. You got weaker and weaker, until your heart or lungs just gave out for good. It was not contagious and not curable, not even by us. Mars has been far more daring in its genetic engineering than has Earth. We had to be, in order to survive, once the reinforcement ships stopped coming. And we've been incredibly lucky, with only minor failures or side effects. But much as we'd modified the human body, we still didn't know enough to do much with the brain. David Hansen's brain was essentially the same as mine, and it was killing him. He'd been in cold sleep for the voyage out and that had halted the blight, but now he couldn't have much time left.

Put yourself in his place. Eight years old—sixteen in E-years—and exiled, dying.

I shuddered.

"Don't do it," Barbara said. "You're an adult, your mom can't make you."

"My mom doesn't make me do anything," I said, which was true. "She only reminds me about the First Principle. Gently."

"That's worse."

"Much worse."

"How many times did you play him?"

"Six."

"How many did you lose?"

"Six."

Barb grimaced. "Did he ever mention . . . you know. . . ."

"The bug recos? No. He doesn't mention anything, not directly. He just hints at nasty stuff. His parents are never around because they leave him alone all the time."

"I'd leave him alone, too. He's shit."

"While we play he has the link screen on an Earther news feed.

It shows disaster after disaster. Yesterday it was all these children dying in some settlement called Africa and the bodies just stacked in a huge pit—you can't imagine how big—and set on fire to—"

"Don't tell me. The Earthers are all rotten, we already knew that. Gina, you should—oh, number three bot's hit something!"

We were on excavation duty. First-year workers always do jobs in pairs, even when the job mostly consists of watching screens and adjusting bot performance. Barb and I sat in the dusty little Level 6 control room, deep underground, near the end of our shift. She had her boots up on the back of my chair. Two chairs and the control console nearly filled the space, but Barb had jammed in Jiji's bed as well. The mebio lay asleep, his tail curled around him. I'd left Fuzz-Ball at home. This was a work shift, after all; sometimes Barb can seem a little immature.

The excavation bots were a mile away, at the end of the new tunnels. Excavation goes on all the time on Mars. We dig out new rooms shielded by tons of rock from the planet's yearly ten rems of radiation. We dig wells to the underground aquifers. But this particular project was a first: a ten-mile tunnel from Mangala to the nearest town, Kasei. Eventually the tunnel would have a little train running along it. Someday underground trains would connect all the settlements in the Valles Marineris.

I studied the data from the bot. "Whatever it hit is harder than the surrounding rock. An igneous form we haven't cataloged yet? Look at this Cixin-scale reading, it—"

Barb's boots left the back of my chair and hit the floor with a resounding *thump*! "Let's go see!"

"You know we're not supposed to do that. For any anomaly we're supposed to call Dr. Alvero and—"

"Oh, for once don't be such a good girl, Gina!"

Barb's eyes sparkled. Her comment rankled. And somewhere deep inside, I felt—even while knowing it made no sense—that I had already paid out enough goodness by playing chess with David Hansen. Besides, I was curious to go into the tunnel, too. I'd never seen it live. And it wasn't as if we didn't know everything about proper suiting up for unpressurized areas. We'd had that drill since we were five.

"Okay," I said, "but let me run the diagnostics first to make sure it's not just a bot malfunction."

It wasn't. The bot had hit something too hard even to dent, although it kept on trying, its diamond-fiber arm scrabbling against the whatever-it-was. Excavation bots are pretty stupid. I turned it off and we took the suits from their closet. Behind the closet was a small air lock, and behind that the start of the tunnel.

The ceiling was higher than it looked on the control screen, and a lot dustier. Minuscule particles of rock choked the air. *Fines*, we called them on the surface, but I couldn't remember if it was the same for underground particulates. All at once this didn't seem like such a good idea.

"Barb—"

"Come on!" she said over her suit radio. She bolted forward, and I followed.

The tunnel was about three meters wide. The first part had been reinforced by a construction bot, which we passed, busily working, about two-thirds of the way along. After that the walls were rough rock, sometimes with different colored strata briefly lit by my head-lamp before we moved on. My uneasiness grew, although I couldn't have said why.

A mile underground seems a lot longer than a mile on the surface.

When we reached the end, we both stood silent until Barb breathed, "Look at that."

"It's got to be a . . ." A what? Inspiration came to me. "A piece of exploratory junk from a few centuries ago. You know, Precollapse, when Earth was sending those piddly little bots to Mars and maybe one of them fell into a hole and then the tectonic plates shifted and it got squashed—"

"Into a perfectly flat impenetrable wall?" Barb said scornfully. She uses scorn as a shield. She always has.

The excavation bot stood frozen in the position I'd turned it off, which somehow made it look as dumbstruck as we were. It had uncovered a square meter of metal. The metal, which should have been scarred by tectonic shifts and rusted by aquifer drips and canted by erosion, gleamed a smooth dull gold. Without thinking I put my glove on it. The gloves are heated, of course, but not as well as the suits, or they'd be too inflexible. Crisscrosses of heating element lace the supple metallic fabric. Through my glove I could feel the metal's piercing cold.

Of course it was cold. This was deep underground in the Martian autumn. Everything was cold.

This was colder.

That made no sense.

"This makes no *sense*," Barb said scornfully. "Is there some part of the tunnel project we weren't told about?"

The tunnel project was open knowledge, like nearly every other project on Mars. You can't build trust any other way among scientific groups, among settlements, among variations in Martian culture.

That's why we have the First Principle. *Put yourself in their place.*

"I think," I said, "we better go back and call Dr. Alvero."

For once, Barb didn't argue.

Mom wasn't home when I got off shift, which is rare. She generally wants to hear about my day. Well, she would hear soon enough. Dr. Alvero had called half the xenologists on Mars and they were all rushing to the excavation tunnel by elevator or rover or dirigible. Those that were too far away were glued to the link.

"Is it—what *is* it?" Barb had asked, and I was glad because I couldn't speak myself.

"How could we know yet?" Dr. Alvero said sternly. I could read that sternness; he was a friend of Mom's, and I'd sat with him at dinner in the mess hall lots of times. He was excited and hiding it; he was insisting on proper scientific skepticism; he was aware that Barb and I had seriously violated regs during his shift as captain.

Barb didn't believe in proper scientific skepticism. She blurted, "Is it ancient Martians? Or aliens?"

Irritation replaced sternness. "Don't be premature, young woman. And don't finish your shift; that's not necessary now. Sign out and, please, don't say anything to anyone about this, at least for now."

"But will you tell us if it turns out to be—"

"Come *on*, Barb!" I said, tugging on her arm before Dr. Alvero could lose his temper. And if the smooth gold wall did mean aliens, everybody would know soon enough—

Aliens.

Halfway back to our rooms, I stopped dead. The terraces around me seemed to waver. *Aliens.* Was that possible? Microbial fossils had been found on Mars, but only microbial fossils. Somewhere in the long distant past, life had started here, and then had shivered to a halt. Climate change or radiation or something—my mind had gone numb. The life on Mars was *us*. This was our planet, my home. Arrivals from Earth were bad enough. But aliens—

It was one of those ideas too big and all-encompassing for the mind to hold onto. Like one's own death.

I had stumbled the rest of the way back to our rooms, as if I were as clumsy in Martian gravity as David Hansen. Now I didn't want to be alone. I scooped FuzzBall from her basket and squeezed her tight. But she didn't like that and yelped. And anyway, a mebio wasn't what I wanted. What did I want?

I wanted my life to stay the same.

Maybe it would. Maybe the smooth gold wall wasn't anything that would change anything. After all, it had probably been there already for a long, long time, doing nothing. Maybe our life on Mars could just go on the way it always had, unlike life on Earth that just got worse and worse, rising oceans and dying oceans and too much CO_2 and stupid ugly biowars and—

Put yourself in their place. And *I want things to stay the same.*

I went to play chess with David Hansen.

The first thing he said was, "What's that?" Until he did, I hadn't realized I was still holding FuzzBall.

"Oh, hell, you might be allergic, I shouldn't bring her in here, sorry. . . ."

"No, let me see it. Bring it here."

I didn't like his commanding tone but I brought FuzzBall to him anyway. David was out of bed, sitting in a chair with the chess set on a little table beside him. He'd been waiting for me. He looked stronger than last time. When he held out his arms for FuzzBall, I gave her to him.

"What *is* it?"

"A mebio. Part mechanical, part genetically engineered biological. *Not* a 'bug.'" I thought he might react to that, but he was too busy petting FuzzBall, who purred in his arms, little traitor. Well, she was pretty cute, even to an Earther.

"It looks sort of like a cat. Is it a cat?"

"I don't know what genes they started with, but DNA is amazingly adaptable. She eats fines."

He looked up. I'd never seen that expression on his face before: open and gentle. He looked almost like a Martian. He said, "What are fines?"

"The bits of dust that get into everything, no matter how hard you try to make a tight seal. Mebios keep it under control."

"You force her to eat dust?"

"Nobody forces her to do anything. She's engineered to lick them up, and the saliva-fines mass is shunted to the mechanical part of her crop, where it can easily be removed. Here, I'll show you."

"No! Don't!" Abruptly he dropped FuzzBall to the floor. She yelped in protest, then began licking the polished stone. "Get it out of here. It's just another freak. Like you."

The gentle look was gone. David stared at me like he hated me. I knew he was going to say it a full three seconds before he did.

"Bug."

Something inside me snapped. The find in the tunnel, the repulsive recos, even the chess games I'd lost, one after another. The big and the small all mixed up, and all sauced with David's contempt and my fear. My vision went red. I picked up the chessboard and threw it at him.

The board struck the side of his head in a rain of pawns and rooks and bishops. FuzzBall ran for the door, snarling. But David *smiled*. Blood streamed down his neck and soaked into his shirt. He said quietly, "Too bad you couldn't throw it harder."

I stared at him, stomped out, and burst into tears.

When Mom finally arrived home from her lab, she rushed straight into my alcove. "Gina! Are you all right?"

I hadn't been able to sleep, but the sudden light disoriented me. Blinking, I tried to see if she knew about Barb and me breaking regs. Of course she knew. Her face wrinkled into dozens of concerned little crevasses.

"I'm fine, Mom. And I know we shouldn't have—"

"But are you *all right*? I couldn't leave earlier, the oocytes—"

I held out my arms, like I was three years old again. She sat on the edge of my bed and held me. That was what I needed, what David Hansen didn't have; someone who cared more about him than about work, or even about Mars. My voice came out thick. "Is it . . . aliens, Mom?"

She laughed, a strangled sort of laugh, but I understood it. The situation was too weird to be quite real—even though it was real. She said, "They don't know. And I don't think we'll know for a long time. Maybe not ever."

That hadn't occurred to me. "Why not?" Mom was calmer now, and that made me calmer. I let go of her, a little ashamed of my lapse back into childhood.

"Well, think about it, Gina. From its position, that thing has lain deep underground for a long time—we'll know how long once we date the metal, if we can, or at least the rock seal over it. A very long time, and if it *is* alien, no aliens have emerged from it. So probably there's nothing biologically complex in there, or there was once and isn't anymore. But unless the thing spontaneously opens, we're not going to open it. Would you? Who knows what contaminating microbes we might let out, or what effect they'd have? Our Mars is fragile, you know that."

I did. Humans didn't evolve here—school studies constantly emphasized that, and so did everybody else—and we had to be careful. One slip and the "planet not indigenous to us" would snatch at a life, a town, the entire human population. I knew it, but I had trouble feeling it deep in my bones. Mars didn't feel "not indigenous" to me. It felt like home.

I said, "So the council will just leave the . . . the alien thing there at the end of the tunnel? Forever?"

She smiled. "Forever is a long time. But, probably, yes."

"Mom—"

"Yes, honey?"

But all at once I didn't want to tell her about David Hansen, the bug recos, throwing the chessboard. After all, I wasn't really three years old. "Nothing."

"All right." She hugged me and left.

The alien artifacts, or biologicals, or whatever they were, would stay sealed. David Hansen would not want any more chess, not after I'd clobbered him with the board. Dr. Alvero would, as shift captain, discipline Barb and me, but that was minor. Mom wasn't angry. I was able to sleep.

I was wrong about David. He called the next day. "You're supposed to be here to play me."

My belly sank.

"Gina? Did you hear me? Your mother *said*."

"You sound like a baby when you say that."

"Get up here."

And I did. From guilt, from duty, from training: *Put yourself in his place*. The problem was, the First Principle was correct. It was the only way to make a Martian settlement work. But I didn't have to like it.

David looked stronger than I'd ever seen him. To my surprise, his elaborate chessboard was already in midgame. As usual there was no sign of either of his parents. I said, "You playing someone else?"

"No, stupid. This is a famous game—the 'Immortal Game' between Adolf Anderssen and Lionel Kieseritzky hundreds of years ago. White to move. Go ahead."

Despite myself, I studied the board. "Pawn to d4."

"No. Anderssen played knight to d5."

The move didn't make sense. This unknown "Anderssen" was ignoring the upcoming threat to his rook. David grinned. "Want to see the rest of it?"

I nodded. He played out the game. White gave away both rooks, his queen, and a bishop—and still got a checkmate, using only minor pieces. It was unexpected. It was beautiful.

David said, "He used a suicide tactic. Kill everything he has to get all the way home."

"I can see that."

"Can you? Gina, I want you to do something for me. I think

I might have been wrong about Mars. I want to see it. Take me outside."

Talk about unexpected! "I can't do that."

"Yes, you can. You're an adult here, and so am I. I researched it. We don't need permission to suit up and go out, but I don't know the way or the air lock codes. There are codes, aren't there, so that little kids can't get out by mistake."

"I'm not taking you outside. Ask your parents."

He did that contemptuous thing with his tongue, and then a hand gesture I knew was considered really filthy on Earth. I hated that I was shocked. He said, as if the word was killing him, "Please."

"No."

He started to curse me then, using some words I knew, some I'd only seen in bug recos, some I'd never heard. I was glad. His foulness finally dissolved my duty, set me free. Nobody ever has to put up with that kind of abuse. I shouted at the top of my voice, startling him, "I could never be in your place!"

In the momentary silence that followed, I left.

The dull gold artifact was measured, photographed, assayed, and put through every possible test to see what was inside. Nothing yielded any useful information, not even internal imaging, which revealed only indistinct shadows. Bots carefully scraped away the rock on the thing's six sides, none of which bore any markings. A perfect cube, the artifact was made of a substance unknown to either Earth or Martian scientists. Geologists determined that rock around it had shifted several thousand years ago; before that the artifact had lain on or near the Martian surface. Images of it became the most accessed data in the solar system.

On Earth a rising ocean, clogged with the out-of-control algal blooms that had killed the rest of its marine life, broke through the levees around a major settlement called New York. The water rushed in. In the floods and panic and contamination, two million people died.

I played and replayed the Anderssen-Kieseritzky Immortal Game, looking for something I could not have named. The stupid game even invaded my dreams. *Knight takes g7, King to d8. . .* Not that I was sleeping all that well anyway.

I didn't see David Hansen, but I heard about him. In a settlement as small as Mangala, gossip is as pervasive as fines. His mother was out on a long-explore; she would not return for the rest of the year. David's father was in Mangala but spent all his days and most of his nights at the lab. After all, wasn't his son supposed to be an adult, here on Mars? I looked up the Hansens on the link. They did not come from New York. They had lived somewhere called Illinois, a place that had undergone rapid desertification during the recent round of massive climate shifts. The link, calling up Earther feeds from its data base, showed me kilometer after kilometer of dry, cracked, withered ground leading to a barren lakeshore.

"Gina," Mom said one day over a very late dinner, just before mess closed down, "there's talk of . . . of certain recos that have been fed illegally to Mars."

I picked up a forkful of soypeach and kept my gaze on it. Ordinarily I like soypeach.

"You saw them," Mom said flatly.

"Yes."

She put down her fork. "'Bug' recos."

"Yes."

"Why didn't you tell me?"

I shrugged. I was an adult; I didn't have to tell her everything.

"Vile, ugly, stupid things—that's what those recos are. From ignorant and diseased minds."

"Yes," I said for the third time, and finally I could look up at her. "I'm sorry."

"*You're* sorry? Dear heart, you have nothing to be sorry for. It's the people who made those recos who should be—is that why you've been looking so tense and preoccupied the last few weeks? I've been worried about you. Ever since you stopped playing chess with David Hansen—was it David who showed you those recos? Was it?"

"No, Mom. I saw them before he even arrived." All at once the tension in my head—and of course Mom had noticed it, she loved me—shot up several levels.

"So David Hansen had nothing to do with it?"

How to answer that? It was too complicated. I said, "Mom—is the council really never going to open that alien thing?"

She stared at me. "What's that got to do with David Hansen?"

"Nothing—I just—never mind. How is he?"

"Doing really well. His brain blight might even be in remission. There are a few rare cases of that on record. If he's one, it's a great chance for up-close study, maybe even to learn something significant about the immune system. DNA is infinitely adaptable."

My linkcom sounded. When I accessed the message, David Hansen's face stared at me, surrounded by waist-high plants. I recognized them: my mother's genemod wheat, modified for nutrient-enhanced Martian soil. David was out in the farm.

Instead of speaking, he used the linkcom's text function, which no one ever does except for data transmission. I had to squint at the tiny letters: "Come right now and alone or bishop to e7."

I stood, my legs shaky, and said, "Barb wants me. See you later?"

"Sure," Mom said. "Have fun."

I made myself not run out of the mess. Bishop to e7 was the last move in Anderssen's immortal game with Kieseritzky. David's words filled my head: *"He used a suicide tactic. Kill everything he has to get all the way home."*

I raced along the underground tunnel from Level 5 to the farm, then up the stairs instead of taking the elevator to the air lock. The farm is pressurized, but the atmospheric mix is different from the town, with more CO_2 to aid plant growth. People can breathe it, but just barely and not for too long. Suits hang along the wall beside the air lock. I hesitated, knowing I should put one on, but I didn't want to take the time. Instead I just grabbed a helmet and rushed into the air lock. It filled agonizingly slowly with the farm air. *Come on come on . . .*

Dusk filled the hot air of the farm, steamy and rich with the scents of plants, loam, water. No one else was around at this hour, and without a suit I had no headlamp. It didn't matter. I had played here, taken botany lessons here, done work shifts here my entire life. Mom was a plant geneticist. I knew every inch of the farm, and I raced sure-footed over the narrow paths between crop beds and mini-fields and hydroponic vats and dwarf fruit trees. The sky beyond the low plastic dome was clear, and Phobos shone above me amid the earliest and brightest stars.

David stood, also unsuited, between two mini-fields of Mom's wheat, where the path ended at the far dome wall. Beyond the dome the Martian surface, rock and fines, was shrouded in shadows.

David's back was to the wall. He held the detached cutting arm of a bot, sharper than any razor.

"David," I said softly, as if sound might somehow jar him into action.

"Don't try to stop me."

"You want me to stop you, or you wouldn't have linked me. You'd have just done it."

He laughed. The laugh shivered along my bones. "Is that what you think, Gina? You're wrong. I linked you because I hate you, hate this place, hate all you bugs—do you know how repulsive you look to me? I can never belong here, never, and I can't . . . can't go . . . home . . ."

He started to cry. I moved faster than I have ever moved before. Somehow—how?—I knew that he could not let me see him cry.

Time seemed to stop, quiver, slow down. I had the weird sensation of seeing us both from the outside, each movement as clear and distinct as a coming-of-age dance: *Gina leaps forward. David thrusts the cutter behind him at the dome wall. Gina closes the distance between them. The wall of tough piezoelectric plastic rips and air rushes out. Gina is upon David. He screams and whips around the arm holding the cutter. He's clumsy in this gravity. She clutches his body in her big arms, so much stronger than his. Her small arms grasp at the cutter. She feels it slice deep into her thigh before he drops it. Gina screams. They both drop to the ground.*

Time returned to normal. Alarms shrieked. A repair bot threw itself at the hole where the air whooshed out. With my small arms I clamped the helmet over David's head and the emergency seal molded itself roughly to his shoulders. Then I saw my own blood streaming down my thigh, and everything went dark.

"Shock," Barb said. "Your mom said it was only shock." Her face was as white as the sheet that lay over me in the infirmary. She was my first visitor except for Mom, but I knew all my other friends would come as soon as they were allowed.

"David?" I croaked. My lungs needed more time to fully recover, but they would. You're not supposed to run and fight and bleed while breathing that much CO_2.

Barb grimaced. "His father took the fucker to Kasei. They have psychiatric facilities there, you know, that we don't. If you ask me, he doesn't need psychiatric help, he needs—"

"Don't."

"All right." She leaned closer. "But why did you do it, Gina? Why save his life? You could have been killed, and he's worthless scum."

"No." I couldn't say more. So we sat in silence, my friend and I, and she held my hand, and I could still feel my mother's arms around me from before she left for her work shift, and I knew why the aliens, or their biologicals, or their machines, stayed inside the dull gold artifact.

It's the same reason we won't ever open it: whatever is inside might cause contamination because it does not belong here. No one else believes this theory. "Gina, sweetheart," Mom said gently when I'd croaked this out to her an hour ago, "think. If that were true, the aliens wouldn't have taken all the trouble to come here in the first place. They must have meant to establish some sort of presence on Mars, or why bother?"

My throat wouldn't let me reply, but I think I know the answer. The aliens *did* mean to establish themselves here. But once they arrived, they discovered that they couldn't. It was not home. It would never be home. They discovered that they were not as adaptable as they'd hoped, and so they committed a sort of suicide, an act of despair.

Or maybe that isn't it at all. Maybe it wasn't an act of despair but of altruism. They landed and discovered they could not survive on Mars. Their craft was damaged, or there weren't the right resources here, or they didn't have the right science to adapt Martian resources to their needs. So they took the only kind of victory they could achieve: leaving Mars uncontaminated for those who could adapt to it. *"A suicide tactic. Kill everything he has to get all the way home."* Maybe the aliens, too, gained a kind of win, that of doing the right thing for us, who would travel here from Earth so much later. *Put yourself in their place.*

I don't know which idea is true, anymore than I know what will happen to David Hansen. His mind is indeed diseased, but not with brain blight. Maybe they can fix his hatred of us, maybe not. Maybe *fix* is the wrong word. DNA might be infinitely adaptable, but I don't know if human minds are. If he returns to Mangala, I'll play chess with him and take him places and try to help him adjust. Carefully. However, no matter what any of us do, David might always feel like an alien on Mars.

But I am a Martian, and this is my home, and I am in my right place.

"Oh, I meant to tell you," Barb says, "the animal wizards have designed the next generation of mebios, and you won't believe how cute they are."

"Yes," I croaked. "I would."

up, rotating my wrist in the strap that held it onto the armrest so that I didn't accidentally break my nose with my own hand when we "clawed our way out of the gravity well." (This was a phrase from the briefing seminars that they liked to repeat a lot. It had a lot of macho going for it.)

The pove smelled like garbage. There, I said it. No nice way of saying it. Like the smell out of the trash chute at the end of our property line. It had been my job to haul our monster-sized tie-and-toss bags to the curb every day and toss them down that chute and into the tunnel system that took them out to the Spruce Sunset Meadows recycling center, which was actually *outside* the Spruce Sunset Meadows wall, all the way in Springville, where there was a gigantic megaprison. The prisoners sorted all our trash for us, which was good for the environment, since they sorted it into about four hundred different categories for recycling, and good for us because it meant we didn't have to do all that separating in our kitchen. On the other hand, it did mean that we had to have a double crosscut shredder for anything like a bill or a legal document so that some crim didn't use it to steal our identities when he got out of jail. I always wondered how they handled the confetti that came out of the shredder, if they had to pick up each little dot of it with their fingernails and drop it into a big hopper labeled PAPER.

Mom and Dad were forward in the adults' cabin, where they were being served fake no-booze Champagne (no one was allowed to touch alcohol for seventy-two hours before lift—this was also from the briefing, and had been accompanied by graphic images of free-fall vomit), far from the howling, spitting kiddilees.

The announcements played twice, once in English and once in "Simplified English," for the foreigners. Simplified English had been new to me when I entered the program, but I soon got used to it, words of one or two syllables drawn from a vocab of five thousand or so. I sometimes even found myself chatting in it over dinner with my parents, which drove them crazy. But Simplified was the official mission language, which had been decreed by the Mars Corp in its charter on the sensible grounds that we couldn't have a new world with a hundred stupid complicated languages, but English was as stupid and complicated as they come—"the tough coughs as he ploughs the dough"—so Simplified was the right compromise.

The pove listened closely to both sets of announcements, like he was anxious to learn Real English so he could stop being such a pove, but I knew it was a lost cause. Poves are poves are poves. Once you're born a pove, you get all the lessons of being a pove, the idea that the world owes you a living, that you can just get by being lazy and begging, and it's nearly impossible to unlearn that lesson. But he'd have to, if he was going to make it on Mars. No handouts on Mars, pove!

They played the liftoff countdown through the PA in the cabin, and at first we all laughed and counted down with it, like it was New Year's Eve: *10, 9, 8 . . .*

But by *4,* no one was counting along. The whole ship was rumbling like a dragon, shaking slightly, feeling full of *potential*, like it had its legs coiled underneath it and it was getting ready to jump, which it was. And when it did—*3*—we would be under way, on a one-way journey to an alien world, and we would never see the green hills of Earth again.

At *2,* I started crying, really bawling, though I couldn't tell you why. Screw the Earth, anyway, the crummy old planet with its environmental bellyaching, its teeming anthills of poves and refugees and crazy religious people with their suicide bombs. But it was Earth, my Earth, my homeworld, and—

1.

I wasn't the only one crying. We were all sobbing, and the only reason it didn't sound like a nursery school before nap time was that the engines were *so damned loud* you'd couldn't hear it if you threw back your head and screamed as loud as you could. The pove next to me was crying, too, and I wondered if his parents were forward, or whether he was one of the orphans the Mars Charity put on board the ship to show what a great bunch of people they all were. *We* all were.

And then we were boosting. It was like a thousand hands on every centimeter of me, pushing as hard as they could, even on the back of my throat, on my tongue, on my nose, on my *lungs*, and it didn't *stop*, it got *worse* and *worse* and *worse* and then

everything

went

black.

The next thing I knew, the pressure was off, and I seemed to be falling in no particular direction. I had just enough time to open my eyes and see the loose ends of my face mask straps floating around my head and think, *Free fall!* and then my stomach decided to send everything it had up to have a look at the wonder of space travel. I gagged and tried to pitch forward, but the straps held me in.

Mars, Inc. had anticipated this, of course. Us kiddilees hadn't eaten or drunk anything for twenty-four hours—the grown-ups ate like hogs, but they had the antinausea injections that weren't kid-safe. My stomach was practically empty, except for some stringy green mucous and bile that tasted like—well, it tasted like *puke!*—and it burned in my throat and sinuses. A little escaped my lips and floated up my nose and back down my throat and I started to choke.

I wasn't the only one. Lots of people were making gagging noises and choking noises. The blob of puke was lodged in my windpipe and I could only get whistling sips of air past it, and I was seeing stars. There weren't any space attendants nearby, and even though I was mashing the call button, I couldn't hear anyone rushing to my aid.

Then there were small, calloused fingers at my straps, undogging my shoulders, arms, wrists, forehead, so that I could lean forward—the falling feeling worse than ever, my stomach churning. A small, strong fist thumped me between the shoulders and I coughed convulsively and the puke was back in my mouth and I spat it out and saw it wobble away like a jellyfish.

It was only then that I saw *whose* small hands had been on me. The pove, who had somehow slipped his bonds and had hooked his foot through one of his straps so that he was able to maneuver while floating above me. He smiled at me as my puke-jellyfish hit him in the chest, leaving a splotch like a greasy paintball hit.

"You okay?" he said. He had a funny convenience-store-clerk accent, clipped but somehow liquid.

"Fine," I said, and it came out with a rasp from my burning throat. He had drifted so that he was upside down, his face bobbing centimeters from mine. "Thanks." It was disorienting. He had toothpaste breath. It made me conscious of the fact that my breath smelled like a dead bear's butthole.

He put a hand out. "Vijay Mukherjee," he said.

"David Brionn Oglethorpe Smith," I said. He snorted. I was used to that. I waited until he'd finished snickering and said, "The Third." It's true. Great-grandad had been the first, converted from Brian to Brionn by a Marine induction sergeant who couldn't spell, and I was the third to bear his name. It was silly and long and weird, but it was mine, and no one else had a name like it (except Dad and Great-grandad, of course).

I still felt like I was falling, but it wasn't as unpleasant as it had been, and I could see where it would stop feeling like falling and start feeling like flying, eventually. "Thanks," I said, then "sorry," gesturing at his stained shirt. He waved off my apology.

"Think nothing of it. We're going into space together, my friend! We can't let little things get to us!" He shook my hand again. He had calloused fingers, but a soft handshake, limp and a little damp. Everyone I knew shook hands like they meant it. But this pove—Vijay!—had rescued me from my choking and hadn't put up a fuss when I puked on him. (A nasty part of me wondered if his slum or whatever wasn't carpeted in worse things than puke). I could live with a damp handshake.

The space attendant finally showed up and demanded to know what we were doing out of our straps and then didn't want to listen when he explained. The spacer—who floated through the air with the greatest of ease—strapped us back in without missing a word in his lecture on shuttle safety.

I turned my head to look at Vijay and I could see that he was doing the same. "Thanks again," I said, my voice muffled by my mask, which reeked of barf.

He gave me another thumbs-up, and then we boosted again and were pushed back into the chairs.

Debarking at Eagle's Nest Station was a lot simpler than boarding had been on Earth. The space attendants swarmed us and bound us wrist-and-foot to our neighbors with soft bungee cords in chains of ten kids. Then they simply grabbed the lead kid and towed the whole chain along the length of the shuttle, through grown-up territory, through the air lock, and into the station's mustering area. We were cut loose and then each of us was issued a set of one-size-fits-all Velcro gloves and slippers, and we struggled into them, some of us flying off into the low ceiling, which might as well have been the floor, except that no one was standing on it at the moment.

It was all pretty chaotic. Every few seconds, ten more colonists came through the air lock, pushing us all farther in, and anyone who wasn't Velcroed down drifted away, and it soon became clear that there just wouldn't be enough room in the mustering area for all of us, but more people started coming out, and I couldn't find Mom or Dad in the press, and then Vijay plucked his way along the carpet to me and said, "Come on, it's too crowded on this wall, let's stand on one of the others," which sounded like a crazy plan but I couldn't say exactly why, so we pushed off together and grabbed the ceiling with toes and hands, laughing as we were skidding and ripped around until we were standing upside down (relative to everyone else, though I still felt like I was falling in every direction at once). At first people stared at us in that familiar hey-you-stupid-kids-cut-it-out way, but as the room grew more and more crowded, many of the other kids and then some of the grown-ups joined us on the "ceiling."

I knew some of the other kids from orientation. There was the big, butchy red-haired boy who liked to mouth off, but who was looking as pukey as I felt. There was the shy girl with the incredible movie-star face and big, wide-set violet eyes, who wasn't looking shy at all now, but was looking frankly and unashamedly at the upside down adults below her, peering through the seaweed tangle of hair that floated around her head. There was the dreamy girl who never turned her earphones off—you could tell, even though they were implants, because she was always doing this head-bobbing thing to the rhythm—now wide awake and plucking her way across the ceiling on her hands, feet brushing the hair of the adults "below."

I spotted Mom and Dad just before the space attendants pushed through the last tensome and dogged the air lock. As it sealed, the air pressure in the room changed slightly and I realized with a shiver that the funny-looking door I'd passed through wasn't just a *door*, it was a door *between two spaceships* and that the only thing that had stopped me from being sucked into space where my lungs and eyeballs would explode while my body turned into a freeze-dried popsicle had been some accordioned metal, rubber, and plastic. And now that was gone, and the shuttle that had lifted us to *Eagle's Nest* was floating through that same void.

The same void that I was going the spend the next six months sailing through in a tin can whose thin skin would be all that stood between me and total assplosion.

A space attendant standing *sideways*, sticking out of the wall like a thumbtack, touched an invisible button on her work space and a two-note whistle sounded. "Colonists, attention please." Her voice was amplified and came from every corner of the room. It was the same system they used in orientation: the room's cameras knew where the speaker was and tuned an array of directional mics to follow them, so that you could speak without the inconvenience of a mic. "Colonists?" she said again, when the chatter barely dimmed. It was as loud as a rocket engine (well, not quite) from all the talking. She twiddled an invisible knob, using some hand jive the ship's computer understood. "COLONISTS," she said again, her voice so loud it actually made we want to go to the toilet as it vibrated the poo I hadn't realized was lurking up my colon.

The silence was thunderous. My ears rang. "Welcome to *Eagle's Nest*," she said, "I am Lainie. Just Lainie. As in 'Lainie Lainie, no complainy.' I am your mommy for the next six glorious months aboard the *Eagle*, and it will be my job to head off any potential strife before it rises to the level of complaint. We live by a strict 'no whining' ethic on Mars—that's why you signed up to go—and it's never too soon to start practicing." She gestured at the kids and the few adults on the "ceiling." "I see that some of you have already gotten into the no-complainy state of mind and solved your own problems by your own wits. Good people of upside down land, I salute you." She ripped off a perfect navy salute. Her uniform was vaguely naval, though Mars Colony didn't have a navy or an army. It had a security force, of course, contracted for out of the colonial fees and charged with enforcing our Mutual Code of Conduct and Respect. But Lainie didn't talk like one of the meatheads who worked security around the Mars, Inc. properties; she talked like a Marsy, smart and confident and assertive. Like my parents and all their friends.

"Now, we are just about ready to move you from the *Nest* straight onto the *Eagle*. We've been making her ready for days now, and she is just in her final inspection from the International Space Agency—" She squeaked out "International Space Agency" in a pinched, cartoony voice, the way every Martian did. No one liked the pencil pushers at the ISA, with all their stupid rules. "And then we can get you aboard. We didn't anticipate this delay, and unfortunately, we can't let you wander around the *Nest*. This is a working jobsite, and there's no way you could be safely permitted to move about freely, much as we'd like to let you." She drew a breath and said, in one long word, "Marsincdeeplyregretstheinconvenience," and grinned. More than a few people chuckled with her. Phrases like "deeply regrets the inconvenience" were the kind of thing we were going to Mars to escape.

"It shouldn't be very long folks. In the meantime, think happy thoughts, talk among yourselves, mingle. These are the people you'll be spending the next six months with. These are the people you'll be sharing a planet with for the rest of your *lives*."

Okay, an admission. I'm not much of a Martian. Martians are supposed to be full of colonial pluck, ready to grab Earth's neighboring planet with both hands and *head butt* that mother into submission. We are the winners, humanity's best hope for surviving once stupid Earth is used up by the poves and the stupids. We're all rich, of course, and that's how you know we're winners. We didn't whine like all the poves who claim that the world owes them a living. We made our own fortunes on Earth and now we're off to set up a new planet that'll be as great as the Earth could be, if only you left all the whiners out.

But I'm not much of a Martian. I'm not much of a winner. I guess that makes me a loser.

Here's the thing: my grades are okay, Bs and B plusses, except for a C in American history, which, honestly, I deserved. I think I slept through more than half those classes. *I* would have given me a D minus.

Here's the thing: I'm not the popular kid. I'm not even the popular kid's best friend. I'm the kid that the popular kid's best friend used to play with before he made friends with the popular kid. I'm not the last picked for teams, but I'm the last picked from the kids who aren't total spazzes or fat or handicapable or whatever.

Here's the thing: the only place I'm not a loser is when I'm playing Martian Chronicles, the Mars Colony game that I've lived, breathed, eaten, and shat for the past five years. The reason for this is that I am a stone Martian Chronicles *monster freak*. I can play MC for eighteen hours without coming up for air, bringing it with me to the toilet and the table. There's something that just *fits* in the game, which sounds kind of boring from the outside: you are a Mars colonist and you have to build your homestead, sell your wares and services, work to elect sympathetic officials (or become an official yourself), and try to get your neighbors to see things your way when it comes to the day-to-day running of Ares City.

Boring, right? Wrong. The game is all about figuring out what everyone else wants, and how to make them feel like they're getting it, even though *you're* really the one getting what *you* want. I have a huge fortune in MC. I'm a ray-gun millionaire. (The Mars, Inc. company scrip—our money—is called "the ray gun," or "the Martian ray gun" if you're feeling formal. There's even a ray gun on every bill, stylized and old-fashioned and cool.) Not real money, but I know that if I can do it in MC, I'll be able to do it on Mars. And then I won't be a loser anymore, and I'll be a real Martian.

I am self-aware enough to know how pathetic this sounds. And I'm pathetic enough that I don't care.

The *Eagle* took on her passengers after three long hours stuck in the *Eagle's Nest* mustering area. For a group of no-whiners, there was a lot of complaining about the strange, lengthy time stuck there in zero-gee (not technically zero, as orientation had reminded us, just microgravity but I couldn't tell the difference), waving back and forth in the air-recirculator's breeze like a bed of sea kelp. They whined about the wait. They whined about the line for the toilet. Then they *saw* the toilet—a kind of giant vacuum cleaner you stuck your whole ass into—and they whined about *that*. The only ones who weren't whining were the kids who were hanging from the ceiling and the adults who'd joined us. We were having too much fun in upside down land to worry about the toilets or the wait. And there was plenty of room on the roof.

"What's your corp?" the girl with the violet eyes said, with no preamble at all. She was asking about Martian Chronicles—specifically, what my corporate affiliation was in-game. That is, which team I played for.

"DBOS-Corp," I said casually. She had thrown up on the shuttle, too—I could tell by the flecks of dried puke down the front of her shirt.

She nodded sagely. "I hear good things about it, but isn't it a hard company to ladder up in? Super-competitive?"

"I don't really need to worry about that," I said. "I'm the CEO." It didn't come out as casual as I'd hoped, because I caught someone's floating, gelatinous sneeze in the eye as I said it and ended up twitching and flinching away.

She cocked her head at me. "If you're lying, I'll find out as soon as we get our cabins. And then I'll spend the next six months making fun of you."

I held up two fingers in an obsolete Boy Scout salute. "I swear by Ares, God of War. May he strike me down with, uh, lightning?" (I wasn't really clear on what Ares—the Greek name for Mars—did in the course of his war-godly duties.)

"Okay, that's impressive."

"Seriously," said a voice from a few centimeters "over" my head. I looked up and found Vijay floating in space just "above" (Okay, I'm going to stop with the "above" and "over" and "below" quotes. There was no up or down, okay?) "That is fantastic. Really top-hole."

He'd taken off his light jacket and twisted it into a rope with one of his Velcro gloves safety-pinned to the end of the sleeve and stuck to the bulkhead's surface. In effect, he'd created an anchor line, and he was using it to fly around the middle of the room like a super-hero.

Violet-eyes's face twisted up like, *Who's the pove?* and I said, "This is Vijay. He flies. Apparently."

Vijay stuck his hand out and she took it. "Helene Gonzales-Ginsburg," she said.

"I'm Dave," I said, feeling like I was falling behind.

"Dave Smith," Vijay said, inches from my ear. "I should have made the connection when you told me your name. Well, that *is* interesting!"

"What corp do *you* work for?" Helene said, pointedly.

"Oh," he said, airily, "I work for the auditor-general."

Now it was my turn to boggle. The AGs were one of the exalted heights that every player secretly aspired to. They only recruited players with absolutely, positively *impeccable* reps, and gave them the power to kick open the doors of any corp, any meeting, and go over its books with a fine-tooth comb and confiscate any money that wasn't properly accounted for. They could take away your corporate charter, bust your character down to the bottom rank. You didn't get to be an AG without playing a long, hard, *tight* game that made you a lot more friends than enemies. I was a pretty top dog, but Vijay was a minor *god*. Whoa.

"Work for?" Helene said. "What does that mean, work for? You snitch for them for money?"

"No," he said. "I am a senior auditor." We both boggled. A bit of drool actually attained separation and liftoff from my lip, forming a glossy sphere that drifted off toward one of the air-recirc vents. Senior auditor! He wasn't just a god, he was a *major* god.

Suddenly I felt very self-conscious. Vijay could buy or sell us all ten times over in MC.

But then I realized that I could probably buy and sell Vijay ten times over in real life. It's a kind of nasty, ungenerous thought, but it made me feel better. And worse.

"Of course," he said, "that's all just for another three months."

Three months. Turnaround. In three months, we'd stop facing Earth and the ship would spin around to face Mars. In three months, we'd be closer to Mars than to Earth, and the light-speed lag would hit a brutal one hundred seconds, making the game almost unplayable. So in three months, the ship's network array will cut over to Mars and we'll all start fresh, new characters on the Mars servers.

Yes, Martian Chronicles is big on Mars. Yes, they actually play a life-on-Mars simulator *on Mars*. Except, of course, on Mars, it *means something*, because the best lessons learned on Mars server are actually turned into policies for Mars government.

In three months, we'd all start over as noobs in the Martian Chronicles. And three months after *that*, we'd touch down and we'd all be noobs on *Mars*. I was abandoning DBOS-Corp. Vijay was abandoning his position as senior auditor. Thousands of hours flushed down the toilet.

"Who do you play for, Helene?" I said.

She grinned, not looking shy at all anymore. "I'm a raider," she said.

We both drew back from her involuntarily, and I lost my balance and ended up standing on my head for a moment while I sorted myself out.

A raider! They were the scum of Mars. They'd borrow a giant amount of money and use it to buy up a majority share of a corp, then they'd vote that the corp should take on their debt. Then they'd sell off all the corp's assets to pay the debts, leaving behind a hollow shell, sucked as dry as a bug in a spider's web. It was great for the "investors" who loaned the raiders their initial stake—they could take millions of player-hours' worth of work and turn it into a nice fat bank balance for themselves. Was it "legal"? Well, no one would send you to jail for it. And it was an open secret that some of the biggest corps had been founded by—or had bankrolled—raiders. If an auditor caught raiders in the act, he could bust up the party, but it was all part of the game. That didn't change the fact that I was instantly tempted to punch Helene in her movie-star nose and then push her out the air lock.

She giggled.

"You should see the look on your face! Come on, it's just a game." They always said that. "Besides, maybe I'll change my ways when we hit apogee. Start clean on Mars as a goody-two-shoes corporate worker bee."

Vijay nodded. "And maybe I'll be a raider," he said.

I swallowed. I wanted to say something like, "I will be a CEO. I have always been a CEO. It's all I ever wanted to be." But "it's just a game" didn't allow me to say anything like that. There was one place in the world—and off the world—where I wasn't a loser, and that was in the Martian Chronicles. I'd come to grips with the fact that I was going to have to abandon my beautiful, perfect corporation in ninety days, but only by promising myself that I'd start building a new corp on day ninety-one.

"It's just a game," I said.

The *Eagle* had only been finished two weeks before we boarded, the last carpets laid, the last bunks prepared, the last safety checks completed. But it still smelled like people had been sweating freely in its corridors for generations. Smelled like a cross between the locker room and the garbage-filled green canal outside of the wall of Spruce Sunset Meadows on a hot day.

The Smell—it deserved the capital S—traveled like a sneaky fart into the *Eagle's Nest* in small gusts as the colonists mustered in groups of ten through the far air lock, just as they had entered by the opposite lock. Each time the lock cycled, a little bit more of that toxic air puffed out, until the room was choking on putrescence. Dad broke off from the intense conversation he'd been having with his buddies and gestured impatiently for me to join him and led me to the lock. He had a look on his face of steadfast refusal to face reality. He was not going to admit that the spaceship we were about to take up residence in had a Smell. We were going to *Mars* and it was all going to be so freaking *awesome* that it was impossible to even take notice of any imperfection, not even a Smell with its own capital letter. No whining!

Mom took my hand and helped me down onto the same local vertical as them and we Velcro-shuffled our way to the lock, *rip, rip, rip*, a family hand-in-hand, with our space-bags slung over our shoulders, about to become pioneers, about to leave behind Earth and all its authorities and laws and rules and governments. We were going to a place where we could be Free, with a capital F, and if Free had a Smell, so be it.

The air lock closed behind us; the equalization hiss was the only sound in the lock. There were ten of us, and I noticed that Vijay was part of our gang and managed to nod at him and he nodded back. Now that the lock was sealed, we were officially, irrevocably *gone*. When the International Space Agency completed its certification tour of the *Eagle*, they completed their duty to the citizens of Earth's nations, and now they had no more authority over us. No one on Earth did. We were in space, and we were a new human race, free as almost no human being had ever been free. No one had any claim over us or our work or our freedom except for our peers, the people we'd elected to go to an alien world with. We were off to start anew.

And we couldn't arrive a moment too soon.

Spaceships suck. You probably didn't realize that, but they do. Spaceships are small, cramped, smelly, and crowded. Our cabin—the room that Mom, Dad, and I would spend the next six months in—was smaller than the mudroom at home, where we took our boots and coats off before going into the house. All the furniture folded away into the walls, and there was no toilet or shower. We had to share the communal toilets at the end of the hallway. Supposedly, there was one toilet for every six people, which someone had calculated was optimal. At home, we had four toilets for three people, not counting the one in the basement. And anyway, Helene did a count once we were under way and calculated that there was one toilet for every *twelve* people, not that any of the grown-ups would listen to her.

The toilets had a double Smell—that putrid human smell that got worse, not better, as time went by (as though my nose was bravely refusing to get used to it, sacrificing itself by insisting on staying totally revolted by it so that I would know that I should get out ASAP), and the lesser smell of the air-freshener that squirted constantly out of little misters around the giant vacuum cleaner head that we stuck our butts into. That was like the smell of bubble gum, times one million, and it clung to your clothes after you used the head so that you smelled it for hours.

Yes, we were pioneers. Pioneers had never had it very comfortable.

"They drove covered wagons across America," my Dad said. "They were killed by bandits, by Indians, by disease. They starved. They baked. They froze. They drowned." Dad's grandparents came to America from Spain and Holland. They were middle-class architects who met at university and married and moved to San Diego because they wanted to live by the Pacific Ocean, and they did for most of their lives, retiring to Arizona just before most of San Diego ended up underwater. The closest anyone in my ancestry had come to a covered wagon was a business-class seat on a British Airways 777 to LAX.

"Yup," I said. "They sure did. Nevertheless, Dad, you have to admit that this ship is kind of crappy. None of the carpets are laid straight. Half the doors don't close right. Your bed falls off the wall every time you fold it out."

He grinned a little. "Yeah, okay, it's not exactly the *Queen Mary*. But it's not supposed to be. It's supposed to get us from Earth to Mars in one piece. If you don't like the room, there's always the lounge."

Junior Colonists (yes, seriously, "Junior Colonists") had their own lounges, three of them, one on each deck. These were compara-tively large spaces in the center of the ship, where there was almost no gravity. The *Eagle* was a big spinning doughnut, with lots of centripetal force—which feels a lot like gravity—around the edges, and almost none in the middle. The floaty parts in the middle were mostly shunned by grown-ups, who found them a little ulpy-gulpy and were prone to losing their lunches in the middle of our play areas. That was fine by us.

The JC lounges were pretty big to start with, but the absence of gravity made them even bigger, because it meant that we could use the ceilings, walls, and middle as functional space, and we did. At any time of the "day" or "night"—the ship had a twenty-four-Mar-tian-hour clock that the colonists stuck to—you'd find it full of kids, most of us in our teens (the little 'uns had supervised play areas that parents took turns overseeing). We'd be flying around the space with fins on our hands and long bungee cords around our waists, or we'd be tethered to something, with our faces masked by goggles and our hands running up and down virtual keyboards suspended in midair.

I never gamed with goggles and virtual keyboards at home, but then, I never had to. My Martian Chronicles competition had all been physically separated from me, but now they were literally on every side of me, and if I'd used even a small screen, dozens of people would have been able to shoulder-surf me.

"Good morning, boss," Helene said, her voice so clear through my headset that she might have been right beside me. Then she tapped me on the shoulder and I shoved my goggles up on my fore-head and realized that she *was* right beside me, floating in space side-ways to me, lazily sculling the air with her hand-fins to keep herself from drifting away on the air currents. I suppressed a scowl.

"Good morning, Helene. Why have we abandoned operational security on this fine day?"

Helene was supposedly going straight. She had vowed that she would give up raiding forever once we made Marsfall, and go into legit business. This had cheered Vijay and me no end, and, at Vijay's insistence, I had given her some minor status in DBOS-Corp, so that she could get some experience working for a living instead of destroying things. But she was a total loose cannon. She knew that we only talked business through the game to avoid being overheard. The game had good crypto protecting our conversations, something that was totally lacking in the cheek-by-jowl (by-butt-by-knee) atmosphere of the JC lounges.

But she wanted to actually *talk*, face-to-face.

"You're supposed to have been this big deal raider," I said. "How did you survive? You've got the secrecy instincts of an elephant."

She shrugged, which caused her to start spinning in slow circles, which she seemed to enjoy. She'd shaved her head after the first day in space and kept it clean to the scalp, something that a lot of other kids had done since. "I suppose I managed to keep it on the down-low when it mattered and ignored it when it didn't."

"This is exactly the kind of thing that's going to get you in trouble when you go to work for some corp Mars-side," I said, aware that I was lecturing, but unable to stop myself. "Companies need to have policies; employees need to obey those policies. It's fine to have ideas of your own, to try to get them circulated within the company and adopted. But you can't just go rogue whenever an idea comes into your shiny bald head."

She rubbed her gleaming noggin—she must shave it every day to keep it so shiny. "You seriously get off on this? Seriously? Role-playing that you're some bigshot in a suit telling other people what to do and amassing a fortune?"

She'd hinted many times that she thought that straight Martian Chronicles players were suckers and drones, but this was the first time she'd come out and said it to my face. She had that same lazy smile and didn't seem to be intending offense, but it got my back up. I swallowed a couple times. "I get off on *making things*. I pay a good salary to people to help me create amazing things that succeed, that make money and make people happy. Making things together requires that you give up some of your individual freedom in order to help the company succeed. If you don't want to do that, you shouldn't take a job."

"Okay," she said. "I won't take the job. Thanks for the memories!" She gave no impression of being upset. She never showed much emotion beyond a kind of lighthearted, detached amusement.

I was so shocked that I just watched her grab hold of her bungee, use it to pull herself to the bulkhead, where she could get her legs coiled under herself, and then push off and go sailing away through the lounge, dodging and weaving between the players with their goggles, and the other fliers who were generally a lot less reckless than she was.

Vijay plucked his way along the wall to me, taking dainty, quick Velcroized steps that seemed ridiculous but actually got him around the space with a lot of speed and control. "What was that?" he said, drawing level with me and stopping his motion with a single finger pressed lightly against my shoulder.

I became aware that I was snorting hot air from my nose like a cartoon bull with a head cold. I made myself stop. "She quit," I said. "Because I asked her to adhere to corp policy." I shrugged my shoulders. "I guess there's no helping some people. She must have been born to be a raider."

Vijay pressed his lips together and managed to look both disapproving and nonjudgmental at the same time. I don't know how he did it, but he did. After a week on the *Eagle*, Vijay seemed to have worked out where all the angles were—he was bunking in a hardship-case dorm with thirty other poves, but he knew which dining room served the biggest portions, which gangways were fastest, which viewing ports were most likely to be free.

No one apart from Helene and I talked to him. We might have been the only ones who *saw* him; peoples' eyes just slid over the poves like they were invisible. Vijay never gave any sign that he minded. He used his invisibility to get into places where we couldn't go, and he always had a fun adventure—what he called a "good wheeze"—up his sleeve.

"Well, I suppose she'll have to figure it all out when we get to Mars, anyway," he said. "As will we all."

"What does that mean? I know how to build a corp. I've done it before. I'll do it again."

"But you'll be a different kind of person on Mars than you were on Earth. You'll be an immigrant. A newcomer. You won't have any assets. You will be a pove, if you'll forgive the expression."

I had never called him a pove. I was raised better than that. But we both knew that he was a pove and I wasn't.

"Don't be ridiculous," I said. "I can't be a pove."

"Why not? If you don't have money, you are poor. You have poverty. You are a pove."

What a stupid day this was turning out to be. First Helene's temper tantrum and now Vijay was trying to needle me. "In the first place, no one is an immigrant on Mars. An immigrant is someone who comes to your place—your country or planet—to live. But Mars *is* our country. Mars, Inc. and its stakeholders—that's us—own it.

"In the second place, a pove isn't someone who's poor. A pove is someone who refuses to stop being poor. They want handouts, not work. Their governments have told them that they have the right to food and shelter, so they want what's theirs by right."

Now, I had heard and said these words hundreds of times. They were part of every civics class I'd ever taken. They were repeated several times a day through the Mars, Inc. orientation. But I have to say, I never really thought about what it would be like to hear those words if you *were* a pove. Not until they came out of my mouth on that day.

I felt the blush burning in my cheeks. "I mean, Vijay, not you, obviously. Obviously you *want* to work, you *want* to get out, and see, you did! You're smart and motivated. That's how you became an auditor. It's how you got to get on the *Eagle*."

He cocked his head. "Dave," he said. "You never asked where my parents were."

I swallowed. "No," I said. "I mean, I figured that you had to be an orphan—"

"Oh, yes, I am an orphan. That's because when I was ten, a P&G neutraceutical plant near my village leaked seventy thousand tons of toxic fumes into the air. It killed over 95 percent of the people for two hundred kilometers around. Many of them worked at the plant, or provided services to the people who did. The company argued that the division that owned that factory was totally separate from P&G, even though P&G was the majority shareholder in it, and its only customer was P&G. Because of this, the Bangladeshi court was only able to render judgment on this 'separate company,' which was practically bankrupt at that point. Luckily, there weren't many of us alive. The ones who lived got enough money to go to a good school and not to one of the bad orphanages where the survival rate is about the same as that of people living in the toxic plume of a P&G plant."

I tried not to show how much this shocked me. It practically *skewered* me. It was so much goddamned *reality*. Made everything I knew seem so . . . fake. Pointless. Like I'd been complaining about a splinter in my toe and this guy had had both of his feet eaten off by a tiger. So first I felt surprised. Then embarrassed. Then angry, though I didn't know at who or what. Maybe my parents for keeping me from reality, though hell knew that I wouldn't want to live through what Vijay had been through.

"Dave," he said. "Please, calm down." Made me wonder what my face had been doing. I hadn't said anything. "I just wanted you to see that people aren't just poor because they're lazy. Some people work as hard as mules, every day of the week, and die poor." Unbidden, the thought rose to my mind, *They must be stupid then. It's not enough to work hard. You have to work hard doing something valuable.* "Some people work hard as mules and get hit by a bus or a chemical leak. Some people sit around on their fat asses all day and get rich." I saw that some heads turned when he said this. Statements like that one were about the worst thing you could say to a Mars colonist.

I knew what I was supposed to say here. It was drilled into me. I said it. "If someone figures out how to do more with less, that tells us that he's doing something *right*, and he should be rewarded for figuring stuff like that out. We don't want people to just work harder—we want people to work *better*."

He nodded. "Of course, Dave. That's what we're told. But Helene is a raider and she's figured out a way to get a lot of money without working hard at all, by ruining the hard and valuable work of others. Where does she fit in?"

I swallowed. "I suppose that's why it's not illegal. But—" I fumbled for the argument. Lots of people were listening. I felt like I was divulging corporate secrets to my competition, even though nothing we were saying had to do with my business. "Just because it's legal doesn't mean it's good."

"No," Vijay said. "But you just said that anyone who figures out how to make more money with less work should be rewarded."

I wanted to sink through the floor. I felt like everyone who was listening in could see that I really was just a loser, one of those people who didn't really understand everything that Mars Colony stood for, not in my heart. I should have had some decent arguments right there on the tip of my tongue. But all I had was ashamed, furious blushing.

"Listen, *pove*," said a voice from below me, loud enough to be heard around the room. "You're a *guest* here. Nobody wants to hear your opinion on what successful people deserve or don't deserve. Why don't you go hang out with your own kind?" It was Liam, the redheaded mouthy kid. He ran an investment bank in Martian Chronicles, moving giant chunks of money around on behalf of big corps and big players. He was always too friendly with me, and too loud, but he also managed to make me feel like I had to go along with him or he might punch me in the gut. Not that I'd ever seen him be violent—he was just, you know, *intense*.

Vijay nodded his head, not ducking it, but nodding, as if Liam was confirming something he'd suspected all along, which somehow made Liam seem like even more of a jackass. "As you say," he said, and took off into the middle of the room, using a hard shove to get himself moving and steering himself expertly through the crowd. Liam swiped at his ankle as he passed, but missed.

Liam righted himself relative to me, so that we were face-to-face. "You need a better class of friend, Smith. Judge a man by the company he keeps. You're going to have to get yourself set up again Mars-side and the impression you make on this ship will follow you around for the rest of your life. Just some friendly advice from your banker."

You're not my banker, I didn't say. And I also didn't say, *You're not my friend*. And also not, *The impression that'll follow you around for the rest of your life is going to be of a big-mouth jerk*.

And also, I didn't say, *Vijay's my friend and I'm proud to be his*.

Instead, I plastered a smile on my face and waved vaguely at him and plucked my way along the wall to the hatch and made for the gravity in the outer rings.

Helene came and got me a couple days later, rescuing me from a truly epic sulk in my parents' cabin.

"You look like Martian crap," she said.

"How's that different from Terran crap?" I asked her.

"It's redder, with a slightly longer day. Also, less gravity."

My father chuckled and my mother smiled and I heard the klaxon go off in the back of my head, the one that went ALERT! ALERT! PARENTS ARE ABOUT TO SAY SOMETHING LIKE "IS THIS YOUR LITTLE GIRLFRIEND, DAVID?"

"Mom-Dad-this-is-Helene-we're-going-out-now-'kay-bye," I said and grabbed Helene and dragged her down the corridor as fast as I could. From behind me, I heard my parents call sarcastically, "Nice to meet you, Helene!" and "Come by anytime," and other parents looked at us from their bunks through their open doors as we tore ass toward the hatch that led in-ship, toward the low-grav zones.

"What is it?" I asked, when we were through the air lock that separated the decks.

"I've been leaving you messages in-game but you haven't answered them. Finally, I decided to see when you'd last logged in and I saw that it had been like seventy-two hours ago and I decided you must have something terminal so I came to find you so I could tell you my secret before you died."

"What secret?"

"You're really a crown prince who was hidden away by the king and queen, sent to live with a provincial bourgeois family so that the evil grand vizier couldn't catch you. You are the rightful heir to the ancient kingdom of Freedonia."

"You're weird."

She bowed. "Indeed. So, what is it? Cholera? Plague? The crushing ennui of daily existence in a futile and uncaring universe?"

I squirmed. The deck we were on was lightly trafficked—it had a different night than we did, everybody slept in shifts—and semideserted at this hour. I was conscious of the fact that Helene was very pretty and somehow managed not to smell like the Smell, but rather like something slightly floral and nice. I was conscious of the fact that we were alone. I was conscious of the fact that the last time I'd spoken with Helene, I'd chased her off by treating her to an uninvited lecture on corporate responsibility.

"I just didn't feel like coming out," I mumbled, staring at my shoes.

"Oh, right then," she said. "Okay, back you go. See you later."

She began to walk away. I stared at her retreating back.

"Wait!" I said.

She looked over her shoulder at me. "Yes?"

"I feel like coming out now," I said.

"Oh, all right then. Let's go find Vijay."

I felt weirdly disappointed. Helene wanted to hang out with me *and* Vijay, which suggested that the half-formed romantic suspicion I'd felt was totally unfounded. Of course. Why would someone as pretty as Helene want anything romantic to do with someone like me? Besides, she was as weird as a sack of snakes; there was no way to predict what was going on in her pointy little head.

I knew, approximately speaking, where Vijay's quarters were. The "scholarship" bunkroom—the place where poves who'd been lucky enough to get a free ride on the *Eagle* slept—was also at the ship's hub, where there was no gravity to speak of. This allowed for a much higher density of humanity—you didn't need bunks, just loosely tethered cocoons where people slept. Vijay had told us about it with a shrug, as if to say that it wasn't any worse than his Bangladeshi orphanage, but I'd had a vision of a huge space, in perpetual twilight, where insectile sacks filled with softly breathing people drifted silently into one another, and it had given me a shiver.

"You're sure he's not in the JC lounge?" I asked.

"No, he stopped showing up two days ago. The lag was killing him." The farther we got from Earth, the laggier the game got, as our play traffic had to traverse the widening light-speed gap between us and the servers twice, once in each direction. Almost immediately after takeoff, we'd lost real-time voice communications with the dirt-side players. We could leave them voice mails and they could reply the same way, but that was all.

Then we lost real-time graphics. Rather than flying through a constantly updated, pin-sharp rendering of the Mars of Martian Chronicles as it was, we saw it in blocky, symbolic graphics covered in glyphs warning us that these buildings and people and vehicles might or might not still be there.

Finally, the game turned into a set of spreadsheets that were updated once every minute, filled with vital statistics about market activity, sales, mergers, acquisitions, corporate raids . . . And as we sped farther and farther from our worn-out mother planet, the update lag would be worse and worse. Until apogee, the point where we were an equal distance from Earth and Mars, when our antennae would be reversed and we'd begin three months' worth of reverse flight, finally slowing down enough to put us at a relative standstill by the time we reached our new home. At Turnaround, the ship's networks would change over to the Martian Internet, a system that was almost entirely separate from Earth's spam-riddled cesspool. The two networks could barely communicate with one another— for one thing, Martian computers reckoned time differently, count- ing by Martian seconds, which were 1.025 Earth seconds long (just as the Martian day was 2.5 percent longer than the Earth day).

"So, if you're sure he's not in the JC lounge, are you *also* sure he's in his quarters? You know Vijay, he could be anywhere."

"It's the tail end of his sleep cycle. He's due to wake up in about thirty minutes. He'll be there."

The pove quarters announced themselves with their own Smell, a Smell distinct from the overarching Smell of the *Eagle*. This was the smell of people stuck together so close that every fart blew directly into someone's face; every toe dangled tantalizing inches from someone's nose; every armpit was wafting its perfume into someone else's breakfast. As we neared it, we heard the Hum, the perpetual sound of a thousand people whispering, trying not to wake the others who were on sleep shift.

The dim room was just as I'd imagined it. Unsurprising, since my impressions were based on candid photos posted to the ship's blog, snapped by colonists who'd snuck down to see how the other half lived. It really *was* like looking in on a termite's nest or the underside of a rotten log, a squirming mass of half-seen humanity wrapped in gauzy harnesses.

"Looks like the povetowns in Martian Chronicles, doesn't it?" Helene said, in a normal conversational voice that cut through the Hum like a cymbal crash. I squirmed with embarrassment, mostly because I'd been thinking just that. You could always tell when a Martian Chronicles player was a pove, because they built houses and businesses that looked like the pove slums you saw in the news. They were too close together, and they ran businesses right out of their residences, and they always tried to do three thousand things at once—jetpack repair, accounting services, hairdressing, space suit designs, all with enthusiastic, badly spelled signage.

"I guess," I mumbled and squinted into the darkness. There was a pove sitting by the door, a man with a little cracked palmtop clipped to his flowing white shift. Apparently the backlight had gone—he was reading it by the light leaking in from the doorway, which we were blocking by standing there, gawping. He made an impatient gesture at us. "Come in, come in," he said in accented English. Maybe he was African? It sounded like the African accents in the games I played.

We scooted past him, and were enveloped in the close, over-breathed air of the pove quarters. I had the same feeling I got when I stumbled into povetowns in Martian Chronicles: claustrophobia, nausea, and an awful, nagging guilt. And then anger. Why were we taking the poves to Mars anyway?

Meanwhile, Helene was floating through the space, peering at peoples' faces, looking for Vijay. "Found him," she sang out, again too loud for the space, and people rolled over in their cocoons and gave us dirty looks. I drifted over to her, grinned weakly at Vijay, who was scrubbing at his eyes with his long, skinny hands.

"Hello," he whispered. "Funny meeting you here." He struggled out of his cocoon and I saw that he was wearing gray underpants and a T-shirt, and I looked away as he snagged his clothes from the ditty-bag under the cocoon and pulled them on.

"Toilet," he said, and led us out of poveland. There was a huge line for the nearest toilet, but he sailed past it and led us down a maintenance corridor that was barely wide enough to pass through, even turned sideways. "'Scuse me," he said, and ducked into a niche I hadn't even seen. A moment later, I heard the pee-plus-vacuum sound of a low-gee toilet. "I think they used this while they were building the *Eagle*," he called over the noise, seemingly unembarrassed by having an audience for his toilet experience. "It's not even on the as-built drawings. But they must have had a toilet while they were working, after they pressurized her." Before pressure, everyone would have worked in space suits and gone in a diaper. He emerged, fastidiously wiping his fingers on a sani-wipe that he tucked in the waistband of his loose cotton pants. "Okay," he said. "Onward, stout comrades!"

He led us farther up the corridor and I felt myself growing heavier, a sense of *downhill* that told me we were headed into the higher-gee outer rings. I heard muffled conversations from beyond the thin bulkhead—snatches of conversation in Simplified English and then in Spanish, which the crew spoke when there weren't any colonists around. They were mostly Mexican, poves, really, and they were getting a free ride to Mars and a free start as colonists in exchange for driving the big tin can across the solar system for us.

"Where are we?" Helene said in her stupid loud voice.

"Quietly, please," Vijay said, without rancor. "Crew quarters. This corridor goes all the way from the center to the outer ring. This is about as far as you can go before you start sliding downhill, though. I thought it'd be fun to come back sometime and do it again with pitons and ropes, see if we can get all the way down to the passenger decks without falling straight down and breaking both legs."

"That *does* sound like fun," Helene said. "Count me in."

"You two," I said. But it *did* sound like fun. We had *months* left in this tin can. And spending it all playing Martian Chronicles didn't sound nearly as much fun as it had before we'd actually left for Mars. "Okay, Vijay, you're officially the coolest guy in outer space. Can we go now? It'd be nice to actually be able to see you guys, rather than the backs of your heads." We were all turned sideways, remember. There wasn't even enough room to turn our heads.

"Don't you want to know what I learned here in my secret perch in crew territory?" He was barely speaking above a whisper—we were all keeping it quiet—but he managed to convey unholy glee.

"Do tell," Helene hissed in a very loud whisper—like a whispered shout. The voices outside the walls got quieter, and we all held our breath for a second. Then they got louder again.

"Well, I speak some Spanish," Vijay said. "Just a little, but it's helpful in Martian Chronicles to be able to audit a company's books in the language that they're kept in. And there are so many Mexican and South American corps now in MC—"

"Farmers," I snorted. Everyone knew that the Spanish-speaking corps were just fronts for "farmers"—players that did mind-numbing, repetitive tasks in-game to amass wealth that they could sell to real players who didn't want their transactions to show up on the official registry.

I could hear Vijay's silence from farther up the corridor, just make out his shoulders tightening. "Many of them are very good firms," he said. "Operating under the highest ethical standards."

I opened my mouth to say something that would defend my position, but Helene spoke before I could. "You were saying, Vijay?"

"Yes. Well, the thing is, the crew are very active MC players. And they have access to the Martian Internet."

"Jesus," I said. "That must be laggy as hell."

"Oh yes," Vijay said. "About two hundred seconds of network delay. But that's plenty fast enough to let them get a look at Martian Chronicles."

"They're logging in?"

"Oh, yes. Logging in and even joining up with corps. They want to be sure that by the time they land, they have a good position. Think about it. Once we hit apogee and switch the *Eagle*'s main systems over to the Martian Internet, there's going to be a thousand colonists all trying to get in with the corps or found their own, all at once. They're beating the rush."

"But that's cheating!" I said, too loud, and again the voices from outside dipped.

"Go," whispered Vijay. "Quietly."

Quietly, we backed down the corridor, turning around to face the way we were going only when we reached Vijay's secret toilet. We popped back out near poveland, and Vijay floated up onto the ceiling and gestured to us to join him. We put our faces close together and spoke softly.

"I'm sorry," I said. "But it *is* cheating."

"No it's not," Helene said. "It's just taking advantage of circumstances. Look at the colonists who went up on the *Falcon*." That was the first Mars, Inc. colony ship, which had made the voyage ten years before. "They got to set up Mars-side Martian Chronicles without anyone else in the way. They had a totally blank world. They could mine the best mineral deposits, grab the best mountains to hollow out and pressurize, stake out the best oxygen patches. Are they cheating? Should they have waited for us to get there before they started?"

I swallowed. "It's not the same thing," I said, but I didn't sound very convincing.

Helene waved her hand at me in a dismissive, floppy gesture.

"What did you find out from them, Vijay?" But before he could speak she put her finger to her lips. "Dave, you might want to move out of earshot until we're done here. Wouldn't want you to get tainted by all this cheating."

"Children," Vijay said, with mock sternness. "Enough."

I glared at Helene, who smiled at me with so much dimple and lip action that I felt myself blushing.

"Sorry," I mumbled.

"Now, what I discovered was this. The Mars-side game is almost nothing like the game we play. It's a lot meaner, and raiding is the order of the day. Four corps control the entire show, and every corp has to pay tribute to one of them for a license to operate, or face financial ruin. The four main corps hate each other, but they'll work in concert to destroy any independent corp that threatens their arrangement—anything it takes: price-fixing, unfair advertising, market lockouts. . . ." He went on, rattling off a long list of sins that only auditors truly understood. Basically, these were all the ways that a corp could try *too* hard, like when all the corps in one sector, like oxygen, make exclusive deals with all the Mars habitats to supply their air at a discount on the condition that the habitats agree not to buy water from some other corp. This was strictly forbidden on Martian Chronicles—Earth-side, at least—though of course people were always trying it.

"So that's the shape of things," he concluded. "The *Eagle*'s crew are trying to work out—from the spreadsheets and news bulletins they're getting from the Mars servers—which of the four corps they should go to work for. They've decided to offer themselves as a team, thinking that they'll get higher wages if they all stand together."

I shook my head. "That's collusion!" I said. If there was one thing that was even more against the rules I'd always lived under than unfair competition, it was labor collusion, when a bunch of workers decided in secret to hold out for a higher wage, or to stop some of their friends from being fired or having their hours cut. It wasn't just illegal in Martian Chronicles—it was illegal on *Mars*, one of the fundamental tenets of Mars, Inc.'s charter. Totally free labor markets!

"It's a different game on Mars," Vijay said. "Besides, what's really wrong with it? A company puts a lot of workers together so that it can earn more profits—why shouldn't workers get together to earn more wages?"

Helene raised her eyebrows at me, as though to say, *Do you have an answer? One that you're okay saying in front of Vijay?*

I tightened my lips. "Vijay, can I say something to you without worrying that you'll be offended?"

He smiled and bobbed up and down in the null-gee. "Of course, Dave. You're my friend. Let it all hang out."

"What you're talking about is pure pove talk. The world has two kinds of people in it: whiners and winners. A winner goes out and starts a company and figures out how to make as much as possible. A whiner complains that the winner isn't paying him enough and, rather than starting his own company, complains and demands more money from the winner. The real way to get higher pay is to take a risk, start your own business, make something important in the world." I checked to see if he was offended. He was floating upside down, so it was hard to tell if he was smiling or not.

I continued: "Okay, so this is why you can always find the poves in Martian Chronicles. They're the ones bitching about the unfairness of everything instead of *doing something*. It's why there are so many poor people on Earth. It's a thought virus they all catch from their society, demanding that the world provide for them instead of providing for themselves. And it's the job of the doers and the winners to ignore the whiners and go on doing and winning so that the whiners will have somewhere to work."

Vijay was looking at me with something like a mild smile on his face. I replayed my words and heard just how offensive they might sound to someone like Vijay. "Look," I said, no longer meeting his gaze. "Look. I'm not saying it's genetic—no one is saying that poor people are inherently *inferior* or anything. But it's a disease, and you catch it from the people around you."

Helene shook her head at me. "You really believe everything your dad tells you, don't you?"

I nearly turned around and left then, but I was still keenly aware of the loneliness I'd experienced for the three days I'd spent locked up in my parents' cabin. So I stood my ground and pretended I hadn't heard her.

Vijay said, "I've heard this theory before. There's only one thing I wonder about. Maybe you could help me with it."

"Go ahead," I said.

"Can you explain where the people who died in the P&G leak were whiners?"

I shook my head. "No, of course not, but—"

"Do you have any idea how many workers I've met who are missing fingers or eyes or hands? How many of them were called whiners and sent away because they asked their employers for compensation because the machines mutilated them?"

I shook my head again. "You don't get it—"

"No," Vijay said, and I heard that the calm voice he used—that he *always* used—was just a tight belt cinched around an enormous pool of anger. That Vijay was *angry* at me, at us, at the colonists. "No, Dave. I *do* get it. Do you know what cognitive dissonance is?"

We'd studied it in school, but I hadn't paid a lot of attention. "It's like when you believe something and the facts don't agree with it."

"That's right. So say, for example, that you believe that the world is fair, but when you look around it, you see that you have so very much more than everyone else." I could see where this was going. I began to walk away, but he floated and skipped after me, continuing to talk. "So you have cognitive dissonance. How can the world be fair if you have more than everyone else? It must be *fair for you to have more*, then, right? And how can that be? It can only be if you are better than everyone else—and everyone else is therefore worse than you—"

I reached a hatch and passed through it and moved out toward the living quarters, downhill in the gravity.

For some reason, there were tears in my eyes.

I didn't go back to the Junior Colonists' lounge for a whole week. Instead, I spent the time with my dad, who seemed pleasantly surprised that his son wanted to hang out with him. It made me feel bad, like I'd been neglecting him. But it also made me ask myself why my father didn't think it was weird that I wasn't spending any time with kids my age. Dad had always been busy on Earth, traveling half the time for work, spending his time at home with his computer over his face, barking angrily at it while his hands worked the keyboard like a mad player attacking a church organ.

I didn't mind, to be honest. Actually, I preferred it to those times when Dad decided to get all dadlike and insist on throwing a ball with me or take me to some kind of sports match or play some game on the big living-room screen with me. It wasn't that it wasn't fun, but there was always a moment when we stopped talking about the game or the project and found ourselves sitting in awkward silence, trying to pretend that the reason we had nothing to say was that we were concentrating too hard on the matter at hand.

On Earth, Dad had been a hotshot statistical risk analyst. This is not an easy thing to explain. But basically, what he did was tried to figure out how to balance investments to minimize risk. Say there's an industry that benefits when someone finds a better way of growing wheat—the bread industry, say. And then there's another industry that suffers when someone finds a better way of growing wheat, like, maybe, I don't know, the corn industry? I forget how he explained this, to be honest, but this is generally the idea. So what he does is figures out how to invest some money in both industries, so that if someone finds a better wheat-growing technique, the investment in bread pays out, and if no one invents it, the investment in corn pays out. That's the rough idea. What he did was like ten million times more complicated, though.

And anyway, it doesn't really matter now. Now we're going to Mars, and there are no risk analysts. When we got to Mars, Dad was going to have to start a new business, or start a job, or something. He had bought us into the gold tier for Mars settlements—that meant that we were going to get our own private pressurized space, six months' worth of food vouchers, and a million Martian ray guns (this sounds like a lot, but keep in mind that a pressure suit costs MRG450,000 at last count). For this, he traded everything—every penny we had, our house, our furniture, our savings, everything. What were we going to do with it anyway? It wasn't like we could take it to Mars. Our personal luggage allowance was limited to fifteen kilos each.

"Dad," I said, as we loitered in one of the corridors, nodding amiably at the other colonists as they went past on their way to the toilets or the common rooms or wherever it was everyone else always seemed to be going.

He didn't hear me. He was looking into space, lips pursed, brows furrowed. It was the expression he'd worn back in his office when he'd been neck-deep in work, computer plastered across his face, only his lips and nose visible. It was weird to see him making that face without a computer. More than weird. Scary. Like he was seeing into a world I couldn't see.

"Everything okay, Dad?" I'd never asked him that before.

"What? Oh, yes, sorry. I was a million miles away."

"Fifteen million miles," I said. "According to the morning *Barsoom*." That was the ship's blog, written by some crew member in Simplified. "But we're closing fast. Mars in forty-nine days."

"Right!" he said. "Right. Exciting, huh?"

He said it so unconvincingly that my heart nearly broke. For years, he'd been talking about Mars and how great it would be when we got there. He hated Earth, hated all the rules and regulations, all the whiners who wanted him to invest in "ethical" funds that gave up on profits so that other whiners would get paid more. Mars was like some kind of promised land that we were headed to, a better world for people like us.

"Exciting," I said. He looked away. "Dad, you don't seem so excited, though."

He put on a big, fake grin. "I'm excited, son. It's just . . . You know. Space travel isn't as glamorous as I thought it would be. You know me. I'm no good at sitting idle. I'm just itching to get some work done."

"How about starting something up with someone onboard? I heard that lots of people are starting their own little corps. You know, hit the ground running." I couldn't believe I was lecturing *Dad* about business. It was quite a switch from the years and years of Dad telling me that I should be more entrepreneurial, play a harder game of Martian Chronicles.

"Yeah," he said. "Yeah. Well, that's something I've been think-ing about. But you know, I'm investigating opportunities. Don't want to jump into something that turns out to be a bust."

"Dad, what's going on? Back on Earth you were always telling me to seize the opportunity, fail fast, move on. Why are you being so . . ." I wanted to say *scared*, but Dad's face had gone all furious, the way it did, so I didn't finish the sentence.

"There's some things you don't understand, kid, believe it or not. Some things that you're going to have to age a year or two before you can grok 'em. Why don't you run along and play, sonny?" He said it in the tone he used when he was telling off some idiot who just didn't get it, someone who was a whiner or a bureaucrat. He often asked those people, *What planet are you living on?* Which I'd always thought was funny. After all, he was the one who wanted to leave the planet and go to a better one.

It wasn't funny now. I slunk away to the room and found Mom.

One of the other moms had come over to our cabin for a chat. All the moms in our corridor had found each other shortly after launch, and it seemed to me that they'd nearly instantaneously formed a tight social club. I kind of envied them the ease with which they came together as a group. It reminded me of when I'd been a little kid at after-school programs and the moms would all be in this tight cluster, chatting away merrily, even as the dads stood off in quiet clumps of two or three, twitching impatiently at their computers.

Mom and her friend Ms. Bonilla, who spoke Simplified mostly, though Mom said she could also speak French and Portuguese as well as her native Spanish, smiled at me as I entered. I wanted to say something like, "Mom, is Dad losing his freaking mind?" but I couldn't say that in front of company.

"Hello, David," Ms. Bonilla said. She was very pretty and seemed young, and I remembered Mom telling me that she'd had a ton of surgery and took pills all the time to keep up her appearance, because "Mexican companies are even harder on aging women in the boardroom than American ones." Dad had made a face at that—it was getting into whining territory, and the *Eagle* was a no whining zone.

"Good day, Ms. Bonilla," I said. That's what we'd all settled on onboard the *Eagle*, where it was always morning for someone, always afternoon or evening or midnight for someone else, depending on which sleep schedule you kept.

Mom cocked her head at me. "Things not so good with your father, David?" Of course she knew. She spent more time with him than I did.

"Always the same for Mr. Bonilla," Ms. Bonilla said. "All the men. It is the no-activity. They can't live with no-activity." A lot of Simplified was like that, taking a word like "activity" and making its opposite by putting "no-" in front of it.

Mom sighed. "David's father has it big-big. From big-big important to small-small no-important. Making him crazy."

"Mars," Ms. Bonilla said. I remembered that she had been a "big-big important" too—the head of a giant cement company—but somehow she was coping okay in transit.

"Mars," Mom agreed. Mom liked to pore over the *Ares Plain Dealer—Colonist Edition* issues that came in over the ship's radio, especially the want ads. "My husband wants start a corp on Mars. Not me. I say work for some time, see how all is, then start a corp. Why run without looking?"

"But Dad is—"

"He's crazy. It's temporary. There are many no-knowns about Mars. He wants information. Wants to try things. Can't do either. Your father is big-big information processor. Without information, he starves. He's big crazy with hunger. Understand that, David. He's not angry with you. Just frustrated with the delay."

That settled it. But if Ms. Bonilla wasn't there, I would have said, "How come so many *other* dads manage to cope? Why are there are all these other dads out there trying to form corps and get ready to hit Mars running?" But not in front of company.

There wasn't anything to say to Mom. Dad didn't want to talk to me. My only friends onboard weren't talking to me (or was it me who wasn't talking to them?). There was only one thing left to do: get back into the game.

Here's how you get to Mars: first, you boost for a couple hours at one gee, which gets your ship really *moving*. Since there's nothing in space to stop it—except a few stray hydrogen atoms and the odd gust of solar wind—it'll just coast Marsward pretty much forever. So you switch the engines off and ride your momentum ever and ever Marsward. If you've timed it all correctly, Mars should also be moving toward *you*, swinging around the sun at 13.3 km/s and closing fast.

Once you're closer to Mars than you are to Earth, you flip the ship over, so that your main antenna array is pointed at the red planet, and reboot the ship's computers, bringing them back online running a Mars-compliant OS that runs on Martian time. Then, about ninety days later, you turn the engines back and boost *away* from Mars for a few hours, because 13.3 km/s and closing fast is *fast*—fast enough to turn your rocket into a cloud of atoms and a giant shockwave if you run *into* Mars instead of going into a gentle orbit around Phobos Base for transfer to a ground shuttle.

We were almost at Turnaround, which meant that we were nearly equidistant from Mars and the Earth. That meant that almost no one was playing the game anymore, because it was at 640 seconds of latency, meaning that a message sent to Earth took 320 seconds to get there and 320 seconds to get back, which made playing the game nearly impossible.

I'd planned to do an orderly shutdown of DBOS-Corp long before this, liquidating my shares and giving the proceeds to a charity that helped new players get established in the game, then leaving my lieutenants to break up the firm's assets according to their share-blocks and either merge with other corps or try to make it on their own. Without my authorization, none of that would be possible, and the company would just putter on for a couple months until the fact that there was no one at the steering wheel caught up with it and it crashed. I'd put far too much work into it to allow that to happen.

Or at least, that's how I'd felt when we left for Mars. Now, in the middle of the black and endless sky, it was hard to figure out what was so important about this imaginary company and its imaginary money. But there was a certain peace in shuffling the paper for my old, familiar company, making the spreadsheets dance to their traditional tunes. I was breaking up my stock, modifying the board, changing the org chart to shuffle corporate officers around. My lieutenants had been sending me increasingly worried notes by long-delayed e-mail, asking me when I'd get around to this, promising (good naturedly) to give me a real thumping when *they* got to Mars if I didn't see to this in good time. Well, now they'd be happy. I fired off the signed orders to the Earth-side game server and waited patiently while the speed of light oozed its way across the reaches of outer space and over to planet Earth and then back again.

But then it was done and the strings were cut. I was free. My company was no longer mine. I was, as of this moment, not a player in either the Earth-side or the Mars-side Martian Chronicles. I found I was pretty happy.

I set off down the corridor, whistling, heading for one of the observation decks, where there was a huge video-wall that displayed the view of the space before us, Mars glowing with enhanced color. I was whistling "The Red Hills of Mars," a folk song that I'd learned at Mars camp when I was all of six years old, and as I made my way along, someone else joined in, her whistle a very tuneful trill.

Yes, her. It was a grown-up. In a uniform. Specifically, it was Lainie, as in Lainie Lainie No Complainy, making her way down the same corridor just a meter or two behind me. She smiled at me as she drew near, her normal theatrical scowl disappearing. "You sure seem happy about something," she said.

I shrugged. I never knew what to say to Lainie. She was everywhere, all the time, and always seemed to know the gossip before any of the colonists did. She was the only one on the ship who'd actually *been* to Mars: she'd lived there for ten years and returned to Earth on the first ship back to retrieve and orient the next batch of colonists.

"Just closed out my Martian Chronicles account," I said. "It's kind of nice not to have to worry about it for a while, at least until Turnaround."

She nodded. "David Smith, right? DBOS-Corp?"

"You know it?" I couldn't believe it.

"Oh, sure. There's only a thousand of you here—I know a lot about all of you." She tapped her temple. "Trick memory. But you stand out, of course. DBOS-Corp, that's a legend."

I shook my head. "Not a lot of grown-ups pay attention to Martian Chronicles," I said. "You really play?"

"I played on the Mars-side server," she said. "Lots of us did. Gave us something to do, helped us get to know each other after we made planetfall. And so I looked up the game when I got to Earth, watched it. Didn't play, though—no time, not while we were getting the *Eagle* ready."

I said, very carefully, "I hear it's a very different kind of game on Mars." I didn't want her to know about Vijay's eavesdropping, but I also felt a weird kind of kinship with her, wanted to open up to her.

"Oh, you hear, do you?" Her face was still friendly, but I could hear a hint of the familiar sternness in her voice. "People do talk."

I was self-conscious, like I'd said too much, blown it. I started to mumble an apology and move on, but Lainie stopped me. "David," she said, her voice low. "I know how rumors spread. I wouldn't want you going away with the wrong impression. Why don't you stop by my cabin during office hours, and we'll chat about this?" She looked away, checking her work space—Lainie and the crew all had work spaces on the *Eagle*, the rest of us had to use handheld computers— and said, "Start in an hour. I'll book you in for my first slot, okay?" It wasn't really a question.

"Okay," I said, and felt a jet of sick fear. Spreading dispiriting rumors was one of the worst kinds of whining on the *Eagle*, and Lainie had lots of punishments, big and small, that she could use to discipline offenders.

The next hour was an agony of worry. I didn't want to go home, didn't want to go to the JC lounge, didn't want to run into anyone I knew, so I ended up hanging around Lainie's cabin, on Deck One, the crew deck, waiting for her hours to start. As soon as the clock ticked over to ship's 1100h, her door clunked open and there she was, still in her crisp ship's uniform, clean lines and a single gold braid around her left bicep. "Mr. Smith," she said. "How good of you to come." She stood aside and ushered me in.

Her quarters were twice as big as the cabin that my whole family shared, and it felt very spacious, even though our house back on Earth had had bathrooms bigger than her entire cabin (she had her own bathroom, I noticed). She had a little writing desk and some pieces of red Martian rock in a frame over her folded-up bunk. The room was as neat as a pin, not a single thing out of place, no dust or dirt. Compared to the rest of *Eagle*—grubby, buckled—it was like an operating theater. "Sit, please," she said, gesturing at a round fold-out seat. She rummaged in a small fridge and withdrew two cold bulbs of orange juice and passed one to me. "Thirsty air on this ship," she said, cracking the seal on hers. "We keep using water for reaction mass as we go, which means the air's going to get drier and drier. By the time we make Mars, you're going to be as desiccated as a mummy. Drink up!" She slurped at her bulb. I cracked my own and drank it.

"Look," I said, still feeling scared, "I'm sorry if I said too much. I know I shouldn't be passing rumors—" She waved at me impatiently.

"Forget that. That's not why you're here. Listen, David, you've been kicking ass on MC for years. You're about to start over in a new world, start *everything* over. And as you've heard, things on Mars are *different*. Not just on Mars, but in the Mars-side Martian Chronicles. Do you understand what things are like there?"

"I think so," I said, carefully. "No whiners, right? No poves. Succeeding on your merits?"

Her expression was unreadable. Amusement? Anger? Impossible to say. "Yes, David. But here's the thing: there's always winners and losers, you understand that?"

I nodded. "Sure."

"Even on Mars."

I nodded again, more slowly. "What do you mean by that?"

"You've heard how things are on the Mars-side game?"

"I've heard . . . things."

"What things?"

"Um. That a few companies control the whole game. That no one can get ahead unless they pay off the big guys."

She nodded. "That's one way of putting it. Another way of putting it is that there are some very, very successful people on Mars. These people saw the opportunity, took it, and made sure that they'd keep it for as long as they could. They're playing the game better and harder than anyone else."

"Wait," I said, confused. "Are you talking about Martian Chronicles or Mars?"

She gave me that mysterious look again. "There isn't really a difference on Mars. Martian Chronicles, Martian life. Why bother coming up with a functional stock market, communications system, and banking system when MC has it all built in? Martian Chronicles was built to model the kind of society that Mars, Inc. and Mars Colony were hoping to build. Why wouldn't you use it as the template for the actual Mars Colony?"

I tried to take this all in. "But it's just a game—"

She looked impatient. "*Just* a game? What is any of this except for a game? Why am I dressed up like a member of some kind of space navy? Why do people who have all the money they could ever spend try to earn more? Why don't you stab your friend when he gets on your nerves? It's all a game, it's all rules, it's all play. It may not always be fun, but games aren't just about fun."

I struggled to get my mind around this. "The *game* is *life* on Mars?"

Her impatience grew. "Look, David, I'm talking to you today

because I thought you'd be a smart kid. If you're just going to sit there boggling at me, you can go back to your quarters. Get with the program, will you?"

Now I felt scared again. "Okay, okay. I see. The game is life. Life is the game. Got you."

"Good. Now, when we flip the antennas around, you're going to get your account on the Martian servers and you're going to start over as a total noob. You're going to have to figure out how to survive in a game that's plenty rougher than any you've ever played. There's a pretty good chance it's going to chew you up and spit you out. It's going to do that to a lot of you. And as you know, I'm in charge of heading off whining, making sure it doesn't happen. So I'm here to help you avoid getting into the kind of situation where you'll be whining."

I couldn't figure out what she was talking about, but I didn't want to seem dumb, so I kept my mouth shut and nodded.

"Here's the thing. There's a thousand colonists headed to Mars. You're going to double Mars's population. But let's be frank here. You're latecomers. The people who've been Mars-side for ten years, those people took a much bigger risk than you're taking. So they're earning a greater reward, too. That's only fair. It's a meritocracy, after all. But I know people. They whine. They complain. Even colonists. Especially colonists—when they discover that colonial life is harder than they reckoned for. And when colonists get too upset about their bad luck . . . . Well, let's just say that on Mars, as on Earth, there are plenty of people who are willing to take by force that which they can't earn by their wits. And we can't have that. We especially can't have that when a thousand new chums are fresh off the boat. That's a volatile situation."

My mouth was dry. I drank more OJ. It tasted metallic, like everything on the ship, having been reconstituted with water from the ship's condensers. "Sound, um, complicated."

"It's not complicated," she said. She managed to make me feel stupid every time she spoke. "It's simple. The thing is, we want to head off any feeling that new colonists can't make it on Mars. We need an example of how fair things can be, if you're the right kind of plucky adventurer with the right entrepreneurial spirit. We need a poster child for success in the second wave. This isn't complicated, David."

I reached for the OJ, but my bulb was empty. "So—" I stopped. "You want to set me up as a what? As a success?"

She smiled condescendingly. "We're going to start up DBOS-Corp on Mars. It'll be a very successful corp from the get-go. You'll have lots of great contracts in hand the second you make Marsfall. Those contracts will pay off big, and bigger. You can hire your friends. Hell, you can hire your *father*. You will be a symbol of the fairness of Martian society. You'll have some silent investors who'll help you get by, starting you out with decent capital and contacts, and who'll take a piece of the action. This is a good deal, David. You've proved that you can build a business once before. It's absolutely plausible that you'd do it again. And having a fifteen-year-old millionaire is going to be *great* news. Everyone's going to go nuts for it. You'll be a hero."

The word *millionaire* hit me like an electric jolt, made me understand the scope of what was being discussed here.

"Lainie," I said, and it came out in a croak. I cleared my throat. "Lainie. That's really, really wonderful, but—"

She cocked her head. "I'm surprised that there's a 'but' here,

David. This isn't the kind of opportunity that comes along very often. I thought you were a businessman, the kind of person who seized the moment. Hell, we did a *lot* of research into this. Went deep on all the colonists. There were fifty potential candidates, but you were the clear winner. Were we wrong?"

I remembered who I had been. What I had been. DBOS-Corp was one of the biggest, most successful corps in the history of MC. I'd built it with fair play, hard work, and smarts. And luck, of course. I wasn't just a little kid. I was a success. I was smart. I had done something extraordinary. And I didn't let anyone push me around. I sat up straighter.

"Lainie, you've made your offer, but I don't make snap decisions. I think things over. This is no exception. I'll get back to you."

She nodded and dropped her offended expression. "Okay, that's fair. Mind you, if you say a word about this to anyone, I'll push you out the air lock." She smiled when she said it, but not very much. "Ha-ha. Only serious."

There was a magic time there, after the latency to Earth became too high to play on its server, and while we were still getting close enough to Mars to do anything except look at slowly updating spreadsheets from there, when nobody thought about Martian Chronicles.

I trickled back into the Junior Colonists' lounge by dribs and drabs, coming in for a few minutes at a time, keeping mostly to myself, though I nodded affably enough at anyone who nodded at me, even Helene and Vijay, who seemed to be up to something intense in their private corner. I didn't care. I didn't care about anything.

Here's what I sent to Lainie the day after she made her extraordinary offer:

Dear Lainie:

In regards to our meeting yesterday:

I have carefully considered your generous offer, and on reflection, I have decided to take you up on it. I am looking forward to a long, profitable relationship.

> *Sincerely,*
> *David Brionn Oglethorpe Smith, III*
> *CEO, DBOS-Corp (Mars)*
> *CEO (ret'd), DBOS-Corp (Earth)*

Not that I didn't agonize over it. I wanted to make it on Mars because I was smarter and better, not because I just got lucky. But I didn't *just* get lucky. Lainie's syndicate picked me because of the job I'd done running DBOS-Corp on Earth. And let's be honest: if the only way to win the game was to get in good with the big guns, I'd be crazy *not* to get in good with them. There's no nobility in failing. Plus, I'd get to hire my Dad, which would be just delicious. Boy, was I *ever* looking forward to that.

That's really what got me. Daydreaming about what it would be like after Marsfall, when we'd all pour out onto that strange world, bounding high in the fractional gravity, our body clocks already adjusted to the Martian day from three months with the *Eagle*'s systems running on Mars standard. We'd go to our housing, grubby new chums around the sophisticated, happy, settled Martians, and we'd start to try to find our fortunes. No whining allowed! Even when there were no fortunes to be had, no whining allowed! There my pals, my father and mother, and everyone would be, trying to find a way to get ahead on their new planet, where all the good opportunities seemed to have been taken, and there *I'd* be, rebuilding Oglethorp Corp, catching all these great breaks, growing more profitable, growing bigger, getting famous. Being a poster child. A hero.

And I could be generous! I could welcome in the new colonists, give them positions in my big, successful corp. Even Helene and Vijay, who'd come to see me as the kind of titan of business I'd always known I could be. I'd been shocked by the idea that on Mars, Martian Chronicles didn't just influence life, it *was* life. But after giving it some thought, I realized that I'd always been better at MC than real life, so why shouldn't I be glad that I was heading to the place where Martian Chronicles ruled?

Nobody was thinking about Martian Chronicles in the Junior Colonists' lounge. Not even me. Once I sent that note to Lainie, I realized that there was no way I could possibly end up as a debt-haunted drone in someone else's corp, and my subconscious mind stopped worrying about it. The crazy anxiety dreams I'd been having ended. The fact that Dad was still all tied up in knots didn't faze me. My future was set.

The second day after apogee, I drifted into the Junior Colonists' lounge. It was my morning, along with a third of the ship's population's—I was on second shift, which ran from ship's 0800 to 1600. I had a couple of my computers with me, a handheld and a bigger control unit that I used to drive my goggles and other devices. Both had just received Mars OS, the Martian operating system that ran on Martian time and used Martian protocols and converted over the whole interface, spell-checker, and everything, to Simplified English. In theory, it ran on everything that was computerized—phones, handhelds, tape-measures, music players, PCs, pedometers, headphones, cameras. . . .

But in practice, Mars OS didn't work as well as we'd been told it would. Lainie just shrugged her shoulders at the complaining colonists and told them, "No whining, gang. The engineers who built Mars OS have been *living on Mars for the past ten years*. Technology has moved on. The source code is on the ship's server. Some of you are wicked techie. Figure it out. Or throw away your gewgaws and get used to living with fewer gadgets—or hell, wait until we make Marsfall and see if anyone's made a Martian replacement you can buy."

So *that*'s what we were mostly thinking about in the JC lounge— how to get all our toys working again. Most of the cheap handheld devices were DOA, which was especially hard on us kids, since no one wanted to be a dork carrying around a huge computer that you needed a handbag or a backpack for. If you couldn't wear it around your wrist or neck, or shove it in a back pocket, you wouldn't be caught dead carrying it.

The kids who were really into the tech side of things had suddenly become monster rock gods, able to lay hands on your precious device and bring it back to life with a few incantations. They were charging all the market could bear for it, too—getting some of the best stuff on the ship, filling huge, floating low-gee net-bags with booty: painting kits, knifes and multitools, jewelry, prize T-shirts, musical instruments . . . The pathetic possessions we were able to squeeze into our luggage allowances. A lot of kids were way pissed at them, accusing them of gouging, but I shrugged and went back to our room for my harmonica and my set of permanent grease pencils. If they could do it and I couldn't, why shouldn't they charge all the market could bear for it?

Besides, once DBOS-Corp was running hot and black on Mars, I'd be able to buy back my stuff and more.

But as I lined up to hand over my treasures, Vijay and Helene drifted over to me. They were bungeed together, which was a convenient way to stay close enough to speak quietly amid all the eddies, breezes, and drifting debris in the JC lounge. As they neared me, Helene held out her hand, as though she wanted me to help her brake so that they could join me in waiting in line. I was unexpectedly glad to see that hand. I'd missed them more than I'd dared admit to myself.

I took Helene's hand and braced myself to help absorb their minimal inertia. As our fingers made contact, Helene whipped her arm up, keeping a tight grip on my hand, and jerked me out of the queue. We began to do slow doughnuts in the JC lounge, dizzying whirls that stopped only when we reached a bulkhead and Vijay stopped me.

I went from glad to furious in three nauseous circles around the JC lounge. Once we were Velcroed down, I glared at them. "I'd been waiting in line for an *hour*," I hissed. "Now you've blown it." That was the line rule on the *Eagle*: get out of line, lose your place. And the *Eagle* was all lines.

Helene crossed her eyes at me and stuck out her tongue. "First of all, it's nice to see you too, stranger. Second, who cares about the line? Third, *I* can fix your stupid computers, and I won't charge you anything for the favor. Fourth, we've got lots to talk about."

I took a moment to absorb all of this. "You can fix my computers?"

She rolled her eyes. "Duh. I've been fooling around with Mars OS for years. I can't believe the rest of you didn't bother! It's the bloody *operating system* that our new planet runs on! Knowing how it works is as important as knowing how to work a rebreather or patch a cold-suit. Give." She held out her hand. I passed her my handheld and my main computer pack and some of my peripherals. She pulled a chopstick out of her hair and stuck one end of it—it was tipped with memory pins, I saw—into the handheld and began to poke at it. "You've got your data backed up?" she said. I nodded. She stuck the tip of her tongue out of one corner of her mouth and unfolded a keyboard and screen from her back pocket and rubbed them against the handheld to get them connected, and then went to work.

Vijay had been silent until now. Finally, he said, "Dave, I'm very glad we found you. We have something we would like to discuss with you, in the utmost confidence." We were tethered to a relatively deserted stretch of bulkhead in the JC lounge—"deserted" for the JC lounge would have been "crowded" anywhere Earthside except for a mega stadium concert.

"Here?"

He smiled. "My place," he said.

He led us back down his private maintenance corridor, where his tiny leftover toilet was. We were strung out sideways again, Helene behind me and Vijay in front of me, and I hunched over a bit, so that we could see each other.

"You're a very mysterious person sometimes, Vijay," I said, trying for a joke and failing. Vijay did me the courtesy of a weak smile.

"You know what the crew are planning to do with MC?" he said. "You remember? Forming a syndicate? Offering their labor as a package?"

"I remember," I said. "It's totally illegal. And doomed. If the MC market is as tough as they say it is, the big corps will laugh them off and then crush them like bugs."

"I agree," Helene said.

"Me, too," Vijay said. "The problem is, they're not thinking big enough. Look, these syndicates have clobbered competition on Mars. They have the whole thing sewn up. But there are only a thousand Martians today, plus a few kids born Mars-side. We're about to double their population. That is going to be massively destabilizing." I started to get déjà vu. And I started to get uncomfortable. Didn't I just have this conversation with Lainie?

"Here's the thing. When the markets there go into chaos, all bets are off. If there was a leadership team with a new corp, a better corp, one that would give the new chums a better deal than the syndicates would, well—"

"Who wouldn't join it?" Helene said behind me. I wished I could see her face.

"Even the old timers who are at the bottom of the food chain. Imagine if there was a trio—a former senior auditor, a former high-powered raider, and a former successful CEO. Imagine the power of a trio running a company with the integrity of the auditor general, the guts of a raider, the acumen of a leading CEO! We wouldn't have to take whatever deal the syndicates there are offering. We could topple the syndicates, institute a fair, competitive market—"

My mouth was dry. The thing was, it was a good plan. A *wonderful* plan. If they'd made me this offer before Lainie had made hers, I would have jumped at it in a second (and that's without knowing that MC *was* real life on Mars). But now that I'd made my deal with Lainie, I had already committed to the same syndicate Vijay and Helene were planning on destroying.

I had a momentary vision of going to Lainie with this, telling her that I had two clever friends who'd be perfect at helping provide cover for her plan. We could start our radical, destabilizing corp, bring all the new chums into it, let everyone think that we were destroying the old order, and meanwhile, we'd be taking our own orders from the syndicate. We would *be* the syndicate.

But there were so many ways that could go wrong. Could I trust Helene? She was a raider, after all—she specialized in dismantling corps without regard for the work that went into them. Could I trust *Vijay*? You don't get to be an auditor without being stiff-necked about the rules and regulations. And what if Lainie said that she didn't want any "help" from my friends? What if she made good on her promise to shove me out the air lock for discussing it? (No, I didn't really think she was serious about spacing me, but with Lainie, there was always a tiny corner of me that believed she meant it).

And there I was, trying to talk myself out of trusting my only two real friends for millions of kilometers in all directions. I felt, I don't know, *disembodied*, like I was hovering over myself, watching myself decide to turn my back on my buddies.

I wanted to turn and run, but in the narrow slip space with Helene behind me and Vijay before me, there was no way I *could*. And there was a better me, the me that wasn't floating above myself but was *in* myself, sweating so hard it ran down into my eyes, that needed to talk.

"I need to talk to you," I said.

"We *are* talking," Helene said from behind me.

I ignored her. My eyes were locked on Vijay's. "What did you call it, 'utmost confidence'? I need to talk to both of you in *utmost confidence*."

Vijay looked grave. "Sounds like you have a secret."

Helene sighed. "How come everyone's got a big, dark secret around here?"

Dad burst into the cabin, outraged. "Is it true?" he said, his eyes red-rimmed, burning, his chest heaving. Mom leapt off the bunk where she'd been working with some of the ship's polymer maintenance putty to make one of her little abstract sculptures.

"David, please, calm yourself," she said, in her I-really-mean-it voice. We all listened when Mom used that tone. It made Dad pull up short like he'd been whacked over the nose with a rolled-up magazine.

He took a deep breath. "Sorry," he said. "Sorry. Okay.

"I have just heard the most remarkable rumor about our son here," he said, gesturing at me. "A truly incredible rumor."

Mom started to say something, but I got to my feet and she stopped.

"It's true," I said.

"What's true?" Mom said.

I reached for my handheld and dialed up the ad we'd sent to every mailbox on the *Eagle*:

MEMBERS NEEDED

Announcing an altogether new kind of corp: The Martian New Chums Co-operative is open to anyone who is willing to work for the cause of a fair deal for all Martians.

WHY?

Because the deck is stacked on Mars. Four large companies monopolize all the wealth, power, and privilege on our new home, and when you land, you can expect to spend the rest of your life working your guts out for the new aristocrats. You may think that this only applies in Martian Chronicles, but we've got news for you: life on Mars IS THE MARTIAN CHRONICLES. No one's mentioned it to us yet (I wonder why not?) but it makes sense, doesn't it? After all, why set up a government, stock exchange, messaging system, and all the other machinery of society when you've got a perfectly good one sitting right there on your game server?

Oh yes, there's LOTS they haven't told you about life on Mars.

Rather than whining about it, we're DOING SOMETHING ABOUT IT.

The New Chums Co-op will not trade with the cartels. We will make our own oxygen, generate our own power, and manufacture our own goods, buying and selling from anyone except the cartel. We won't have the same stuff, but your ray guns will go to fellow New Chums, and their ray guns will go back to you, and we'll all prosper together. We'll be a democracy: one member, one vote. And we'll help each other.

Want to join? Great! The New Chums Co-op will begin signing on members in seventy-two hours, which should give you plenty of time to get your kids to show you how to use Martian Chronicles, get you set up with an account on the Mars server, and verify what you've read here.

In the meantime, watch out for dirty tricks from Mars, Inc.! Watch out for unexplained network outages. Watch out for your fellow colonists being arrested in the name of "preserving morale."

Aren't you old enough to make up your own mind about what's

true and what isn't? Do you really want a big-daddy corporation locking up people who say things that it disagrees with?

Membership opens in SEVENTY-TWO HOURS! Meantime, any questions: ask the Co-op's founders:

Vijay Mukherjee (senior auditor, retired)

David Brionn Oglethorpe Smith, III (CEO, DBOS-Corp, retired)

Helene Gonzales-Ginsburg (liquidity specialist, retired)

PS: If we get arrested, the Co-op is still on. Organize yourselves. No whining!

Mom looked at me as if I'd sprouted another head and three extra arms. Dad was trembling slightly, suddenly looking much, much older.

I leaned back in my seat. I'd known this was coming, had feared it, had come through the fear. It was a relief to have it out in the open after all the stress of wondering what would happen when my parents found out. When the whole ship found out. Helene had said to me, "The fear of the consequences are always worse than the consequences themselves."

"I don't think they can afford to arrest us, not after everyone on the ship has read it," I said, trying to sound casual, trying to convince myself that I was calm.

Dad slumped. "I can't believe that you—"

Mom put her hand on his arm. "Is it true, David?"

"Which part?" I said, again, trying for a nonchalance I didn't feel.

"All of it!" I could see that, beneath her calm exterior, she was ready to lose her cool.

"All of it is true," I said. "Mars is run by four corps, and everyone works for them. You can verify it for yourself—just create a

Martian Chronicles account and start looking around. And yes, Mars runs on the Martian Chronicles server. Have a look and you can see it: our quarters are assigned, in the Burroughs warren, the spaceport is booked for the *Eagle*'s arrival. The city hall forum is full of people talking about real life." We had decided not to mention Lainie's offer to me. I had promised her that I'd keep it a secret, and I didn't want her to be able to go around telling everyone that I didn't honor my promises. I needed to be squeaky clean if I was going to be on the Co-op's steering committee. "And it's true that we've started the Co-op. Technically, it's just another corp, but Vijay structured the bylaws so that it gets to run like a co-operative. He's good at that sort of thing."

"Vijay?" Mom said.

"The pove," Dad said. "The one he pals around with." He sounded shell-shocked.

"We're all poves now, Dad." I swallowed, looked into his eyes. It was hard to do. "We're headed to Mars to clean the toilets. That's the thing that we discovered. And the people Mars-side, they're fine with that. After all, if we were too good for toilet cleaning, we would have been in the *first* wave. They'll say that they're too good to clean toilets, and they'll prove it by pointing out that we're all broke and the only jobs they have for us are the worst, crappiest jobs. Anyone who disagrees will be a whiner."

That had been the real surprise, once Mars OS was running on all my devices: the message boards filled with Martians fantasizing about how great it would be once the next wave of colonists arrived, how they'd be able to "solve the labor shortage" and finally hire people at "affordable wages" to do the real work of running the colony.

A tear slid down Dad's cheek. "David, you're making trouble for us, for our family—"

Mom pulled him into a hug. "Shh," she said. "Sounds like trouble was already there." Dad kind of collapsed into her arms and she met my eyes and made a little scooting gesture behind his back. I took the hint and left.

Standing outside the door was Lainie. She was perfectly composed, leaning against the corridor wall. There was no one else in the corridor. Lainie had that effect on people—if you saw her standing somewhere, you'd go somewhere else.

"Hello, David," she said.

I'd talked this over with Helene and Vijay, too. Helene had been busted dozens of times, and Vijay had made plenty of busts. They knew how it went.

I nodded and held my wrists out, as though for handcuffs.

She smiled and shook her head. "Oh, I'm not going to put you in the brig, young Mr. Smith. Not at all. The last thing I want to do is create a martyr for your little cause on Mars."

(When I told Vijay about this, he nodded curtly and said, "Smart.")

"But I just want to put a little whisper into your ear, a little seed of doubt for you to remember when we land on Mars, when the people I work for take *serious* steps to ensure that you don't upset the apple-cart. You ready for it?"

I nodded, not trusting myself to speak—barely trusting myself not to wet my pants.

"It's this: you could have been a king. A CEO. Rich. Famous. Powerful. Admired. You could have had it all. But now, no matter what happens, no matter whether your little 'co-op' is crushed or soldiers on raggedly, you will always be a pove, and a leader of poves."

She whispered it like a curse, and I knew she was right.

They arrested us forty-eight hours after Marsfall. Every Co-op member. *Conspiracy in restraint of trade.*

We put up quite a defense and accused Mars, Inc. of the cardinal sin of "whining" at every turn.

And they did let us go, eventually. And by the time they did, nearly every New Chum had signed up for the Co-op, and the game got really, really *fun*.

CORY DOCTOROW (www.craphound.com) is a science fiction author, activist, journalist, and blogger—the coeditor of Boing Boing (boingboing.net), and the author of the bestselling novel YA *Little Brother*. His new novel is *For the Win*. He is the former European director of the Electronic Frontier Foundation and cofounded the UK Open Rights Group. Born in Toronto, Canada, he now lives in London.

AUTHOR'S NOTE

There's a certain circularity to the argument that goes, "We have to get off this planet, we're using it up!" I often hear it from people who are comfortable with using the planet up to get off-planet, which, to me, sounds a lot like, "I have to eat all the cookies, because once the cookies are gone, I won't have any cookies!"

Space exploration is great for science and for our dreams, and it spins off some cool technologies, but it will not reduce population pressure on Earth (you'd have to march people into spaceships at breakneck speed to make any significant dent in population growth and you could feed, clothe, and house a person for years for what it costs to lift her space suit into low Earth orbit).

Space colonization fantasies are all too often silent on the question of what happens to the world's majority of poor people when the rich folks have buggered off to the stars after expending the planet to get there.

GOODNIGHT MOONS

❖

Ellen Klages

'd always dreamed of living on Mars. From the first time I went to the library in Omaha and found the books with rocket ships on their spines, discovered Bradbury and Heinlein and Robinson. Later, I heard real scientists on the news saying it could happen—would happen—in my lifetime.

I didn't want to stay behind and watch.

A big dream, but I was disciplined, focused. I took physics and chemistry, ran track after school, spent my evenings stargazing from the garage roof—and my nights reading science fiction under the covers. I graduated valedictorian, with a full scholarship to MIT, and got a doctorate in mechanical engineering, then stayed on for a second degree in astrobotany. We'd need to grow food, once we arrived.

My husband was an electronics genius, but a small flaw in Pete Morrison's left eardrum grounded him early in the NASA program. We lived outside of Houston while I trained: endurance, microgravity, EVA simulations. I even survived the "vomit comet" with flying colors.

When they announced the team for the Mars mission, I made the list. Four men and two women: Archie, Paolo, Rajuk, Tom, Chandra, and I were overnight celebrities. Interviews, photos, talk shows—everyone wanted to know how it felt to be the first humans to go to another planet.

Our last public appearance was at the launch of the *Sacagawea* with her payload of hydrogen and the gas extractor that would fuel our trip back. She would be waiting for us when we landed, in another thirty months. Once she was up, we disappeared for two years of training and maneuvers in Antarctica and the Gobi desert, the most extreme conditions Earth could offer.

Pete and I said our farewells the night before the launch team was sequestered for the final countdown week. Champagne (for him), filet mignon, red roses, and a king-size bed. Then I was isolated with the others at the base, given so many last-minute shots, tests, and dry runs that I felt like a check mark on an endless to-do list.

But I made it. On a sunny Tuesday morning, the *Conestoga* roared up into a bright blue sky. Billions of people watched us set out for a new world.

Free fall was a relief after the crush of the launch. We'd be floating in zero-g for seven months. Archie and Paolo were a little green around the gills at first, but they got their sea legs soon enough. For me, it was as easy as swimming.

The tedium of a long voyage set in once we established our routine. Cramped quarters, precious little privacy, and not much to do once we were past the moon. I checked my instruments, sent data packets back to Mission Control, took my turn in the galley. Then on day 37, I tossed my cookies so suddenly there wasn't even time to grab a barf bag. Everyone laughed, no one harder than Paolo and Archie.

For three days, nothing wanted to stay down. Didn't feel like zero-g effects. More like a bug. Chandra, the medical officer, took my vitals. No fever, blood pressure normal—for these conditions. When she took an EPT stick from the supply closet, I laughed. "No way. Brand-new implant when we got back from the desert."

"Just a precaution," she said. "By the book. Anything abdominal I can rule out is a plus."

The only plus was the symbol on the stick. The second stick as well.

"Jeez." Chandra whistled through her teeth. "Protocol says—"

"I know." Pregnant personnel are restricted to ground duty. Pregnant personnel assigned to flight missions are immediately reassigned. That was why we both had the implants. A one-in-a-million chance, but mine was defective.

Human error? Technical glitch? For two years, we'd gone over every phase of the mission, tens of thousands of parts, maneuvers, systems—anything could go wrong at any time. We had reams of contingency plans. Every snafu had some kind of back-up. Except this.

I zipped up my flight suit. "You have to tell Tom," I said. Another protocol. Information that might affect the crew or the mission had to be relayed to the captain.

"Yeah."

"Wait till tomorrow? I need to tell Pete first."

She put her hand on my arm. "Okay." She hesitated. "There's only one option. You know that."

I nodded. If one crew member becomes unfit to serve, the mission is aborted. It had happened once on the space station. Appendicitis. The whole crew had to evacuate back to Earth. And that wasn't possible for us, not in an orbital transit. Earth wouldn't be in the same position as when we'd left, and we didn't have enough fuel to realign. I *had* to be fit for duty. "Tomorrow," I said.

My bunk was the only private place. I pulled the curtain across and leaned against the bulkhead, my hand on my still-flat belly. Chandra was right. And, in theory, that was a choice I'd always supported. So why did I feel like I had to pick—my dreams or my future?

This was an exploration mission. Seventeen months on the surface. We didn't have the supplies or the technology or the infrastructure to start colonizing. That was decades down the road, and only if *we* succeeded.

When the communication window opened, I sent a message to my husband. I told him what had happened and what I had to do. The fourteen-minute delay for his reply seemed endless. And when it arrived, the words on the screen surprised me. "Can't let you do that, Zoë," it said.

Before I could type my reply, the next message arrived. That one was from CNN, asking for confirmation.

Then all hell broke loose.

Tom and the rest of the crew stared at me as the queue backed up with message after message. Mission Control was furious. Two different generals sent conflicting orders from millions of miles away.

But the public response was instant and overwhelming. News sites headlined, WELCOME, FIRST MARTIAN BABY! Within an hour, I was the hot topic of blogs, newscasts, and water cooler discussions all over the globe. A contest offered a million dollars for the person who named THE FIRST CITIZEN OF SPACE. It was a circus—and NASA had never been so popular.

The furor showed no signs of dying down, but at least Earth continued to rotate, and we lost the comm signal after a few hours. I went to my bunk, but didn't sleep much. When I got up, the screen held a terse communiqué from Mission Control: "Seventh crew member authorized."

I was relieved. I was scared. The rest of the crew did their best to hide their feelings. An order was an order.

The Surgeon General issued a statement. Barring any complications, the likelihood of transit-oriented problems in the next six months was low. The fetus was in a water-filled sac, exactly the sort of environment the crew had trained in for zero-g. As long as radiation levels were closely monitored, she believed a full-term pregnancy was entirely possible. Deceleration and landing, however, would require further consideration.

Would I still fit in my landing couch? What about my pressure suit—it wasn't designed to stretch. I'd never paid much attention in home economics, but the suit was just engineering, and I was able to make some alterations.

A few days shy of my eighth month, we began the descent to the surface. The baby kicked the whole way down. Fortunately, the landing was textbook: no system failures, no injuries, no unexpected terrain. And out the porthole, we could see the *Sacagawea* a hundred meters away, plumes of vapor wafting from its lower vents. Our ride home.

That first night, Rajuk broke out the bottle of whiskey he'd smuggled on board, and we toasted our places in history. I drank my share; all the medical texts said it wouldn't make much difference, not at that stage. No one knew what difference cosmic radiation and zero-g had already made.

The baby and the planet were both terrae incognitae.

I had studied Mars for more than twenty years. I wasn't prepared for how eerily beautiful and utterly alien it was. Everything was shades of reddish brown, no greens or blues. The horizon was too close, the sky too uniform, the lighting flat. Daylight was butterscotch, as if it were always afternoon, half an hour before dusk. At night, the two small, lumpy moons rose into the starry blackness, Phobos slowly in the west, tiny Deimos in the east.

I was, of course, restricted to the ship. For two weeks I had to watch as the others took turns out on the dusty metallic surface, kicking up puffs of iron oxide with every step. I could feel the floor vibrate as they opened the cargo bay, unloaded the rover, began to set up a base. It took a full day to anchor the *Conestoga*, turning her from a spaceship into a permanent habitat, for us, for future crews.

We had all cross-trained in each others' fields, so I was busy checking schematics, logging soil samples, monitoring pressure levels and hatch seals. I gave hand signals through the porthole as Tom and Paolo unrolled my inflatable greenhouse and moved the equipment in. As soon as they connected it to the Hab and its atmosphere, I started my own work.

The first seedlings were unfurling in the hydroponic tank when my water broke.

Chandra had set up the medical facility as soon as we landed; everything was ready. Like the Russians' rats', which gestated in zero-g, my labor was long and slow. The gravity of Mars—only one third Earth's—meant less strain, but less pull when I pushed. Finally, on day 266 of the mission, Mars day 52, I heard a loud, strong cry.

"It's a girl," Chandra said a moment later. I saw a red, wrinkled face, then she was on the counter, being weighed and measured and tested. "Only five pounds, a little underweight, but otherwise she seems remarkably healthy." Chandra laid her on my chest.

A few days later, a woman in Indiana would win a million dollars for naming my baby Virginia Dare Morrison—the first child born in the New World. But as she lay there, suckling for the first time, I murmured, "Podkayne of Mars," and we just called her Poddy.

The *Conestoga* had not been stocked with infant necessities, so we had to make do. T-shirts were diapers. Archie made a mobile from some color-coded spare parts and dental floss, dangling it above the hammock that hung in my bunk. A blanket became a snugglie; while I worked, I carried her like a papoose from another, older frontier.

I breast-fed her for the first eight months, no extra draw on the closely measured rations. She got sponge baths, just like the rest of us. When she was teething, her cries filled the Hab—the bunks were only soundproofed enough to offer a bit of privacy—and the rest of the crew grumbled about lost sleep. But they watched her when it was my turn in the rotation to be outside, and she heard lullabies in four different languages.

Martian gravity is kind to toddlers. At thirteen months, Poddy massed eighteen pounds, but her chubby legs only had to support six as she pulled herself up and began to walk. It's impossible to child-proof a spacecraft, but we blocked off the lab and the stairs to the upper level of the Hab, and strung tether cords across the hatchways. She could climb like a monkey.

She bounced and hopped the length of the greenhouse, laughing at the top of her lungs and bounding about in a way no Earth baby could. I sent vids to Pete, and they were replayed everywhere; a dance called the Poddy Hop was the new craze. Plans were made for a homecoming tour the next year: First Martian Returns.

But that *was* a problem, said the doctors.

Martian gravity *might* turn out to be sufficient for healthy growth. No one knew. Poddy's stats were being studied by scientists everywhere, and would provide the data for future missions. But travel in zero-g was not a possibility, not at her age. She was still developing—bones and muscles, neurons and connections. She would never recover from seven months in free fall.

Every member of the crew already had muscle-mass and bone loss from the trip out. I'd known from day one that once the mission was over, I'd spend the next two years in hospitals and gyms trying to get as much of it back as I could.

For Poddy, they said, the loss would be irreversible. Mission Control advised: further study needed.

A month before takeoff, I got their final verdict.

Poddy could not return to Earth.

If she did, even as an adult, she would never walk again. She would be crippled by the physics of her home planet, always in excruciating pain, crushed by the mass of her own body. Her lungs might collapse, her heart might not take the strain.

"We had not planned for children," Mission Control's message ended. "We're sorry."

I read the message three times, then picked her up and kissed her hair. I'd always dreamed of living on Mars.

Future missions would bring supplies, they promised. Clothes, shoes, a helmet, a modified pressure suit with expandable sections and room to grow. From now on, they would carry extra milk and vitamins, educational materials, toys and games. Engineers had begun working on a small-scale rover. Whatever she needed.

The next ship should arrive in seven months.

Tom reassigned duties for a five-person crew. By the time the *Sacagawea* was ready for launch, Poddy was talking. Just simple words. *Mama, Hab, juice.* She waved her tiny fingers at the porthole as her aunt and uncles boarded: *Bye-bye Chanda, bye-bye Tom. Bye-bye.*

We would never see them again.

Like my great-grandmother, I was a pioneer woman, alone on the frontier. Isolated, self-sufficient by necessity. Did it matter, I wondered as I heated up our supper, whether it was a hundred miles of prairie, a thousand miles of ocean, or millions of miles of space that separated me from everything and everyone I had known?

I read to Poddy, after the meal. A picture book, uploaded a week before, drawings in primary colors of things she would never see: *tree, cat, house, father.* For her, Earth was make-believe, a fantasy world with funny green grass and the wrong color sky

On the first of two hundred cold, black nights, Deimos and Phobos low in the sky, I sat by the porthole and cuddled my daughter, whispering as I rocked her to sleep.

Goodnight, Poddy.

Goodnight, moons.

ELLEN KLAGES is the author of two acclaimed novels for younger readers: *The Green Glass Sea*, which won the Scott O'Dell Award, the New Mexico Book Award, and the Lopez Award, and *White Sands, Red Menace*, which won the California and New Mexico Book Awards. Her short stories have been published in eight countries and have been nominated for the Nebula, Hugo, World Fantasy, and Campbell awards. Her story "Basement Magic" won a Nebula in 2005. She lives in San Francisco, in a small house full of strange and wondrous things.

Her Web site is www.ellenklages.com.

AUTHOR'S NOTE

Seeking inspiration for this story, I ate a Mars bar, reread *The Martian Chronicles* and *Little House on the Prairie*, then had lunch with a rocket scientist.

THE TASTE OF PROMISES

❁

Rachel Swirsky

They approached the settlement at dusk. Tiro switched the skipper to silent mode, grateful he wouldn't have to spend another night strapped in, using just enough fuel to stay warm and breathing.

A message from Tiro's little brother, Eo, scrolled across his visor. *Are we there yet?*

Tiro rolled his eyes at Eo's impatience. *Just about,* he subvocalized, watching his suit's internal processor translate the words into text.

Is it someplace good? asked Eo.

I think so. Be quiet and let me check it out.

It was a big settlement. Three vast domes rose above the landscape like glass hills. Semipermanent structures clustered around them, warehouses and vehicle storage buildings constructed from frozen dirt. Light illuminated the footpaths, creating a faintly glowing labyrinth between buildings.

For such a big place, it seemed strangely deserted. There should

have been volunteer patrols, weapon caches, watchtowers where settlers would take turns on duty to scan for thieves or poachers or,
worse, gang convoys studded with skulls.

On Mars, civilization only extended as far as the pressure seals
on the domes of official colonies sponsored by Earth governments.
Settlers who left the government shelters gained the freedom to
claim homesteads from the vast tracts of empty land, but they lost
the protection of settled society. It could be a hard life on the wild
frontier. Everyone feared the gang convoys that sold whole settlements into slavery, slaughtering those who weren't strong enough to
work in the mines.

Tiro eyed the settlement nervously. He messaged Eo: *Do you see
any security?*

After a pause, his brother replied, *A few charge guns in the domes.*
Nothing else? Too weird.
Maybe their God doesn't like weapons.
Maybe.

Tiro could explore more after nightfall, but in the meantime, he
decided to investigate the warehouses. No one stored anything valuable outside, but Tiro was skilled at living off things other people
didn't value.

He parked the skipper, sealed his helmet onto his suit, and got
out. Nearby, there was an igloo made from frozen dirt. He ducked
inside; crates filled the cramped space from floor to ceiling, leaving
Tiro barely any room to stand. He pulled down the nearest crate
and braced himself against the wall to pry it open. His jaw dropped.

Eo? he sent. *Did you check all their computers for security?*
Yeah. The word flashed resentfully.
You sure?

Eo inserted a picture of a kid blowing a raspberry.

Sorry. I'm just having trouble believing we struck gold.

You found gold???

Food! wrote Tiro. *Crates and crates of frozen rations.*

Eo sent a picture of a dancing kid. Tiro grinned.

Tiro hauled the crate back to the skipper. A few trips back and forth and he'd be set. He could even sell the extra and buy rooms for the rest of the trip.

His thoughts were full of good food and warm beds when he caught sight of four men clustered around the warehouse entrance, their faceplates reflecting the darkening sky so he couldn't make out their faces. *I thought there was no security!* he messaged Eo.

There wasn't!! Eo messaged back.

Tiro flattened against the wall.

What're you gonna do? asked Eo.

I don't know, said Tiro. *Shut up and let me think.*

Tiro figured he could make it the ten meters back to the skipper, but he doubted the skipper could outrun the settlement's vehicles. His only option was to get out of sight. Slowly, he started scooting along the wall.

By his second step, he knew he'd been caught. "Did you see that?" one man mumbled to another. The second reacted with fighter's instincts, whipping out his flashlight like a gun.

"Who are you?" the man demanded, voice gruff through the suit's transmitter. "Are you a scout? Who are you leading here?"

Tiro winced as bright light shone into his eyes. *Get out!* he messaged Eo. *Quick! Get into their systems.*

But—

Go!

The man with the flashlight crouched like a cat and leapt. Dust flew into the air as he landed beside Tiro. "Who are you?" he repeated.

Tiro shrank away. "I didn't mean any harm."

The man twisted Tiro's arm painfully behind his back. "Go on. Keep lying. We'll get the truth either way."

The man with the flashlight was their leader. The others called him Jirair.

They marched Tiro into the smallest of the three domes. "Nothing to see! Get home!" Jirair bellowed. Settlers flashed alarmed looks their way before dispersing.

They halted in front of a squat building, metal beams glistening in the newly fallen darkness. One man removed Tiro's helmet. Another opened a reinforced door and shoved him inside. He tumbled headfirst into the dark, falling against the wall with a thud.

Someone switched on a light. The dank cell was floored with dirt. Manacles gleamed on the wall.

Tiro tried to edge away. Jirair gestured to his men. They chained Tiro's wrists and ankles.

Jirair pulled off his helmet. Underneath, he looked surprisingly young, maybe twenty years old. His scarlet hair stuck out in stylized spikes.

"Get the nerve ripper."

"The nerve ripper!" repeated a man leaning against the wall. "I love the nerve ripper."

"Think he'll be able to walk afterward?" asked the short man beside him.

The first one laughed. "Depends on how much he lies!"

The man who'd thrown Tiro inside the cell fidgeted uncomfortably. "Come on, Jirair. He's just a kid."

"Just a kid?" Jirair turned, lips peeled back to show his teeth. "Gangs use kids as scouts all the time. You want that to happen here?"

The man shook his head silently.

"Then get the nerve ripper," he repeated. The man rushed away.

Tiro struggled. His chains clanged as they reached their full extension. He tapped the bud implanted in his wrist that let Eo monitor his life signs. Tiro used it when he wanted Eo's attention— but this time, there was no answering pulse.

Eo was safe. That was what Tiro wanted, of course, but it didn't make him feel any less alone.

Jirair paced in front of Tiro. "I'll ask again. Who are you leading here?"

"I'm just a scavenger," Tiro said.

"Petty criminals know to stay away from us. You're no scavenger. Why are you here? Did you come to steal our seeds?"

"Your . . . seeds?"

"Where are you from?"

"New Virginia."

"Who did you bring with you?"

Tiro's heart pounded. "No one."

"No one?"

"No one!"

Jirair shot him a disdainful look. "Only fools travel alone on Mars." He burst into motion, punching the wall in a sudden fury. "You poachers! You think your lives are the only ones that matter! Do you think we don't know what you're up to?"

Tiro whimpered.

"Calm down, Jirair," came a woman's voice from the back of the room. "There's no need to act the fool."

Jirair whipped around. "What are you doing here, Sahar?"

A woman moved forward. Layers of heavy gray clothing swathed her from neck to ankles, but her head was shaved bald. "Naghmeh said you were up to your old tricks." She looked Tiro over, gray eyes shining from her angular face. "How old are you?"

"Eighteen," Tiro said.

"There is no possibility that you are eighteen."

"Sixteen."

Sahar scrutinized Tiro's face. "Possibly."

"It doesn't matter how old he is," Jirair said. "I'm in charge of security. If you have a problem with it, run against me next cycle."

Sahar lifted a hand in objection. "I'm here on Naghmeh's behalf, not mine. She says the boy's not alone."

"I knew it!" shouted Jirair.

Sahar moved smoothly past him, coming to Tiro's side. She held up a data globe. Its readout lights flashed in morse code. *S.O.S.*

"Who is this?" Sahar asked.

Tiro slumped. "My brother."

Sahar instructed the men to unlock Tiro's restraints. Rubbing his wrists, Tiro collected his helmet and followed Sahar out of the cell and down the glowing path to the dome exit.

"What did he threaten you with? Iron drops? The pain candle?"

"Nerve ripper," Tiro mumbled, heart still pounding.

"There's no such thing. He was trying to scare you." Faint light illuminated her harsh features. "Jirair's a good man. He'd be harmless in any other job, but give him security work, and he starts to think like a tyrant. He thinks the only way to protect the colony is to act like a bully. I argued against electing him, but too many people think aggression is the same as defense."

They approached an air lock leading out of the dome. Sahar used her retinal scan to open an adjacent storage locker. It was filled with space suits. Sahar began putting one on over her clothes. "Put your helmet back on," she instructed.

Tiro hesitated. "Where are we going?"

Sahar gave him an amused look. "You're bold for a prisoner, aren't you? I'm giving you a room in my compound tonight."

"Aren't you worried I'm a gang scout?"

"Are you a gang scout?"

"No."

Sahar paused to adjust her suit. "Naghmeh says you are who you say you are. A teenager making a suicidally stupid journey alone— well, almost alone—from New Virginia to Kaseishi."

"Who's Naghmeh?"

Sahar grunted impatiently. "Enough for now," she said, sealing her helmet.

Tiro sealed his, too, and they made their way outside. The lights lining the path shone like fairies at their feet as they hiked to the largest dome.

They stopped at a small, dimly lit dome entrance. Sahar spoke through her transmitter. "This is my door. It has security you can't break, even with your brother's help. Do not try to go through without me."

Once they were inside, Sahar started removing her suit. She glanced at Tiro. "Don't you want to get out of that thing?"

Tiro paused. He'd been traveling for so long that his suit felt like a second skin, but it would feel good to wear just a shirt and pants again. He stripped down, enjoying the sensation of air on his arms—until he noticed Sahar tossing his discarded suit into a bin in the storage locker.

"What are you doing?" he demanded.

"A little insurance," she said, locking the crate.

Sahar started toward a large building. Fuming, Tiro followed.

The structure was larger than any private building Tiro had ever seen. He gaped as Sahar opened the door onto an unbelievably enormous room.

It smelled of baking bread. Bowls of fruits and vegetables glistened on the counters that ranged across the back wall. Chairs sat stacked on two long, parallel tables, each of which could seat at least twenty.

"You live here?" he asked.

"I do," said Sahar, heading up the immense staircase that stretched away from the dining hall. She took a right from the first floor landing and opened one of what seemed like an infinity of doors, revealing a narrow bedchamber.

She nudged Tiro inside. "You'll sleep here until your arbitration with our elders. I'm locking you in tonight, but I'll come by in the morning for breakfast."

Hesitantly, Tiro reached toward the polished headboard. "What's this made of?"

"Wood. From settlement trees."

"You harvest *wood*?" Tiro asked incredulously.

This elicited a genuine smile. "Get some sleep."

Tiro turned. "Wait!"

Sahar stopped with her hand on the door. "Yes?"

"Please. My brother. Can't you give him back?"

"I'm sorry—"

"Please!"

"We'll return him after arbitration."

Tiro started toward Sahar. "When will that be?"

"A few days. . . ."

"But he's never spent the night alone!"

Sahar held out her hand to prevent Tiro from coming further. "Calm down."

Tiro stopped advancing. He dropped his balled fists to his sides.

When Sahar seemed satisfied that he'd regained his self-control, she continued. "Your brother will be fine. He'll stay with Naghmeh until your arbitration."

Tiro's patience snapped. "Who's Naghmeh?"

Sahar paused. "My daughter," she answered at last. "She was lifted, too."

Tiro was too surprised to know how to respond.

Sahar closed the door.

Tiro had hazy memories of the day Eo was born: the blue blanket his aunt shipped from Earth for the new baby, the red bag his mother packed for the hospital, the burned toast his father made for breakfast. He didn't remember putting on a space suit and trying to run away, but that was what his parents always told stories about. "At first, Tiro wanted to get away from Eo so badly that he ran away from home," his dad would say. "Now they're inseparable."

At first Eo seemed healthy, but soon he stopped eating. His stomach swelled. One night their father found blood in Eo's diaper, and then it was back to the hospital for test after test. By the end, they'd plugged him into machines that breathed for him and machines that pumped his heart, even machines that spun tendrils into his brain.

Tiro didn't remember any of that. He did remember his parents taking him to the hospital where they put his hands into gloves mounted in a clear plastic wall so he could touch his brother one last time. His mother cried because it was so sterile and remote, but Tiro didn't feel that way. To him, it felt like touching anyone through a space suit. Just part of growing up on Mars.

Scientists had never reached a consensus on how lifting occurred. They did identify the responsible technology: a recently introduced monitoring system intended to track global mental function. The system kept records of brain activity for physician review and, over time, these created a holistic representation of the brain in motion.

Dead patients' records were dumped into the hospital system. When cognitive development specialist Dr. Joshua Roanoke went to access the records for his research, he discovered the presence of distinct personalities haunting the system like ghosts. He told the press, "It's as if the children have been lifted from their bodies and moved into the machines."

Only patients in a narrow age range seemed to be susceptible. Dr. Roanoke hypothesized that, in order to transfer successfully, infants had to possess a concept of object permanence but still be in the sensorimotor stage. Except for the fact that affected infants fell roughly into the predicted age range of three to twenty-four months, no proof had been uncovered to substantiate his claim.

While scientists argued over how the lifted children had been created, politicians debated what to do with them. Mars was still recovering from high profile technological disasters: six hundred colonists had died at Juel when a new biotic system poisoned the air instead of providing oxygen, and another two thousand died planet-wide when an innovative dome synthetic developed microscopic fractures. The technophobic climate combined with calls from a number of dominant religions for the lifted children to be exorcised so they could properly enter the afterlife.

The governments of Mandela and Marston—the other two colonies that had used the brain monitoring technology—ordered their hospitals to purge the lifted children. Working under more stringent property laws, New Virginia ruled that the lifted children were equivalent to remains and left it to the parents to dispose of them. All three governments placed heavy restrictions on the brain monitors to prevent further incidents.

Average citizens called the lifted children ghosts. They told each other horror stories about haunted machines.

Most parents, already grieving, had their children's remnants wiped. A few brought them home.

"Even if it's only an echo, how can we throw that away?" asked Tiro's mom. "He's our little boy."

Eo grew on the home computer. He navigated data streams like a rafter in white water, skimming through the public nets with abandon. He pulled pranks on the neighbors' private machines, too, until their parents lectured him about trespassing.

Their family shaped itself around Eo. All day, they laughed at jokes he sent their visors. During the evenings, they watched movies he spliced together from free footage on the nets. At night, Tiro wore his visor to bed so he and Eo would never be apart.

Everyone adored Eo, but their father still drank in the evenings, his expression tired and forlorn. Once, Tiro asked what was wrong. His father gave him the saddest look he'd ever seen. "I want what any father wants. For both my sons to become men."

Tiro went to their mother. "Doesn't Dad love Eo?"

She sighed. "Of course we love Eo, but it's hard. We'd give anything to fix what happened. To make him what he should be."

Tiro never forgot what his parents wanted for Eo. A body, so he could be a man.

Tiro was still sleeping when Sahar returned. She wore even more gray this time, a heavy ankle-length dress. She led him downstairs to the kitchen where she picked up a basket of red fruit.

"We'll eat outside," she said.

Tiro blinked as they emerged into brightness. Trees arrowed toward the dome, branches woven into a dense canopy. Creepers garlanded the trunks with emerald, scarlet, and amber leaves.

Tiro wandered, dazed by the mingling scents of flowers and wet leaves. He paused beside a whip-slender sapling that was putting out new fronds. "I've seen these in New Virginia."

Sahar was crouched a meter away, spreading a blanket over the grasses. She looked up. "Those are comfort palms. We export the seeds."

"People pull off the fronds to wrap up in. They keep you pretty warm."

Sahar settled on the blanket. "That's why we made them. All our plants are engineered to be useful. We call it anthropocentric ecology. Once there's a thick enough atmosphere to sustain life, we'll seed our plants across Mars. Think about it. Our jungles won't be hostile. They'll be full of plants that exist in symbiosis with us, that help us survive and prosper."

Tiro kicked a clump of bluish weeds. They released a pleasant almond scent. "What's the point? It'll be centuries before plants can live outside."

Sahar held up a chiding finger. "It'll take centuries under the plans made by government colonies. They've introduced oxygen-generating and nitrogen-fixing microbes, but we can do better than that. We're engineering microbes with more efficient metabolisms. Once they're ready to be released, our new strains will accomplish the process in decades."

"Why can you do that better than the colonies?"

"We have better computers." Sahar smiled. "But more about that later." She pulled a fruit from her basket and held it out to Tiro. "Try a promise. They're superficially a mix of pomegranates and apples, blended with more supplementary genomes than I can remember. They're calorie rich and extremely nutritious. Humans can survive on them for weeks at a time."

Tiro took the fruit. The first bite was a perfect, pulpy mix of sweet and acrid. His spine prickled. "Why are you telling me all this?"

"Why are you going to Kaseishi?"

"Didn't my brother tell you?"

"I want to hear it from you."

Tiro hesitated, choosing words carefully. "We heard there's an engineer there who can make special mechanical bodies."

He stopped. "Yes?" Sahar prompted.

"Ones that lifted kids can move into," said Tiro. "To make them normal."

"It's only worked once. It may not work again. The integrated body frames were built to interact with computers, you know, not for lifted kids."

Tiro said nothing.

"How are you going to afford one?"

Tiro shrugged. "We'll figure it out."

"Your brother said you had a plan."

Tiro clenched his fists in frustration. What was the point being careful if Eo told them everything? "Kaseishi takes contracts for indentured servants, okay? If someone buys my labor for ten years, I can get a body for Eo."

Sahar ignored his exasperation. "If I accessed your records from New Virginia, how old would they say you were?"

"Sixteen."

"Really."

"Okay, fourteen. But that's old enough! I'm a man. I can sign my own contracts."

Sahar's eyes narrowed. "You look like you have African ancestors. If you're from New Virginia then your parents or grandparents probably came from the United States. Am I right?"

"Yeah. So?"

"So you've probably got a family history of slavery. I can't imagine your ancestors would be happy about one of their sons selling his freedom." She gestured to herself. "My people are Parsi. For generations, they were marginalized in India. We know what it is to be not-quite-people under the law." She paused. "What do your parents think?"

Tiro thought fast. "They're dead."

"Are they?"

"I have to do it for Eo."

"What if it's not the best thing for him?"

"He needs a body!"

"My daughter runs this settlement. The computer enhances her so she thinks faster than any human, and she enhances the computer so it works better than anything on Mars or on Earth." She paused, eyes searching Tiro's face for his reaction. "Do you understand what that means? It's a gift beyond measure. With Naghmeh's help, any plant I design can become reality in months. Without her, I'd have been lucky to construct even one species. That comfort palm, for instance. That would be my life's work."

"That's nice for you and Naghmeh, but Eo needs a body."

"Does he? Or do you need one for him?"

Tiro turned away, flaming with anger. Sahar called after him. "Think, Tiro! What does your brother know about flesh and bones? Are you doing this for him or for you?"

"I'm doing it for Eo!" Red anger flowed through Tiro's face and fists. He bolted into the trees, feet pounding across springy ground cover. At first he was surprised that Sahar let him run—but then, where could he go? She'd taken his suit.

He slowed in the middle of a grove and sat among the fallen leaves, trailing his fingers through the wet soil.

He remembered when his parents had first read about the mechanical bodies. They spent weeks arguing over their finances, trying to conjure what they needed. His father examined Kaseishi's laws and discovered the corporations there had agitated to legalize indentured servitude so they could bring up the droves of willing but impoverished workers from Earth and force them to repay their travel costs. He considered selling himself, but he was too old to get a contract.

"I'll do it," Tiro had said.

Both his parents looked at him like he'd just turned pink and sprouted wings.

"The devil you will," said his mother.

His father just shook his head, slowly. "No, Tiro. We won't sell one son's potential for the other's."

So Tiro ran away. What was ten years of his life if it could buy Eo's humanity?

Tiro didn't know how much time had passed before he heard Sahar's footsteps. He looked up. She held out her hand to help him stand.

"I shouldn't have pushed so fast," she said. "I'm passionate about what I do, about Mars and plants and Naghmeh. Please accept my apologies."

Every morning, Tiro asked when his arbitration would be. Every morning, Sahar answered, "Not yet. You need more food and rest anyway."

She took him to look at water-filled flowers that could be plucked and used as canisters, and at creepers that froze into durable ropes. She showed him how they planned to incorporate mechanical elements into future plants, such as trees that could monitor human heart rates and issue distress signals.

Tiro asked whether they could change humans the way they were changing plants. "I'd like to live in the cold. Or maybe you could make us fly . . ."

"Perhaps once the atmosphere is ready," said Sahar. "For now, we have more than enough to do."

Tiro enjoyed helping Sahar plant seedlings. Infant plants couldn't save lives, but they were fragile and green. He loved wriggling his fingers like worms in the dirt.

Sahar told him about the settlement. "Things have changed since Naghmeh integrated with the computer. We have more money now, more time, more knowledge. If people hadn't reacted ignorantly to the lifted children, more settlements could prosper as we do."

The settlement had welcomed Naghmeh by agreement of the elders and also by popular vote. Some of the population had been ready to surrender total control to Naghmeh, while others worried about what would happen if they allowed a child—however mechanically enhanced—to take authority over delicate systems like life support. In the end, they compromised, walling off a section of the system where Naghmeh could live, separated from processes that could threaten the settlers' lives.

"The settlers here are good people," said Sahar.

"Except Jirair," grumbled Tiro.

Sahar looked chagrined. "Some people are damaged by their pasts. There's a lot they can do with psychological programming these days, but . . . Jirair was your age when he came here as a runaway. He'd been kidnapped by a gang who murdered his parents and forced him to scout for new victims. He's convinced the same thing will happen here. The settlement has always weathered strikes by poachers, but three years ago, a gang convoy mounted a full attack. Naghmeh dealt with them. But ever since then, Jirair has seen any traveler, even merchants, as a threat. His housemates say he wakes screaming from dreams where we've all been slaughtered."

Tiro rubbed his wrists, remembering the manacles. "He still shouldn't treat people like that."

Sahar looked away. "Some people think anything is justified if they're certain they're right."

That night, Sahar warned him that she'd be coming early the next morning. "Why?" asked Tiro. "Is it my arbitration?"

Sahar shook her head. "It's time you met Naghmeh."

Sahar woke Tiro before dawn. They navigated the maze of her house, finally emerging on a rooftop observatory beneath the translucent curve of the dome.

"Naghmeh is everywhere the computer is, of course," Sahar said, "but the settlers prefer their privacy, so we ask her to speak only in certain places. This is my favorite, close to the sky."

"How do I talk to her?" Tiro asked.

"Just talk."

Tiro edged forward. "Hi."

A breathy voice whispered from the nearby audio outputs. "Hi."

"Why does she sound like that?" Tiro asked Sahar.

Sahar shrugged. "Caprice."

Tiro wandered between shining pieces of observatory equipment. "Sahar says you're with my brother."

"I am." With a laugh, she added, "He's sparkly!"

"Sparkly?"

"All over spark-raining! Showers and showers. Luminosity spikes like radiant flow."

Tiro balked. He looked at Sahar for an explanation.

"They see things differently than we do," said Sahar.

"I guess so." Tiro wondered if Eo saw things differently, too. He never said so, but was he trying to make himself seem normal for his family? Tiro looked up at one of the speakers. "Can I talk to my brother?"

A whir. "Later, maybe," said Naghmeh.

"What are you two doing together?"

"I'm showing him around. We go here. We go there." The outputs blared a bash song overlaid by high-pitched chatter. Noise-makers sounded in the background. "It's a party!"

"Are you showing him how to make plants?"

The party noises disappeared. The voice became whiny. "We just want to play. I work hard enough, don't I?"

"Doesn't the computer do the work?"

An elephant brayed, which seemed to be the equivalent of Eo's icon of a kid blowing a raspberry. "Isn't your body doing your breathing?"

"You work very hard," interjected Sahar with a peacemaker's tone.

"Eo's more interested in learning about machines anyway," said Naghmeh.

"Naghmeh," Sahar went on, "what would you think if someone said you could have a body?"

"A me-extension to make me mobile?"

"No, a human kind of body, not part of the network."

"A me-extension would be vroom! Mobile-network-me could prank and chat and fun." She paused. "Work more, too, if I had body *and* network."

"But humans can't do that. This body would do only what humans can. Would you want that?"

"For keeps or for play?"

"Keeps. You couldn't leave. You'd be in the body all the time."

"Why?"

"So you could think and act like we do."

"There's no scarcity of you, but there's scarcity of me. You should give up your bodies and live with me."

"There's nothing you'd want about being in a body?"

A pause. "Might be fun a while."

"But not forever?"

"Forever?" Naghmeh's voice rose with distress. "Why be small in oneplace onemind onethought?"

A cacophony of bird and animal noises poured from the outputs.

"Why trapbe?" asked Naghmeh. "Why cagebe? Why prisonbe?"

The screeches grew deafening. Eo had never acted like this. Was this what Sahar meant by seeing things differently? Would Eo be like this if they let him stay on the networks? Tiro slapped his hands over his ears, but the noise kept mounting.

"Naghmeh!" shouted Sahar. "Please! Quiet down!"

The noise waned, replaced by quiet keening. Sahar paced to one of the outputs, running her fingers over the mesh as if caressing an infant's cheek. "Shh, Naghmeh. I'm sorry we upset you."

When Sahar came to Tiro's room later, her eyes were red.

"Is Naghmeh okay?" Tiro asked.

Sahar nodded. Her fingers fretted at her cuffs, nails bitten and raw. "Do you understand now why you can't force Eo into a body?"

Tiro didn't want to meet her gaze. "He has to become what he was supposed to be."

Sahar's expression looked almost as sad as his father's. Wordlessly, she turned and left him alone.

The next day, the elders scheduled Tiro's arbitration.

Sahar pestered him so much that Tiro didn't even feel relieved when she returned his space suit.

"You need to reconsider," she pleaded. "You're acting like Jirair.

You know that? You're so certain it's right for Eo to have a body that you'll do anything to get him one, even hurt him."

"You just want Eo to grow your plants," Tiro snapped, switching off his receiver.

The second dome was smaller than Sahar's. Rows of flowers created a maze of red, blue, and yellow. The hexagonal meeting-house rose above the other buildings like a megalith.

They stopped by the entrance to remove their suits. Sahar shot Tiro a worried look that would have annoyed him if his heart hadn't been pounding.

Inside, a smoky scent drifted toward the exposed rafters. The three elders sat on wooden stools, their gray robes sweeping the floor.

Sahar bowed from the waist. "This is Tiro. His brother is the lifted child—"

"Thank you, Sahar," said the female elder on the right. "You may go now."

Sahar opened her mouth to object, but reconsidered. "I bid you good judgment." She bowed again before departing.

The door closed, leaving silence in its wake. Tiro shifted, waiting for the elders to speak.

"I'm sorry I stole the food," he ventured. "After I finish in Kaseishi, I'll come work it off."

The elders exchanged glances. The man on the left said, "Sahar and Naghmeh spoke on your behalf. Accept it as our gift."

A prickle crept up Tiro's spine. "Why?"

The middle elder leaned forward, the beaded ends of his braids clattering across his back. "We hope you'll feel grateful and return with your brother," he said. "We would also welcome your parents."

"They're dead," said Tiro.

"They aren't."

"They—"

The left-hand elder lifted his palm to halt Tiro's protest. "We understand why you lied. We don't begin adulthood at fourteen here. But you are not one of us, and we accept that our rules don't apply."

"Though Sahar does not," interjected the woman. "She wanted us to permit her to contact your parents."

The middle elder pinned Tiro with a firm gaze. "It would violate our ethics to do as she asked. Nevertheless, we urge you to consider our offer."

Tiro swallowed. "Thank you, but my brother and I must go to Kaseishi."

With a sigh, the middle elder reached into his voluminous sleeve. He withdrew a data globe. "You may use this at any interface to speak with your brother."

Uneasily, Tiro reached for the globe. "Is that all?"

The middle elder nodded. "That is all."

Tiro's fingers closed around the globe. He fled before the elders could change their minds.

Once outside, he rushed to put on his suit. He ran for the nearest interface, forcing the globe into its input recess.

The globe lit up. Text scrolled across his visor. *Tiro!*

Eo! Are you okay?

Did you know we can race more than a thousand times per second? I beat Naghmeh more than half the time! She showed me this engine trick that works out-world, too, and—

Race what? said Tiro. *Never mind. Tell me later. We have to go now.*

Blankness followed.

Come on, Eo, get in the globe. We have to go to Kaseishi.

Maybe later, wrote Eo. *I'm having fun.*

We won't be able to go later.

But I like Naghmeh.

We don't have time! Tiro stopped, breathing deeply to calm himself. Now wasn't the time to upset Eo. *Can we talk alone? I don't want anyone listening. This is private, you know?*

A brothers thing? asked Eo.

A brothers thing, Tiro agreed. *Please move into the globe?*

The lights on the data globe blinked rapidly as Eo moved inside. Tiro waited until they held a steady color before yanking the globe from its recess. He switched it into energy-saving mode. The lights dimmed as it entered hibernation.

"Sorry, Eo," Tiro whispered.

Hastily, he sealed his helmet and headed for the nearest exit. He had to reach the skipper before Sahar or Naghmeh realized what he'd done.

When the settlement was out of sight, Tiro placed the data globe in the skipper's pit. Its lights brightened, but no words appeared on Tiro's visor.

Eo? wrote Tiro. *Come on, talk to me.*

Nothing crossed Tiro's vision but endless dust.

I'm doing this for you, Eo. You were born into a body. You should have the chance to grow up in one. It's what our parents want.

Nothing appeared. Hours passed under the skipper's wheels.

They stopped at dusk. Tiro warmed some frozen rations from Sahar's settlement. After supper, he strapped himself into the driver's seat, lowering the skipper's energy output to the minimum required for heat and oxygen.

He woke to see the sun's rays mounting the horizon. The stale air smelled of food and plastic. He considered breakfast, but didn't want to stay in one place any longer. He initialized the skipper and started driving.

At first, Tiro had been enraptured by the landscape's shifting, ruddy hues. Now, travel just made him tired. As morning seeped into afternoon, he began to drowse.

Sometime later, he woke with a start. Text scrolled across his vision. *Tiro.* He blinked, wondering if he was dreaming—but no, it was real. *Tiro, stop the skipper. Go to low energy. Now!*

Tiro didn't pause to think. His hands moved rapidly across the machinery, cutting the skipper into silent mode. He shivered as the nonessential heating dissipated, leaving bitter cold.

What is it, Eo? Tiro asked.

Gang convoy, wrote Eo. *They'll be visible in . . . 20 . . . 17 . . . 15 . . .*

Gang convoy? Where?

Northeast. 5 . . . 3 . . .

Tiro shrank in his seat as the convoy rumbled past. Skippers zoomed alongside thunders and ground-eaters. Some vehicles were huge, armored like enormous beetles. All were painted red as Mars dust, the color of the landscape, the color of blood.

They're headed toward Sahar's settlement, Tiro wrote when they were past.

I know, wrote Eo.

We're lucky they didn't see us.

I know that, too.

There's no point in going back. There's nothing we can do.

Eo fell silent.

Tiro swallowed. *The gang will be there long before we can. Everyone would be dead by the time we arrived.*

That would be true, wrote Eo, *except Naghmeh taught me how to make the skipper go a lot faster.*

A lot faster?

Eo sent an enormous, toothy grin. *Ohhhhhhhhh yeah.*

They parked the skipper behind the warehouses. Jirair lay panting in the dirt nearby, a comfort palm frond wrapped around his leg.

"You," said Jirair as Tiro approached. "The elders said they invited you to stay. You came back?"

Tiro nodded. Now didn't seem like the time to get into why he'd run away.

"I guess you're as good as one of us now. For as long as there is an us." He jerked his head toward Tiro's skipper. "Get out before you get killed."

"You're injured," Tiro said.

"My suit is ripped. Not that it'll matter when I run out of oxygen . . ."

Tiro hated being forced to help Jirair, but he knelt beside him anyway and plugged their suits together. "If you need more air, find my skipper. It has a two week supply. Will the palm keep your suit sealed?"

Jirair nodded, savoring a deep breath.

"Where are the others?"

"Hostage in the garden dome. I kept running while they shot at me, grabbed a frond, and got out. I'd rather die out here than . . ." He trailed off.

Tiro looked up at the domes. The gang vehicles were parked around them in an enormous red mass, like fire ants swarming a kill.

"Can you walk?" Tiro asked Jirair. "I'll need help."

Tiro offered his hand to help Jirair stand. After a moment's hesitation, Jirair accepted, but as he pushed onto his bad leg, something made a snapping sound.

Jirair choked off a scream. Panting with pain he said, "I warned them! I told them the gang would come back. I told them Naghmeh can't be our only protection. They wouldn't listen." Jirair punched the igloo wall, dislodging a cascade of ice.

"Then tell me what to do."

"There's nothing. They're trained fighters."

"There must be something. Tell me what you know."

"There's nothing! Naghmeh runs all our security. They've trapped her."

"How?"

Tiro coaxed the story from him. Three years ago, a gang convoy had attacked the settlement. Naghmeh took control of their network. She fired their weapons randomly, killing some, disabling others, and forcing the rest to hurl their defenses away. She used the vehicles to herd the infantry, the drivers helpless to control their rebeling machines.

Jirair had warned the settlers that the gang would nurse a grudge. "A well-trained force they could have understood," Jirair said. "But this was an insult, a challenge to their prowess."

Sahar and other respected settlers had argued that it didn't matter. Naghmeh's relationship with the settlement computer was unique. As long as they didn't know what Naghmeh was, they couldn't fight her.

They remained confident when the convoy began offering a reward for information about settlement security. But someone— no one knew who—had betrayed them all.

The gang arrived with a program that was designed to invade the network and seek Nagmeh out, enfolding her in a coded prison that protected itself by creating the illusion that it was the portion of the system where Naghmeh lived. Naghmeh didn't even know she was trapped.

"I've seen these work on simple AIs," Jirair said, "but never something sophisticated enough to fool Naghmeh. They must have bought the technology from Earth. The settlement's not *that* wealthy. . . . They must really want us dead. . . ." He shook his head, his expression hard-worn beneath his visor. "If you could get her back in control—but you can't."

Jirair must have been in considerable pain from his wound, but the plight of the colony seemed to be causing him even more pain than that. Tiro almost understood why Jirair had threatened to torture him. Sometimes you'd do anything to protect what you loved.

He glanced at his brother's data globe, strengthening his resolve. "Maybe I can."

Can they trap you like they did Naghmeh? Tiro asked as he trudged toward the domes.

They don't even know I'm here. Get me to an interface.

They'll know you're there if you get into the network. They got Naghmeh and she's been doing this a lot longer than you!

She didn't know they were coming. The gang could trap me now because I don't have any defenses, but if I get into the network, I can trounce them. Just get me to an interface!

Luck was with them for now. The attackers had been warned to expect one computer enhanced by a lifted child. They would never expect a second.

Sneaking through the vehicle perimeter was easier than Tiro thought it would be. The drivers were relying on their vehicles' security. Eo confused the scans, telling Tiro when to duck to avoid visual confirmation sweeps.

Isn't it dangerous for you to interfere with their systems? asked Tiro. *Won't they find you?*

Not if we move fast.

They emerged near Sahar's dome. Tiro searched for her private entrance. She had told him it was guarded by security that even his brother couldn't break. If that meant Naghmeh, then it would be undefended now. But what if it wasn't?

Detect anything? Tiro asked.

No, said Eo, but Tiro couldn't help thinking of the last time he'd been wrong.

The air lock opened with a smooth hiss. Tiro's heart pounded as he went through both doors and entered the dome, the ground cover springy beneath his boots. He opened his helmet's circulation to admit dome air, inhaling the scent of flowers.

Now that they'd made it inside, Tiro could feel his perceptions growing sharper as his body flooded with adrenaline. He looked up uneasily at Sahar's enormous house.

His visor flashed with Eo's alarm. *You're not going in there!*

When I was staying in this dome with Sahar, I only saw one interface. He craned his neck upward. *It's on the roof.*

There are gangsters in there!!

Can you tell me where they are?

If they're carrying things connected to the network.

Are they?

Eo seemed loath to admit it. *They have wrist chatters.*

Eo continued to convey his misgivings by sending a stream of anxious faces, but he assembled a floor plan for Tiro with the gangsters' locations marked by moving red dots. One stood in the entryway, blocking the stairs. Tiro began searching the deadfall for something to use as a club.

Suddenly, the gangster veered into the hallway. Tiro straightened. *What did you do?*

Sent a fake letter to his chatter. He thinks it's from a woman upstairs.

Tiro blinked as Eo's message scrolled across his visor, virtually steaming with innuendo.

Where did you learn that? asked Tiro.

Never mind, it'll get you in!

Tiro entered and ran upstairs without pausing to think. Each of his footsteps seemed to boom on the wood like strikes on a bass drum.

He wove through the mazelike corridors, darting left and right as needed. Eo sent more fake messages, but not all the gangsters took predictable courses. Tiro hid whenever one turned an unexpected corner, willing himself to be invisible among the shadows. On the third floor, he crouched behind a door for an agonizing fifteen minutes while two gangsters finished playing dice. Eo sent a letter to one of their chatters, but the woman only glanced at it and laughed, blanking out its screen for the rest of their game.

Finally, Tiro emerged in front of the narrow, rickety staircase leading to the roof. *Stop*, Eo warned as Tiro put his hand on the railing. *There's someone up there.*

Tiro's stomach churned. *Can you get rid of him?*

No prob, Eo replied, smugly.

A minute passed. *Eo?* Tiro prompted.

His visor flashed red. *They figured out I was faking messages! They're looking for me!*

They can't find you if you don't do anything else, right?

I don't know!

Calm down, Tiro directed with more confidence then he felt. *I'll take care of it.*

Ignoring Eo's protests, Tiro started upstairs.

When he reached the top, he pressed himself into the shadow of the open door and peered out. At night, the observatory was full of glints and shadows. A tall man in leather sat beside one of the telescopes, eating a promise fruit. An illegal compressed-gas projectile gun sat in his holster. The interface lay beyond him, its recess gleaming like water in an oasis.

Tiro's heart thumped. The man was sleek, with runner's muscles, built for speed as well as strength. There was no way to get past him.

Tiro cleared his throat. He'd always been good at thinking up lies. His father said they flowed from his mouth like scat from a pig's anus. Thinking of lies was easy. It was convincing people to believe them that was hard.

"Hey there!" he shouted, coming into the light. "I'm Tiro. I'm the one who gave you the info on the lifted kid. Where's my reward?"

The gangster looked up at him, slowly. He set aside his half-eaten promise fruit and got to his feet. "No you're not," he said, flicking his gaze up and down Tiro's body. "We've got the woman outside. Some religious bat."

"Yeah, but I gave her the information."

"Yeah?" echoed the gangster. "Why would a kid turn in his settlement? They send you to bed without supper?"

Tiro swallowed, trying to conceal his shaking hands. "They made me work with the lifted kid because we're the same age. They think they can give her friends like a normal person. But she's an abomination. She's just a copy of some poor dead kid, keeping its soul from going to the afterlife."

A flash of darkness crossed Tiro's visor, Eo's expression of pain. Eo had been told he wasn't a real person all his life, by strangers, by the news. Maybe even by his family—did Eo think that's what they were saying when they wanted to get him a body?

Tiro wished he could comfort Eo, but he didn't dare send him a message.

The pirate circled Tiro, coming between him and the door. "Why didn't Benita tell us about you then?"

Tiro darted a glance over his shoulder at the recess. He hoped he'd seem to be looking for an escape route. He backed a few steps away from the gangster as if afraid, moving toward his goal.

"I . . . don't know . . ." he stammered. "Maybe she forgot."

The gangster advanced. "Forgot. Sure. Or maybe you don't want to go to the mines?"

Tiro kept walking fearfully backward.

"Want to know what happened to Benita? She's dead. If she betrayed you, she'd betray us, too. So we killed her. Now tell me how you got up here."

That was enough. Tiro turned to run, palming his brother's data globe. He was halfway across the roof. Could he make it the rest of the way?

"Stop," the gangster shouted. Tiro's feet slammed against the wood. He heard the smack of metal on plastic as the gangster drew his gun. He hardly registered the blast of pain that erupted in his side as he twisted in midair, his arm sweeping outward to toss the globe the last few centimeters into the recess. He crashed to the ground. The gangster's boots struck the boards as he approached for a final shot, but already the data globe's lights were pricking the darkness with blue and yellow.

A child's voice sputtered from the audio outputs. "I don't like all this violence."

The gangster shouted with pain as his gun's internal chip heated the metal until it was excruciating. The gun clattered to the floor.

"That's better," Eo continued. "Can you take it from here, Naghmeh, or do I have to do everything?"

Tiro twisted to get a better look at Sahar as she entered his room. "Did you bring another plant book?"

"Don't," she said, setting a bowl of mushroom soup on his nightstand. "You'll hurt yourself."

"I'm fine," Tiro grumbled, but Sahar bent to inspect his wound anyway. Before condemning Tiro to three weeks' bed rest, the settlement's physician had said that the bullet had missed his major organs, but made a major mess.

"You finished the volume on diseases already?" Sahar asked.

"What else do I have to do?"

"I should shoot all my apprentices."

Sahar wore her clothes from the garden. Traces of soil on her boots and cuffs gave her a budding, green smell. Tiro hissed as she touched a tender spot.

"Are you done yet?"

"Momentarily." Sahar completed her inspection and withdrew, letting Tiro tug down his shirt. She paused. "We heard from your parents."

Tiro's mouth went dry. "What did they say?"

"They're furious," she said. "But they'll get over it." She went on, "They want to know how you survived, and what you were thinking, and how you're going to pay them back for their skipper. They also want you to know they've quit their jobs in New Virginia and they'll be here in a month."

Tiro sat up. "They're coming?"

Sahar grinned. "We're offering them large salaries, rewarding work, and a place where both of their children can grow as they are. How could they refuse?"

Tiro matched her grin. For a moment, he was ecstatic, but then a sliver of worry worked its way inside. He slumped onto the bed, his smile gone.

Sahar frowned. "What's wrong? Are you in pain?"

Tiro shook his head.

"I thought you'd be happy your parents were coming."

"I am. It's just . . ." Tiro trailed off.

Sahar sat beside him on the bed. "You must have known Eo wouldn't leave if you let him back into the system."

"I didn't think I had a choice. The gang . . . but I didn't have to come back. I could have kept driving."

"So why did you come back?"

"I think, in the back of my mind, what you said about me and Jirair got to me. I'm not him. I couldn't hurt Eo, not even for his own good. I had to let him choose."

"And now you wish you hadn't."

"No!" Tiro looked up to see if he'd upset Sahar, but she stared back with placid gray eyes. "It's just, sometimes . . ."

Sahar sighed. "Sometimes you listen to them talk and play, and you realize they're not like you, and they won't ever be. They're themselves—and that's good. . . . But sometimes it breaks your heart."

Tiro nodded silently.

Later, when Tiro recovered, he and Eo would commune on the rooftop observatory. He'd tell Eo all about working with plants while Eo went into flights about mechanics and computing that he could never hope to understand. Tiro would start sleeping in his visor again so that they could spend their nights together as they always had.

But just now, Tiro was afraid he'd cry if he spoke. He closed his eyes, letting Sahar stroke his hair as he mourned the way he hadn't known how to the first time he lost his brother's body.

RACHEL SWIRSKY is a Californian short story writer whose work has appeared on www.Tor.com, in *Subterranean* magazine and *Fantasy* magazine, and in a number of year's best anthologies. Her latest nonwriting project is trying to tame a litter of feral kittens so they can be adopted out as house pets.

AUTHOR'S NOTE

I started working on "The Taste of Promises" by asking my friends what books I should read about Mars. One title kept coming up: Robert Zubrin's *How to Live on Mars: A Trusty Guidebook to Surviving and Thriving on the Red Planet.* This witty, fast-paced book was a tremendously fun read and helped me to shape some ideas about what life might be like on a settled Mars.

Some of my other inspirations came from online reading. For instance, Growth Assembly (http://www.pohflepp.com/?q=growthassembly) considers creating plants that would be engineered to grow product parts. I played with this idea to come up with anthropocentric ecology. I also read about soft mobile morphing robots, which are robots made of materials that can deform and change shape so that the robot can travel through narrow crevices. That got me thinking about what kinds of robots we'd have in the future, which got me thinking about mechanical intelligences, which got me thinking about lifted kids.

This whole process is pretty different from the way I normally start stories. I know that a lot of other science fiction writers start out by finding a nifty technology. Personally, I usually start writing when I find a kind of character or situation that I don't think has been written about enough, or that's always written about in a way that irritates me. These kinds of stories come to me with the plots and characters already established. It was interesting to write a piece and discover who and what it was about along the way.

DIGGING

Ian McDonald

Tash was wise to the ways of wind. She knew its many musics:
sometimes like a flute across the pipes and tubes; sometimes
a snare-drum rattle in the guylines and cable stays or a death
drone-moan from the turbine gantries and a scream of sand
past the irised-shut windows when the equinox dust storms blew
for weeks on end. From the rails and drive bogies of the scoopline
the wind drew a wail like a demon choir and from the buckets set a
clattering clicking rattle so that she imagined tiny clockwork angels
scampering up and down the hundreds of kilometers of conveyor
belts. In the storm-season gales, it came screaming in across Isidis's
billion-year-dead impact basin, clawing at the eaves and gables of
West Diggory, tearing at the tiered roofs so hard Tash feared it would
rip them right off and send them tumbling end over end down,
down into the depths of the Big Dig. That would be the worst thing.
Everyone would die badly: eyeballs and fingertips and lips exploding, cheeks bursting with red veins. She had nightmares about suddenly looking up to see the roof ripping away and the naked sky and

the air all blowing away in one huge shout of exhalation. Then your eyeballs exploded. She imagined how that would sound. Two soft popping squelches. Then In-brother Yoche told her you couldn't hear your eyeballs exploding because the air would be too thin, and the whole story was a legend of mischievous Grandparents and Sub-aunts who liked to scare under-fours. But it made her think about how fragile West Diggory was and the other three stations of the Big Dig. Spindly and top-heavy, domes piled upon half-domes upon semi-domes, swooping wing roofs and perilous balconies, all resting on the finger-thin cantilevers that connected the great Excavating City to the traction bogies. Like big spiders. Tash knew spiders. She had seen spiders in a book and once, in a piece of video excitedly shot by Lady-cousin Nairne in North Cutter, a real spider, in a real web, trembling in the perennial beat of the buckets working up the scoopline from the head of the Big Dig, five kilometers downslope. Lady-cousin Nairne had poked at the spider with her fingers—fat and brown as bread in high magnification. The spider had frozen, then scuttled for the corner of the window frame, curled into a tiny balls of legs, and refused to do anything for the rest of the day. The next day when Nairne and her camera returned it was dead dead dead, dried into a little desiccated husk of shell. It must have come in a crate in the supply run down from the High Orbital, though every-thing they shipped from orbit was supposed to be clean. Beyond the window where the little translucent corpse hung vibrating in its web, red rock and wind and the endless march of the buckets along the rails of the excavating conveyor. Buckets and wind. Tied together. Wind; Fact one: when the buckets ceased, then and only then would the wind stop. Fact two: all Tash's life it had blown in the same direction—downhill.

Tash Gelem-Opunyo was wise to the ways of wind, and buckets, and random spiders, and on Moving Day the wind was a long, many-part harmony for pipes drawn from the sand-polished steels rails, a flutter of the kites and blessing banners and wind socks and lucky fish that West Diggory flew from every rooftop and pylon and stanchion, a sudden caress of a veering eddy in the small of her back that made Tash shiver and stand upright on the high veranda in her psuit, a too-intimate touch. She was getting too big for the old psuit. It was tight and chafed in the wrong places. Tight it had to be, a stretch-skin of gas-impermeable fabric, but Things were Showing. My How You've Grown Things, that Haramwe Odonye, who was an Out-cousin in from A.R.E.A. and thus allowed to Notice such things, Noticed, and Commented On. Last Moving Day, half a long-year before, in an attempt to camouflage the bumps and creases and curves, she had drawn all over the hi-visibility skin with marker pen. There were more animals on her skin than on the whole of Mars.

Up and out on Moving Day, that was the tradition. From the very, very old to the very, very, young, blinking up out of their pressure cocoons; every soul in West Diggory came out onto the balconies and galleries and walkways. Safety was part of the routine— with every half-year wrench of West Diggory's thousand of tons of architecture into movement the possibility increased that a joint might split or a pressure dome shatter. Eyeball-squelch-pop time. But safety was only a small part. Movement was what West Diggory was for; like the wind, downward, ever downward.

The Terrace of the Grand Regard was the highest point on West Diggory; only the banners of the Isidis Planitia Excavating Company, eternally billowing in the unvarying downslope wind, and the wind turbines stood higher. Climbing the ladders Tash felt

Out-cousin Haramwe's eyes on her, watching from the Boys' Pavilion. His boy-gaze drew the other young males onto their high and rickety terrace. The psuit was indeed tight, but good tight. Tash enjoyed how it moved with her, holding her in where she wanted to be held, emphasising what she wanted emphasised.

"Hey, good snake!" Out-cousin Haramwe called on the common channel. On her seventh and a half birthday Tash had drawn a dream snake on her psuit skin, a diamond pattern loop with its tail at the base of her spine, curled around the left curve of her ass and its head buried in her inner thigh. It had been exciting to draw. It was more exciting to wear on Moving Day, the only time she ever wore the psuit.

"Are you ogling my ophidian?" Tash taunted back to the hoots of the other boys as she climbed up onto Gallery of Exalted Vistas to be with her sisters and cousin and In-cousins and Out-cousins, all the many ways in which Tash could be related in a gene pool of only two thousand people. The guys hooted. Tash shimmied her shoulders, where little birds were drawn. The boys liked her insulting them in words they didn't understand. *Listen well, look well. I'm the best show on Mars.*

A thousand banners rattled in the unending wind. Kites dipped and fluttered, painted with birds and butterflies and stranger aerial creatures that had only existed in the legends of distant Earth. Streamers pointed the way to West Diggory: downhill, always downhill. The lines of buckets full of Martian soil marched up the conveyor from the dig point, invisible over the close horizon, under the legs of West Diggory, toward the unseen summit of Mount Incredible, where they tipped their load on its ever growing summit before cycling back down the underside of the conveyor. The story was that the freshly dug regolith at the bottom of the hole was the color of gold: exposure to the atmosphere on its long journey upslope turned it Mars red. She turned to better feel the shape of the wind on every part of her body. This psuit so needed replacing. There was more to her shiver than just the caress of air in motion. Wind and words: they were the same stuff. If she threw big and fancy words, words that gave her joy and made her laugh from the shape they made from moving air, it was because they were living wind itself.

A shiver ran up through the catwalk grills and railings and into Tash Gelem-Opunyo. The engineers were running up the traction generators; West Diggory shuddered and thrummed as the toka-maks drew resonances and steel harmonies from its girders and cantilevers. Tash's molars ached, then there was a jolt that threw old and young alike off balance, grasping for handrails, stanchions, cables, one another. There was a immense shriek like a new moon being pulled live from the body of the world. Shuddering creaks, each so loud Tash could hear them through her ear protectors. Steel wheels turned, grinding on sand. West Diggory began to move. People waved their hands and cheered; the noise reduction circuits on the common channel brought the din down to a surge of delighted gig-gling. The wheels, each taller than Tash, ground 'round, slow as growing. West Diggory, perched on its cantilevers, inched down its eighteen tracks, tentative as an old woman stepping from a diggler. This was motion on the glacial, the geological scale. It would take ten hours for West Diggory to make its scheduled descent into the Big Dig. You had to be sure to have eaten and drunk enough, because it wasn't safe to go inside. Tash had breakfasted lightly at the commons in the Raven Sorority, where the In-daughters lived together after they turned five. The semizoic fabric absorbed everything without stink or stain but it was far from cool to piss your suit. Unless you were up and out on a job. Then it was mandatory.

Music trilled on the common channel, a cheery little toe-tapper. Tash gritted her teeth. She knew what it heralded: the West Diggory Down. No one knew when, where, or who had started the tradition of the Moving Day dance: Tash suspected it was a joke that no one had recognized and so became literal. She slid behind a stanchion as her Raven sisters formed up, and the boys up on the Boys' Pavilion bowed and raised their hands. Slip away, slip away before it starts. Up the steps and along the clattering catwalk to the Outermost Preview. From this distant perch, a birdcage of steel at the end of a slender pier, a lantern suspended over the sand, Tash surveyed all West Diggory, her domes and gantries and pods and tubes and flapping banners and her citizens—so few of them, Tash thought—formed up into lines and squares for the dance. She tuned out the common channel. Strange, them stepping gaily, hand in hand, up and down the lines, do-si-do in psuits and face masks and total silence. The olds seemed to enjoy it. They had no dignity. Look how fat some of them were in their psuits. Tash turned away from the rituals of West Diggory to the great, subtle slope of the Big Dig, following the lines up the slope. She was on the edge of the age when you could leave West Diggory, but she had heard that up there, beyond Mount Incredible, the small world curved away so quickly in all directions that the horizon was only three kilometers distant. The Big Dig held different horizons. It was huge cone sunk into the surface of a sphere. An alternative geometry worked here. The world didn't curve away, it curved inward, a circle over three hundred kilometer 'round where it met the surface of Mars. The world radiated outward: Tash could follow the radiating spokes of the scooplines all the way of the edge of the world, and beyond, to the encircling ring-mountain of Mount Incredible that reached the edge of space. Peering along the curve of the Big Dig through the dust haze constantly thrown up by the ceaseless excavating, she could just make out the sun-glitter from the gantries of North Cutter, which, like West Diggory, was making its slow descent deeper into the pit. A flicker of thought would up the magnification on her visor and she would be able to look clear across eighty kilometers of airspace to A.R.E.A and spy on whatever celebrations they held there, at the first and greatest of the Excavating Cities on Moving Day. Maybe she might see a girl like herself, balanced on some high and perilous perch, looking out across the bowl of the world.

The figures on the platforms and terraces broke apart, bowed to each other, lost all pattern and rhythm, and became random again. Moving Day Down was over for another half-year. Tash flicked on the common channel. Tash liked to be apart, different, a girl of words and wit, but she also loved to be immersed in West Diggory's never-ending babble of chat and gossip and jokes and family news. Together, the Excavating Cities had a population of less than two thousand humans. Small, complex societies, isolated from the rest of the planet, gush words like springs, like torrents and floods. The river of words, the only river that Mars knew. Tash's psuit circuitry was smart enough to adjust the voices so that they spoke at the volume and distance they would have in atmosphere. Undifferentiated, the flood of West Diggory voices would have overwhelmed her. She turned her head this way, that way. Eavesdropping. There was Leyta Soshinwe-Opunyo, queen-beeing again. Tash had seen pictures of bees like she had seen birds. On Arrival Day, when the Excavating Cities finally reached the bottom of the Big Dig, there would be birds, and bees, and even spiders. There was Great-Out-aunt Yoto, seeming enthusiastic but always seasoned with a pinch of criticism: oh, and another thing—people weren't performing the dance moves right, the engineers had mistuned the tokamaks, and her titanium hip was aching, was it her or did more bits fall off West Diggory every time? They would never have allowed that in Southdelving, her family home. A sudden two-tone siren cut across the four hundred voices of West Diggory. Emergency teams slapped their psuits to warning yellow and rushed to their positions. Every-one hurried to the muster points, then relaxed as the medics discov-ered the nature of the emergency. The common channel flooded with laughter. Haramwe Odonye, during a particularly energetic caper in the West Diggory Down, had slipped and sprained his ankle.

Big Dig Figs and Facts

Population: 1,833, divided between the four Excavating Cities of (clockwise) Southdelving, West Diggory, North Cutter, and A.R.E.A (Ares Reengineering of Environment and Atmosphere). Total Martian population: 5,217.

Elevation: at the digging head as of Martian Year 112, Janulum 1: minus twenty three kilometers below Martian Mean Gravity Surface (no sea level). Same date, highest point of Mount Impossible: fifteen kilome-ters above MGS.

Diameter of the Big Dig at Martian MGS: 516 kilometers.

Circumference of the Big Dig at Martian MGS: 1,622 kilometers.

Angle of Big Dig Excavation Surface: 5.754 degrees. That's pretty gentle. The scoopline can't handle more than an 8 degree slope. To the casual human eye—one that hasn't grown up inside the gentle dish of the Big Dig—that would look almost flat. But it's not flat. That's why it's the key figure: those 5.754 degrees are going to make Mars habitable.

Date of commencement of the Big Dig: AlterMarch 23, Martian Year 70. Two thirty in the afternoon, on schedule, the scooplines excavated and the bucket teeth took their first bites of Isidis Planitia.

Volume of the Big Dig: as of above date: 1,813,000 cubic kilometers. All piled up neatly into Mount Impossible, the ring-shaped mountain that surrounds the Big Dig like the wall of an old impact crater. Not entirely surrounds. Mount Impossible has been constructed with four huge valleys: Windrush, Zephyr, Cyroco, and Storm of the Black Plums: howling, wind-haunted, storm-scoured canyons—the same wind that sings over the tombs of the diggers who have died in the course of the great excavation and unfailingly stirs the flags and streamers of the mobile cities far below.

Total mass of Martian surface excavated in the Big Dig to date: 7.1 x 10^{15} tons.

Big Dig Figs and Facts. The numbers that shape Tash's world.

Tash was in the Orangery when the call came down through the rows of breadfruit trees. Like the Moving Day dance, the name Orangery was generally considered another joke that had run away and taken up residence in the ventilators and crawl spaces and power conduits of the Excavating City, as this baroque glass dome had never grown oranges. The rows of breadfruit and plantains and bananas and other high-carb staples gave camouflage and opportunity for West Diggory's young people to meet and talk and scheme and flirt.

"Milaba wants to see Tash, pass it on."

"Sweto, tell Chunye that Milaba wants to see Tash."

"Qori, have you seen Tash?"

"I think she was down in the plantains, but she might have moved on to the breadfruit."

"Well, tell her Milaba wants to see her."

By leaps and misunderstandings, by staggers and misapprehensions, by devious spirals of who liked whom and who was talking to whom and who wasn't and who was hooking up with whom and who had finished with whom, the message spiraled in along the web of leaf mold–smelling plants to Tash, spraying the breadfruit. A simple call, a message would have reached her directly, but where there are only a hundred of you, true social networking is mouth-to-mouth.

In-aunt Milaba. She was a legend, a statue of woman, gracious and noble, adored far beyond West Diggory. Her dark skin was lustrous as night, her soul as star-filled. To be in her presence was to be blessed in ways you would not immediately understand, but more thrilling to Tash was that In-aunt Milaba was the chief service engineer for the northwest sector scooplines. The summons to her office, a little glass and aluminium bubble like a bunion on one of West Diggory's steel feet, could mean only one thing. Out. Out and up.

"So Haramwe sprained his ankle."

Every part of In-aunt Milaba's tiny office, from the hand-carved olivine desk to the carafe of water that stood on it, shook to the rattle of the buckets hurtling up the scoopline. Milaba raised an eyebrow. Tash realised a response was due.

"Are his injuries debilitating?"

"Debilitating." Milaba gave a flicker of a smile. "You could say that. He'll be out for a week or so. He came down heavily, silly boy. Showing off. When is your birthday?" Tash's heart leapt.

She knew. Everyone knew everything, all the time. The game was pretending not to know.

"Octobril fifth."

"Three months." Milaba appeared to consider for a moment. "Peyko Ruebens-Opollo says for all your fancy talk you've a good head and better sense and do what you're told. That's good, because I don't need attitude problems or last-minute good ideas when I'm out on the line."

For once the words failed Tash. They hissed from her like air from a ruptured atmosphere cell. She waved her hands in speechless delight.

"I'm taking a diggler up Line 12 to Windrush Valley. The feed tokamaks have been fluctuating nastily. Probably a soft fail in a command chip set; they get a lot of radiation up there. Now, I need someone with me to hold things and make tea and generally make intelligent conversation. Are you interested?"

Still the words would not come. The rule was that you did not leave the Excavating Cities until you were eight, when you were technically an adult. Rules broke and bent with the frequency of scoopline breakdowns but three months was a significant proportion of the long Martian year. Out. Out and up. Up the line, into the windy valley. In a diggler, with In-aunt Milaba.

"Yes, oh yes, I'd love to," Tash finally squeaked. Now Milaba unleashed the full radiance of her smile, and it was like sunrise, it was solstice lights, it was the warmth of the glow-lamps in the Orangery. *I say you are an adult citizen of West Diggory, Tash Gelem-Opunyo,* the smile said, *and if I say it, all say it.*

"Be at the Outlock 12 at fourteen o'clock," Milaba said. "You do know how to make tea, don't you?"

Still not got it? It's easy, easy easy easy. Easy as a heezy, which is a digger saying. A heezy is the lever on a scoopline bucket that, when struck by the dohbrin (which is a different type of lever found at the load-off end of the scoopline) tips the contents of the bucket down Mount Incredible. Heezy peasy easy. It's all because air has weight. Air's not nothing. It's gas—in Mars's case, carbon dioxide, nitrogen, argon, oxygen, and the leaked breathings from the hundred-and-something years that humans have scratched and scrabbled clawholds on its red earth. It has mass. It has weight. And it flows, the same way that water flows, to the lowest point. Wind is air flowing. People say, *No one knows why the wind blows.* That's stupid nonsense. Wind blows from high to low, high pressure to low pressure, high altitude to low altitude; down the slopes of mountains, through canyons and valleys. The air pressure at the bottom of the great and primeval rift of Valles Marineris is ten times that in the long-cold volcanic calderas atop Olympus Mons. Titanic gales and fog blow through that valley. The fog is because the atmospheric pressure at the bottom of the valley is enough just enough—to allow water to exist as vapor. But that's still not enough to support big life. That's like higher than Earth's highest mountain. That's fingertip-lip-exploding, eyeball-squelching, cheek-bursting pressure. Bug life, yes, big life, no. That's not enough to make Mars a green paradise, a home for humanity, a fertile pool of life beyond little blue Earth. What you need is deep. Thirty kilometers deep. Deeper than any place on Earth is deep. Deeper than even Olympus Mons, mightiest mountain on all the worlds, is high. And because air has weight, because atmosphere flows and the wind blows, gas will fill up the hole. That's the wind that rattles the banners and turns the rotors of West Diggory. As the gas flows the pressure grows, until the day comes when the atmospheric pressure at the bottom of the hole is enough for you to walk around without a psuit, in just your skin if you have the urge and your skin is pretty enough. Earth atmospheric pressure. Pressure, that's always been the problem with making Mars habitable. Get all the gas into one place. When you've got enough of it, turning it into something you can breath is the easy bit. That's just bugs and plants and life.

Thirty kilometers deep. The scooplines are at minus twenty-six kilometers. That's another five M-years before they hit atmospheric baseline. Then they'll level out the floor of the crater, take away some of the sides, expand the flat area, though it will all seem so flat, the atmospheric gradient so subtle, that you will seem to be walking out into breathlessness and light-headedness rather than ascending into it. Fifty years after her In-grandfather Tayhum made the first incision, the Big Dig will be dug. Tash will be seventeen and a half in Earth years when the wind rushing down the sides of the Big Dig finally fails and the rotors stop and the banners fall and the Excavating Cities finally come to a rest.

Twenty-six kilometers up slope, In-aunt Milaba gave the sign for Tash to throw the levers to disengage the diggler from the scoopline. Thus far the big world of outside had been a thumping disappointment to Tash. She had yet to be outside, properly outside, two-figures-in-a-Mars-scape outside, shiver-in-your-psuit outside. She had transited from plastic bubble by plastic tube to plastic bubble connected by its grip on the scoopline to home.

This was what Tash Gelem-Opunyo saw from the transparent bubble of the diggler. Sand sand sand sand sand, a rock there, sand sand sand rock rock, oh, some pebbles! Sand grit sand more grit something between pebble and grit, something between grit and sand, a bit of old abandoned machinery, wow wow wow! Dust drifted up around it. Sand. Sand. Sand. West Diggory was still visible, down the dwindling thread of the scoopline, now truly the size of a spider. The enormous, horizonless perspectives robbed Tash of anything by which she could judge movement. The sand, the buckets, the unchanging gentle gradient that went up halfway to space. Only by squinting down through the floor glass at the blurred, grainy surface did she get any sense of movement.

Twenty-six vertical kilometers equaled two hundred sixty surface kilometers equaled five and a half hours in a plastic bubble with a relative you've grown up in enforced proximity with but until now never really known or talked to. Everyone loves In-aunt Milaba the Magnificent, that's the legend, but after five hours, aunt and niece, Tash began to wonder if this was another wind-whisper legend blown around the corners and crannies of West Diggory. She was beautiful, a feast for the eye and soul, all those things an eight-year-old-girl hopes for herself (and did Tash not share the DNA—given that the Excavating Cities gene pool was shallow as a spit, hence all the careful arrangements of In-relatives and Out-relatives and who would be sent to one of the other Excavating Cities and who would stay), all those things a girl of almost-eight wants for herself, but try as she might, and did, Tash could not engage her. Fancy funny words of the type Tash treasured. Poems. Puns. Riddles. Guessing games. Break-the-code-games. Allusions and circumspect questions. Direct questions. To them all In-aunt Milaba shook her head and smiled and bent over the controls and the monitors and checked her kit and said not a word. So tea, lots of tea, and muttering little rhymes to the rhythm of the huge balloon wheels as the scoopline hauled Diggler Six up the side of the biggest excavation in the solar system.

But now they were released from the scoopline, and Milaba

was standing at the steering column, driving the diggler under its own power. It was still sand sand sand and occasional rock, but Tash knew a gnaw of excitement. She was free, disconnected from the umbilicals of life for the first time. She was out in the wild world. The scoopline dwindled to a thread, to invisibility behind her; ahead she saw a notch on the edge of vision. Windrush Valley. All the windblown words stopped. A flaw in the horizon. A place beyond the Big Dig. Beyond that declivity was the whole curved world. In the silence In-aunt Milaba turned from the control column.

"I think you could have a go now."

So this was what she had been waiting for: Tash to run out of words and finally listen.

The diggler was ridiculously simple to drive. Plant your feet firmly at the drive column. Push forward to feed power to the traction motors in the wheel hubs. Pull back to brake. Yaw to steer. There was even a little holder on the side of the drive column for your tea. Tash giggled with nervous glee as she gingerly pushed forward the stick, and the bubble of pressure glass slung between the giant orange tires stuttered forward. Within thirty seconds she had it. Thirty seconds later she was pushing it, sneaking the speed bar up, looking for places where she could make the diggler skip over rocks.

"I'd go easy on that throttle," Milaba said. "The battery life is eight hours. That's why we ride the scoopline up and down again. You don't want to get stuck up here with night coming down, no traction, and no heat."

Tash eased the stick back, but not before the diggler hit the small boulder at which she had discreetly aimed and bounced all four wheels in the air. Milaba smiled that morning-sun smile. Then shoulder by shoulder they stood at the controls and rode up into the orange valley. The land rose up on either side, higher as they drove deeper, kilometers high. The mountains felt like oppression to Tash, shouldering close and ominous, their heights breathless and haunted with dark things that lived in the sky. At the same time she felt hideously small and exposed in the fragile glass ornament of the diggler. The wind was rising; she could feel the diggler shake on its suspension, hear the shriek and moan through the cables. The controls fought her, but she pushed the little bubble deeper and deeper into Windrush Valley. When her forearms ached and the sinews on her neck stood out from fighting the atmosphere of Mars pouring through this two-kilometer wide notch in Mount Incredible, Milaba leaned over and tapped a preprogrammed course into the computer.

"Suit up," she said. "We'll be there in ten minutes."

The tokamak station was a wind-scoured blister of construction plastic hunkering between a boulder field and a stretch of polished olivine. It was only when the diggler slowed to a stop and fired sand anchors that Tash realized that it was near and smaller than she had thought. It was not a distant vast city; the power plant was only slightly higher than the diggler's mammoth wheels. The wind rotor, spinning as if it would suddenly leap from its pylon and spin madly away through the upper air, was no bigger than her outstretched hands.

"Mask sealed?"

Tash ran her fingers around the join with her psuit hood and give In-aunt Milaba two thumbs up. "I'm DPing the diggler." There was a high pitched shriek of air being vented into the tanks, a whistle that ebbed into silence as the pressure dropped to match the outside environment. The scribbled-over psuit felt tight and stuff. This was true eyeball-squelch altitude. Then Milaba popped the door and Tash followed her out and down the ladder onto the wild surface of Mars.

Gods and teeth, but the wind was brutal. Tash balled her fists and squared her shoulders and lowered her head to battle through it to the yellow and blue chevronned tokamak station. She could feel the sand whipping across the skin of her psuit. She didn't like to think of the semizoic skin abrading, cell by cell. She imagined it wailing in pain. A tap on the shoulder, Milaba gestured for her to hook her safety line onto the door winch. Then In-aunt and In-niece punched through the big wind to the shelter of the tokamak shell. Out. Out in the world. Up high. If Tash kept walking into the wind she would pass through Windrush Valley and come to a place where the world curved away from her, not toward her. The desire to do it was unbearable. Out of the hole. All it would take would be one foot in front of another. They would take her all the way around the world and back again, to this place. The gale of possibility died. It was all only ever circles. Milaba tapped her again on the shoulder to remind her that there was work to be done here. Tash took the unitool and unscrewed the inspection hatch. Milaba plugged in her diagnosticators. She was glorious to watch at work, easy and absorbed. But it was long work and Tash's attention wandered to the little meandering dust-dervishes that spun up into a small tornado for a few seconds, staggered down the valley, and collapsed into swirling sand.

"Willie-willies," Milaba said. "You want to be careful with those, they're tricksy. As I thought." She pointed at the readout. "A hard fail in the chip set." She pulled a new blade out of her thigh pouch and slid it into the control unit. Lights flashed green. Inside its shielded dome the tokamak grumbled and woke up with a shiver that sent the dust rising from the ground. Tash watched the wind whirl into a dozen dust devils dancing around each other. "Just going to check the supply line. You stay here." She headed up the valley along the line of the power cable. The dust devils swirled in toward one another. They merged. They fused. They became one, a true dust demon.

"Looks all right!" In-aunt Milaba called.

"Milaba, I don't like the look . . ." The dust demon spun toward Tash, then at the last moment veered away and tracked up the valley. "Milaba!"

Milaba hesitated. The hesitation was death. The dust demon bore down on her; she tried to throw herself away but it spun over her, lifted her, threw her hard and far, smashed her down onto the smooth polished olivine. Tash saw her faceplate shatter in a spray of shards and water vapor. It was random, it was mad, it was a chance in a billion, it can't happen, it was an affront to order and reason, but it had and there Milaba lay on the hard olivine.

"Oh my gods oh my gods oh my gods!" For a moment Tash was paralyzed, for a moment she did not know what to do, that she could do anything, that she must do something. Then she was running up the valley. The dust demon veered toward Tash. Tash shrieked, then it staggered away, broke itself on the boulders, and spun down to dust again. The psuit would seal automatically, but In-aunt Milaba had moments before her eyeballs froze. "Oh help help help help help," Tash cried, her hands pressed to Milaba's face, trying to will heat into it. Then she saw the red button on the safety line harness. She hit it and was almost jolted off her feet as the winch on the diggler reeled Milaba in. Tash hit the emergency channel.

"This is Diggler Six this is Diggler Six in Windrush Valley. This is an emergency." Of course it is—it's the emergency channel. She tried to calm her voice as the winch lifted the limp Milaba into the air. "We have a suit DP situation. We have a suit DP."

"Hello, Diggler Six. This is Diggory West Emergency Services. Please identify yourself."

"This is Tash Gelem-Opunyo. It's Milaba."

"Tash. Control here." Tash recognised Out-uncle Yoyote's voice. "Get back. Get back here. You should have enough power, we'll send another diggler up the line to meet you, but you, darling, you have to do it. We can't get to you in time. It's up to you. Get back to us. It's all you can do."

Of course. It was. All she could do. No rescue swooping from the skies, in a world where nothing could fly. No speed-star scorching up the slope of the Big Dig in a world where the scoopline was the fastest means of transport. She was on her own.

It took all her strength to swing Milaba through the hatch into the diggler cab and seal the lock. Tash almost popped her faceplate. Almost. She repressurized the diggler. The air shriek built to a painful screech then stopped. But Milaba was so still, so cold. Her face was white with frost where her breath had frozen into her skin. It would never be the same again. Tash knelt, turned her cheek to her In-aunt's lips. A whisper a sigh a suspicion a susurration. She was breathing. But it was cold so cold death cold Mars cold in the diggler. Tash slapped the heater up to the maximum and jigged around the tiny cab. Condensation turned the windows opaque, then cleared. Back. She had to get back. Was there an auto-return program? Where would she find it? Where would she even begin looking? Wasting precious instants, wasting precious instants. Tash took the control column, stamped on the pedal to release the anchors, and engaged the traction motors. Turning was difficult. Turning was scary. Turning forced a small moan of fear when the wind got under the diggler and she felt the right side lift. If it went over here, they were both dead. This was not fun driving. There was no glee, no whee! at every bounce Tash tensed and clenched, fearful that the diggler would roll over and shatter like an egg, smash an axle, any number of new terrors that only appear when your life depends on everything working perfectly. *Come on come on come on.* The battery gauge was dwindling with terrifying speed. This was outside. This was the horizoned world. Where was the scoopline? Surely it hadn't been this far. *Come on come on come on.* A line on the sand. But so far. Power at 12 percent. Where had it gone, what had she used it on? The heating blast? The emergency reP? The burn on the winch? Call home. That would be sensible. That would be the act of a girl with a good head and better sense who did what she was told. But it would use power. Batteries at 7 percent, but now she could see the scoopline, the laden buckets above, the empty buckets below, bucket after bucket after bucket. She drove the diggler on. Matching velocities with the scoopline was teeth-gritting, nerve-stretching work. Tash had to drop the diggler into the space between the buckets and hold exact speed. A push too fast would ride up on the preceding bucket. Too slow and she would be rear-ended by the bucket behind. And ever edging inward, inward, closer to the line as the batteries slid from green to red. Lights flashes. Tash threw the lever. The shackle engaged. Tash rolled away from the drive column to Milaba on the floor.

"Tash." A whisper a sigh a suspicion a susurration.

"It's all right, it's all right, don't talk, we're on the scoopline."

"Tash, are my eyes open?"

"Yes, they are."

A tiny sigh.

"Then I can't see. Tash, talk to me."

"What about?"

"I don't know. Anything. Everything. Just talk to me. We're on the line, did you say?"

"We're on the line. We're going home."

"Five hours then. Talk to me."

So she did. Tash pulled cushions and mats around her into a nest and sat holding her In-aunt's head, and she talked. She talked about her friends and her In-sisters and her Out-sisters and who would go away from West Diggory and who would stay. She talked about boys and how she liked them looking at her but still wanted to be different and special, not to be taken-for-granted, funny Tash, odd Tash. She talked about whether she would marry, which she didn't think she would, not as far as she could see, and what she would do then if she didn't. She talked about the things she loved, like swimming and cooking vegetables and drawing and words words words. She talked about how she loved the sound and shape of words, the sound of them as something quite different from what they meant and how you could put them together to say things that could not possibly be, and how the words came to her, like they were blown on the wind, shaped from wind, the wind brought to life. She talked of these in words that weren't clever or mouth-filling, words said quietly and simply and honestly, saying what she thought and how she felt. Tash saw then a richer lode in words; beyond the beauty of their sounds and shapes and patterns was a deeper beauty of the truth they could shape. They could tell what it was to be Tash

Gelem-Opunyo. Words could fly the banners and turn the rotors of a life. Milaba squeezed her hand and pushed her broken lips into a smile and creased the corner of her white, frost-burned eyes.

The emergency channel chimed. Yoyote had her on visual: they were about twenty kilometers downslope from her. They were coming to get her. They would be safe soon. Well done. And there was other news, news that made his voice sound strange to Tash in Diggler Six, like he was dead and walking and talking and about to cry all at the same time. A command had come in from Iridis Excavation Command, from the High Orbital, ultimately all the way from Earth and the Iridis Development Consortium. There had been a political shift. The faction that was up was down and the faction that was down was up. The Big Dig was canceled.

From here, every way was up. There had been no official announcement from the Council of Diggers for ceremonials or small mournings: in their ones and two, their families and kinship groups and sororities and fraternities the people of West Diggory had decided to share the news that their world was ending, and to see the bottom of it; the base that had been their striving for three generations; the machine head. Dig Zero. Minimum elevation. So they took digglers or rode down the scoopline to the bottom of the Big Dig and looked around them and looked around at the digging heads of the scooplines, stilled and frozen for the first time in memory, buckets filled with their last bite of Mars turned toward the sky. As they grew accustomed to the sights and wonders of the dig head, for not one in fifty of the Excavating Cities' populations worked at the minimum elevation, they saw in the distance, between the black scoopline, groups and families and societies from North Cutter and Southdelving and A.R.E.A. They waved to each other, greeting relatives they had not seen in years; the common channel was a flock of voices. Tash stood with her Raven Sorority sisters. They positioned themselves around her, even queen-bee Leyta. Tash was a brief heroine— perhaps the last one the Big Dig would ever have. In-aunt Milaba had been taken to the main medical facility at A.R.E.A where they were growing new irises for her frost-blinded eyes. Her face would be scarred and patched with ugly white, but her smile would always be beautiful. So the In-sisters and In-cousins stood around Tash, needing to be down at zero but not knowing why, or what to do now. The boys from the Black Obsidian Fraternity waved and came across the sand to join the girls. *So few of us, really,* Tash thought.

"Why?" Out-cousin Sebben asked.

"Environment," said Sweto, and in the same transmission, Qori said "Cost."

"Are they going to take us all back to Earth?" Chunye asked.

"No, they're never going to do that," Haramwe said. He walked with a stick, which made him look like an old man but at the same interesting and attractive. "That would cost too much."

"We couldn't anyway," Sweto said. "The gravity down there would kill us. We can't live anywhere but here. This is our home."

"We're Martians," Tash said. Then she put her hands up to her face mask.

"What are you doing?" Chunye, always the nervous In-cousin, cried in alarm.

"I just want to know," Tash said. "I just want to feel it, like it should be." Three taps, and the faceplate fell into her waiting hands. The air was cold, shakingly cold, and still too thin to breathe, and anyway, to breathe was to die on lungfuls of carbon dioxide, but she could feel the wind, the real wind, the true wind in her face. Tash exhaled gently into the atmosphere gathered at the bottom of the Big Dig. The world still sloped gently away from her, all the way up the sky. Tears would freeze in an instant so she kept them to herself. Then Tash clapped the plate back over her face and fastened it to the psuit hood with her clever fingers.

"So, what do we do now?" whiny Chunye asked. Tash knelt. She pushed her fingers into the soft regolith. What else was there? What else had their ever been? A message had come down from Mount Incredible, from High Orbital, from a world on the other side of the sky, from people who had never seen this, whose horizons were always curved away from them. Who were they to say? What wind blew their words and made them so strong? Here were people, whole cities, an entire civilization, in a hole. This was Mars.

"We do what we know best," Tash said, scooping up pale golden Mars in her gloved hand. "We put it all back again."

IAN MCDONALD lives in Northern Ireland, just outside Belfast. He sold his first story in 1983 and bought a guitar with the proceeds, perhaps the only rock 'n' roll thing he ever did. Since then he's written thirteen novels, three story collections and diverse other pieces, and has been nominated for every major science fiction/ fantasy award—and even won a couple. In his day job he works in television development—where do you think all those dreadful reality shows come from? His current novel is *The Dervish House*, set in near future Istanbul.

He blogs at http://ianmcdonald.livejournal.com.

AUTHOR'S NOTE

A large part of the job of the writer is to remember, and to remember incorrectly. The most interesting ideas come from half-remembered factoids: ones where you can't quite recall where they came from, if you've got them right, if you ever heard them at all, or if you conflated them with other half-remembered factoids. This idea came from something I may have heard, read, seen on the subject of terraforming Mars, the simple, titanic job of making an uninhabitable planet habitable. It may have been a post, a comment, all I remember was that it said dig a big hole. The rest just flows naturally. Of course this appeals to me because it's the most environmentally outrageous way of terraforming a world—or rather, a bit of a world. It somehow seems more environmentally destructive than transforming an entire planet, though if you think about it, it isn't. There's still wild Mars left. So it's a story about how complex it can be growing up in a confined space and how much you can see and what lies over that horizon. It's about learning about disappointments, and how much of life consists of digging holes and then filling them in again.

LARP ON MARS

✦

Chris Roberson

W hen they first found the body, but before they realized whose it was, Ravi was quick to point out that if the other two had listened to *him* they'd still be back home playing Battlesnakes.

"Ri-ight," Penn said, shuffling back and forth, clearly debating with himself whether they should get any closer to the body than they already had. "I forgot. You've *never* had a bad idea."

Whenever things went wrong Ravi was always been quick to say it wasn't his fault. It *had* been his fault that they'd been grounded inside the hab the last time around, though: a fact that he conveniently forgot whenever the subject came up.

"Guys?" Jace shone the light from his helmet lamp at the body, the broken length of plastic with the wrapped-fabric hilt still held in his hand, then looked back to his two friends. "If we count this as treasure, that means the quest is over, right?"

"If it is," Ravi shot back, "we should *totally* share the experience points."

That the three were friends was more a product of proximity than of preference. Still, they made the most of it. During school hours when they were logged onto the classroom, they interacted with students and teachers from all over Mars, but when the bell rang and the school day was over, it was just the three of them. The only other kids living at the O. H. Morton Research Facility down on the southern slopes of the Hellas Planitia were barely out of diapers, like Penn's baby brother and Jace's cousin.

Theoretically they could have interacted online with anyone they wanted, even as far away as Earth if they didn't mind the communication lag, but in practice it wasn't worth the effort. Ravi had tried to maintain a long-distance relationship with one of their classmates, a girl named Claire who lived in the shadow of Olympus Mons on the far side of the planet, but had quickly discovered it was too much trouble to keep going.

For three people pretty much forced by circumstances to be friends, though, they were lucky that they shared as much in common as they did. Jace didn't understand what Ravi liked about the novels of R. R. Bonaventure, and Ravi couldn't *stand* the Thunderskull videos that Penn was always raving about, but by and large they at least *tolerated* each other's interests and passions. And there was one passion in particular that all three of them shared: gaming.

"Okay, okay, we'll go already," Ravi had said, after the other two had voted down his Battlesnakes suggestion. "But if we're going, I'm voting for Boy Detectives."

Jace and Penn hadn't even bothered to deliberate, but replied in unison without hesitation. "Lame."

"Okay, then." Ravi crossed his hands over his thin chest and glared across the clubhouse floor. "What do *you* want to do, then?"

The "clubhouse" was really just a disused corner of one of the older storage zubrins. Their parents had assigned the space to the three friends years ago, probably more to get the kids out of their hair than to reward their good grades, which was the purported justification. It had just been an empty space, dimly lit and powdered with a thin covering of red dust that had worked its way inside through the air lock cycling over countless years. Once the three had outfitted it with tables and chairs lugged through the umbilicus that connected the zubrin to the rest of the habitat and brought in storage containers to hold all of their books, videos, and games, it was more than adequate to their needs.

(Penn's father had kidded them when they were first setting up the clubhouse, asking if they weren't afraid of O. H. Morton's ghost. But they'd already studied early exploration in their Martian history course and knew all about the early settler who'd gone missing during a surveying expedition out on the surface, back when there'd only been a handful of zubrins and unmanned generators on site. And they also knew enough from their Metaphysics & Philosophy course to doubt seriously that the disembodied shade of Oliver Hazard Morton haunted the research facility that now bore his name. Not that it wouldn't have made life a whole lot more interesting if he *did*.)

"How about SuperSpies?" Jace proposed. "We'll be out near the caves, right? So we can use one of them as the setting. Make it the secret volcano base of a mad scientist bent on world domination. It'd be perfect!"

Penn and Ravi exchanged a glance. They both enjoyed a bit of superspy action now and again, but they'd just finished off a *long* campaign of tabletop SuperSpies the day before and were getting a little sick of it.

Jace didn't need it spelled out for him. He could see it in their faces. "Okay, maybe not. . . ." he said, dispirited.

A long silence stretched out as the three considered their options. They'd been gaming together for so long, and so often, that there wasn't much they hadn't already beaten into the ground like tent stakes.

"I've got it!" Penn said, snapping his fingers, a wide grin spreading across his face. "Epic Quest!"

If there was one thing that the three friends shared, in addition to a physical mailing address and a passion for gaming, it was a love of fantasy. Even Penn, who much preferred video to text, had read his way through the core works: Tolkien, Moorcock, Wynne Jones, Nix. And while Jace didn't share Ravi's affection for the novels of Bonaventure, they both devoured any and all fantasy comics they could find: Japanese demon-slayer manga, Australian sword-and-sorcery comics, Finnish adventure-fantasy albums. If it involved magic or monsters, sorcery or swords, elves or vampires, or any combination of the sort, it was golden in their eyes.

And those games that managed to combine their love of fantasy and their passion for gaming? Those weren't just golden, those were *iridium*. Real-time strategy games, turn-based combat, virtual simulators, and tabletop spoken-word role-play. Puzzle-based spell games, hack-and-slash melees, hunt-and-seek dungeon crawls, and magicians' duels in unreal realms.

But best of all were those rare games that allowed them to get out of the habs and onto the surface—albeit in constrictive "walker" suits—to get up and *move* for a change, away from the stale recirculated air of the clubhouse. And best of *those* was the *LARPing*.

"Okay, we should just keep this simple," Ravi had said as the trio trekked south toward the lava-tube caves. "I'll take a few pics while you two make some quick observations, and then we're good to go."

The assignment from their science class had only called for them to do a research paper on some geological feature of the Martian surface. It could have been as easy as doing a few minutes worth of searching online and then cobbling together a hasty few paragraphs. And under normal circumstances, that would have been precisely what they'd have done. Another thing the three friends had in common was that science was their *least* favorite subject in school, and one or more of them was always in danger of flunking at any given time. This semester, in fact, all three of them had stayed right at the borderline between pass and fail, which was one of the principal motivations for taking on the extra-credit portion of the assignment.

The *other* reason, though, was that the extra-credit required them to go *outside*.

"How come *you* get to take the pics?" Jace asked, struggling a bit with the awkward load of the three plastic swords he carried. "You didn't even want to *do* this, remember?"

"Right!" Penn said. "And as the GM, shouldn't *I* be the one to scout the area in advance?"

It was true, as Game Master that *was* Penn's prerogative. More than that, though, was a fact that none of them seemed to feel it was worth saying out loud. Namely, that they wouldn't even *need* to do an extra-credit school assignment to go outside if not for Ravi, and the disaster that their *last* LARPing outing had turned into.

"Okay, okay," Ravi said, holding up his gloved hands in surrender. "You take the pics, Penn. Satisfied?"

Jace, as the injured party in the last LARPing outing, grumbled a bit under his breath that it really should have been *him* with the cushy job, but he didn't care enough to start a fight over it.

They'd been grounded in the hab ever since Jace got a rip in his walker during their last LARPing campaign. They'd been doing a round of Ninjas & Samurai that time around, using long lengths of metal wrenched off some disused shelving as makeshift swords, and everything had been going fine until Penn zigged when he should have zagged, putting more force behind a parry than was actually necessary, and his "sword" whacked hard against Jace's upper arm. The rip in the constrictive fabric of Jace's walker went from his shoulder down past his elbow, and by the time the three of them were back through the air locks into the habitat, the low air pressure outside had raised a wicked bruise down the length of Jace's arm that took *months* to heal fully.

It could have been worse, though. If they'd been up on the dunes out toward Barnard when the walker got cut, Jace might not have survived long enough to make it back to the habitat.

The unanimous order from their parents had been that there was to be no more "monkeying around" outside. (Jace tried to explain to his mother that they weren't "playing," but had been "gaming," a subtle but distinct difference. She didn't seem particularly swayed by the argument.) But it wasn't like the three friends had to be told twice. The whole thing had freaked them out pretty good, Jace especially. So for a long time, several months in fact, they'd stayed inside the habitat in their free time, meeting in the clubhouse to game, read, and watch videos.

But they could only watch so many episodes of their favorite anime series, or hit the dee on their palmtops to see if they made their saving throw so many times before it all began to wear a little thin.

Only the fact that one or all of them might fail science if they weren't able to do some primary research out on the surface meant that they weren't still cooped up inside.

Even so, the makeshift swords that they'd be using for this campaign *weren't* made out of metal. They'd learned *that* lesson already. Instead, they'd used pliant plastic cut from the lids of storage containers, too blunted and soft even to scrape the fabric of their walkers, much less cut through.

And to be on the safe side, they'd brought three complete patch kits, just in case.

"That should do it," Penn said, switching his helmetcam from static back to standby. "You guys got what you need?"

Ravi and Jace were sprawled on the red sands near the entrance to the largest of the caves. "Yeah, yeah," Ravi said, waving his hand dismissively. "'Lava tubes are formed when the tops and sides of a lava flow cool faster the interior, then the interior lava pours out and a hollow tube is left behind, blah-blah-blah.' We *got* it already."

Jace tapped the side of his helmet. "We should have enough." Once they got back home, their palmtops would transcribe into text everything they'd recorded on their helmet mics, and they could simply cobble the text together with Penn's images and they'd be done.

"Then I think we're ready to start." Penn rubbed his gloved hands together, a wicked smile on his face.

"I'm *hungry*," Ravi said.

The other two ignored him. They'd all known going in that all they'd have to drink was stale recirc from the packs on their backs, and that eating would be out of the question unless they wanted to lug a pressure tent out with them and go to the trouble of putting it up. The chance to do whatever they wanted was *well* worth the price of skipping a meal.

"Ready when you are, Penn." Jace climbed to his feet, dusting red sand off his legs and backside.

"Yeah, okay," Ravi said, standing up slowly. "Let's get to it."

Penn picked up the wrapped-handled plastic swords and passed them out to the group. "What we're looking at today is a dungeon crawl, plain and simple."

"Seriously?" Jace arched an eyebrow behind his helmet's face shield.

"Ah," Penn answered, his grin growing even more wicked. "But this is a dungeon crawl with a *twist*."

He paused a beat, while the other two looked on, waiting for him to continue.

"Two words, guys," Penn said triumphantly. "*Zombie ninjas.*"

As the only three kids anywhere near their age at O. H. Morton, they tended to get on one anothers' nerves from time to time. There were even occasions when they stopped speaking to one another, either collectively or in all possible permutations of any two of them, but those occasions were more the exception than the rule. And in another year or so when they went their separate ways, they all knew that they'd miss these days, if only a little.

Ravi would be heading to Earth for college—provided he didn't flunk science—and had already been accepted by Addis Ababa University in Ethiopia. Penn talked about going to Australia and trying to break into the video business, but didn't have any concrete plans yet. Jace dreamed about becoming a big-time manga star, in Japan maybe, or Finland, but secretly suspected that he'd probably just stay at home on Mars.

Penn had modded some graphics from the online Return of Sauron game, skinned them over logics he'd frankensteined together from a hundred different sources, and was transmitting them directly from the palmtop clipped at his waist to the heads-up displays in everyone's helmets. With their plastic swords tagged as virtual artifacts as well as physical objects, the trio could interact directly with the non-player characters who shambled toward them, parrying the virtual swords of the zombie ninjas with the plastic ones in their own hands. The lack of force-feedback in the lengths of inert plastic meant that the three couldn't *feel* the impacts, but this *was* role-playing, after all.

"Okay," Penn said as they moved deeper into the cave, having fended off the last round of NPC attackers, "now you smell a foul, acrid stench from up ahead that makes your eyes water and sting."

"Can I identify the origin?" Jace asked.

"What's your Perception?" Penn answered.

"Plus Three."

Penn thought for a brief moment. "You'd need to roll a nine."

Jace tapped the palmtop on his belt and scowled as the results of the dee flashed on the corner of everyone's helmet display, a three and a four.

"No," Penn answered, suppressing a grin, "you can't identify the origin."

"I'm preparing magic missile," Ravi said.

Penn sighed. Whenever in doubt, Ravi *always* went with magic missile.

"Okay," he answered, "but that means you lose the initiative."

Ravi grinned. "'That, my friend, is a risk I'm willing to take.'"

"Don't." Jace stopped short, holding up his hand.

"What?" Ravi and Penn turned in his direction.

"Just *don't*, okay. I swear, if you start quoting from Bonaventure novels again, you won't *stop*."

"It's true, Ravi," Penn said. "Last time, I wanted to beat you to death with a chair when you started that crap."

"Fine!" Ravi threw his arms in the air in frustration, the tip of his plastic sword almost reaching the roof of the lava tube overhead. "But I'm still preparing magic missile."

"Shall we continue?" Penn motioned ahead. "And I'll point out that it's getting darker, the deeper into the cave you go." The light from the opening behind them barely reached this far in, and from this point onward they'd need to rely on their helmet lamps.

"Okay," Jace said, switching on his lamp. "I'm lighting a torch and continuing into the cave."

"The scent grows stronger as you proceed," Penn said as they walked on. "Smelling of death and decay."

"Um, guys?" Ravi said as soon as he switched on his own helmet lamp. "Either Penn's graphics are getting *way* better than I thought, or there's something up ahead."

✳ ✳ ✳

And that's when they found the body.

At first, they didn't know whose body it was, and Ravi started in on Battlesnakes again.

"Who is it, do you think?" Penn asked, ignoring Ravi's demand for experience points.

It was a dead person, there was no question about that. The face seen through the helmet's faceplate was like one of the mummies in *Tomb Raiders of the Lost Pyramid*, desiccated and leathery, pulled taut over the bones of the cheek and forehead, lips curled back over a grimacing death grin.

"It's nobody from O. H. Morton, that's for sure," Jace said. The full population of the research facility numbered only in the dozens, and if anyone had disappeared on the surface it was sure the three would have heard about it. "Maybe a researcher from one of the other stations?"

The walker worn by the dead person—the dead *man*, it seemed, given the physique and size of the body—had a large cut in it that went from the right shoulder all the way down to the left hip, continuing a few handspans down the left leg. The three friends knew at a glance that so much flesh exposed to the lower atmospheric pressure on the surface wouldn't just leave a bruise, but would have killed the man in relatively short order.

But there was something odd about the dead man's walker, too, in addition to the clearly fatal tear.

"Look over there," Ravi said, shining his lamp farther down the cave. There was a metal assemblage about twice the length of one of their plastic swords, a kind of tripod with a swivel mount on top. A few steps away was a large piece of machinery, clearly damaged, that seemed to have fallen from the tripod and rolled off a short distance.

"Maybe he was setting that thing up, and when that—whatever that thing is—fell off, it hit him and ripped his walker?"

Before either of the other two could answer, a host of zombie ninjas swarmed out of the darkness, swinging their blades overhead and moaning for blood and brains.

"Penn, do you mind?" Jace looked up from the dead man's body with an annoyed expression on his face.

"Sorry," Penn said sheepishly, and then tapped his palmtop to shut down the NPCs altogether.

"How long do you think he's been down here?" Jace said, once the zombie ninjas had disappeared from view. In the thin, dry atmosphere of Mars things tended to rot very, *very* slowly. When they were just kids, the three had done an experiment in their science class where they left a sandwich, an orange, and various other organics out on the surface and then charted the course of decay and decomposition over time. It had been a few years, but so far the food looked pretty much like it had the day they put it out.

"A *long* time," Penn answered. "I mean, look at that walker he's wearing. Doesn't have a built-in recirc system, and check out the helmet lamp. That's a *halogen* bulb. When was the last time you saw one of *those*?"

Ravi was still looking back and forth between the broken machinery and the dead man, a look of extreme concentration on his face. "Um, guys?"

The other two glanced in his direction.

"I don't think that he was *from* O. H. Morton. I think that he *was* O. H. Morton."

A silence fell over the three friends as they considered the idea, staring down at the dead man in the antique walker.

"Wow," Jace said in a quiet voice.

"Guys, if that *is* . . ." Penn began, then faltered. "I mean . . . He was born on Earth, right? He was one of the first settlers on Mars. One of the *pioneers*."

"The trip back then took *ages*," Ravi said in breathless wonder. "They used to use . . . use . . . what where those things called again?"

"Hohmann transfer orbit," Jace said, after a few moments' thought. He was the farthest from the pass-fail borderline in their science class, largely because he'd reluctantly done an extra-credit assignment on transit times between Mars and the other celestial bodies early in the semester. "They used to call it 'The Long Way Around.' Now they use . . . um . . . wait a minute, um . . . *brachisto-chrone* trajectories, where the ship just flies straight at the destination, accelerating full out the first half of the trip and decelerating the rest of the way. But back then it didn't take two weeks to get here from Earth, but nearly two *years*."

"And when they got here," Penn said, "there was nothing *here*. No habs, nothing."

"There were the zubrins they sent ahead," Ravi said. "With the automated factories already manufacturing oxygen and water and stuff."

"Yeah, but no *people*," Penn answered.

"Wow," Ravi said, whistling low. "They must have gotten *bored*."

"I don't know, guys." Jace was thoughtful. "Sounds kind of . . . *cool*."

They considered trying to carry the body back to the hab, and possibly the old broken machinery as well, but none of them looked forward to the long walk lugging the awkward load. In the end, they called ahead to their parents, told them what they'd found, and started back.

By the time they got back home, it was already a big deal. In the end, they didn't even have to write their extra-credit report on surface geology, but got full marks just for telling the class about their experience in the cave. (Luckily, Penn had thought to take a few pics of the body and the machinery, which saved them a lot of description.)

The governor of Mars came down from the capital for the dedication ceremony of the new historical landmark, and the three were made to pose with him in front of the remains of the long-lost explorer. When the pics and video of the ceremony were posted online, along with a heavily edited version of their school report, the three became celebrities, for a few hours at least, mentioned in posts from as far away as Earth and even Titan.

By the following week, though, things went back to normal, and everyone seemed mostly to have forgotten the whole thing. But the three friends hadn't.

"So what do you guys want to do?" Ravi asked, putting his palmtop down on the table. He'd just finished Jeremy Stone's *Termination Shock*, about interstellar explorers of the far future, and had to admit grudgingly that he might like it better than Bonaventure's fantasy epics.

"We could watch another episode of *Space Man*," Penn suggested from the other side of the clubhouse. He'd become *obsessed* with the Australian adventure anime *The Adventures of Space Man* in the last few days and couldn't shut up about it.

"Yeah, maybe," Jace said, looking up from his palmtop. He'd

been spending all of his free time on extra-credit assignments for their science class, and when the instructor ran out of work for him to do Jace had started reading his way through the library. For days, he'd been boring everyone with the latest tidbit about quantum computing that he'd just read. "It's kind of repetitive, though. Maybe some gaming?"

The other two brightened at the suggestion, but their enthusiasm dimmed when the debate about just what game to play dragged out into interminable indecision. None of the old games really interested anyone. They all just seemed so . . . *boring*.

"Oh, hey!" Jace said, after another lingering silence. "I got a mail from this kid online about a new role-playing game we could check out. Earth Force Z?"

"Based on the manga?" Ravi asked.

"Yeah," Jace answered. The long-running manga series was all about the space forces of a future Earth defending the solar system against the predations of an invading alien armada. "The science in the manga isn't as good as it could be, but the ship designs are pretty cool."

Ravi shrugged. "Sure, why not?"

Penn sat up, looking interested. "Let's give it a shot."

The three friends dragged their chairs over to the table while Jace called up the rules and game stats on his palmtop. There were complications involved in computing orbital trajectories in the game mechanics, it seemed, but they'd get the hang of it soon enough. It was only science, after all.

For the moment, at least, fantasy was just not going to be enough.

CHRIS ROBERSON has worked as a baker, taught middle school history, been a product support engineer, and given change at an arcade. His work is heavily influenced by the pulp adventure classics of the 1940s and 1950s. He has published a number of books, including *Here, There & Everywhere*; *Set the Seas on Fire*; *The Dragon's Nine Sons*; *End of the Century*; *Iron Jaw and Hummingbird*; *Three Unbroken*; and the comic book series Cinderella: From Fabletown with Love and I, Zombie.

He has been a finalist for the World Fantasy Award four times—once each for writing and editing, and twice for publishing—twice a finalist for the John W. Campbell Award for Best New Writer, and four times for the Sidewise Award for Best Alternate History (winning the Short Form in 2004 with his story "O One" and the Long Form in 2008 with his novel *The Dragon's Nine Sons*). Chris and his wife, Allison Baker, live in Austin, Texas, with their daughter, Georgia.

His Web site is www.chrisroberson.net.

AUTHOR'S NOTE

I grew up in Texas, in a landscape dotted with relics and reminders of the days when the area had been a frontier. But my friends and I didn't have any real interest in pioneer days, or "cowboys and Indians," or anything to do with the history that surrounded us. We were more interested in superhero comics and Japanese anime and role-playing games. Thinking about the kids who might one day grow up on a colonized Mars, I realized that they probably wouldn't be any more interested in their pioneering ancestors than my friends and I had been about the Europeans who had settled our state (or the Native Americans they displaced). But they should be interested, just like we should have been.

MARTIAN HEART

John Barnes

Okay, botterogator, I agreed to this. Now you're supposed to guide me to tell my story to *inspire a new generation of Martians*. It is so weird that there *is* a new generation of Martians. So hit me with the questions, or whatever it is you do.

Do I want to be *consistent with previous public statements*?

Well, every time they ask me where I got all the money and got to be such a big turd in the toilet that is Mars, I always say Samantha was my inspiration. So let's check that box for tentatively consistent.

Thinking about Sam always gives me weird thoughts. And here are two: one, before her, I would not have known what either *tentatively* or *consistent* even meant. Two, in these pictures, Samantha looks younger than my granddaughter is now.

So weird. She *was*.

We were in bed in our place under an old underpass in LA when the sweeps busted in, grabbed us up, and dragged us to the processing station. No good lying about whether we had family—they had our retinas and knew we were strays. Since I was seventeen and Sam was fifteen, they couldn't make any of our family pay for re-edj.

So they gave us fifteen minutes on the bench there to decide between twenty years in the forces, ten years in the glowies, or going out to Mars on this opposition and coming back on the third one after, in six and a half years.

They didn't tell you, and it wasn't well-known, that even people without the genetic defect suffered too much cardiac atrophy in that time to safely come back to Earth. The people that went to Mars didn't have family or friends to write back to, and the settlement program was so new it didn't seem strange that nobody knew a returned Martian.

"Crap," I said.

"Well, at least it's a future." Sam worried about the future a lot more than me. "If we enlist, there's no guarantee we'll be assigned together, unless we're married, and they don't let you get married till you've been in for three. We'd have to write each other letters—"

"Sam," I said, "I can't write to you or read your letters if you send me any. You know that."

"They'd make you learn."

I tried not to shudder visibly; she'd get mad if I let her see that I didn't really want to learn. "Also, that thing you always say about out of sight, that'd happen. I'd have another girlfriend in like, not long. I just would. I know we're all true love and everything but I would."

"The spirit is willing but the flesh is *more* willing." She always made those little jokes that only she got. "Okay, then, no forces for us."

"Screw glowies," I said. Back in those days right after the baby nukes had landed all over the place, the Decon Admin needed people to operate shovels, hoes, and detectors. I quoted this one hook from our favorite music. *"Sterile or dead or kids with three heads."*

"And we *can* get married going to Mars," Sam said, "and then they *can't* separate us. True love forever, baby." Sam always had all the ideas.

So, botterogator, check that box for *putting a priority on family/love*. I guess since that new box popped up as soon as I said, *Sam always had all the ideas,* that means you want more about that? Yeah, now it's bright and bouncing. Okay, more about how she had all the ideas.

Really all the ideas I ever had were about eating, getting high, and scoring ass. Hunh. Red light. Guess that wasn't what you wanted for the new generation of Martians.

Sam was different. Everybody I knew was thinking about the next party or at most the next week or the next boy or girl, but Sam thought about *everything.* I know it's a stupid example, but once back in LA, she came into our squat and found me fucking with the fusion box, just to mess with it. "That supplies all our power for music, light, heat, net, and everything, and you can't fix it if you break it, and it's not broke, so, Cap, what the fuck are you doing?"

See, I didn't even have ideas *that* good.

So a year later, there on the bench, our getting married was her having another idea and me going along with it, which was always how things worked, when they worked. Ten minutes later we registered as married.

Orientation for Mars was ten days. The first day they gave us shots, bleached our tats into white blotches on our skin, and shaved our heads. They stuck us in ugly dumb coveralls and didn't let us have real clothes that said anything, which they said was so we wouldn't know who'd been what on Earth. I think it was more so we all looked like transportees.

The second day, and every day after, they tried to pound some knowledge into us. It was almost interesting. Sam was in with the people that could read, and she seemed to know more than I did afterward. Maybe there was something to that reading stuff, or it might also have been that freaky, powerful memory of hers.

Once we were erased and oriented, they loaded Sam and me into a two-person cube on a dumpround to Mars. Minutes after the booster released us and we were ballistic, an older guy, some asshole, tried to come into our cube and tell us this was going to be his space all to himself, and I punched him hard enough to take him out; I don't think he had his balance for centrifigrav yet.

Two of his buds jumped in. I got into it with them too—I was hot, they were pissing me off, I wasn't figuring odds. Then some guys from the cubes around me came in with me, and together we beat the other side's ass bloody.

In the middle of the victory whooping, Sam shouted for quiet. She announced, "Everyone stays in their same quarters. Everyone draws their own rations. Everyone takes your turn, and *just* your turn, at the info screens. And nobody doesn't pay for protection or nothing."

One of the assholes, harmless now because I had at least ten good guys at my back, sneered, "Hey, little bitch. You running for Transportee Council?"

"Sure, why not?"

She won too.

The Transportee Council stayed in charge for the whole trip. People ate and slept in peace, and no crazy-asses broke into the server array, which is what caused most lost dumprounds. They told us in orientation, but a lot of transportees didn't listen, or didn't understand, or just didn't believe that a dumpround didn't have any fuel to go back to Earth; a dumpround flew like a cannon ball, with just a few little jets to guide it in and out of the aerobrakes and steer it to the parachute field.

The same people who thought there was a steering wheel in the server array compartment, or maybe a reverse gear or just a big button that said TAKE US BACK TO EARTH, didn't know that the server array also ran the air-making machinery and the food dispensary and everything that kept people alive.

I'm sure we had as many idiots as any other dumpround, but we made it just fine; that was all Sam, who ran the TC and kept the TC running the dumpround. The eighty-eight people on International Mars Transport 2082/4/288 (which is what they called our dumpround; it was the 288th one fired off that April) all walked out of the dumpround on Mars carrying our complete, unlooted kits, and the militia that always stood by in case a dumpround landing involved hostages, arrests, or serious injuries didn't have a thing to do about us.

The five months in the dumpround were when I learned to read, and that has helped me so much—oh, hey, another box bumping up and down! Okay, botterogator, literacy as a positive value coming right up, all hot and ready for the new generation of Martians to suck inspiration from.

Hey, if you don't like irony, don't flash red lights at me, just edit it out. Yeah, authorize editing.

Anyway, with my info screen time, Sam made me do an hour of reading lessons for every two hours of games. Plus she coached me a lot. After a while the reading was more interesting than the games, and she was doing TC business so much of the time, and I didn't really have any other friends, so I just sat and worked on the reading. By the time we landed, I'd read four actual books, not just kid books I mean.

We came down on the parachute field at Olympic City, an over-dignified name for what, in those long-ago days, was just two office buildings, a general store, and a nine-room hotel connected by pressurized tubes. The tiny pressurized facility was surrounded by a few thousand coffinsquats hooked into its pay air and power, and many thousand more running on their own fusion boxes. Olympica, to the south, was just a line of bluffs under a slope reaching way up into the sky.

It was the beginning of northern summer prospecting season. Sam towed me from lender to lender, coaching me on looking like a good bet to someone that would trust us with a share-deal on a prospecting gig. At the time I just thought rocks were, you know, rocks. No idea that some of them were ores, or that Mars was so poor in so many ores because it was dead tectonically.

So while she talked to bankers, private lenders, brokers, and plain old loan sharks, I dummied up and did my best to look like what she told them I was, a hard worker who would do what Sam told me. "Cap is quiet but he thinks, and we're a team."

She said that so often that after a while I believed it myself. Back at our coffinsquat every night, she'd make me do all the tutorials and read like crazy about rocks and ores. Now I can't remember how it was to not know something, like not being able to read, or recognize ore, or go through a balance sheet, or anything else I learned later.

Two days till we'd've gone into the labor pool and been shipped south to build roads and impoundments, and this CitiWells franchise broker, Hsieh Chi, called us back, and said we just felt lucky to him, and he had a quota to make, so what the hell.

Sam named our prospector gig the *Goodspeed* after something she'd read in a poem someplace, and we loaded up, got going, did what the software told us, and did okay that first summer around the North Pole, mostly.

Goodspeed was old and broke down continually, but Sam was a good directions-reader, and no matter how frustrating it got, I'd keep trying to do what she was reading to me—sometimes we both had to go to the dictionary, I mean who knew what a flange, a fairing, or a flashing was?—and sooner or later we'd get it figured out and roll again.

Yeah, botterogator, you can check that box for persistence in the face of adversity. Back then I'd've said I was just too dumb to quit if Sam didn't, and Sam was too stubborn.

Up there in the months and months of midnight sun, we found ore, and learned more and more about telling ore from not-ore. The gig's hopper filled up, gradually, from surface rock finds. Toward the end of that summer—it seemed so weird that Martian summers were twice as long as on Earth even after we read up about why— we even found an old volcanic vent and turned up some peridot, agate, amethyst, jasper, and garnet, along with three real honest-to-god impact diamonds that made us feel brilliant. By the time we got back from the summer prospecting, we were able to pay off Hsieh Chi's shares, with enough left over to buy the gig and put new treads on it. We could spare a little to rehab the cabin too; *Goodspeed* went from our dumpy old gig to our home, I guess. At least in Sam's mind. I wasn't so sure that home meant a lot to me.

Botterogator if you want me to inspire the new generation of Martians, you have to let me tell the truth. Sam cared about having a home, I didn't. You can flash your damn red light. It's true.

Anyway, while the fitters rebuilt *Goodspeed*, we stayed in a rented cabinsquat, sleeping in, reading, and eating food we didn't cook. We soaked in the hot tub at the Riebecker Olympic every single day—the only way Sam got warm. Up north, she had thought she was cold all the time because we were always working, she was small, and she just couldn't keep weight on no matter how much she ate, but even loafing around Olympic City, where the most vigorous thing we did was nap in the artificial sun room, or maybe lift a heavy spoon, she still didn't warm up.

We worried that she might have pneumonia or TB or something she'd brought from Earth, but the diagnostic machines found nothing unusual except being out of shape. But Sam had been doing so much hard physical work, her biceps and abs were like rocks, she was *strong*. So we gave up on the diagnosis machines, because that made no sense.

Nowadays everyone knows about "Martian heart," but back then nobody knew that hearts atrophy and deposit more plaque in lower gravity as the circulation slows down and the calcium that should be depositing into bones accumulates in the blood. Let alone that maybe a third of the human race have genes that make it happen so fast.

At the time, with no cases identified, it wasn't even a research subject; so many people got sick and died in the first couple decades of settlement, often in their first Martian year, and to the diagnostic machines it was all a job, ho hum, another day, another skinny nine-teen-year-old dead of a heart attack. Besides, *all* the transportees, not just the ones that died, ate so much carb-and-fat food, because it was cheap. Why *wouldn't* there be more heart attacks? There were always more transportees coming, so put up another site about healthful eating for Mars, and find something else to worry about.

Checking the diagnosis machine was everything we could afford to do, anyway, but it seemed like only a small, annoying worry. After all, we'd done well, bought our own gig, were better geared up, knew more what we were doing. We set out with pretty high hopes.

Goodspeed was kind of a dumb name for a prospector's gig. At best it could make maybe 40 km/hr, which is not what you call roaring fast. Antarctic summer prospecting started with a long, dull drive down to Promethei Lingula, driving south out of northern autumn and into southern spring. The Interpolar Highway in those days was a gig track weaving southward across the shield from Olympic City to the Great Marineris Bridge. There was about 100 km of pavement, sort of, before and after the bridge, and then another gig track angling southeast to wrap around Hellas, where a lot of surface prospectors liked to work, and there was a fair bit of seasonal construction to be done on the city they were building in the western wall.

But we were going far south of Hellas. I asked Sam about that. "If you're cold all the time, why are we going all the way to the edge of the south polar cap? I mean, wouldn't it be nicer to maybe work the Valles Marineris or someplace near the equator, where you could stay a little warmer?"

"Cap, what's the temperature in here, in the gig cabin?"

"Twenty-two C," I said, "do you feel cold?"

"Yeah, I do, and that's my point," she said. I reached to adjust the temperature, and she stopped me. "What I mean is, that's room temperature, babe, and it's the same temperature it is in my suit, and in the fingers and toes of my suit, and everywhere. The cold isn't outside, and it doesn't matter whether it's the temperature of a warm day on Earth or there's CO_2 snow falling, the cold's in here, in me, ever since we came to Mars."

The drive was around 10,000 km as the road ran, but mostly it was pleasant, just making sure the gig stayed on the trail as we rolled past the huge volcanoes, the stunning view of Marineris from that hundred-mile-long bridge, and then all that ridge and peak country down south.

Mostly Sam slept while I drove. Often I rested a hand on her neck or forehead as she dozed in the co-driver's chair. Sometimes she shivered; I wondered if it was a long-running flu. I made her put on a mask and get extra oxygen, and that helped, but every few weeks I had to up her oxygen mix again.

All the way down I practiced pronouncing Promethei Lingula, especially after we rounded Hellas, because Sam looked a little sicker every week, and I was so afraid she'd need help and I wouldn't be able to make a distress call.

Sam figured Promethei Lingula was too far for most people—they'd rather pick through Hellas's or Argyre's crater walls, looking for chunks of something worthwhile thrown up from deep underground in those impacts, and of course the real gamblers always wanted to work Hellas because one big Hellas Diamond was five years' income.

Sam already knew what it would take me fifteen marsyears to learn: she believed in making a good bet that nobody else was making. Her idea was that a shallow valley like the Promethei Lingula in the Antarctic highlands might have more stuff swept down by the glaciers, and maybe even some of the kinds of exposed veins that really old mountains had on Earth.

As for what went wrong, well, nothing except our luck; nowadays I own three big veins down there. No, botterogator, I don't feel like telling you a damned thing about what I own, you're authorized to just look all that up. I don't see that owning stuff is inspiring. I want to talk about Sam.

We didn't find any veins, or much of anything else, that first southern summer. And meanwhile Sam's health deteriorated.

By the time we were into Promethei Lingula, I was fixing most meals and doing almost all the maintenance. After the first weeks I did all the exosuit work, because her suit couldn't seem to keep her warm, even on hundred percent oxygen. She wore gloves and extra socks even inside. She didn't move much, but her mind was as good as ever, and with her writing the search patterns and me going out and grabbing the rocks, we could still've been okay.

Except we needed to be as lucky as we'd been up in Boreas, and we just weren't.

Look here, botterogator, you can't make me say luck had nothing to do with it. Luck always has a shitload to do with it. Keep this quibbling up and just see if I inspire *any* new Martians.

Sometimes there'd be a whole day when there wasn't a rock that was worth tossing in the hopper, or I'd cover a hundred km of nothing but common basalts and granites. Sam thought her poor concentration made her write bad search patterns, but it wasn't that; it was plain bad luck.

Autumn came, and with it some dust storms and a sun that spiraled closer to the horizon every day, so that everything was dimmer. It was time to head north; we could sell the load, such as it was, at the depot at Hellas, but by the time we got to the Bouches de Marineris, it wouldn't cover more than a few weeks of prospecting. We might have to mortgage again; Hsieh Chi, unfortunately, was in the Vikingsburg pen for embezzling. "Maybe we could hustle someone, like we did him."

"Maybe *I* could, babe," Sam said. "You know the business a lot better, but you're still nobody's sales guy, Cap. We've got food enough for another four months out here, and we still have credit because we're working and we haven't had to report our hold weight. Lots of gigs stay out for extra time—some even overwinter—and nobody can tell whether that's because they're way behind like us, or they've found a major vein and they're exploiting it. So we can head back north, use up two months of supplies to get there, buy about a month of supplies with the cargo, go on short term credit only, and try to get lucky in one month. Or we can stay here right till we have just enough food to run for the Hellas depot, put in four months, and have four times the chance. If it don't work *Goodspeed*'ll be just as lost either way."

"It's going to get dark and cold," I pointed out. "Very dark and cold. And you're tired and cold all the time now."

"Dark and cold *outside the cabin*," she said. Her face had the stubborn set that meant this was going to be useless. "And maybe the dark'll make me eat more. All the perpetual daylight, maybe that's what's screwing my system up. We'll try the Bouches du Marineris next time, maybe those nice regular equatorial days'll get my internal clock working again. But for right now, let's stay here. Sure, it'll get darker, and the storms can get bad—"

"Bad as in we could get buried, pierced by a rock on the wind, maybe even flipped if the wind gets in under the hull," I pointed out. "Bad as in us and the sensors can only see what the spotlights can light. There's a reason why prospecting is a summer job."

She was quiet about that for so long I thought a miracle had happened and I'd won an argument.

Then she said, "Cap, I like it here in *Goodspeed*. It's home. It's ours. I know I'm sick, and all I can do these days is sleep, but I don't want to go to some hospital and have you only visit on your days off from a labor crew. *Goodspeed* is ours and I want to live here and try to keep it."

So I said yes.

For a while things got better. The first fall storms were water snow, not CO_2. I watched the weather reports and we were always buttoned up tight for every storm, screens out and treads sealed against the fine dust. In those brief weeks between midnight sun and endless night, when the sun rises and sets daily in the Promethei Lingula, the thin coat of snow and frost actually made the darker rocks stand out on the surface, and there were more good ones to find too.

Sam was cold all the time; sometimes she'd cry with just wanting to be warm. She'd eat, when I stood over her and made her, but she had no appetite. I also knew how she thought: food was the bottleneck. A fusion box supplied centuries of power to move, to compress and process the Martian air into breathability, to extract and purify water. But we couldn't grow food, and unlike spare parts or medical care we might need now and then, we needed food every day, so food would be the thing we ran out of first. (Except maybe luck, and we were already out of that). Since she didn't want the food anyway, she thought if she didn't eat we could stay out and give our luck more of a chance to turn.

The sun set for good; so far south, Phobos was below the horizon; cloud cover settled in to block the stars. It was darker than anywhere I'd ever been. We stayed.

There was more ore in the hold but not enough more. Still no vein. We had a little luck at the mouth of one dry wash with a couple tons of ore in small chunks, but it played out in less than three weeks.

Next place that looked at all worth trying was 140 km south, almost at the edge of the permanent cap, crazy and scary to try, but what the hell, everything about this was crazy and scary.

The sky had cleared for the first time in weeks when we arrived. With just a little CO_2 frost, it was easy to find rocks—the hot lights zapped the dry ice right off them. I found one nice big chunk of wolfenite, the size of an old trunk, right off the bat, and then two smaller ones; somewhere up the glacial slopes from here, there was a vein, perhaps not under permanent ice. I started the analytic program mapping slopes and finds, and went out in the suit to see if I could find and mark more rocks.

Markeb, which I'd learned to pick out of the bunched triangles of the constellation Vela, was just about dead overhead; it's the south pole star on Mars. It had been a while since I'd seen the stars, and I'd learned more about what I was looking at. I picked out the Coal Sack, the Southern Cross, and the Magellanic Clouds easily, though honestly, on a clear night at the Martian south pole, that's like being able to find an elephant in a bathtub.

I went inside; the analysis program was saying that probably the wolfenite had come from way up under the glacier, so no luck there, but also that there might be a fair amount of it lying out here in the alluvial fan, so at least we'd pick up something here. I stood up from the terminal; I'd fix dinner, then wake Sam, feed her, and tell her the semi-good news.

When I came in with the tray, Sam was curled up, shivering and crying. I made her eat all her soup and bread, and plugged her in to breathe straight body-temperature oxygen. When she was feeling better, or at least saying she was, I took her up into the bubble to look at the stars with the lights off. She seemed to enjoy that, especially that I could point to things and show them to her, because it meant I'd been studying and learning.

Yeah, botterogator, reinforce that learning leads to success. Sam'd like that.

"Cap," she said, "this is the worst it's been, babe. I don't think there's anything on Mars that can fix me. I just keep getting colder and weaker. I'm so sorry—"

"I'm starting for Hellas as soon as we get you wrapped up and have pure oxygen going into you in the bed. I'll drive as long as I can safely, then—"

"It won't make any difference. You'll never get me there, not alive," she said. "Babe, the onboard diagnostic kit isn't perfect but it's good enough to show I've got the heart of a ninety-year-old cardiac patient. And all the indicators have gotten worse in just the last hundred hours or so. Whatever I've got, it's killing me." She reached out and stroked my tear-soaked face. "Poor Cap. Make me two promises."

"I'll love you forever."

"I know. I don't need you to promise that. First promise, no matter where you end up, or doing what, you *learn*. Study whatever you can study, acquire whatever you can acquire, feed your mind, babe. That's the most important."

I nodded. I was crying pretty hard.

"The other one is kind of weird . . . well, it's silly."

"If it's for you, I'll do it. I promise."

She gasped, trying to pull in more oxygen than her lungs could hold. Her eyes were flowing too. "I'm scared to be buried out in the

cold and the dark, and I can't *stand* the idea of freezing solid. So . . .
don't bury me. Cremate me. I want to be *warm*."

"But you can't cremate a person on Mars," I protested. "There's
not enough air to support a fire, and—"

"You promised," she said, and died.

I spent the next hour doing everything the first aid program said
to do. When she was cold and stiff, I knew it had really happened.

I didn't care about *Goodspeed* anymore. I'd sell it at Hellas depot,
buy passage to some city where I could work, start over. I didn't
want to be in our home for weeks with Sam's body, but I didn't have
the money to call in a mission to retrieve her, and anyway they'd just
do the most economical thing—bury her right here, practically at
the South Pole, in the icy night.

I curled up in my bunk and just cried for hours, then let myself
fall asleep. That just made it worse; now that she was past rigor
mortis she was soft to the touch, more like herself, and I couldn't
stand to store her in the cold, either, not after what I had promised.
I washed her, brushed her hair, put her in a body bag, and set her in
one of the dry storage compartments with the door closed; maybe I'd
think of something before she started to smell.

Driving north, I don't think I really wanted to live, myself. I
stayed up too long, ate and drank too little, just wanting the journey
to be over with. I remember I drove right through at least one bad
storm at peak speed, more than enough to shatter a tread on a stone
or to go into a sudden crevasse or destroy myself in all kinds of ways.
For days in a row, in that endless black darkness, I woke up in the
driver's chair after having fallen asleep while the deadman stopped
the gig.

I didn't care. I wanted out of the dark.

About the fifth day, *Goodspeed*'s forward left steering tread went off a drop-off of three meters or so. The gig flipped over forward to the left, crashing onto its back. Force of habit had me strapped into the seat, and wearing my suit, the two things that the manuals the insurance company said were what you had to be doing any time the gig was moving if you didn't want to void your policy. Sam had made a big deal about that too.

So after rolling, *Goodspeed* came to a stop on its back, and all the lights went out. When I finished screaming with rage and disappointment and everything else, there was still enough air (though I could feel it leaking) for me to be conscious.

I put on my helmet and turned on the headlamp.

I had a full capacitor charge on the suit, but *Goodspeed*'s fusion box had shut down. That meant seventeen hours of being alive unless I could replace it with another fusion box, but both the compartment where the two spare fusion boxes were stored, and the repair access to replace them, were on the top rear surface of the gig. I climbed outside, wincing at letting the last of the cabin air out, and poked around. The gig was resting on exactly the hatches I would have needed to open.

Seventeen—well, sixteen, now—hours. And one big promise to keep.

The air extractors on the gig had been running, as they always did, right up till the accident; the tanks were full of liquid oxygen. I could transfer it to my suit through the emergency valving, live for some days that way. There were enough suit rations to make it a real race between starvation and suffocation. The suit radio wasn't going to reach anywhere that could do me any good; for long distance it depended on a relay through the gig, and the relay's antenna was under the overturned gig.

Sam was dead. *Goodspeed* was dead. And for every practical purpose, so was I.

Neither *Goodspeed* nor I really needed that oxygen anymore, *but Sam does*, I realized. I could at least shift the tanks around, and I had the mining charges we used for breaking up big rocks.

I carried Sam's body into the oxygen storage, set her between two of the tanks, and hugged the body bag one more time. I don't know if I was afraid she'd look awful, or afraid she would look alive and asleep, but I was afraid to unzip the bag.

I set the timer on a mining charge, put that on top of her, and piled the rest of the charges on top. My little pile of bombs filled most of the space between the two oxygen tanks. Then I wrestled four more tanks to lie on the heap crosswise and stacked flammable stuff from the kitchen like flour, sugar, cornmeal, and jugs of cooking oil on top of those, to make sure the fire burned long and hot enough.

My watch said I still had five minutes till the timer went off.

I still don't know why I left the gig. I'd been planning to die there, cremated with Sam, but maybe I just wanted to see if I did the job right or something—as if I could try again, perhaps, if it didn't work? Whatever the reason, I bounded away to what seemed like a reasonable distance.

I looked up; the stars were out. I wept so hard I feared I would miss seeing them in the blur. They were so beautiful, and it had been so long.

Twenty kilograms of high explosive was enough energy to shatter all the LOX tanks and heat all the oxygen white hot. Organic stuff doesn't just burn in white-hot oxygen; it explodes and vaporizes, and besides fifty kilograms of Sam, I'd loaded in a good six hundred kilograms of other organics.

I figured all that out a long time later. In the first quarter second after the mining charge went off, things were happening pretty fast. A big piece of the observation bubble—smooth enough not to cut my suit and kill me, but hard enough to send me a couple meters into the air and backward by a good thirty meters—slapped me over and sent me rolling down the back side of the ridge on which I sat, smashed up badly and unconscious, but alive.

I think I dreamed about Sam, as I gradually came back to consciousness.

Now, look here, botterogator, of course I'd like to be able, for the sake of the new generation of Martians, to tell you I dreamed about her giving me earnest how-to-succeed advice, and that I made a vow there in dreamland to succeed and be worthy of her and all that. But in fact it was mostly just dreams of holding her and being held, and about laughing together. Sorry if that's not on the list.

The day came when I woke up and realized I'd seen the medic before. Not long after that I stayed awake long enough to say "hello." Eventually I learned that a survey satellite had picked up the exploding gig, and shot pictures because that bright light was unusual. An AI identified a shape in the dust as a human body lying outside, and dispatched an autorescue—a rocket with a people-grabbing arm. The autorescue flew out of Olympic City's launch pad on a ballistic trajectory, landed not far from me, crept over to my not-yet-out-of-air, not-yet-frozen body, grabbed me with a mechanical arm, and stuffed me into its hold. It took off again, flew to the hospital, and handed me over to the doctor.

Total cost of one autorescue mission, and two weeks in a human-contact hospital—which the insurance company refused to cover because I'd deliberately blown up the gig—was maybe twenty successful prospecting runs' worth. So as soon as I could move, they indentured me and, since I was in no shape to do grunt-and-strain stuff for a while, they found a little prospector's supply company that wanted a human manager for an office at the Hellas depot. I learned the job—it wasn't hard—and grew with the company, eventually as Mars's first indentured CEO.

I took other jobs, bookkeeping, supervising, cartography, anything where I could earn wages with which to pay off the indenture faster, especially jobs I could do online in my nominal hours off. At every job, because I'd promised Sam, I learned as much as I could. Eventually, a few days before my forty-third birthday, I paid off the indenture, quit all those jobs, and went into business for myself.

By that time I knew how the money moved, and for what, in practically every significant business on Mars. I'd had a lot of time to plan and think too.

So that was it. I kept my word—oh, all right, botterogator, let's check that box too. Keeping promises is important to success. After all, here I am.

Sixty-two earthyears later, I know, because everyone does, that a drug that costs almost nothing, which everyone takes now, could have kept Sam alive. A little money a year, if anyone'd known, and Sam and me could've been celebrating anniversaries for decades, and we'd've been richer, with Sam's brains on the job too. And botterogator, you'd be talking to her, and probably learning more too.

Or is that what I think now?

Remembering Sam, over the years, I've thought of five hundred things I could have done instead of what I did, and maybe I'd have succeeded as much with those too.

But the main question I think about is only—did she *mean* it? Did she see something in me that would make my bad start work out as well as it did? Was she just an idealistic smart girl playing house with the most cooperative boy she could find? Would she have wanted me to marry again and have children, did she intend me to get rich?

Every so often I regret that I didn't really fulfill that second promise, an irony I can appreciate now: she feared the icy grave, but since she burned to mostly water and carbon dioxide, on Mars she became mostly snow. And molecules are so small, and distribute so evenly, that whenever the snow falls, I know there's a little of her in it, sticking to my suit, piling on my helmet, coating me as I stand in the quiet and watch it come down.

Did she dream me into existence? I kept my promises, and they made me who I am . . . and was that what she wanted? If I am only the accidental whim of a smart teenage girl with romantic notions, what would I have been without the whim, the notions, or Sam?

Tell you what, botterogator, and you pass this on to the new generation of Martians: it's funny how one little promise, to someone or something a bit better than yourself, can turn into something as real as Samantha City, whose lights at night fill the crater that spreads out before me from my balcony all the way to the horizon.

Nowadays I have to walk for an hour, in the other direction out beyond the crater wall, till the false dawn of the city lights is gone, and I can walk till dawn or hunger turns me homeward again.

Botterogator, you can turn off the damn stupid flashing lights. That's all you're getting out of me. I'm going for a walk; it's snowing.

JOHN BARNES has commercially published twenty-eight volumes of fiction, probably twenty-nine by the time you read this, including science fiction, men's action adventure, two collaborations with astronaut Buzz Aldrin, a collection of short stories and essays, one fantasy, and one mainstream novel. He has done a rather large number of occasionally peculiar things for money, mainly in business consulting, academic teaching, and show business, fields which overlap more than you'd think. Since 2001, he has lived in Denver, Colorado, where he has a wonderful girlfriend, an average income, and a bad attitude, which he feels is actually the best permutation.

AUTHOR'S NOTE

I don't know where stories come from, much of the time; this one had a more tangled genesis than most. Mars stories, I think, should be frontier stories, mainly because of my strong sense that by the time there are cities on Mars, they will be essentially like large luxury hotels, where nothing much interesting usually happens (well, extramarital affairs and international intrigue, but those aren't what I usually like to write stories about). I was thinking about things that would be hard to do on a Martian frontier and scribbled out a list; after a while I settled on "cremation." That, of course, brought me to the single best-known poem about a difficult cremation of which I am aware, and there, anyway, was the beginning of an outline.

Somehow in my mind that connected with Eric Hoffer's observation that happy, successful people don't go to frontiers. That in turn got me thinking about the students I teach at a career college, who have essentially been brought up by a mixture of peer culture, mass culture, and government services; in particular I thought about the strict, harsh code of honor that many of them live by, in which personal loyalty to peers is the highest and sometimes only value, which very likely helps to keep them trapped and broke, but also keeps them alive and determined. That brought me back to the Robert Service poem, with its emphasis on keeping promises, and somewhere eventually to the thought that many people have been made by a promise they kept, and more by the keeping than by what they promised, or who they promised it to. That, and perhaps a difficult drive through Kansas ground blizzards (on Christmas Day, which again intersected with the poem), which made me reflect on keeping your word when it is inconvenient, and perhaps a dozen other things that I'm not consciously aware of, finally gave me an ending to this story.

DISCOVERING LIFE

Kim Stanley Robinson

The final approach to the Jet Propulsion Laboratory, a narrow road running up the flank of the ugly brown mountains overlooking Los Angeles, is a fine road in ordinary circumstances, but when something newsworthy occurs it is inadequate to handle the influx of media visitors. On this morning the line of cars and trailers extended down from the security gate almost to the freeway off-ramp, and Bill Dawkins watched the temperature gauge of his old Ford Escort rise as he inched forward, all the vehicles adding to the smog that already made the air a tangible gray mist. Eventually he passed the security guards and drove up to the employee parking lot, then walked down past the guest parking lot overflowing with TV trailers topped by satellite dishes. Surely every language and nation in the world was represented, all bringing their own equipment of course.

Inside the entry building Bill turned right and looked in the press conference room, also jammed to overflowing. A row of Bill's colleagues sat up on the stage behind a long table crowded with mics, facing the cameras and lights and reporters. Bill's friend Mike Collinsworth was answering a question about contamination, trying to look like he was enjoying himself. But very few scientists like other scientists listening in on them when they are explaining things to nonscientists, because then there is someone there to witness just how gross their gross simplifications are; so an affair like this was by its very nature embarrassing. And to complicate the situation, this press corps was a very mixed crowd, ranging from experts who in some senses (social context, historical background) knew more than the scientists themselves, all the way to TV faces who could barely read their prompters. That plus the emotional load of the subject matter, amounting almost to hysteria, gave the event an excruciating quality that Bill found perversely fascinating to watch.

A telegenic young woman got the nod from John and took the radio mic being passed around. "What does this discovery mean to you?" she asked. "What do you think the meaning of this discovery will be?"

The seven men on stage looked at each other, and the crowd laughed. John said, "Mike?" and Mike made a face that got another laugh. But John knew his crew; Mike was a smart-ass in real life, indeed Bill could imagine some of his characteristic answers scorching the air—It means I have to answer stupid questions in front of billions of people; It means I can stop working eighty-hour weeks and see what a real life is like again—but Mike was also good at the PR stuff, and with a straight face he answered the second of the questions, which Bill would have thought was the harder of the two.

"Well, the meaning of it depends, to some extent, on what the exobiologists find out when they investigate the organisms more fully. If the organisms follow the same biochemical principles as life on Earth, then it's possible they are a kind of cousin to terran life, bounced on meteorites from Mars to here, or here to Mars. If that's the case then it's possible that DNA analysis will even be able to determine about when the two families parted company, and which planet has the older population. We may find out that we're all Martians originally."

He waited for the obligatory laugh. "On the other hand, the investigation may show a completely alien biochemistry, indicating a separate origin. That's a very different scenario." Now Mike paused, realizing he was at the edge of his sound bite envelope, and also of deep waters. He decided to cut it short. "Either way that turns out, we'll know that life is very adaptable, and that it can either cross space between planets or begin twice in the same solar system, so either way we'll be safer in assuming that life is fairly widespread in the universe."

Bill smiled. Mike was good; the answer provided a quick summary of the situation, bullet points, potential headlines: "BACTERIA ON MARS PROVES LIFE IS COMMON IN THE UNIVERSE." Which wasn't exactly true, but there was no winning the sound bite game.

Bill left the room and crossed the little plaza, then entered the big building forming the north flank of the compound. Upstairs the little offices and cubicles all had their doors open and portable TVs on, all tuned to the press conference just a hundred yards away; there was a holiday atmosphere, including streamers and balloons, but Bill couldn't feel it somehow. There on the screens under the CNN logo his friends were being played up as heroes, young devoted rocket scientists replacing astronauts by necessity as the exploration of Mars proceeded robotically—silly, but very much preferable to the situation when things went wrong, when they were portrayed as harried geek rocket scientists not quite up to the task, which was the extremely important (though underfunded) task of teleoperating the exploration of the cosmos from their desks. They had played both roles several times at JPL and had come to understand that for the media and perhaps the public there was no middle ground, no recognition that they were just people doing their jobs, difficult but interesting jobs in difficult but not intolerable circumstances. No, for the world they were a biannual nine-hours' wonder, either nerdy heroes or nerdy goats, and the next day forgotten.

That was just the way it was, and not what was bothering Bill. He felt at loose ends. Mission accomplished, his to-do list almost empty; it left him feeling somewhat empty, but that was not it either. He still had phone and e-mail media questions waiting, and he worked through those on automatic pilot, his answers honed by the previous week's work. The lander had drilled down and secured a soil sample from under the sands at the mouth of Shalbatana Vallis, where thermal sensors had detected heat from a volcanic vent, which meant the permafrost ice in that region had liquid percolations in it. The sample had been placed in a metal sphere that had been hermetically sealed and boosted to Martian orbit. After a rendezvous with an orbiter, it had been flown back to Earth and released in such a manner that it had dropped into Earth's atmosphere without orbiting at all and slammed into Utah's Dugway Proving Grounds a mere ten yards from its target. An artificial meteorite, yes. No, the ball could not have broken on impact; it had been engineered for that impact, indeed could have withstood striking a sidewalk or a wall of steel, and had been recovered intact in the little crater it had made—recovered by robot and flown robotically to Johnson

Space Center in Houston, where it had been placed inside hermetically sealed chambers in sealed labs in sealed buildings before being opened, everything having been designed for just this purpose. No, they did not need to sterilize Dugway, or all of Utah, they did not need to nuke Houston (not to kill Martian bacteria anyway), and all was well; the alien life was safely locked away and could not get out. People were safe.

Bill answered a lot of questions like these, feeling that there were many people out there who badly needed a better education in risk assessment. They got in their cars and drove on freeways, smoking cigarettes and holding high-energy radio transmitters against their heads in order to get to newsrooms where they were greatly concerned to find out if they were in danger from microbacteria locked away behind triple hermetic seals in Houston. By the time Bill broke for lunch he was feeling more depressed than irritated. People were ignorant, short-sighted, poorly educated, fearful, superstitious, deeply enmeshed in magical thinking of all kinds. And yet that was not really what was bothering him either.

Mike was in the cafeteria, hungrily downing his lunchtime array of flavinoids and antioxidants, and Bill joined him, feeling cheered. Mike was giving them a low-voiced recap of the morning's press conference (many journalists were in the JPL cafeteria on guest passes). "What is the meaning of life?" Mike whispered urgently. "It means metabolism, it means hunger at lunchtime, please God let us eat, that's what it means." Then the TVs overhead began to show the press conference in Houston, and like everyone else they watched and listened to the tiny figures on the screen. The exobiologists at Johnson Space Center were making their initial report: the Martian bacteria were around one hundred nanometers long, bigger than the

fossil nanobacteria tentatively identified in ALH 84001 (the meteorite found in the Antarctic in 1984), but smaller than most terran
bacteria; they were single-celled, they contained proteins, ribosomes,
DNA strands composed of base pairs of adenine, thymine, guanine,
and cytosine—

"Cousins," Mike declared.

—the DNA resembled certain terran organisms like the
Columbia basement archaea *Methanospirillum jacobii*, thus possibly
they were the descendant of a common ancestor—

"Cousins!"

—very possibly mitochondrial DNA analysis would reveal
when the split had happened. "Separated at birth," one of the
Johnson scientists offered, to laughter. They were just like the JPL
scientists in their on-screen performances. Spontaneous generation
versus panspermia, frequent transpermia between Earth and Mars;
all these concepts poured out in an half-digested rush, and people
would still be calling for the nuclear destruction of Houston and
Utah in order to save the world from alien infection, from androm-
eda strains, from fictional infections—infictions, as Mike said with
a grin.

The Johnson scientists nattered on solemnly, happy still to be
in the limelight; it had been an oddity of NASA policy to place the
Mars effort so entirely at JPL, in effect concentrating one of the
major endeavors of human history in one small university lab, with
many competing labs out there like baby birds in the federal nest,
ready to peck JPL's eyes out if given the chance. Now the exobiol-
ogy teams at Johnson and AMES were finally involved, and it was
no longer just JPL's show, although they were still headquarters and
had engineered the sample-return operation just as they had all the
previous Martian landers. This diffusion of the project was a relief

of course, but could also be seen as a disappointment—the end of an era. But no—watching the TV Bill could tell that wasn't what was bothering him either.

Mike returned with Bill and Nassim to their offices, and they continued to watch the Johnson press conference on a desk TV in Nassim's. Apparently the sample contained more than one species, perhaps as many as five, maybe more. They just didn't know yet. They thought they could keep them all alive in Mars jars, but weren't sure. They were sure that they had the organisms contained, and that there was no danger.

Someone asked about ramifications for the human exploration of Mars, and the answers were scattered. "Very severely problematized," someone said; it would be a matter for discussion at the very highest levels, NASA of course but also NSF, the National Academy of Sciences, the International Astronomical Union, various UN bodies—in short, the scientific government of the world.

Mike laughed. "The human mission people must be freaking out."

Nassim nodded. "The Ad Martem Club has already declared that these things are only bacteria, like bathroom scum—we kill billions of them every day, they're no impediment to us conquering Mars."

"They can't be serious."

"They are serious, but crazy. We won't be setting foot there for a very long time. If ever."

Suddenly Bill understood. "That would be sad," he said. "I'm a humans-to-Mars guy myself."

Mike grinned and shook his head. "You'd better not be in too much of a hurry."

✳ ✳ ✳

Bill went back in his office. He cleaned up a little, then called Eleanor's office, wanting to talk to her, wanting to say, "We did it, the mission is a success and the dream has therefore been shattered," but she wasn't in. He left a message that he would be home around the usual time, then concentrated on his to-do list, no longer adding things to the bottom faster than he took them off at the top, trying to occupy his mind but failing. The realization was sinking in that he had always thought that their work was about going to Mars, about making a better world there; this was how he had justified everything about his life—the killing hours of the job, the looks on his family's faces, Eleanor's being fully sympathetic but disappointed, frustrated that it had turned out this way, the two of them caught despite their best efforts in a kind of 1950s marriage, the husband gone all day every day. Except of course that Eleanor worked long hours too, so that their kids had always been day care and after-school care kids, all day every weekday. Once Bill had dropped Joe, their younger one, off at day care on a Monday morning, and looking back through the window he had seen an expression on the boy's face—of abandonment and stoic solitude, of facing another ten hours at the same old place, to be gotten through somehow like everyone else—a look which on the face of a three-year-old had pierced Bill to the heart. And all that—all the time he had put in, all those days and years, had been so that one day humans would inhabit Mars and make a decent civilization at last; his whole life burned in a cubicle because the start of this great project was so tenuous, because so few people believed or understood, so that it was down to them, one little lab trying its best to execute the "faster better cheaper" plan which contained within it (as they often pointed out) a contradiction of the second law of thermodynamics among other problems, a plan that they knew could only really achieve two out of the three qualities in any real-world combination, but making the attempt anyway, finding that the only true "cheaper" involved was the cost of their own labor and the quality of their own lives, rocket scientists running like squirrels in cages to make the inhabitation of Mars a reality—a project which only the future Martians of some distant century would truly appreciate and honor. Except now there weren't going to be any future Martians.

Then it was after six, and he was out in the evening smog with Mike and Nassim, carpooling home. They got on the 210 freeway and rolled along quite nicely until the carpool lane stalled with all the rest, because of the intersection of 210 and 110, and then they were into stop-and-go like everyone else, the long lines of cars brake-lighting forward in that accordion pattern of acceleration and deceleration so familiar to them all. The average speed on the LA freeway system was now eleven miles per hour, low enough to make them and many other Angelenos try the surface streets instead, but Nassim's computer modeling and their empirical trials had made it clear that for any drive over five miles long the clogged freeways were still faster than the clogged streets.

"Well, another red-letter day," Mike announced and pulled a bottle of Scotch from his daypack. He snapped open the cap and took a swig, then passed the bottle to Bill and Nassim. This was something he did on ceremonial occasions, after all the great JPL successes or disasters, and though both Bill and Nassim found it alarming, they did not refuse quick pulls. Mike took another one before twisting the cap very tightly on the bottle and stuffing it back inside his daypack, actions which appeared to give him the feeling he had returned the bottle to a legally sealed state. Bill and Nassim had mocked him before for this belief, and now Nassim said, "Why don't you just carry a little soldering iron with you so you can reseal it properly."

"Ha-ha."

"Or adopt the NASA solution," Bill said. "Take your swigs and then throw the bottle overboard."

"Ha-ha. Now don't be biting the hand that feeds you."

"That's the hand people always bite."

Mike stared at him. "You're not happy about this big discovery, are you Bill?"

"No!" Bill said, sitting there with his foot on the brake. "No! I always thought we were the—the bringing of the inhabitation of Mars. I thought that people would go on to live there and terraform the planet, you know, establish a whole *world* there, a second strand of history, and we would always be back at the start of it all. And now these damn bacteria are there already, and we may never land there at all. We'll stay here and leave Mars to the Martians, the bacterial Martians—"

"The little red natives—"

"And so we're at the start of nothing! We're the start of a dead end."

"Balderdash," Mike said.

And Bill's spirits rose a bit; he felt a glow like the Scotch run through him; he might have slaved away in a cubicle burning ten years of his life on the start of a dead-end project, a project that would never be enacted, but at least he had been able to work on it with people like these, like brothers to him now after all the years, brilliant weird guys who would use the word *balderdash* in conversation in all seriousness, because (in Mike's case) he read Victorian boy's literature for entertainment, among other odd habits, a guy whose real self had not in the slightest way appeared on TV while playing the Earnest Rocket Scientist, stupid role created by the media's questions and expectations, all of them playing their stupid roles in precisely the stupid soap opera way that Bill had dreamed they were going to escape someday: What does life *mean* to you, Dr. Labcoat, what does this discovery *mean*; Well, it means we have burned up our lives on a dead-end project. "What do you mean, balderdash!" Bill exclaimed. "They'll make Mars a nature preserve! A bacterial nature preserve, for God's sake! No one will risk even *landing* there, much less terraforming the place!"

"Sure they will," Mike said. "People will go there. Eventually. They'll settle, they'll terraform—just like you've been dreaming. It might take longer than you were thinking, but you were never going to be one of the ones going anyway, so what's the rush? It'll happen."

"I don't think so," Bill said.

"Sure it will. Whichever way it happens, it'll happen."

"Oh, thank you! Thank you very much! Whichever way it happens, it'll happen? That's so very helpful!"

"Not your most testable hypothesis," Nassim noted.

Mike grinned. "You don't have to test it, it's that good."

Harshly Bill laughed. "Too bad you didn't tell the reporter that! Whatever happens will happen! This discovery means whatever it means!" And then they were all cackling. "This discovery means that there's life on Mars!" "This discovery means whatever you want it to mean!" "That's how meaning always means!"

Their mirth subsided. They were still stuck in stop-and-go traffic, in the rows of red blinks on the vast viaduct slashing through the city, under a sour milk sky.

"Well, shit," Mike said, waving at the view. "I guess we'll just have to terraform Earth instead."

KIM STANLEY ROBINSON grew up in Orange County, California, and attended UC San Diego and Boston University. His first novel, *The Wild Shore*, appeared in 1984, the first of his Orange County trilogy, reflecting his interest in utopian and ecological issues. It was followed by *The Gold Coast* (1988) and *Pacific Edge* (1990), the last the winner of the John W. Campbell Memorial Award.

Robinson is best known for his trilogy about terraforming Mars: Nebula winner *Red Mars* (1992), and Hugo and Locus award winners *Green Mars* (1993) and *Blue Mars* (1996). A collection of related material, *The Martians* (1999), also won the Locus Award. Near-future ecological thriller *Antarctica* (1997) was the result of a National Science Foundation grant that sent Robinson to Antarctica as writer-in-residence, while Locus Award winner *The Years of Rice and Salt* (2002) was a major alternate history about the development of science. His most recent works are the science fiction trilogy Science in the Capital (*Forty Signs of Rain, Fifty Degrees Below,* and *Sixty Days and Counting*) and the novel *Galileo's Dream.* A new collection, *The Best of Kim Stanley Robinson*, is forthcoming.

A reference Web site for his work can be found at www.kimstanleyrobinson.info.

AUTHOR'S NOTE

Jane Johnson, my friend and editor at HarperCollins UK, asked me for a story for a private volume celebrating the fifth anniversary of her imprint HarperVoyager. I had visited JPL in Pasadena a few times in the previous years, and the recent claim by NASA scientists in Houston that they had found signs of fossil bacteria in a Martian meteorite had surprised everyone. The story was then included in the American paperback edition of *The Martians*, in 2000.

I wouldn't be surprised if one day this one came to pass. Seasonal appearances of methane on Mars seem to suggest life may be there.

ACKNOWLEDGMENTS

An anthology is not assembled by one person, neatly and tidily, working in idyllic isolation (at least, not in my experience). Rather it's the incredibly fortunate outcome of the efforts of a village of talented and giving people.

Life on Mars would not exist without the efforts of the remarkable Sharyn November or my indefatigable agent Howard Morhaim. I am grateful to them both. I would also like to thank Stephan Martiniere for *another* remarkable cover and say how grateful I am to each and every one of the book's contributors who really were far kinder and more patient than I had any right to hope.

I would also like to acknowledge the efforts of Jack Dann, Cat Sparks, Tansy Rayner Roberts, Alisa Krasnostein, Katie Menick, James Patrick Kelly, Garth Nix, and Gary K. Wolfe, all of whom provided critical assistance when it was needed.

Finally, as always, I would like to thank my wife, Marianne, and my daughters, Jessica and Sophie, who allow me to steal time from them to do books like this one. It's a gift I intend to repay.

ABOUT THE EDITOR

JONATHAN STRAHAN is an editor, anthologist, and critic. He was born in Belfast, Northern Ireland, in 1964, and moved to Perth, Western Australia, in 1968. He graduated from the University of Western Australia with a bachelor of arts in 1986. In 1990 he cofounded a small press journal, *Eidolon,* and worked on it as coeditor and copublisher until 1999. He was also copublisher of Eidolon Books.

In 1997 Jonathan started worked for *Locus: The Newspaper of the Science Fiction Field* as an assistant editor. He wrote a regular review column for the magazine until March 1998 and has been the magazine's reviews editor since January 2002. His reviews and criticism have also appeared in *Eidolon, Eidolon: SF Online, Ticonderoga Online*, and *Foundation*. Jonathan has won the William J. Atheling Jr. Award for Criticism and Review and the Australian National Science Fiction Ditmar Award.

As a freelance editor, Jonathan has edited or coedited more than a dozen reprint and original anthologies, which have been published in Australia and the United States. These include various "year's best" annuals, *The Locus Awards* (with Charles N. Brown), *The New Space Opera* (with Gardner Dozois), and the ongoing Eclipse series. As a book editor, he has also edited *The Jack Vance Treasury* and *Ascendancies: The Best of Bruce Sterling*. In 1999 Jonathan founded The Coode Street Press, which published the one-shot review zine *The Coode Street Review of Science Fiction* and copublished Terry Dowling's *Antique Futures*. The Coode Street Press is currently inactive.

Jonathan married former *Locus* managing editor Marianne Jablon in 1999, and they live in Perth, Western Australia, with their two daughters, Jessica and Sophie.

His Web site is www.jonathanstrahan.com.au.